THE ACTION MA

Denton Farr has eve...
a fine woman. So why plan the peri...
heist? Why do something that would bring the
federals and the syndicate howling after him; why
try a stunt that could easily get him killed and
certainly send him up for the rest of his life? The
action. There's something special about the way
his body feels—something different about the air it
breathes—when he has action. That it is
unnecessary doesn't matter. It is action. And why
the hell does he want to climb that mountain?
Because it is there. Yes, this is the heist will provide
all the action that Farr will ever need…

TERROR TOURNAMENT

Ex-cop Burl Stannard has been hired as security to
protect the take at a 3-day pro-amateur golf
tournament. All he has to do is ride shotgun with
the money to the bank. But something goes wrong.
Three men pull up in a golf cart and crash their
car. Shots are exchanged. A fellow ex-cop and one
of the thieves are killed. When Stannard comes to,
the $400,00 is gone, and no clues in sight—not
even the body of the dead criminal. Who could
have pulled off such a perfect heist? The more
Stannard digs, the more it begins to look like an
inside job—but everyone involved has an airtight
alibi!

The Action Man

Terror Tournament

BY JAY FLYNN

Introduction by Bill Pronzini

STARK
HOUSE

Stark House Press • Eureka California

THE ACTION MAN / TERROR TOURNAMENT

Published by Stark House Press
1315 H Street
Eureka, CA 95501, USA
griffinskye3@sbcglobal.net
www.starkhousepress.com

THE ACTION MAN
Originally published in paperback by Avon Books, New York,
and copyright © 1961 by Jay Flynn.

TERROR TOURNAMENT
Originally published in hardback by Mystery House, New York,
as by J. M. Flynn and copyright © 1959 by J. M. Flynn. Reprinted in
paperback in an abridged edition by Ace Books, New York, 1959.

"That Was Flynn" copyright © 1988 by Bill Pronzini. First appeared in
Mystery Scene #13, reprinted by permission of the author.

ISBN-13: 978-1-944520-56-4

Book design by Mark Shepard, SHEPGRAPHICS.COM
Cover art by Rupam Grimoeuvre
Proofreading by Bill Kelly

First Stark House Press Edition: December 2018

FIRST EDITION

Contents

Contents

That Was Flynn

by Bill Pronzini

Jay Flynn was a character. The tragicomic variety, with accent on the tragic.

In many ways he was a throwback, a stereotype. Hard-drinking, rough-living, blarney-spouting Boston Irishman. Ex-GI, newspaperman (ten years as a crime reporter on the *Portland Express*, Portland, Maine; stints on the *San Jose Mercury* and other California papers), bartender, editor, mystery writer, sex novelist, bootlegger, security guard, caretaker, and (so he claimed) prisoner in a hell-hole Mexican jail on a trumped-up charge and "writer-in-residence" at a Nevada whorehouse.

A screw-up of the first rank, with sometimes hilarious results. Lousy luck with women and games of chance, much of it of his own making. Restless, peripatetic; "everybody's got to be someplace," he said once, "but it don't always have to be the same damn place." Lazy, ambitious, apathetic, energetic, generous, selfish, cynical, sentimental, don't-give-a-damn, care-too-much – all the schizophrenic contradictions that make up most of us, but that in him seemed magnified to an even greater degree. As has been said about Hemingway, he was just a little larger – and just a little smaller – than life.

There is a schizophrenic quality to his fiction as well. He was like the proverbial little girl: When he was good he was very good, but when he was bad he was very, very bad. His characters and his plots, like Flynn himself, were full of BS and on the screwball side. Big, tough, occasionally inept Irish heroes with names like McHugh, Tighe Slattery, Joe Mannix (no relation or resemblance to the Mike Conners TV character), Burdis Gannon, Matt Tara, Burl Stannard, John Christian Fifer.

Beautiful, willing, treacherous women. Ultra-nasty villains. Action fast and furious – and scatterbrained and often implausible. Storylines, some solidly constructed and some riddled with holes, involving elaborate capers, hijackings, modern-day bootlegging, the hot-car racket, military-base intrigue, the Mafia, vigilante cops and serial killers, Nazi war spoils, spy stuff, even a treasure hidden inside an Irish pub's thirty-foot, hand-carved mahogany bar. Typical paperback fare of the sixties and seventies, in one sense; atypical, in another, because of Flynn's slightly skewed perceptions and not inconsiderable (when he worked at it) storytelling skills.

His first published work and only published short story, "The Badger Game," as by Jay Flynn, appeared in the November 1956 issue of the hard-boiled, J.D.-oriented mystery magazine, *Guilty*; his first novel, *The Deadly Boodle*, as by J. M. Flynn, was an Ace Double two years later. The short story isn't such-a-much; the novel is a pretty fair maiden effort.

There is a similar dichotomy among his six other Ace Doubles published between 1959 and 1961, all as by J. M. Flynn. Four are varying degrees of good: *The Hot Chariot, Ring Around a Rogue, Drink with the Dead, The Girl from Las Vegas.* The other two, *One for the Death House* and *Deep Six*, are rather awful.

His best novels of the period are the pair of capers in this volume, *Terror Tournament* and *The Action Man*, and the five titles that comprise his series featuring an off-the-wall San Francisco bar owner and secret agent named McHugh. *Terror Tournament* (Bouregy, 1959, his only hardcover) is an effective tale of the carefully planned heist of the gate receipts of a golf tournament modeled after the one at Pebble Beach. Even better – his magnum opus, in fact – is *The Action Man* (Avon, 1961, as by Jay Flynn). The caper here is a bank heist, and its mastermind, anti-hero Denton Farr, is Flynn's most complex and believable protagonist. A high level of suspense and a savagely ironic ending are two of the novel's other pluses.

If Denton Farr is Flynn's most complex and believable character, McHugh is his most memorable. In *McHugh, A Body for McHugh, It's Murder McHugh, Viva McHugh!*, and *The Five Faces of Murder* (Avon, 1959-62, all as by Jay Flynn), this two-fisted Irish-American James Bond blithely brawls and blusters his way through dizzy plot-swirls concerning a missing electronics expert, Mafia hit men, a couple of Navy flyers mysteriously AWOL in Mexico, a Caribbean island dictator and his army of thugs, and a fortune in hidden Nazi loot.

Along the way he drinks prodigious amounts of booze, trades quips with his fellow agent, Bud Chapman, and his boss, General Burton Harts, and has more problems than sack time with bevies of good and bad women. None of his adventures make much sense, really, but there is a good deal of energy in each, plus plenty of sly humor, breakneck pacing, and some lean, evocative writing. As in the barbed narrative hook that opens *It's Murder McHugh*:

> McHugh pushed the Polish girl away and went on watching the door of the cantina. He wished Bramhall would show up. It would be even better if Long was with him.
> That would make his job easier, because he could kill both of them at the same time.

(Flynn once told me that the McHugh series was the result of a drunken lunch with his agent and an editor at Avon. The agent, he said, began extolling the virtues of "a great new series" Flynn had concocted, and did

such a good selling job that afterward the three of them lurched back to
the Avon offices, where the editor immediately put through a request for
a three-book contract. The only problem was, Flynn had not concocted
anything at this point; had never heard the name McHugh until his silver-
tongued agent mentioned it, nor had any idea of who or what McHugh
was going to be. This anecdote may be true and it may be apocryphal. With
Flynn, you just never knew what was fact and what was bullshit.)

I read most of his Ace and Avon novels, either when they were first published or at some point in the sixties. One of my favorites was *Drink with
the Dead*, which has a modern-day bootlegging theme, and in early 1969
I recommended it to friend and fellow writer Jeff Wallmann. Jeff liked it
so much he suggested we write a story with a similar theme, which we pro-
ceeded to do. The result, "Day of the Moon," was published in *Alfred
Hitchcock's Mystery Magazine* in 1970 under our William Jeffrey pseudonym. Much later, we expanded the story into a novel that was first published under the same title and same pseudonym.

One evening after we'd written the story, over too many drinks in Wallmann's house near San Francisco, we got to talking about Flynn and his
work; to wondering why he hadn't published a new novel in seven years;
and whether or not he was still living on the Monterey Peninsula, where
much of his fiction was set and where a brief bio in one of the Ace Doubles said he made his home. As a lark, we began that night to track him
down. It took us a while, following a cold and circuitous trail, but we finally found him – not on the Monterey Peninsula but in a V.A. facility in
Portland, Maine. On the phone he claimed to be recuperating from a buck-
shot wound – in the ass, no less – administered by an irate husband. He
also claimed to be writing a new McHugh novel to pay his medical expenses, which proved definitely to be hooey because no such book was ever
published.

That was Flynn.

I exchanged a couple of letters with him shortly afterward, but at that
point none of us seemed inclined to keep up a regular correspondence. It
would be almost two years before Wallmann and I got to know Flynn well.
And how that came about requires a couple of paragraphs of relevant au-
tobiography.

In mid-1969 Jeff and I succumbed to an offer to write sex books for an
outfit called Liverpool Library Press, aka LLP – partly for the money, which
was top market dollar in those days ($1200 per title), and partly because
it enabled us to finance our legitimate work. Soon we were collaborating
on a book every two months for LLP. We churned them out in four or five
days of intensive effort, so we could spend the rest of our time writing fiction we cared about.

Late that year LLP moved its base of operations from California to the Mediterranean island of Majorca, where the high-rolling publisher (an Ivy-League American) had rented a palatial villa. For tax and other reasons he preferred his writers to also live on Majorca – or at least somewhere in Europe – and so he offered to pay the way of anyone who was willing to make the move. Wallmann and I were willing. We took a freighter for Amsterdam in February of 1970, and we arrived on Majorca in a broken-down VW station wagon five weeks later.

Neither of us remembers corresponding with Flynn while we were on Majorca; and we have only dim recollections of receiving some kind of communication from him at Christmas of 1970, when we returned to California for a brief holiday visit. But we're both sure that after we moved from Majorca to a small Bavarian town near Munich in the spring of 1971, we were not only in touch with him again but exchanging frequent letters.

Toward the end of that year Flynn wrote saying he was broke and looking for work – a letter that arrived at about the same time LLP's publisher decided to move his headquarters to Paris and to increase the number of books he was publishing. LLP was in need of writers; Flynn was in need of work, and claimed to have been writing sex books off and on since his legitimate paperback markets dried up in 1962 (which was probably true). So we got them together, Flynn submitted some sample material, and LLP put him on the payroll.

It was six months or so before the publisher offered to pay his way to Europe. By that time Jeff had made up his mind to move again, this time to France. He and Flynn arrived in Paris not long apart, and met there for the first time in the fall of 1972.

I was doing well enough with legitimate fiction by then to quit the sex-book racket, and I opted to get married and to stay in West Germany. But I continued to correspond with Flynn, and the better I got to know him through his letters (he wrote great letters), the more he intrigued me. I used him as the model for the boozy ex-pulp writer, Russell Dancer, who first appeared in the "Nameless Detective" novel, *Undercurrent*, in 1973 and who made encore appearances in *Hoodwink, Bones*, and *Nightshades*. There are a number of differences between Dancer and Flynn, but none of them is fundamental; the lines Dancer speaks in the four "Nameless" novels either were or might have been spoken by Flynn.

He stayed in Paris for a while, at LLP's expense, and then moved to Majorca, at least in part because Wallmann and I had extolled the island's virtues to him on numerous occasions. He somehow managed to rent the same small villa Jeff and I had occupied in Palma Nova, and stayed there for about a year, getting himself into and out of a series of minor misadventures with LLP (he was fired at least once, briefly, for delivering "unacceptable" material), a group of other LLP writers living on the island, and the owners of several bars and discos. Then his wanderlust got the best of him, and he hied himself off to Monte Carlo, near where Jeff and his girlfriend had moved from Paris.

In Monte Carlo, Flynn fell passionately in love with a 25-year-old suicidal West German beautician named Hildegarde. But their romance didn't last long; she threw him over for a randy Bulgarian and went back to Germany. This so upset Flynn that he, too, fled Monte Carlo. He went first to Ireland, on the mistaken assumption that any writer could live there cheaply and tax-free. When he found out that in order to obtain the tax-free status he would have to exchange his American citizenship for an Irish one, he figured it was time to return to the States. Specifically, to New York to look for writing work, since the bottom was already beginning to drop out of the sex-book market.

He took a room in Rosoff's, an old and now-defunct hotel-and-restaurant on West 43rd just off Times Square, and managed to scrounge up a contract to write several books in the then popular Lassiter paperback western series. The job didn't last long; he screwed up somehow on one of his manuscripts and was fired. But it so happened that Wallmann arrived in New York just about then, on a business trip; and Jeff, who was doing a book for Belmont-Tower, one of the lower echelon paperback houses, learned that B-T was in need of an assistant editor and house writer. He recommended Flynn, and Flynn got the dual job.

This was 1975. By which time I had been back in the U.S. myself for well over a year, living in San Francisco and also making periodic business trips to New York. So it was in Rosoff's in early '75 that Flynn and I finally came face to face.

He was shorter than I had envisioned him, less bulky, not at all imposing. No outstanding features, except maybe for a bristly salt-and-pepper mustache. I was vaguely disappointed. Flynn in person was nowhere near as impressive as he was in the abstract.

Over the next couple of years we got together every time I went to Manhattan. On one occasion he took me up to see his ex-agent (they were still friendly even though they could no longer work together) because the agent kept a bottle of 30-year-old Scotch for after-hours visitors and why pay for cheap booze, Flynn said, when you could get vintage stuff free? Mostly, though, we sat in the bar at Rosoff's and drank cheap liquor and talked shop. One of the things we talked about – and wrote each other about from time to time – was collaborating on a novel, but somehow we never got together on a mutually appealing idea. I wish we had; the finished product may not have been much good, but it would have been interesting.

Once when I went to see him, he announced that he was on the wagon for good. I asked him why. "Damn croaker said I'd be dead inside a year if I didn't," he said.

Two days later he was drinking again.

But he was still alive and kicking when the year was up.

That was Flynn.

During his association with Belmont-Tower, he published several novels as by Jay Flynn under their B-T and Leisure imprints – all of them pretty bad. Sexed-up westerns about a World War I-era operative for the Gallows Detective Agency, Jim Bannerman; sexed-up adventure tales featuring a drifter named Venable; sexed-up, violent cop melodramas starring San Francisco police sergeant Joe Rigg.

Worst of the lot were the Joe Riggs books. *Trouble Is My Business* (1976, no apologies to Chandler), about a psycho who chopped off his victims' heads with a Bowie knife, which Flynn had the puckish audacity to dedicate to Wallmann and me; and *Blood on Frisco Bay* (1976), a scandalous anti-police diatribe about the murder of a San Francisco socialite. He inscribed my copy of the latter: "For Bill Pronzini – a jolly tosspot [sic] and a hell of a fine friend. After this thing, let on you know me and the S.F.P.D. will have your ass – sit tight." I took his advice and sat tight.

Flynn did publish one reasonably good novel during this period, though it was written a year and a half to two years earlier while he was in Ireland. *Warlock* (Pocket Books, 1976, as by J.M. Flynn) features psychic detective John Christian Fifer and his 15-year-old daughter, Fiona, a full-fledged, spell-casting witch. Fey stuff, mixing crime and fantasy – not wholly successful, but with some of the same positive energy that made his Ace and Avon novels so enjoyable. It was supposed to be the first of a series, and in fact he wrote and delivered a second book; but that second manuscript was close to 200,000 words in length and very eccentric, and when Flynn refused to cut or revise a word, his editor rejected it outright and canceled the series. My copy of *Warlock* carries this inscription: "For Bill Pronzini – who knows where it's at – from the founder of the Day Late & Dollar Short Writers' Assn."

It took Flynn just about two years to wear out his welcome at Belmont-Tower, which for him was quite a long time. One of the reasons for the wear-out was the increasing eccentricity of the contract novels he delivered; another reason was his failure to deliver at all on other contracts; a third reason was that he had begun to foul up on his editorial duties because he was drinking on the job. His bosses knew he had booze stashed in the office; he would get increasingly oiled as each day wore on, without ever leaving the premises. He would also lurch into the john periodically to freshen his breath from a bottle of Listerine he kept in his desk. It took them weeks to figure out that he had his booze in the Listerine bottle and the Listerine stashed somewhere else.

That was Flynn.

After B-T fired him, and he couldn't find any other contract or editorial work, he quit New York and the writing business for good. The first place he went was to Richmond, Virginia, for reasons that never were quite clear to me. Inside of a year he was broke and living on Richmond's skid row, where he reputedly fell in with a bunch of white-lightning bootleggers and for a time ran an illegal "nip shop" for them in the rear of a neighborhood barbershop. Then, also for obscure reasons, he quit the bootleggers and took a legit job as a uniformed security guard – a position that required him to carry a handgun.

One night during a heavy rainstorm, drunk on white-lightning or the like, he noticed that the ceiling of his furnished room was bulging strangely. Maybe he thought he had the DTs and demons were coming after him; maybe he was just too drunk to know what he was doing. In any event he grabbed up his revolver and pumped five shots into the ominous bulge. Whereupon the entire ceiling collapsed and the ensuing deluge of trapped rainwater knocked him flat, broke his leg, and almost drowned him.

That was Flynn.

I had lost touch with him again by this time, but he and Wallmann (who had also returned to the States) continued to exchange an occasional letter. So I found out that after his leg healed Flynn left Richmond, broke and jobless again, and went to Connecticut, where he talked his ex-agent into letting him live on the agent's estate as a nominal caretaker. He stayed out of trouble there, for the most part, but he still and inevitably managed to wear out another welcome. In late January of 1986 he decided to move back to Richmond. But he'd been feeling poorly, he wrote Wallmann just before he left, and so he intended to put himself into a V.A. hospital en route for a checkup.

He never got back to Richmond because he never got out of the hospital. Less than two weeks after his admission, he was dead.

Ironically, it wasn't the booze that killed him; the damn croakers never did get that right. It was cancer. A tumor the size of a beer bottle. Doesn't seem possible, but he was still a relatively young man, still in his fifties. Wallmann and I each thought he was that age the first time we met him, thirteen and ten years earlier.

Yeah, Jay Flynn was a character.

The tragicomic variety, with accent on the tragic.

....

This memoir first appeared in *Mystery Scene* #13.

The Action Man

BY JAY FLYNN

CHAPTER 1

The dawn seeped, thin and gray, through the restless morning fog, lightening the hardly-moving surface of the bay, alerting the birds in the live oaks and pine forests of the hillsides. It caused a rooster to crow and a dog to bark at the rooster. And in the house that backed up on the yard where the dog lived, a man who had slept little because of a colicky baby twisted restlessly and cursed the son-of-a-bitch with quiet competence. At the vast Army training camp a few miles north of Peninsula City, the CQ's yawned, shrugged into their field jackets, lit cigarettes and clumped through the barracks, picking out the bunks which had the o. d. towels knotted at the foot, waking the KP's.

Denton Farr's closed eyes did not respond to the faint lightening of the room, and he was too far away to hear the rooster and the dog and the man who cursed the dog. Denton Farr was asleep in a second-floor apartment above a bar in the heart of the city, six blocks up the hill from the waterfront. He woke to the sound of heavy boots slapping the concrete sidewalk, the sound of motors and tires squealing on the corner, the sound of voices giving crisp orders.

He came awake in the way a cat wakes; the eyes opening and remaining open, the senses of sight and smell and hearing orienting him in that first instant, the trained muscles of his big body controlled, ready. He heard the breathing of the woman whose warm, naked flesh had been fitted against his; he could still feel the pinpoints of heat the firm, erect nipples had left on his back and his nostrils flared at the faintly acrid, musky scent of her. Denton Farr was awake. He was sitting now on the edge of the bed, bare feet on the carpet, watching through the slits of the venetian blinds as his fingers moved toward the night table and the cigarettes.

He watched the doorway of the bank across the street, and the action of the men. There were at least a dozen, and they had come in a fleet of cars. All were in uniform.

Parked immediately in front of the bank door was a sedan marked by military police insignia. On its roof, a red light winked in steady rhythm, painting the slats of the blind, casting barred shadows on Denton Farr's face. He watched two men climb from the car and approach the bank door.

The one who led the way was a solidly built man. Farr squinted, made out the dull silver leaves of a lieutenant colonel on his shoulders. He wore a gunbelt and a service .45 slapped at his broad rump. The second man was taller, leaner, a captain. He carried a sidearm and held a submachine gun in the crook of his arm. The colonel rapped on the heavy glass door with the tip of his swagger stick.

Farr watched four enlisted men get out of a second MP car, saw them pat the holsters on their hips as they moved up behind the two officers.

To either side, fifty or sixty feet away, other MP's took up their posts, looking sharply at the few civilians who were in sight. Farr saw a man who had come out of an all-night restaurant walk slowly toward the scene, then turn back after a word from an MP whose finger rested on the trigger guard of his Thompson.

A civilian appeared at the door of the bank and unlocked it from inside. The lieutenant colonel, the captain and the four enlisted men went inside, and a team of two MP's stepped up to guard either side of the door. At both ends of the street, cars marked with the insignia of the California Highway Patrol moved to block the intersections, their red lights flashing. Gold stars glinted in the early light as the patrolmen, shotguns held easily in their hands, got out and stood beside their cruisers.

A slight movement drew Farr's attention to the roof of the bank. He saw two more soldiers there. They had a water-cooled machine gun set up on a tripod, a belt of ammo dangling from it. He reached, found the woman's thigh, squeezed lightly.

There was a change in the way she breathed; it became deeper, more abrupt. Without waking, she groped for his hand, guided it higher.

Farr pulled his hand away and shook her. Bette Vout sighed and awoke, grudgingly. Her eyelids fluttered. She saw him at the edge of the bed, a lean, dark shape. She made a woman sound in her throat and ended with "... again, Dent?"

He did not smile or look at her. He leaned over to pull the cord that tilted the slats of the blind open. "The Army's taking over the bank. Why?"

"*What?*" Bette rolled up on an elbow, looking. Wheat-blonde hair feathered out from her head and she combed it back with her other hand, yawning, showing good teeth. She was in her late twenties. She had been married once and divorced once and she had come out of the divorce with the bar downstairs. She had a good, long-legged, limber body and a liking for the way a man who knew what he was about could make the body feel. She had liked it so much with Dent Farr that she had sold him a half-interest in the Loving Cup. She had done this because Dent Farr was married to a girl who had a build and a lot of smart, too, and Dent might get so he took her for granted sometime but he'd stick around enough to keep an eye on his investment. She leaned over him, bit his neck with the sharp teeth, ran the tip of her tongue over the taut muscle.

"End of the month. They pay the doggies today."

"Is that so." He found a match, got a cigarette going. "I hear they've got about twenty-five or thirty thousand GI's out there. Should be quite a bit of money."

"I've heard it's up to two million. Depends on how many doggies in the pound, darling."

"And they get it from *that* bank?" He puffed on the cigarette.

She laughed, pulled him down on the bed. "You never heard about it?" She leaned across him, mashing her breasts against the corded muscles of his arm as she took the cigarette and puffed on it. "Forget it, darling. You'd make a lousy bank robber. And I happen to know some pro's have thought about it. Three or four times. It can't be done."

Denton Farr let himself relax. Compartments of his mind which hadn't been called upon to work for over two years were working now. He did some fast mental arithmetic. Of the thirty thousand men at the fort, perhaps one-third would be officers or non-coms who would be paid by check. That would leave twenty thousand, perhaps eighty per cent recruits and twenty per cent cadre who would draw their pay over the table. The average should be at least fifty dollars for each man. It could be closer to seventy-five. Fifty dollars a man would still add up to a nice, round million.

A million dollars would be on its way to the fort built on the rolling hills inland from the sand dunes along the rim of the bay in a few minutes.

It would move with a convoy that was loaded for bear. But it had been sitting across the street in a sleek, glass-and-steel civilian bank all night, maybe longer.

Hell. Denton Farr grinned. Some smart apple was always knocking a bank over.

"They make enough racket," he grumbled. He lay back on the bed, no longer interested in the men who were carrying canvas sacks from the bank to the sedan with the red light on its roof. He finished the cigarette and listened to the slam of doors and the whine of tires against pavement as the convoy moved off.

Bette was at least partly right. Once the Army took over, nobody was going to get close to that payroll. Not without getting to hold a lily he wouldn't smell or see.

Dent Farr felt the old excitement again. The last caper was a long time back, and this bank job was ideal because he had never worked a bank over before.

Denton Farr arranged no more than one crime a year. Between projects he worked hard as a businessman, made legitimate money and carefully broke no laws except those dealing with adultery.

He operated under two simple, basic rules: Never do the same thing twice. Never get caught.

Diverting attention from himself came under the heading of "Never get caught." He had expressed interest in what had happened across the street.

Now he had to make Bette Vout forget this.

He put his mouth against the heat of her throat, sensed the acceleration of her heartbeat with the tip of his tongue.

"I can't sleep," he muttered.

Her hands found him.

He thought about a bunch of doggies cutting up a million bucks.

Farr watched the early sun warm the street. He sat at the small ell of the bar near the front window, the heels of his loafers hooked over the rungs of the stool. He sipped at a bottle of beer he had taken from the cooler behind the bar and chewed thoughtfully on a strip of beef jerky from a cellophane-wrapped pack. The plumbing made slight rumbling sounds and he knew Bette was in the shower upstairs. Traffic on the street was building up with the first cars of soldiers who lived off the post and civilians who worked there, and others employed in the few factories of Peninsula City. It was too early for the business district to be glutted with cars, but in a half-hour or so that would change. The tourists would stream down to the historic waterfront and Fishermen's Wharf, sunburned and outlandishly dressed, swinging their cameras and guidebooks, asking to be shed of the money they had brought from the hot towns of the interior valleys and the mushroom of human fungus that was the Los Angeles area. Farr checked his wrist watch. A few minutes before seven; about time for the first-shift bartender to open up. There would not be much trade for another hour or so, probably, but the early man had to swamp out. The Loving Cup had the stale beer, spilled whisky, and dead cigarette smell of all second-rate bars. It was a dive, but it moved a lot of booze and beer and the percentage was good. It was a soldier's bar, a fisherman's bar, sometimes a tourist bar, and all it had really needed to boost that percentage was a guy who could run it.

Trouble with Bette was she couldn't see spending anything on a dollar that didn't multiply itself inside an hour. She'd fought him on giving Tony, the Dago chef who'd been fired out of better hotels than she'd ever been in, free use of the kitchen in the back, plus his utilities and laundry. It cost them maybe fifty or sixty dollars a month, but where there'd been a slump in the middle of the day three months ago, a couple of thousand dollars a month extra went into the tills behind the bar. She'd fought him on the music at night, saying it wouldn't go in a place like the Cup. It had gone— enough to put on two extra bartenders and three cocktail girls at night. Sure, the Loving Cup was a dive, but it did better and cost less to run than the Tack Room. The Tack Room was a converted stable out in the country. It had atmosphere and high prices and prestige, and the smells were of leather and sweat, fireproofed hay; not like the Loving Cup at all. But the percentage wasn't as good. Not nearly as good.

Jack Anderson unlocked the street door and came in, kicking the stop down to hold it open. He grinned at Denton Farr.

"Smells like a backhouse."

"Looks like one, too. Hi, Jack."

"This is the only dive on the street where the bartender got to swamp out."

"I'll think about a janitor service. If there's one that won't drink up the back bar."

"There isn't. You could get something made to fence the stuff off." He went into the back room, came back with a push broom and a trash can, then began to stack the barstools and sweep out.

"I'll give it some thought."

Dent Farr raised the beer bottle to his lips and emptied it. He popped the last strip of jerky into his mouth and went out to the street as a pair of colored men in neat gray uniforms came out of the bank. They carried cleaning tools and they walked to a panel truck parked a few doors from the Cup. Farr made a mental note of the name of the janitor service painted on the side of the truck. If it was good enough for a bank it should be good enough for the Loving Cup. And there was just a chance it would be good business to do business with an outfit that could get inside that particular bank in the middle of the night. The bank was a big one for Peninsula City. Farr recalled seeing the cleanup crew in there sometimes when the Cup closed up at two in the morning.

One thing for sure—if that Army payroll was ever taken, whoever did it would have to be in and out of the place well before the convoy got there.

He walked to a restaurant that did a big business with the night people: the cops, the fishermen who left the harbor not long after the bars closed, the cabbies and the chippies and the bartenders. He sat at the counter and had steak and fried eggs and hash-browned potatoes and four cups of coffee, and he thought about the possibilities of taking that payroll. It couldn't be easy or it would have been done before. He would have to do a lot of looking—first for the way to do it, then for the right men for the job—and if there wasn't one absolutely certain method of operation to use, and at least one alternate that would give a ninety per cent chance of success and getting away clean, he would have to forget it.

He left the restaurant and walked to the Inside Garage, where the gunmetal-gray Thunderbird was parked. Johnny came from the ramshackle office, smelling of tokay and a little off-brand rye. He leaned against the battered gas pumps and worked up a grin.

"You work worse hours than me, Dent."

"End of the month. Inventory." Farr jingled the keys in his pocket, watching the man with the pasty face and bloated features.

"Save that for Mary Jean."

"You don't think I was?"

"I should give a goddamn." The slack mouth gurgled a laugh but the reddish eyes were sly. "I know you wasn't. Mary Jean called about four. Said she'd tried to raise you at the Cup."

Denton Farr waited without speaking, without a change of expression, for the rest of it.

"I said you went through a half-hour or so before. Said you was thinkin' about feedin' your face and why didn't she try Hermann's. She told me to hell with it, not sayin' hell, you know how your wife is, and she'd expect you when you show. I guessed you might go out to the Tack Room for an inventory there later."

"Good guess, Johnny." Farr took a ten from his wallet, folded it into the pocket of the sweat-stained shirt. "See you."

He walked across the cracked concrete that was stained by decades of oil from leaky motors and weeks of dirt that had been allowed to accumulate, folded himself behind the wheel of the T-bird and warmed the motor. He drove through the sagging overhead door and considered Johnny Emery.

Johnny Emery was a stewbum. He lived on the sauce and he ran a backhouse of a garage, but he was still to be cultivated. The Inside Garage was the fountainhead of everything, active and otherwise, in Peninsula City, and Johnny still had just enough brain to remember it. It was maybe seventy-five years old, a rambling, ramshackle, whitewashed, faded, stained and stunk-up building that had been a livery stable in the old days. It took up most of the center of a large city block, covering maybe an acre and a half. Three bars had their back entrances on the Inside Garage. From its murky innards you could reach any of four hotels, of sorts. It opened on three streets through alleyways, and Johnny ran a wrecker and two ancient ambulances. The whores who worked on the row on Union Street stored their cars there; so did the gamblers and the mayor and the police department. A man who knew what to look for could walk through the Inside Garage, use his eyes, and know just how much action was going in town, who'd taken the heat last, just by looking at the cars.

Denton Farr gave the low-slung car a little more gas and thought it would be a good idea to pick up the contract on the Inside Garage just for insurance. He got out on the county road leading up the valley and let the T-bird out until he reached the blacktop road to the ranch.

He parked beside the Pontiac station wagon in the carport. Emilio, the old *vaquero*, was limping toward the stable, carrying a bucket of oats for the horses. He turned as the car door slammed, grinned with teeth that were white in a wine-red face, and waved without speaking.

Farr walked slowly down the hill, between the scattered live oaks. He leaned on the door of a box stall as Emilio scooped grain into the feedbox. The bronze saddlebred gelding that went almost seventeen hands made rumbles in his throat and burrowed his nose in the box, limber lips reaching out for the kernels.

"Do I throw my hat in first?" Farr asked.

Emilio grinned as he swung the lower half of the door shut and went to the next stall. "Fool if you do, boss. That TV guy, Thomaston, was up."

Dent Farr picked a piece of straw from the manger and sucked on the end. "I understood old Burt was moving down here. He still hot for her?"

"Beats hell outa me." Emilio shoved his crumpled straw hat back on his head. "They sat in there and played the music until almost four. Killed a jug, too. Both *muy borracho* when he shoved off."

"Thanks." He took a five from his wallet, passed it over.

"Buy yourself a jug. Maybe it'll keep you out of the house stock awhile." He walked up to the shake-roofed, thick-walled ranch house that had been built to fit the contours of the hill on this north side of the valley. He entered their bedroom through the patio door.

Mary Jean lay on her side in the bed, covered only by a thin sheet.

Denton Farr shed his clothes, kicked his shoes across the room, slid into the bed. He peeled the sheet back, slapped the tanned firmness of buttocks lightly. "Hey—the old man's home."

The woman shifted restlessly in the bed, drew her legs up under her, sighed. Her dark hair was feathery ink on the white of the pillow. She pretended she was asleep.

Dent Farr grinned, drew the sheet over himself, flattened the pillow under his head and let himself sleep.

CHAPTER 2

He woke to the sound of the big, soft towel rubbing against her body; to the deep, sensuous humming in the tanned column of her throat. He rolled on his back and the sheet slid away from him. He lit a cigarette while he eyed the strong, tapering thighs, the small, erect cones of her breasts. He grinned.

"Come here?"

She studied him with eyes that were a dark, almost violet blue. She knotted the towel around her waist, took a cigarette from the pack on the dressing table and lit it before answering.

"Why?"

He grinned again. Mary Jean had class, the kind a woman is born with; and she had pride. Without knowing why, he realized he liked to smash at that pride in any way he could. He supposed maybe it was because he felt she was stronger than he.

This was the one thing she must not be; and yet if she'd been another Bette Vout he'd never have married her. Bette was a good kid, but she was just another broad whose understanding of and use for men began and ended at the bedroom door. If she couldn't have one, she'd find another. Mary Jean was different. She had accepted him as her man; she would stick to her bargain now, in spite of Burt Thomaston coming back.

Mary Jean had been Burt Thomaston's woman; he met her on account of Thomaston. It had been three years before. He had been looking for one thing—a way to hurt Thomaston and hurt him bad. Thomaston, the chunky tiger of Channel 8, the man with the strong face and the angry black eyes and black hair prematurely peppered with gray; the man who needed nothing other than his self-created role as the Grand Inquisitor; luring victims in front of his camera, slashing them open the way the fat cannery women gut a fish, throwing their guts onto the carpets of a hundred thousand living rooms.

It had been at a time when Denton Farr had been promoting sports-car races, ostensibly for charity. It had been a good gimmick, and Farr always made sure there was something left over for the good cause after his piece had come off the top. The real take had come in another way, milked from the guys who were so loaded they could buy a twelve-grand Ferrari without thinking about which bank account it should come out of. They spent money on their cars and drivers; they would have sold their souls to win one of the small gold cups with the crossed flags on the plaque and their names underneath. Denton Farr didn't have to buy twelve-grand Ferraris and drivers who could boot them up to a hundred and thirty coming out of a curve. All he had to buy was one man in a pit crew, one man with just enough smart to loosen a wire at the right time, throw the hot car just a fraction off its pace. Then the owners would pay off the bets made through a dummy and right away want to get one down for the next stop on the circuit.

Somehow—Denton Farr had never discovered just how—Burt Thomaston had found out about this. The sports-car promotion fed on publicity; Farr had decided to take a chance on a half-hour grilling by the Grand Inquisitor. The studio lights had been bright in his eyes as he sat opposite Thomaston's desk, and Thomaston himself had been invisible because of that damnable desk lamp that glared full in Farr's face throughout the interview. Thomaston showed on the monitor screens only as a dim-lit profile of a vengeful man carrying out his mission of exposing the sins of this world.

He had read sworn statements from several pit-crew boys Farr had bought; he had described graphically the troubles which beset cars which Farr bet against. He even had a couple of taped interviews with coldly furious car owners who had paid off in good faith and had not known they were pigeons until the Grand Inquisitor had shown them how it was done.

And there were the interminable, slashing questions; the questions which could not be answered because any attempt at an answer would make things worse.

And there was the final breaking on the wheel; the calm-voiced reading of a financial statement indicating Denton Farr was worth, conservatively, two hundred thousand dollars. And the reading of a letter from the Welfare Department in San Antonio, Texas, stating that one Mrs. Christy Farr, former wife of Denton Farr, was receiving seventy-seven dollars a month from the county for the support of herself and her minor child; that her former husband had deserted her when she was seven months pregnant and did not in any way contribute to her support or the child's.

That one horrible half-hour had put Denton Farr out of business, and he had been sued by the welfare people for support. He calculated it had cost him at least a hundred thousand dollars.

He had set out to find the one way to hurt this Grand Inquisitor who could not be hurt. He had learned Burt Thomaston's only need beyond himself was Mary Jean.

So he had married Mary Jean. She had known his past and she had not cared; she loved him.

Denton Farr often thought he was in love with her, too.

This he could not permit.

He had realized quickly how Burt Thomaston worshipped the slender, dark-haired woman with the cool, fine body and the agile mind; had realized Thomaston was an incurable romantic who would be happy if Mary Jean was happy, even if this happiness came from a man he personally despised.

So Denton Farr could never allow his wife to be happy.

Now she was standing in the doorway, her body sweet after the shower, the towel knotted over her hips showing damp spots, and her mouth was still forming the "why?" and her eyes were showing the hurt that Denton Farr's grin brought.

"You don't want me. If you did, you wouldn't have to ask."

She opened a wardrobe, selected shorts and a halter from a shelf and put them on without looking at him or expecting an answer.

"Burt was here last night."

"Have a nice time?"

"I just wanted you to know."

"Okay."

"Carmen will be fixing breakfast for me."

"I got breakfast in town."

"Yes." She opened the door, stepped into the hallway. "I guess you get everything in town. You don't have to, Dent."

The cigarette smoke was flat and bitter in his mouth as he watched the door close.

Farr let the bronze horse set his own pace, picking his way along the narrow trail through the oaks and madrone. The shack on the north ridge was a little more than an hour's ride from the house. It was a leaning, sagging structure slapped together years ago as a line camp for cowboys. Now it was unused, except by Denton Farr, or possibly an occasional deer or wild boar hunter who might come on it during the season.

There was a small spring on the hill behind the shack. Farr dropped a rein, rolled up a shirtsleeve and plunged his arm into the cold water. He came up with a bottle of beer and popped its cap with the opener on his pocket knife. He sat on a rock and drank from the bottle. The beer was cold; Farr had packed a case up a couple of months ago and stashed it in the spring for just such days as this one.

He gazed out over the vast country. The rugged green shapes of the Coast Range humped away to the south, incredibly sharp in air that was diamond-clear. They trembled in the waves of heat.

The sight made him think of this payroll caper. In a way, this rugged country and the robbery-to-be could be compared.

Both challenged the utmost in a man, offered the illusion of the impossible, offered vast rewards to one who could make the impossible possible. The mountains covered upwards of two thousand square miles, with the peaks gouging at the sky like shark's teeth. They took the rains from the coastal storms and left the interior valley parched. They were populated heavily by wild creatures—mountain lions, European boar that had roamed southward from the Carmel Valley, the small, nimble coast variety of deer, bobcats, some bear, rattlesnakes. And a few men. Maybe as many as a hundred. Men who were as wild and savage as the animals; men who considered civilization a zoo which must be visited once in a year or once in five years.

Denton Farr was a man who lived fully only when he called upon himself to do something which other men instinctively knew could not be done. He was not rash; he had no desire to die with police bullets in his body or lethal gas administered in the name of the People of the State of California in his lungs, or to live out his days in a cage. But only by living in the shadow of these things could he live at all.

It was not the money. He had, in one place or another, more money than he would ever be likely to need. This small ranch was all the house he could use, the fine horses cost him less than one good car; he could buy his clothes off ready-to-wear racks and they would fit his lean body to perfection. He was even on good terms with the Internal Revenue people.

It bored the pure hell out of him.

He pulled another beer from the spring and watched the gelding crop at the tall grasses around it, grasses that were green and moist, bright on the hillside that had been turned brown weeks ago by the sun. He leaned his back against the warmth of a rock, closed his eyes and drew a mental picture of a map. The map covered the area between the Federal Reserve Bank in San Francisco and Peninsula City and its hinterland. They would move the payroll in an armored car. The armored car would have to take one of the three main routes; it probably carried other shipments than the payroll. The route might be slightly different each time.

The least complicated way would be to ambush that tank somewhere.

But Denton Farr knew this part of California well. The only places where an ambush would be practical would make a getaway virtually impossible. The armored cars were equipped with two-way radios; a couple of seconds would be enough time for the crew to give the alarm. Fewer than a half-dozen roadblocks would take care of the rest.

There would be no possibility of planting a man in the armored car. Any man suitable for the job would have a prison record which routine fingerprints would turn up. Farr could handle that part himself, but it would take the actual operation out of his hands, make it necessary to turn the actual operation over to someone else. And this was something Denton Farr had to do himself. He would need the help of men, but he would have to control them, too.

He concentrated on Peninsula City itself. In theory, escape from a police net there would be impossible. There was one route to the south—a mountain road with no turnoffs that went anywhere for two hundred miles. There was another through the interior valley, but to reach it meant at least a half-hour drive which would take him through the heart of the county seat. The county seat was loaded with cops. City cops, the sheriff's office, Highway Patrol headquarters. To the north and east were the towns sprawled around the rim of the bay.

Even so, a one- or two-man operation might have a chance of making it out with a whole hide. But this would be big, would involve at least a half-dozen men. More than likely, twice that. The exact number would be known only when the job had been figured down to the last detail.

When a man can't run, he has to hide. Hide deep and well.

Denton Farr knew that somewhere in a city of a hundred thousand or more people there would be a place to hide.

He finished the second bottle of beer, tossed it into a gully. He walked to where the gelding cropped grass in the shade of an oak, checked the cinch, picked up the ground rein and swung easily into the saddle.

The question of where and how to go to ground could wait. First there was the problem of getting into that bank and walking out with more than a million bucks. It would take a lot of research.

He turned the horse toward the ranch, gave him his head. Hell, there was no hurry. He could spend a year setting this one up.

CHAPTER 3

Denton Farr spent most of the following month on research.

It was a slow process because he had to do it all himself; had to do it in a way which would not draw suspicion to himself now or later.

Pure circumstance helped establish one of the basic facts; Bette Vout had been right in her guess at the amount of money. A company commander at the training camp had overextended himself. He had not gambled or spent his money on liquor or women and his car was three years old. But his wife had spent more on clothes than a captain's wife should and they had taken a fat loss on the house they sold at the time of his transfer from a post in the East. Buying real estate was a costly proposition around Peninsula City because the military population, with the easy financing available to it, had pushed prices sky high. The captain and his wife had three children, and they had a wide acquaintance with bill collectors. In all, they had owed roughly eight thousand dollars in unsecured debts and there was no way to pay them off.

The captain had picked up his company payroll, a matter of some twelve thousand dollars, and had headed south alone. Three weeks later the FBI found him in San Diego. He had six thousand dollars, a two-year-old Lincoln convertible and a blonde. He was now awaiting court-martial.

Farr heard the details of the case one night when he had gone over to the Tack Room to relieve the bartender there. He got the story from a major stationed at the camp. The major was assigned to the Post Finance office and he had bitched about the mass of paperwork the captain had caused, concluding, "... and on top of it all, the man was incredibly stupid."

"Getting caught is stupid," Farr agreed. He mixed the major another Presbyterian.

"Oh, I don't mean just that," the major snapped. He sipped at his drink with heavy lips. "Man who does something like that expects to be caught. Sometime. A lousy twelve thousand isn't worth it. With not much more effort he could have blown out with ten times as much. Enough to stash away and come back for when they let him out. Know what'll happen to the stupid captain, bartender? The court-martial'll give him ten years busting rocks at Leavenworth. The review board'll cut it to five or six and he probably won't pull more than two. Now me, I wouldn't mind playing boulder polo a couple of years if I had a hundred thousand or so stashed."

Farr grinned. "Maybe you fellows just didn't give him enough. After all, he took off with all he could get his hands on."

The major finished his drink and pushed the glass across the bar for a refill. "Nuts! Know how big that payroll is at the end of the month, bartender? I'll tell you. Since World War II it hasn't been under a million. Last one was a million three-seventy-five thousand, and more often they're a lot bigger. Why didn't he get his hands on *that?*"

"Probably couldn't figure a way. Could you?"

The major was getting a little drunk. He concentrated on lighting a cigarette, smirked and blinked his eyes. "There's a way. The money comes down from the city in an armored car. Just three guys in an armored car. They drive up to the bank, toss the sacks on a handcart and lug it inside like it was nothin'. They should care? It's insured. Then in the mornin' the Army shows up with a half a battalion, I mean ready to fight, an' hauls it off. Not insured then. The general worries."

"Sure. So what's the way?" Farr's hand moved toward the bottle of bourbon in the well in case the major needed more priming.

"Christ, don't ask me. Probably do the goddamn job myself if I could figure it. But there's a way, bartender. Someday, there's a guy who'll want to do that job bad enough he'll figure out a way. An' when he does—" he leaned across the bar and lowered his voice—"I wanna chance to put in with him."

Farr grinned again. The major thought he was being friendly. Farr was thinking what a nice loud splat the major's ass would make on the broad plank floor of the Tack Room if he got knocked off his stool. He moved off down the bar to take care of another customer.

As the days passed, he added bits and pieces to his fund of information. One night in the Loving Cup a couple of off-duty MP's told him how payday had a big drawback for them—they had to go on duty at two in the morning when the payroll convoy made up and then just sit around for a couple of hours while the colonel got his drunken ass out of the rack and put the show on the road.

Farr brought them a round of drinks and in return learned that the rou-

tine was the same each month. The convoy would move out from the camp
a few minutes before four in the morning and meet the sheriff's cars and
Highway Patrol in town. An assistant cashier would admit the officers and
men who were to carry the money into the bank and would open the heavy
vault and check the sacks of money out. Then the vault was closed and the
time lock reset. The convoy would roll, and in a couple of hours the money
would be broken down to the penny to meet company payrolls. And it was
all one big pain in the tail.

Farr spent the day before the next payday locked in the apartment
above the Loving Cup. He brought with him a motion-picture camera with
a fast telephoto lens and plenty of film. He photographed each of the bank
employees as they came and went, and he made slow-motion shots of what
took place each time an armored car pulled up to curbside to make a
pickup or delivery. The one he presumed to be the payroll arrived shortly
before five P.M., as the evening traffic was at its thickest. A driver and guard
rode in front and another guard rode in the van. The driver stood by the
truck while the one who had ridden in back pushed a small hand truck
loaded with canvas sacks into the bank. The other guard walked beside
him, hand on the butt of his revolver. The delivery took less than five minutes. The armored-car crew appeared unconcerned. They had no reason
to worry—there would be no escape through the traffic-glutted streets if
desperate men did hold them up. Denton Farr was reasonably certain not
one of the three guards would try to use his gun if there was trouble.

That night he worked behind the bar until midnight, when he began the
month's-end routine of taking inventory of the stock, timing it so he finished a few minutes after one-thirty. He checked the cash registers, made
up a bank deposit, knotted the strings at the top of the canvas sack and
walked casually across the street to the night depository built into the wall
of the bank. He inserted his key, thrust the sack inside, heard it drop
through the chute, then walked past the front of the building.

Inside, the two janitors were cleaning up. One used a vacuum on the
wine-red rug behind the railing in the officers' section. The other emptied
wastebaskets into a big hamper. At a desk in the far corner, the assistant
cashier who would turn the payroll over to the Army fingered through a
basket of papers.

Denton Farr turned into a recessed doorway that was part of the bank
building. He used a key on a heavy glass door, locked it again behind him
and climbed a flight of stairs to offices built on the second floor. They had
been built with the idea of eventual expansion of the bank's activities. For
the present they were not needed, so they were leased out to a variety of
enterprises. A dentist had one, there were two law firms, a certified public accountant and a property-management operation. And there was the

two-room suite for which Farr had made elaborate arrangements. It had
two advantages. It was situated almost directly over the bank vault and its
windows afforded a view of the street in two directions.

The parted venetian blinds admitted enough light from the street. Farr
stood motionless, just inside the door, his ears alert for any unexpected
sounds, before crossing the room and opening the blinds farther. He
watched the occasional traffic on the street, saw several persons enter the
Loving Cup. Masking the flare with his cupped hands, he lit a cigarette,
then crossed the room to a gray steel desk which had been installed in one
corner. He unlocked the large drawer at the bottom, took out a set of lightweight earphones and unrolled the long cord attached to them as he walked
to the table which dominated the room.

It was nearly a dozen feet long, flanked by heavy chairs. On it were ten
telephones, each equipped with headsets, and a pad of paper and several
sharpened pencils lay beside each. At one end of the table was a device for
automatically recording telephone conversations. The necessary wiring for
all this apparatus was carried across the flooring in a steel conduit which
terminated in a black rectangle, about the size of a cigar box, fastened to
the floor near the end of the table. From it, individual wires led to each of
the phones.

Using a small screwdriver, Denton Farr removed the top of the box and
attached the headset wires to the proper contacts. He adjusted a rheostat
and then checked the recorder to be sure it was operating properly.

Denton Farr removed a silver flask from the pocket and allowed himself a small sip of Scotch before sinking into the upholstered chair behind
the desk. He tilted the blinds slightly, puffed his cigarette and settled
down to wait.

It had cost money to establish this vital observation post. There had been
the not trivial year's lease on the two rooms and the investment in the telephone equipment, ordered through a front man in the name of a vague
company allegedly in the business of making telephone surveys of the
Peninsula area for a national advertising firm. The crew from the phone
company which had done the installing had been sure a new horse parlor
was opening up and this suspicion had been confirmed by prompt and efficient juicing of the vice-squad plainclothesmen who came around to see
what was what. Farr had even arranged to hire several young women to
call telephone numbers at random several hours a day and ask questions,
the answers to which were duly recorded on printed forms. The forms in
turn were mailed every three days to a post-office box in Chicago. This ac-
tivity took place between eight and ten o'clock in the morning and four
and six o'clock in the afternoon, hours which permitted the placing of bets
on horse races in between.

The survey girls thought the operation was legitimate. The bookie believed it to be safely illegitimate and cared not beyond knowing the fix was in good.

Denton Farr himself had converted the equipment to suit his own needs, had removed the junction box and installed under it the leads from the pencil-thin microphones which he had installed in holes drilled in the flooring. By manipulating switches, Farr could listen in to any area of the bank he chose and record what the mikes picked up for future study.

Now he leaned back, crossed his ankles on the desk and tuned in on the janitors. The vacuum cleaner was no longer in use and he could hear the light swishing of push brooms over the tiled floor of the lobby. They were talking about their wives and about a couple of women they knew who were more fun than their wives. The conversation bored Farr and he tried other mikes until he found one which picked up the sounds made by the assistant cashier at his desk. There was the faint scratching of a pen on paper, and, after almost an hour, the man made a phone call, evidently to his family and of absolutely no interest to Farr.

At three-fifteen, there was a rapping on the front door. Farr leaned forward, watched through the window as two uniformed merchant patrol guards were admitted. He listened as they exchanged greetings with the bank man and the janitors. He checked his watch again, then inspected the line to the recorder and turned up the volume on one of the microphones.

At precisely three-thirty, he heard the sound for which he had been waiting—the soft, solid clicking as the time lock on the vault released. In a moment, the soft whirr of metal turning against metal came through the earphones. The cashier was dialing the first numbers of the vault's combination lock. The individual clicks were too quiet, too close together, to be picked up by human ears. But slowed down by the tape and amplified, they would reveal the combination as surely as if Denton Farr had been watching the numbers come up. The cashier would not complete the operation now—he'd leave one or two turns of the dial for the arrival of the Army. They, too, would be recorded.

Farr hoped he would have no need of the combination. Too many things could go wrong with an operation which depended on his opening that immense steel and concrete box downstairs. Much, much better if the banker did the job.

The sounds from the vault area ended. A mike from the rear of the building picked up the clatter of a bolted door being released. Farr, the headset wires trailing behind him, walked into the adjoining room. It overlooked an alleyway which serviced the bank and several other buildings and which, after a couple of turns, led to the Inside Garage.

The door was open and the janitors were hauling the big hamper of trash outside, spilling its contents into a large covered storage box. As he watched, they finished the job and walked back into the bank. The door was closed and locked again.

The time was three forty-three.

Farr closed his eyes as he sat in the chair again. He swallowed a mouthful of whisky and smiled. There was a simple way to accomplish this impossible robbery. Simple if the timing held up. That left only the problem of getting away clean.

He was so engrossed with the mechanics of the getaway that he almost missed hearing the cashier dial the final numbers of the combination as the now-familiar military caravan turned into the street.

The same lieutenant colonel and captain approached the bank. The captain had a Thompson submachine gun.

CHAPTER 4

The Commissioner stirred the tall rum concoction with the colored straws, puckered his wide mouth and looked steadily at Farr with eyes that seemed to be without color. The eyes were recessed under the ledge of the sloping forehead.

Farr moved his feet restlessly under the table. In the mirror behind the booth he watched the red-jacketed bartender wipe a thin-stemmed glass and carefully set it on the back bar. This was the part of the whole thing that he did not like—the bringing in of specialized talent for this job, allotting a slice of his proceeds to the eastern syndicate and the Commissioner. A slice that was sure to be disproportionately large in comparison to the services rendered.

From the start he had realized it would have to be this way.

The Commissioner was deep-chested, powerfully built. He had the look of an insurance salesman who did well enough to take four-month vacations. The appearance was deceptive. For all practical purposes, the Commissioner was forever on vacation. He lived well through arranging work for others. The transportation of hot goods or hot people out of the country. The smuggling in of goods and people who were hot in other countries and who could pay for the necessary services. The employment of a man who could make an incendiary bomb and see that it did its job properly. The Commissioner could provide a platoon of men who could kill with knives, guns, rope, poison or bare hands.

The Commissioner knew and admired Denton Farr.

Now he fitted a cigarette to a short holder, put the holder between his lips and snapped a silver lighter. His voice was almost sad.

"Sorry, Dent. Too hot."

Farr's mouth went thin and tight. The bleat of a fog horn under the Golden Gate irritated him. He gulped the whisky in his glass and rapped it down on the dark wood of the table.

"You think it can't work?" he said curtly.

The Commissioner carefully tapped the new ash from his cigarette. "If anyone else proposed something of this magnitude, I might think that. Knowing you, I feel only the worst conceivable luck could *prevent* it from working. And I say that without knowing exactly what it is you have in mind, although two million dollars spells bank to me."

"Then *why?*"

"The time is wrong. We can live with our opposite numbers in the law-enforcement profession. They're pretty well hemmed in by the rulings of our very liberal courts. However, we can't live with the congressional committees. They accomplish nothing in theory and everything in fact. They expose us by making us take the Fifth. It makes doing business difficult. At the present time we have some nice, steady operations going for us on the Coast. Your caper would get us two million dollars' worth of congressmen. An awful lot of congressmen, Dent. Suppose you make it. We take a half-million. In the end we lose ten times that much. This is just my opinion. I can take it on up the line but I know what the answer will be. A quiet *no* with a lot of authority behind it."

"Meaning the organization will try to stop me if I do it on my own."

"You'd be stopped, Dent."

"You're big enough." Farr was standing now, smiling, picking up the bar check. This was not a case to be argued. "Anyway, Commish, it's been good getting together. Been too long."

The Commissioner put his hand on Farr's shoulder and squeezed with a fraction more power than a friendly gesture required. "It has. I'm really sorry, Dent." He waited while Farr paid the check and they walked out to the steep San Francisco street together. "Look—if it did work out, you'd be too hot for the States for the rest of your life. And the word would get out. No matter where you went, there'd always be somebody waiting to take it away from you."

Farr grinned into the damp coolness of the fog without replying. The message was blunt enough to need no comment.

The Commissioner stopped beside an Imperial hardtop. He unlocked the door, slid into the seat, shut the door behind him and rolled the window down.

"Dent. I mentioned we had some good stuff going for us out here. We could use you."

Farr shook his head and looked for a cruising cab. "I've got a nice clean business going. I don't have to give a damn about congressmen. And I sleep easy." He flagged a Checker, paused a moment as the driver swung the rear door open.

"See you in the spring when you're fat."

The cab squealed its tires on the steep pitch of the hill.

Farr thought about it in the tavern car of the train which took him back to Peninsula City. He estimated that his chances of taking the payroll and keeping it long enough to enjoy it were about one-third of what they had been before he went to see the Commissioner. He had been prepared to take his chances on the police agencies which would dedicate themselves to hunting him down. They had their limits. If he was caught, and providing nobody had been seriously hurt, he could expect to do no more than five years in the joint. He supposed he could pretty much take over the management of any pen they might put him in within six months. The size of his caper would make him high in the ranks of the cons immediately, and in these days of enlightened penology the cons ran the prisons, making them not much more than big hotels with the warden for a manager and the screws for bellhops. Farr imagined he could enjoy himself.

The organization was a different situation. It operated without the law, made its own laws, enforced them with the sure, swift efficiency of the guillotine. If he crossed the organization the Commissioner's associates would hunt him down. They would take what he had taken and they would kill him. Kill him in a slow, painful way that would be a warning to others. They would go a long way, take a long time to do the job.

Farr knew these things. He accepted them.

He sipped a Scotch-on-the-rocks and thought it would probably take a long time to figure out a way to get the organization off his tail.

He was sure they would be watching him, quietly, closely. He was glad he had not gone into detail with the Commissioner.

He recalled their conversation in detail and he decided the Commissioner had been told just enough to send him riding off in four or five wrong directions at once.

The Commish would be thinking about a bank. The Commish also knew that nobody had tapped a bank except during business hours for years and years. The people who make vaults and alarm systems had seen to that. So the Commish would waste a lot of time trying to find out which of several hundred banks was ripe to be taken.

He knew Farr had never set up a caper within fifty miles of wherever he happened to be living at the time. So he might never get around to thinking about Peninsula City at all.

He knew Farr had asked for a first-rate electronics man who could build a couple of radios to order and also a portable jammer to confuse a radar set. Such men are rare; in the whole country, there would probably be no more than a dozen who would do the job. The Commish would know each of these men and all he had to do would be to pass the word to let him know if they were approached.

And there was the matter of the airplane and the man to fly it. Farr had let the Commish think they were vital. The Commish would put in a lot of hours checking around to see which of hundreds of pilots who would fly anything anywhere, if the price was right, were picking up jobs. The Commish would be angry indeed when he discovered the plane was nothing more than an expensive piece of window dressing.

The train clanked to a stop at the Peninsula City station. There was a thin fog hovering around the dirty brown-and-yellow building, and the reflector lights that hung from poles along the track made the place even more dismal than it had a right to be. Farr swung easily from the step of the tavern car and felt his expensive shoes crunch into the gravel of the walkway as he crossed the parking area to the cab stand.

He rode to the Loving Cup and was glad he hadn't said anything to the Commissioner about wanting a doctor, a trash truck, three men to handle the truck and a Negro actor with a lot of brain and a lot of patience.

If he had mentioned these men and the truck, the Commissioner would have figured the key parts of the operation within a few days.

The piano player was taking a break and Bette Vout was having a drink with him. As Farr came in she swung off the stool at the far end of the bar and walked toward him with that leggy strut. The way she carried her body said she hadn't seen him for too long a time, but the full lips did not smile and her eyes were a shade too narrow, too calculating. There were thirty or so men in the Loving Cup and Farr watched their eyes following her. She wore a pale silver sheath that molded the long, tapering thighs, reflecting the pale lights spotted along the walls. She stood close to him, fingers gripping the tight muscles of his upper arms.

"It was getting late. I thought you might not be back."

He trailed his fingers lightly along the curve of her back, touching the nerve centers that were a short fuse for this ripe female body.

"I'm back but I can't stick around."

Her eyes flared in the dim light. "Going up the valley?"

"Yeah. You object?"

"It wouldn't do any good, would it?"

"You don't have to ask."

"I might as well save you a trip. You won't find anyone home."

"No?"

"She's on the town tonight. With one of your favorite people."

"Thomaston?"

"Naturally. And a half-dozen hangers-on. They had a couple of drinks here and moved on a half-hour or so ago. We talked a little, Mary Jean and I. I—I think I like her. Anyway, I came out of it feeling sort of cheap."

Without changing expression, Farr let his hand move around to her side, until his thumb rested in front of and slightly above the bone of her hip. Smiling, he dug thumb and fingers into her flesh until she breathed sharply with the pain and the corners of her mouth went white.

"So you told her all about us. You dumb bitch!"

"No!" She twisted her body, broke away from the pressure. "Of course not, Dent. I think she knew a long time ago. You never seemed to give a damn who saw you coming out of the apartment when the sun was coming up. *Please.*"

"Yeah. Remember, that's not a license to get stupid. How come the party tonight?" Farr realized the knowledge that his wife was out with Burt Thomaston was disturbing him more than it should. He knew Mary Jean. He knew she liked Thomaston, maybe came close to loving him. He also knew she would not go to bed with him as long as she was married to Denton Farr; she would not use his own infidelity as an excuse to play the same game.

So why should it bother him?

There was more to it than his personal dislike, even hatred of Burt Thomaston. He had evened the score with the Grand Inquisitor on the sports-car thing when he took Mary Jean. He would still enjoy putting the blocks to Thomaston any time he had a chance, and he knew Thomaston felt the same toward him. But this was a matter involving no one but themselves. They could hate each others' guts without involving Mary Jean or anyone else.

"The party?" Bette Vout was saying. "Thomaston did his first show from the peninsula tonight, that's why. You knew he was building his home here. He put up a studio as well, and a lot of his shows will be originating there from now on. He didn't grill anybody tonight, at least not very much. He had a few of the peninsula fat cats up, had the cameras show the place off, introduced this one and that one. The idea behind it all was 'here is a very solid citizen; he's really not a bastard at all,' and I think he put it over."

"Yeah." Farr took his hands from her. "I have to go anyway."

Bette Vout took one step back and laughed. It was not a pleasant sound. "I knew you'd do it."

"Do what?" The words were cold, quiet.

"Chase her. You're hooked, Dent. Only you don't know it." She turned and went back to the piano player.

Farr pivoted on his heel and straight-armed the door open.

Johnny Emery smelled of bourbon this time. He was leaning back in the ancient swivel chair in his rat's-nest of an office when Denton Farr walked through the big double door of the Inside Garage. He slammed the drawer that held the bottle into the desk as he watched Farr with red, watery eyes and licked slack lips.

"What'n hell you browned off about?"

"You're loaded again," Farr said curtly. "The T-bird gassed?"

"Sure. Goin' somewheres?"

Farr quelled the urge to pick this drunken slob up, backhand him until his fingers ached and then dump his tail in one of the littered corners. He was sure he would be needing Johnny Emery soon, and needing his Inside Garage. And the only thing wrong with Johnny was too much mouth. Not blabbing mouth, but smart, needling mouth. Drunk or sober, Johnny Emery had never been known to drop a piece of information to the wrong ears.

Farr looked at him and thought: This is the one guy I could tell, 'I'm going to take a bank' and be sure nobody'd get it out of him. Not with thumb-screws, not with boots to the kidneys, probably not even with the fancy truth drugs like Pentothal, because, in Johnny's case, the sauce had permanently fogged the part of a man's mind those drugs work on.

A tube of paper cups lay on top of the water cooler. Farr took a cup, held it under the spigot, pressed the valve and filled it with water. Then he crossed to the desk and yanked the lower drawer open to pick out the cheap blend. Unscrewing the cap, he put the bottle to his lips, swallowed twice and gulped the water as the gagging began.

"Getting soft," he said pleasantly. "Time was when I could swill stuff like this without a chaser."

Johnny Emery reached for the bottle. He drank, blinked his eyes, took his time about replacing the cap. He tossed the bottle into the litter of papers on the desk. "I still got an iron gut. Try the Tack Room."

"Why?"

"That bunch Mary Jean was with said something about going out there."

Farr did not reply immediately. He stood, easy and relaxed against the doorway, his expensive flannel suiting brushing against the grimy, peeling paint. Then he grinned fleetingly, took a bill from his wallet and let it flutter down beside the bottle.

"Buy something that won't take the bottom off an ox."

He folded himself into the Thunderbird and drove to the Tack Room.

They were grouped around the heavy, circular table set in what had once been a box stall. One of the waiters was serving steaks from a big tray set on a folding stand. Burt Thomaston sat beside Mary Jean, and to his right the wine steward was spinning a tall, dark bottle in a silver bucket filled with ice. Thomaston met his eyes as he stepped up to the table. The man's face was a mask. A mask that began to smile in the knowing, half-mocking smile that came into maybe a million living rooms every Thursday night at 10 o'clock. The black eyes flicked around the other faces at the table, returned to Denton Farr. They said there will be no unpleasantness. At least while my distinguished guests are present. And, of course, you will crash my party. With your lovely wife beside me, what else can you do?

"Dent! I'm glad you got back in time."

Mary Jean could say it like she meant it, and Denton Farr thought she probably did at that. The black hair was wound in a Grecian roll and she wore a black dress expertly fitted to the swell of her breasts.

"Hello, Mary Jean. Burt. Gentlemen ..." Farr slid a captain's chair back from a vacant place at the table and turned his professional-host smile on the other men. These were the fat cats Bette Vout had mentioned. The superior court judge, the mayor of Peninsula City, the commanding officer of the fort, the county supervisor from this district. Solid, substantial people who could afford a dinner at the Tack Room even if it didn't go on Burt Thomaston's expense account. With a glance, Denton Farr checked the steaks. He approved. The waiter had informed the chef it was Mary Jean's party, so the steaks were New York cuts, a full two-inches thick, served only with small bowls of clear, strong soup and baked russet potatoes slashed open and covered with melted butter and light cheese. No vegetable. Instead, a candied crab apple. Nothing more was needed.

The wine steward prepared to open the bottle. The label, seen from the corner of his eye for a fraction of a second, alerted Denton Farr.

"*Luigi.*" The word was little more than a whisper.

The wine steward became a statue. Then his dark, expressive eyes moved from the bottle in his hands to Farr's face and they read the message there. A faint smile of anticipation played at the corners of his mouth. Luigi liked Denton Farr; he did not approve of Denton Farr's wife coming to this place with another man who obviously cared much for her.

Luigi prepared himself for the pleasure of seeing Denton Farr make an ass of this Burt Thomaston.

In quiet, fluent Italian, Denton Farr called his wine steward down for permitting such a vintage to be served to this illustrious group. He pointed out that the grapes had been notoriously poor in the particular year represented by the bottle which Luigi held so tenderly; that it appeared on the list only because the tourists who knew no better insisted upon ordering it and, even in the good years, this particular variety traveled poorly and could be enjoyed by one gifted with taste buds on the tip of his tongue only in its own country. He instructed Luigi to remove it forthwith and bring instead the excellent grenache rosé from the small winery in the Los Gatos hills of California.

Luigi bowed himself away from the table, taking the wine with him. Farr looked to Burt Thomaston. The man's brow was furrowed as he struggled with the translation. Farr was sure Thomaston spoke no Italian. Thomaston knew the bastardized Spanish spoken in California and there was— maybe—enough similarity so the chunky man with peppered hair and angry black eyes got a little of the drift. Hell, a deaf mute could have caught on just from watching Luigi. Their faces told him the mayor and the county supervisor had understood none of what he said. The two-star general chewed his lip and there was a faint gleam in his steady eyes. Farr decided he knew the wine, not the language. The judge, a small, swarthy man, was second-generation Italian. He had understood perfectly. And he could be counted upon to pass the story on.

Satisfied, Farr smiled fondly at Burt Thomaston. "Burt, I was forced to give my man hell for not informing you we have a far better wine than anything on the list. I understand you have a real reason to celebrate tonight. Reason to justify tapping the private cellar." He eased himself into the captain's chair as the waiter brought a double martini. "Please don't wait for me. If you don't tear into those steaks, the chef will be out here wanting to know what the hell's wrong."

Thomaston raised his knife with fingers that trembled slightly. He plunged the fork into the steak, watched it run red with blood. "Thank you, Dent."

Denton Farr caught his wife's eyes over the rim of his glass. He winked and sipped his drink, feeling the stem of the glass wet and cold against his fingers.

The waiter brought a steak for Farr and Luigi arrived with the grenache rosé. They talked pleasantly of Burt Thomaston's plans to do all his West Coast shows from the peninsula, of a major golf tournament which would be played next month, of how the area could get rich off the tourists and conventions if the quality of what was offered was kept high and the prices higher to exclude the five-and-dime trade, of how the military population was built-in insurance policy against any real depression.

The judge praised the wine.

Burt Thomaston scowled.

Denton Farr watched the general clean up every scrap of food on the platter. He was mildly pleased. The general had a local reputation as a gourmet.

"I'm afraid we couldn't keep the Tack Room open with the military alone, General," he said. "We seldom see officers below field grade."

The general smiled and dabbed at his mouth with the napkin. "Consider

your prices, sir. But why should you worry? I understand you have a place
called the Loving Cup that's popular with our junior officers and the EM."

"Dent Farr has something for everyone." Burt Thomaston's words were
pleasant but his face was tight, flushed. Mary Jean looked nervously from
him to her husband. "We've got some sports-car races coming up in a few
weeks. Dent had those once."

The faces swiveled to Farr now. Farr met the eyes and he realized these
men did not know the story. It had all happened before he moved to the
peninsula and none of them were in the beret and bucket-seat crowd. He
didn't give much of a damn about any of them, but there was no point in
being revealed as a bastard.

Thomaston was eyeing him with anticipation, not realizing he was
shackled. This was not a studio, dark except for a spotlight burning into
the eyes of his victim. This was the Tack Room and this audience was hap-
pily fed with the best steak on the Coast and mellowed by the best wine,
not bloated with popcorn or pretzels and belching off the gas from cheap
beer and flicking ashes on the rug while their eyes were glued to the glare
of the television screen.

"I promoted the original races a few years ago," Farr told them quietly.
"Burt here was just getting started with his Grand Inquisitor gimmick and
he was hot for stories. Some men who wanted to take over what I'd built
up provided him with one. The Inquisitor format was the same then as it
is now—what it lacks in fact it makes up in venom. None of it could have
been substantiated in a court of law." Farr paused to light a cigarette. "I
thought about suing you, Burt. Even went so far as to get affidavits from
your 'witnesses' admitting they had lied. My lawyers felt they could clean
you out—except that you didn't have enough to make it worthwhile at the
time. We found a better answer. Much better."

Burt Thomaston reached for his glass and drank the wine which he had
not previously touched. "If this is true—and I don't know that it is,
Farr—you can't sue me now that I'm worth something. Statute of limita-
tions expires in one year and—"

"You're so right." Farr summoned the waiter, ordered after-dinner
drinks and asked him to bring a strongbox from the safe in the office.

The drinks came and he studied Mary Jean's face as she lifted a pony glass
of B&B to her mouth. Her blue eyes were dark and they held a message.
*You are being an utter bastard, as always. You were a bastard to come
here in the first place and you were a bastard about the wine and you will
probably be a bastard again and sign the check when this started out as
Burt's party. But whatever you are, my unfaithful bastard of a husband,
you are not stupid. I think Burt was stupid. Stupid and vindictive, and because of that he has dug himself a hole. If he falls into the hole and is sat*

upon by you, dear bastard, I will enjoy it immensely. I will take you home to bed with me and for the first time in much too long a time I will turn you every way but loose.

Farr smiled at his wife and he wanted his wife. He saw the color come up in her face and knew she sensed his wanting.

The waiter brought the small metal box. It had a sturdy lock which Farr opened with a key from his chain. He felt the eyes upon him as he thumbed through envelopes, selected one, took a sheaf of photostats from it. He passed them across the table.

Burt Thomaston pressed them flat on the table, leaning close, smoothing the crease marks. He fished a pair of heavy-rimmed glasses from his breast pocket and put them on.

"Cut through the legalese and it means I own a quarter of the Grand Inquisitor," Farr said dryly. "Your producer was much impressed with what my lawyer showed him. I insisted you shouldn't be told, Burt. I didn't want to inhibit you.

Thomaston's mouth worked but no sound came out. He tried to drink from the empty wine glass, slammed it down and grabbed the King Alphonse which the waiter had left by his coffee cup. He folded the photostats and flipped them toward Farr.

Farr replaced them in the box, locked it. The waiter came to take it away and brought the check. Farr signed it and looked into Mary Jean's eyes as he wrote. He stood. Thomaston's head was slumped between his shoulders and his fingers knotted around his napkin. Farr could see the gleam of sweat on the man's hands. He had humiliated the Grand Inquisitor; it was not something from which he could take pride. Thomaston had gone looking for trouble, he had walked into something that had been waiting a long time and he had been sandbagged. Denton Farr would have enjoyed himself if they had started from scratch, if he had not been the hunter crouching in the blind while the quarry was driven to him. The fact that the quarry had done its own driving didn't make that much difference.

He nodded to the quiet faces around the table. They were faces of men who have just watched a tiger eat a goat. "Gentlemen," he said softly. "Mrs. Farr and I must be leaving. We'd like you to be our guests for the remainder of evening."

The judge, the mayor, the general and the county supervisor stood as Mary Jean did. Burt Thomaston could not get to his feet until Mary Jean was finishing her good-byes and ready to leave. Then he leaned heavily on the table and merely nodded. His eyes slid away from Denton Farr's.

She sat beside him without speaking as the T-bird throbbed along the valley road. Farr smoked a slender, strong, cigar. The bite of the smoke helped him keep his mind on driving. Mary Jean wore no perfume. She liked the clean, slightly musky woman smell of herself and knew she needed nothing more to arouse the instincts of a man. The scent reached his nostrils in spite of the cigar.

He knew how it would be.

She was out of the car before it had fully stopped, her heels rapping at the walk that led directly to their bedroom. Farr got out of the car slowly and followed, fingers loosening his narrow tie, opening the top buttons of his shirt.

She was fast. Her dress, the cobweb underthings, the garter belt and sheer hose were spilled over the corner chair when he closed the door. She came toward him, her body dim in the light that filtered in from the curtained window. He started to shrug out of his jacket and then her arms were around him, her hands pulling the cloth away from him.

She arched herself against him, mouth up, open, wanting his, and her fingers worked quickly at the buttons. She took her mouth away for the seconds she needed to kneel and unlace his shoes and then the taut, wanton young body was tight against him again.

She leaned her weight on him and he fell backward across the low bed. He reached for her and she drew away.

"No!"

"Huh?" He groped for the light shape so close to him. "Hey!"

"Dent—don't." Her breath was quick and hot against his chest. "I thought about this all the way up here. Maybe a long time before that."

"Oh."

"Don't move a muscle. Please. Not until I say to."

Her lips were against his chest. He felt the hot, moist tip of her tongue and the small, sweet pain her teeth made.

He thought he would be out of his mind before she raised her head, put her mouth on his and let him know it was all right now.

She slept with her head in the hollow of his shoulder. Farr had left the bed once, to open the drapes, and now he lay without moving. For a long time, until the sky over the east ridge began to show a gray and then a faint new-day blue, he watched the stars track across the window.

He tried to understand himself. He tried to isolate the reason behind his compulsion to take that payroll.

Not for the money. He didn't expect to run through what he already had in his lifetime. Not for the pleasure of surprising a lot of people who believed such a thing couldn't be done. He was incapable of caring what others thought of or about him.

To prove something to himself? He doubted it. He had successfully planned and executed a variety of crimes already and had not proved much of anything. He had not intended to.

Then why?

He was fat with money, he had this fine woman and everything was going for him. Why do something that would bring the federals and the syndicate howling after him; why try a stunt that could easily get him killed and certainly send him on the dodge for the rest of his life?

The action, then. There was something special about the way his body felt, something different about the air it breathed, about the food it ate and the liquids it drank, when he had action. That it was unnecessary did not matter. It was action.

Why the hell do you want to climb that mountain?

Because it is there.

Denton Farr closed his eyes against the growing light of day and slept.

CHAPTER 5

The guy was stocky, swarthy, with a lot of dark hair carefully fingerwaved into position. A sullen mouth, a suit with too much lapel, a shirt with too much color and a necktie with too much knot.

Denton Farr had not seen him come into the Loving Cup and with the trade building up the way it was he might not have picked him out for a couple of hours. The cocktail girl tipped him when she slid her tray across the bar and called out the order.

"Rye and ginger."

Farr did not turn immediately. He let several seconds go by while he looked for the rye among the glinting bottles of the back bar. The one he picked up had dust on it and he used a towel to wipe it clean before pouring the shot. As he made the highball he finished the story he was telling the fisherman who had the stool next to the waitress's station.

He took more time than was necessary with the cash register, watching in the tinted mirror behind the bar as the girl delivered the drink.

Rye is strictly an East Coast whisky.

In Boston, New York, Philly, you ask the barman for a waterball, ginger high or whatever and it comes up made with a rye or a blend that's on the rye side. Anywhere else in the country and it'll be bourbon.

Farr supposed not one drink in three hundred built at the Cup involved rye. The rye drinker was drinking his rye now, lowering it to the halfway mark in the glass with one swallow. Farr could see that the ashtray on the table was clean except for the single thin cigar tilted up against it, so the guy had just come in. He knew the face from somewhere. Somewhere that was a long time back.

If the guy had asked for Scotch or bourbon, he'd have been just another customer. If Farr had noticed him at all, he'd have pegged him as a small-time punk from the city. Maybe a bookie's runner, maybe a policy bagman, maybe just tied up with the pinball and music-box bunch. A nothing. But he drank rye.

Farr went on making drinks, probing his memory as he fingered ice cubes into glasses, poured whisky over them, added ginger, soda, water, a twist of lemon, a cherry.

Boston.

Eight or nine years ago, when he and the Australian had the Chinese refugee thing going. The Australian had some static with the syndicate, which was what chilled the game anyway, and Rye Drinker had come around a couple of times.

Tony Perisi. One generation away from a pushcart in the North End. A gun, a knife, a set of broken kidneys.

The Commissioner had gone better than three thousand miles on this one and he had picked a guy Farr could make in a minute. Farr smiled. The Commissioner's luck was usually better than that.

So what to do about Tony Perisi?

He could do nothing. Let Perisi wander around trying to figure what the hell was up. But Perisi might be smarter than he looked; he might be just bright enough to get himself into those offices over the bank and dig around until he found the mike wiring. That would be enough for the Commissioner.

He could arrange to have Perisi dropped in the bay. There were guys on the waterfront who would drop the mayor in the bay for a grand and guarantee he wouldn't make a splash. No good. The Commissioner would figure what happened and send somebody else. Farr knew he might not spot the somebody else until it was too late.

He had to do something. Something that was just right. Rough enough to let the Commissioner know Denton Farr was too tough to take in Peninsula City without a pretty bloody time all around. Not so rough that the Commissioner, who had a certain place in the pecking order of the organization to maintain, would have to send in a crew of real heavies to hold that place.

Farr decided the first move should be a long, intimate talk with Tony Perisi. He walked along the bar, poured a straight shot and put it in front of the fisherman he'd told the story to. He was one of the Appromollo brothers. Willie. They had a double-ended trawler and a corrugated-iron shed on the waterfront, and with the help of assorted relatives it made into a pretty good little wholesale fish operation.

Willie Appromollo eyed the shot glass and then Denton Farr.

"Brother Chick around?"

"Uh-huh. 'Cross the street. Pizza."

"How about your panel truck and the shed. Available for a couple of hours?"

Willie lifted the shot glass in callused fingers but did not drink. "Depends. Us too?"

"Sure. I got a tough apple on my tail. I think I should peel him."

Willie studied Denton Farr's face and the faces reflected in the minor behind him. "How tough is this apple?"

"You don't care. He's mine. You and Chick just drive the truck with him nice and quiet in the back. Then you cut up some fish or something at the shed while I talk to this guy in back."

"Maybe. How much?"

"Five bills."

"Apiece?"

Farr lit a cigarette. "For that much I can get him deep-sixed."

Willie drank the whisky. "Okay. How soon?"

"Get Chick and the truck. Around back, in the alley by the Inside Garage. Come in and let me know when you're set."

Willie Appromollo nodded. He swung off the barstool and went out. Denton Farr went upstairs. He put on a sports jacket and slipped a lightweight, stubby revolver into a hip holster.

Bette Vout was on the bed. She wore a sheer bra and panties and she was reading a paperback novel. She saw the gun.

"Dent! Why're you—"

He turned his eyes on her. She went back to the book without finishing the question.

Farr went downstairs and waited until headlights flared in the alleyway behind the building. He saw Willie Appromollo get out of a battered panel truck and slam the door. He picked his way through the couples on the small dance floor, heading for the booth.

Tony Perisi was careless. If he'd taken the next booth over, it would have been impossible to walk up behind him. He was starting on another rye when Farr came up and flipped his jacket back, let his fingers hang close to the butt of the revolver.

"Okay, Tony. Keep the hands on the table and get up slow. Walk out the back door. Do it just right and you might be able to walk back in."

Tony Perisi was a pro. He did exactly as he was told. He knew Denton Farr did not want blood. Not here, anyway. He worked himself out of the booth, kept his hands in sight, stood docilely as Farr shoved him against a wall in the back room and took a switchblade knife and a .32 automatic from him. His opinion of Farr went up when Farr found the tiny .22 holstered in his garter.

He walked out the rear door obediently, and when Farr hit him behind the right ear with the butt of the revolver he fell face-down in a puddle of water and did not move.

Farr called the Appromollo brothers. "Take him down. Tie him up to a chair in the back room. He's big heat, so don't let him see your faces or know where he is. I'll be along."

He watched the panel truck jounce down the alleyway, then went to the Inside Garage. He described Tony Perisi.

"Yeah. He left his wheels here, Dent. The Merc sedan, two down from your Bird." Johnny Emery yawned. "He locked it."

"You've got keys. I want a look."

Emery brought a big ring of keys from the office. Farr had the Merc unlocked quickly. It had California plates, so the Commissioner had probably provided it. Farr went through the glove compartment, ripped the floor mats loose, tore the seats out. He found what he expected to find. Nothing.

Just a twin to the automatic he'd taken off Perisi, in a holster strapped to the underside of the front-seat cushion. He removed the clip, took the gun to a workbench, stripped it down, used a ball peen hammer and small chisel to break the firing mechanism in a way that wouldn't be discovered until Perisi tried to use the gun. He reassembled it, wiped his fingerprints and replaced it under the seat. Johnny Emery had gone back to his office, where he was eyeing the low level of a fifth of cheap rye balefully.

Farr took a ten-dollar bill from his wallet and put it beside the keys. "Lock it up and forget it. That means you never remember."

"Sure, Dent." Johnny folded the ten into his pocket and reached for the bottle.

Farr drove the T-bird to the waterfront. He thought: Two rye drinkers in town. Tony Perisi and Johnny Emery.

It smelled like all fish sheds since the beginning of time. The front room, with two large refrigerated showcases and a running-water tank for crabs and a large scale, was spotlessly clean, smelling of ammonia and fresh sawdust. Willie and Chick Appromollo were gutting a pile of rock cod, their fingers deft with the long, sharp knives. They wore white aprons over short jackets and shapeless slacks of white with thin gray lines.

"He's waitin'. Just now comin' around," Willie said.

He jerked his head toward a door in the rear of the room. Farr opened the door, took a step inside and came back, his nose wrinkling. "Jesus! Fish do smell." He did not like the thought of getting the stink into his expensive clothes. "Got another one of those butcher-boy outfits?"

"In the locker," Chick said. "Got the dough?"

"Not on me. Come by the Cup later, or tomorrow." He went to the locker, picked a jacket and slacks from a shelf and changed in the cubbyhole of an office.

The smell in the back room was overpowering. As Farr shut the door, he thought he'd tell anybody anything they wanted to know if they left him long enough in a room that reeked of dead fish. Anything over an hour would be long enough. He felt the old planks of the floor, soaked through with years of fish oil, sink under his weight. The shed was built up on piles over the water and he could hear the wet slap of the tide against the timbers. Tony Perisi looked awake and unhappy.

His olive complexion had a greenish tinge in the light of the single overhead bulb that swung at the end of a kinked wire. He breathed in shallow gasps and the front of his shirt and suit were stained with vomit. He watched Farr with dark, malevolent eyes, and Farr knew this hoodlum from the East Coast would kill him as soon as he had a chance. Kill him whether the Commissioner wanted it that way or not. Perisi's chunky body strained at the tough strands of fishing line that bound him to the stout wooden chair and he cursed Denton Farr in English and Italian.

Farr slapped his face. The waved hair sprayed out in a wild mop as the chair crashed over. Perisi landed in a pool of water. The water was gray with fish scales. Perisi arched his neck and tried to roll away from it. He had to breathe, and when he breathed he gagged. Farr yanked the chair upright, set it so the light glared full in Perisi's eyes.

He spoke to Perisi in Italian. Not the precise, scholarly Italian he had used with Luigi but the gutter dialects of San Francisco's North Beach and the waterfront of Peninsula City. It is possible to say more obscene things in Italian than in German, French, Spanish and English combined. Many of the expressions cannot be literally translated into the other languages, and so their true meanings can only be comprehended by one born to the tongue. When Farr had finished defiling Perisi, his mother, father, brothers, sisters, aunts, uncles, all other possible relatives and the family dog and cat in Italian, he switched to Slovenian.

He paused momentarily, long enough to know Perisi understood enough of the Slavic dialect to get the point. Farr knew only the viler phrases, courtesy of the Slavs who had the big lettuce deals over around Watsonville in the Pajaro Valley. They picked up where the Italian left off as Farr expressed a poor opinion of Perisi's God.

He watched the man and knew this was the way to do it. Perisi was tough. You grow up in the old brick tenements and filthy gutters of Boston's North End and if you're alive when your eighth birthday comes up you're tough as you will ever need to be. Perisi would not break with a pounding. He had quite likely lived through more physical violence than Denton Farr could ever devise.

But he could not stand bad smells and, while he probably hadn't been to Mass in twenty years, there was still enough of the Holy Roman Church in him so that such fluent blasphemy in a variety of languages would stir the old memories of Hell and *I believe in Almighty God, in Heaven and Earth and*—and that goddamn Commissioner said this was just another guy who might get out of line. He didn't say anything about him being the goddamn Devil.

Denton Farr put a cigarette between Tony Perisi's lips, another in his own mouth and lit them. "Okay, fella. The Commish sent you. Who else did he send and what did he tell you to do?"

Perisi used a phrase which had slipped Dent Farr's mind. But the words were shaky.

Farr smiled with his mouth but the blue eyes were cold as the winter sky above the Matterhorn. He puffed on his cigarette, then went through the door to the shop in front.

"Need a little help?" Willie asked.

"Not yet. Just a bucket and some fish guts. Not too big."

Willie got a tin can. He gutted a fish, hacked at the oozing mess for a moment with his knife and dumped the result into a can.

Farr carried the can into the back room. He circled behind Perisi, took the cigarette from his mouth, slid his hand in front of the man's jaw and pressed a nerve center at the hinge of the jawbone.

Perisi's head came back, rigid. He screamed weakly, and then the scream melted into a horrible, sickly sound. Denton Farr shoved a fistful of fish entrails into the mouth and clamped it shut.

Holding Perisi's mouth closed and pinching off his nostrils until the hoodlum was forced to swallow took all his strength for a full half-minute.

He let the man go and stepped back. There was a retching and Perisi vomited.

Farr waited, the can in his hand. He smiled.

"Speak. This won't kill you, fella, but it'll sure make you unhappy."

Perisi cursed Dent Farr. And then he talked.

"I dunno much. No reason to. The Commissioner calls me out. He says watch you, let him know what you do. He don't say why an' I don' ask. I come alone. If there's anybody else on you, I don' know. I don' guess there is, cause he tells me I might hafta fix you an' he don't seem too worried about nothin'." He shook his head and retched again. "Jeez. I just hit town. Who fingered me, Farr?"

Farr chuckled. "Nobody. I knew you."

"Crap. I never seen you before."

"You don't remember Boston. A long time back. A guy they called the Australian."

Perisi stared hard. "I remember the Australian."

"So do I. And what you did to him." Farr walked from the circle of light to a wooden bench. He picked up a filleting knife.

"*Hey. Good Jes—*"

"Shut up. I'm going to cut you loose, Perisi. There's a sink over in the corner. I'll give you two minutes to use the water on your wrists and get the circulation back." He slashed the fishline.

Perisi stood, flexing himself on his toes to restore the circulation in his legs. Slowly he took off his coat and shirt and then he went to the sink and held his hands under the cold-water tap, massaging them together.

"Time's up." Farr had stripped the thin jacket off. He stood in the circle of hot light, bunched muscles making shadows on his body.

"What's this?" Perisi said. He was stripped to the waist; a waist covered with fat. Not flabby fat but the kind an athlete builds, the kind that can absorb a lot of punishment. Farr held his hands open, waist high. A bead of sweat formed in his right armpit and trickled down his arm. "I'm going to make sure you remember the Australian's friend."

Perisi lowered his head and charged, swinging the short, muscular arms. He was fast, powerful, competent. Before Farr's knee came up, Perisi's fists had jackhammered his ribs a half-dozen times. There was no sense of pain, but there was no breath left in Farr, either.

He gasped. The right knee was coming up and now he laced his fingers together, caught the back of Perisi's head and yanked it down. The knee mashed the aquiline nose flat and came away red with blood. Perisi howled and bored in. He was too close to do much harm but he was also too close for Farr to work on him. Farr pivoted, stepped back, felt his feet slide in the slime of the floor. Perisi lunged for him again but Farr had enough room this time. Fingers stiff, he chopped hard across Perisi's throat, saw the burly man's eyes bug, saw him swallow air. Farr swung a right that landed solidly under the heart. As Perisi collapsed, he caught the black, oily hair and held him up. Just long enough to drive the hard right fist between Perisi's eyes, against the bridge of his nose, into the mouth.

The jawbone broke with a brittle sound and the ruined mouth gushed chunks of teeth in a stream of blood.

Farr let the hair go and Perisi fell on his face into the fish filth of the floor, and he did not move. Farr went to the sink and washed his hands carefully.

He found a thin cotton towel hanging on a rusted nail over the sink and used it to dry himself. He saw the Appromollo brothers by the door. They were looking at Tony Perisi.

"You didn't much like him, I guess," Chick said.

"No." Farr walked past them. In the office he changed back to his own clothes. "Give me about half an hour. Then take him up and dump him where you got him. He's Mafia, so you can get dead if you let it get around you were in on this."

They were damning Dent Farr when he walked from the shed to the car. He went back to the Inside Garage, and he thought something would have to be done about Tony Perisi. If Perisi had the strength to walk around, he would try to find Farr and kill him. He would do it tonight.

Not because of a beating.

Because of a mouthful of fish guts.

It was not difficult to arrange. Bette Vout was downstairs, keeping the bar trade happy. Farr watched the alleyway from an upstairs window until the panel truck, its lights out, pulled in and the Appromollo boys dumped Perisi. Perisi had been lying doggo. He got to his feet and moved painfully toward the Inside Garage as soon as the truck left.

Farr used the telephone, with a handkerchief over the mouthpiece. He told the dispatcher at police headquarters that a hood wanted in a couple of eastern states was hanging around the Inside Garage, that he had a gun.

The radio car couldn't have been much over a block away. It came quickly, quietly, without the flasher or siren, purring through the alley, angling across the doorway of the garage.

Farr saw the two blue-uniformed figures pile out. The cop who had done the driving had his service revolver half out of his holster and his partner was poking the muzzle of an automatic shotgun through the window.

He heard one of them shout at Perisi to get his hands up. He saw Perisi dig for the automatic he'd taken from the Merc sedan.

He imagined he heard the futile click of the broken mechanism an instant before the pistol barked and the shotgun blasted Perisi's stomach open.

He heard the cop who handled the shotgun using the radio, and then the throb of a siren in the distance.

He saw Johnny Emery come out of the office; watched him look, be sick, take a drink from the fifth of rye and be sick again. He watched the stream of people from the back door of the Loving Cup. He decided to go down and see what all the excitement was about.

CHAPTER 6

Farr drifted with the crowd that surged against the circle of police. He saw the crash blanket draped over Tony Perisi's face and knew the shotgun had done its work well. Perisi's body lay on its side, the legs drawn awkwardly toward the torn stomach. The automatic had bounced on the concrete floor and lay a few inches from the dead, clawing fingers. Farr felt nothing, except for a faint satisfaction that Perisi would be making no deathbed statements. A punk was dead. He was long past due. Farr wished the Australian could see it.

Johnny Emery was leaning against the doorframe. He was taking another drink from the bottle and a plainclothes cop was gently taking the bottle from him, walking him toward the office, saying words Denton Farr could not hear. Emery's eyes met his for an instant, and he knew Emery would tell the law only that Perisi had parked his car at the Inside Garage a few hours before. He would say nothing about Farr shaking the car down, doing something to a gun that he took from it and later returned.

Farr breathed deeply and imagined he could still smell the odor of dead fish on himself. When the cops got their initial routine out of the way, they would start wondering why Perisi reeked. Farr went back to the Loving Cup, showered and changed clothes. Most of the curious had been shooed back to the bar by the time he left by the front door. He took a cab to the Tack Room and worked the bar for a while.

He closed the Tack Room at two o'clock in the morning and hitched a ride back to the Inside Garage with one of the bartenders. Johnny Emery had left for the night. A man in greasy coveralls leaned on a pushbroom, staring at the place where Perisi's blood had soaked into the grime of the floor. Farr went to an all-night restaurant and waited for the early edition of Peninsula City's morning paper.

The police had done fairly well, considering the short time which had elapsed. They had a positive identification on Perisi and New York had been able to give them a fast rundown on him.

A punk better off dead.

The police were still trying to find out who had phoned the tip in. Whoever did it obviously knew Perisi—the caller had said he was a hoodlum from the East, and wanted. The captain of inspectors handling the case suggested the caller was someone who wanted Perisi dead. Farr wished he had reported only a man brandishing a gun.

Somebody had administered a competent beating to the victim a short time before his death. The police wondered who. The victim's clothing was saturated with fish oil. Police were checking the waterfront to see if he'd been there. They were sure he had. This did not disturb Farr. The Appromollo brothers would have nothing to say.

It was not perfect, but it was good enough. The Commissioner would wonder, he would ask some questions of his own. But if he sent anyone else down, whoever came would be just a little nervous about tangling with Denton Farr.

Farr slept well and in the morning he ate a large breakfast of hotcakes and ham prepared by Carmen, the Mexican housekeeper-cook. He had a third cup of coffee with Mary Jean and they talked about the shooting of one Tony Perisi by the police.

She wore a pale-yellow housecoat, open at the throat. The morning paper was on the table. She lit a cigarette. "Dent—I wish you'd sell out of the Cup."

"Why?" He knew this had nothing to do with Bette Vout since he had not slept with her since the night of Burt Thomaston's abortive celebration. He knew Mary Jean felt things were going right for them again.

"When something like this can happen right beside the place, it's a place I can do without any part of. And it takes more of your time than it should. Really. The Tack Room I don't mind. It seems to almost run itself. But the Cup—"

Dent Farr grinned and reached over to pinch the roundness of her hip where the housecoat was snug. "The Tack Room is a different type of operation. With the trade it gets, the Cup needs a lot of managing. What do we do if I sell it—live on what comes from the Tack and my piece of Thomaston's show?"

She laughed. It was an easy, happy sound. "I understand Burt tried to break his contract. But Dent—seriously now—we don't need the Cup. You'll get mad, but I worry."

Farr grinned. "Mary Jean, I've been through a couple of wars and an affair with a Spanish countess. I'll survive the Cup."

It ended there. But Farr thought, as he drove into town, that the time was coming to put the Loving Cup in its place. Not immediately, but in a few months. After the payroll caper was out of the way. And if anything went wrong with that, there would be no need to think about the Loving Cup. If the job worked out, he and Mary Jean would have to make themselves scarce for a while anyway. If the cops wouldn't know who to look for, the Commissioner would. And for a couple of million dollars, the Commissioner would look long and hard. The proper place for the Loving Cup was under the management of Denton Farr Properties, Inc. Farr believed in diversified investments, in picking up anything that could be had cheap and built into something good with a little money and time. In just a few years he had accumulated a small plant that turned out a popular line of bar snacks, assorted pieces of real estate, a motel, three party fishing boats, the Tack Room, half the Loving Cup, a quarter horse stallion with a five-hundred-dollar stud fee and some good service-station leases. Once he got each of them working right he turned them over to a retired three-star admiral who ran Denton Farr Properties, Inc., with the aid of a single secretary. Beyond hiring a certified public accountant to keep an eye on the admiral, and signing an occasional paper, Farr did not concern himself with the various operations, except for the two bars.

He was a wealthy man. He had no good reason for wanting the Army payroll. But he was Denton Farr.

He had started a long time ago, in Europe, when it was being torn all to hell and gone by World War II. He was an American university student in Italy when Pearl Harbor came up and he had preferred the hills to the prospect of a concentration camp. He had fought with the guerrillas and been in on the hijacking of a truck convoy that was packing some of Musso's loot out while Musso still expected to make it in one piece. When the shooting died down and the American Military Government bunch took over, somebody had goofed and put him down as a wild Wop who shot at the right people and he got his share of the looting.

After a few months, it was no longer polite to use a gun and it was getting tougher to rathole money back in the States. So Denton Farr had come home.

He had come home knowing an easy way to get money. Find out who's got some, then find a neat way to get it. Neat meaning don't get caught.

He had not been caught. Ever.

There was plenty of money now. But the only thing with any beat to it was the action of going after more.

The captain of inspectors was waiting in the booth to the right as Farr came into the Loving Cup. He had a morning paper, an ashtray overflowing with crushed cigarette butts and a coffee cup half-full of coffee and half-full of good bourbon. His name was Gene Nicholls, and Farr could see he was uncomfortable.

"Hi, Cap." He slid into the booth. "If you boys don't quit blasting guys out back, they'll take all my business away. I had a hell of a nice house here until that happened."

Nicholls was a lanky, balding man with a long face and thinning hair. Now he lit a fresh smoke and took a long pull at the spiked coffee. "You see it, Dent?"

Farr shook his head. "Not until it was over. I was in here. Heard the shooting, but I didn't think much about it until everybody took out the back door."

"Know this Perisi?"

"No. Should I?"

Nicholls scowled. "I don't see how you could. We know he just hit the state two days ago. I thought maybe he came in here last night."

Farr shrugged. "He might have. I was on the bar but I don't remember him. Maybe one of the cocktail girls would."

He hoped he was saying it right, hoped Nicholls hadn't already found someone who remembered seeing him walk up to the booth where Perisi had been sitting. Not much chance, unless Perisi had lied when he said he didn't come to Peninsula City alone. The Loving Cup was a dark hole in the night. A man had to look hard to see who was doing what ten feet distant. And if Nicholls had turned up a witness—so? Perisi had been gunned down by officers of the law. He was a known criminal, a member of the Mafia. Who would blame Denton Farr for denying he had fingered Perisi?

"Were you working the bar when it happened?"

"No. On this side. We had some stray broads and a lot of studs to keep in line."

Captain of Inspectors Gene Nicholls emptied his cup and his cop eyes studied the man opposite him. A man with a pleasant face and a well-concealed hardness. A tiger with a veneer of tabby-cat gentleness. A powerful man with bruised knuckles. Gene Nicholls liked Denton Farr. Hell, every man in the department did. He was good for five hundred tickets to the Policemen's Ball every year, and the tab for the stuff they fed the kids at the Christmas party. He would toss a cop who tried using his badge to cadge a free drink out on the street, and then send him a check for a hundred bucks when he got married. At least a dozen men in the department, turned down by every bank in town and even the loan companies, were buying houses of their own because Dent Farr let them have the down payment on a no-interest note they could take ten years to pay back, if they had to. For guys who were having a tough time bringing up four kids on a take-home of two eighty-five a month, Dent Farr had picked up the cost of babies and funerals. In most cases he did this anonymously. Where it wasn't anonymous it was a confidential matter between Farr and the other party involved.

Denton Farr asked no favors. He even paid his parking tags.

The cops of Peninsula City would fight each other to protect him.

"What happened to your hands, Dent?"

Farr rubbed his knuckles. "Got skinned up stacking beer cases in the storeroom. Why?"

"Well, somebody whaled the piss out of this Perisi. I'd guess they maybe knocked him into a fish bin, too. He was around the waterfront, but nobody's talking down there."

"According to the paper, this was a guy who had some lumps coming."

"I suppose so." Nicholls scowled again.

Denton Farr fished a cigarette out, got it going. He signaled the bartender for two coffees, spiked. He stirred a half-spoonful of sugar into his, then leaned back, waiting for it to cool.

"Let's get it out on the table, Cap. You don't care if I knocked this guy's head loose from between his ears. What's up?"

The thin lips made a weary smile and Nicholls took a report sheet from his pocket, ran his fingers nervously over the creases. "We got a tip this morning. Anonymous, like the one on Perisi."

"I'm it." Farr grinned. "Get on with the hanging."

Nicholls cleared his throat uncomfortably. "Like I said, we got a tip. It was wild enough for the man who took it to call me out of bed right after I got home. I didn't like the sound of it so I phoned San Francisco right away, got their deputy chief out of the sack. Dent, what do you know about the Jamesburg Club?"

"Nothing."

Farr felt the question coming as soon as San Francisco was mentioned. He had a little better than three seconds to prepare himself; he had Gene Nicholls, Captain of Inspectors, on his side.

"Nothing at all?"

Farr chewed his lip and pretended to think. "A private club in the city? Members all over the world, all loaded?"

"That's it."

"And that's about all I know. I'm not that loaded yet."

Nicholls' eyes skipped over the typewritten report. "On the 27th of April, four years ago, an unknown party entered the Jamesburg Club. It's one of those big stone forts in San Fran. Has its own gym, pool, library, dining room and seven floors of posh suites for the members. They travel with a lot of cash and securities and some jewelry, most of which is kept in a vault. It has safety-deposit boxes and the night clerk had one key. Our unknown party somehow contrived to get copies of the other key to each of the boxes, and there's about a hundred. Our unknown party strolled into the place, mugged the night man as he made a fire check on the fourth floor, put him neatly in a broom closet and then took his time and the clerk's key to open those boxes. He got better than a hundred thousand in cash and twice as much in negotiable securities and jewelry. He was never caught. Hell, they don't even know how he got the second keys to those boxes."

Farr tasted his coffee. "And somebody says I'm the guy."

"Yes."

"You know you're not being a smart cop. Instead of telling me this you

should be weaseling around, finding out what I was up to the 27th of April,
four years ago."

"I doubt you could tell me."

"I doubt it, too. But I can prove I was worth a hell of a lot more than
was lifted out of the Jamesburg at the time. And maybe that I was a long
way off."

"Sure. It stinks. Particularly coming right on top of Perisi and all that.
I'll drop it, but if somebody wants to hang you up, they'll try another
agency. Maybe you better be ready for some real questions."

"Sure." Farr stood. "And thanks, Cap."

Farr finished the coffee as Nicholls unfolded his lean frame, nodded and
went out. Somebody wanted to hang him up. High. The Commissioner.
The Commissioner knew how Denton Farr had worked as a desk clerk at
the Jamesburg Club long enough to get duplicates of the strongbox keys
and then returned months later to clean the place out. He had arranged
for the fencing of the jewelry.

But Denton Farr had arranged his own alibi. The police wouldn't be able
to break it and the Commissioner wouldn't be able to break it. He had
managed to get away clean.

Farr guessed the Commissioner must have instructions to stop him before he bought the organization a couple of million dollars worth of congressmen. The Commissioner wouldn't have used the Jamesburg thing
without orders.

And he had used it fast. Much too fast.

Nicholls had said the tip came in right after he went home to bed. And
Nicholls had been at the Inside Garage, looking at what was left of Tony
Perisi.

The Commissioner had not heard about the killing from the newspapers.
There wasn't enough time. And the Commissioner did not stay up until
four in the morning listening to the radio, if the radio stations had had the
story by then.

So somebody had called him from Peninsula City.

Farr guessed Perisi only thought he came alone.

Perisi had been the stalking horse, the goat waiting tied to the stake for
the hunter. But who was the hunter?

Farr considered the odds. They were building up in the wrong direction.
It was time to get a few things straightened out. He walked three blocks
to the bus station and called the Commissioner from a pay phone.

"You know who this is?"

"Yes. The stubborn one."

"I think we should have a talk. A friendly one."

"Do you mean you're beginning to see things from my viewpoint?"

"No. That's why we should get together."

"All right."

"And don't think of doing anything rash. I'm covering myself."

"Naturally."

They met in the bar where the Commissioner had first turned the proposition down. The Commissioner was waiting when Farr came to the booth and sat down. He waited for the bartender to bring a Scotch-and-soda before speaking.

"Dirty pool, Commish. I thought you had ethics."

The Commissioner clucked his tongue. "Was getting the cops to blast the tourist ethical?"

Farr tasted his drink, took his time lighting a thin cigar. "It happened we had an old account on the books. Coming after me with a gun after we settled it was his idea."

He told the Commissioner the essentials of what had happened in Peninsula City and what Perisi had done to the Australian a long time ago.

The Commissioner grinned uncomfortably, finally said, "A man force-fed on the entrails of a fish can lose his perspective and good judgment."

"It didn't happen to you," Farr snapped. "So what's your excuse for tipping the law to the Jamesburg caper?"

The Commissioner laced and unlaced his fingers. "Orders."

"I guess you take orders pretty easy."

"It depends upon who gives them."

Farr's teeth were tight on the cigar. "All right. Now I'm going to give some. You can accept or reject them—I don't much care which. I came to you with a proposition and you didn't just turn it down. You started playing dirty pool. You've lost so far and you'll keep on losing. So. I intend to go through with this bit of business as long as it looks like I can do it and get away clean. You and your syndicate friends will sit back and keep hands off. And be ready to get me out of the country if something goes sour. In return, you will get a quarter split after expenses. How does that sound?"

"Just like it sounded at first." The Commissioner signaled for more drinks. "Dent—I'm for you. I always have been. But the big boys say *no*, and when they speak, I obey. So would you if you had a lick of sense."

Farr shrugged. "All right. What I said still goes. You know I'm on the inside of enough of the action on the West Coast to blow it. Blow it into real small pieces. The old gag of putting it all in writing and rigging it so it comes out if anything happens to me or anyone I care about is still good. And it's all done. You know I don't bluff, Commish. Try me and you'll have a lot more than congressmen to sweat out."

Fresh drinks arrived and the Commissioner wrapped a hand around his, swirling the ice cubes. "I guess you'd do it."

"It's already done."

"Yes. Well, I suppose you win most of the pot. But face it, Dent. You tap a till for better than a million and the organization couldn't cover you if it wanted to. For that kind of loot a lot of rough boys will pretend they don't hear the word."

"If I'm not worried about federals, you think a pack of free-lancing gunsels will make me sweat? You just make sure nobody knows I've got this job working. You've got a big stake in seeing nothing happens to me, Commish." Farr drained his glass and stood. "I'll call you if I need anything."

"Sure. Luck, Dent."

The Commissioner watched Denton Farr's back until he was out the door. Fear and admiration merged in his eyes. He began to think about how to convince his associates they had better lay off.

Farr rode a cab to the Embarcadero. There was no indication that he was followed. He was reasonably sure there would be no further trouble with the Commissioner, at least until the payroll was knocked over. Then it would be six, two and even that the Commissioner would turn his hounds loose. They would try to take the money, but the rules of the game were understood by both sides.

They could grab him, try to make him hand it over. If they tried too hard and he died, they would be killing themselves, too, when his lawyers got around to opening a certain safety-deposit box. So they would be sure to keep him alive.

They could try using Mary Jean as a lever, but the same thing would apply. They would know Denton Farr would personally manage to kill any man who put his hands on Mary Jean.

Farr paid the cabbie and selected a bar at random from several on the wharf. It was a basement affair with a couple of pinball machines to the left of the door and the bar itself along the wall to the right. He saw a couple of tables and a juke box at the rear of the room. The stools in front of the bar were old, with peeling plastic covers, and about half of them were taken. There was not much light. It was another Loving Cup. Farr picked a stool from which he could watch both the door and the people along the bar.

None of the faces turned toward him. They were looking in the other direction where a small group of roughly-dressed men at the far end were giving the barkeep a bad time. The barkeep was a tall, lanky man with sleeves rolled above big wrist bones. He pointed a long finger at the arguing men and said something in a voice pitched low so it did not carry to Farr.

"Yeah? Well you think you can do it, just try comin' out from back of the goddamn bar and we'll see whether—"

It was as if the bartender had leaped from a springboard. He jackknifed his legs and in one smooth leap was standing on the bar. His right foot lashed out and one of the men yelled and windmilled back, upsetting the stool. He fell across one of the tables, upsetting it, and the chairs which had flanked it toppled. The bartender jumped again, in time to the crash. Denton Farr was on his feet, peering into the dimness. There was something old and familiar in what he was seeing as the barman finished it up. The two remaining men were distracted by the cursing of the one on the floor. They did not feel the long fingers clamping around their necks until it was too late.

The wiry arms came together and Farr heard the crack of skull against skull, saw the men drop without sound or struggle. The barman looked at them for a moment, then turned to the man he had kicked, caught his left arm, twisted it behind him, locked it. He marched the man the length of the bar, stopped a few feet from the two steps leading to the door and street, took careful aim and used his foot. There was a sudden shout of pain and the man seemed to soar. He cleared the steps, crashed against the door and spilled face-down onto the sidewalk. The bartender went back, grabbed the unconscious pair by their shirt collars and dragged them to the door. He tossed them out, then turned to look at the people in the bar. Most of them were still on their stools.

"Anyone else?" His voice was a whisper, but it carried. The tone was not unpleasant.

"Getting old, Jim? You used to get a lot more distance out of that foot." Farr was leaning on the bar, grinning.

"Wanta find out?" The barkeep took two steps toward Farr, carrying his weight lightly on the nimble feet. He stared hard for a moment, then grinned with his wide mouth. "Well goddamn!"

Then he and Farr had their arms around each other, pounding each other's backs, blurting the things men say to each other when there's been a long separation.

Farr thought back, decided the last time he'd seen Whispering Jim Oxford had been late 1946, or thereabouts, in Rome—or was it Naples? Oxford had dropped into Italy with an O.S.S. team and he'd made a connection with the guerrilla outfit Farr had been working with. A man of contrasts, a man twisted out of shape by a war. He'd almost made it through medical school at Harvard when some undergrad bash had gotten out of hand. Oxford had been fired out of Harvard into the Army. He'd made the medics, but as an enlisted man instead of an officer. He'd heard somewhere that the O.S.S. would take on a medic if he had certain qualities that would make a good agent, including the willingness to use his trained hands to kill instead of heal. Oxford qualified. He had taken great pleasure in attacking anything that moved. Speaking seldom, he had confided in no one. The long, sensitive fingers could set a demolition charge or cut out a bullet from a man's guts using nothing but a stiletto that happened to be handy. He used his knowledge of the workings of the human body to extract information from men who had once thought they would die before they talked. They invariably died immediately after talking.

Whispering Jim Oxford and Denton Farr had done well in the black market. They had not been friends, but they had been partners and loyal to that partnership.

Now Whispering Jim Oxford, who should be a rich man, was tending bar in an Embarcadero joint.

They sat down and Oxford called to one of the men at the bar to take care of the trade for a while. They had a couple of beers and skimmed over a dozen years. Farr decided Oxford had not changed. If he had not, this could solve a major problem.

Farr looked the bar over. "You broke or something?"

Oxford grinned, drank from his bottle. "Not quite. I've got some dough stashed in Switzerland. Right now I can't get it over here without cutting Uncle in, and I don't feel like going over there. Just more or less killing time here until a score comes up."

"I think I've got something you might want a piece of."

"Oh so?"

"Long odds but a right price."

"Try me."

Farr told him.

"Where do I fit?"

"We go in on the job together. There are five men in the bank. The cashier, two janitors, two private guards."

"The cashier and cleanup boys are nothing. How do we take the guards?"

"We *are* the guards."

Whispering Jim Oxford smiled. "So how do we take the real guards?"

"No strain, unless you've forgotten how to mug a guy and use a hypo."

"I haven't. What's in the needle?"

Farr waved the question off. "How should I know? You're the doctor. If you think sarsaparilla would put them out for four or five hours, use it. We get them out of the way, take their keys. I'll have the right uniforms for us. At just the right time, we show up at the bank and the cashier lets us in to stand by while the time lock is open. One of the janitors will be with us. We give the other one a shot. And the cashier, too, once the door's open."

Oxford thought a moment. "I don't see why we need the janitor."

"Because one of the janitors has to pack that binful of trash out the service door. The take goes out in the trash. We then walk off and disappear."

"And just leave better than a million bucks in a trash-bin? What if a scavenger truck comes along?"

"One will. It'll pick the sacks up and take them just where I want them to go. When it does, we get them back."

"And just how are we sure this truck does what it's supposed to do, and at just the right time?"

"We arrange for the truck. Listen, Jim, I've been over this thing a thousand times. I've figured it all the ways there are. We'll have at least a half-hour, which is *beaucoup* minutes. Only three of us will be on the inside. Us plus the janitor. The guys on the truck, maybe three, but I think we can do it with two, will know what to do but not why they're doing it. There'll be a couple of others to fake a getaway but they don't have to know what they're getting away from. They sure don't have to know us."

"The guy who does the janitor bit will."

"Not face-to-face until that night. And when we go in that door, we'll look like a couple of other guys. I've got plans for that angle, too, because I'm known in Peninsula City. Now, this janitor has to have some talent. I'm arranging for a layout of the alarm system but he'll have to spot the switches. He'll have plenty of time to do it, three or four weeks. We'll let him work through one payroll delivery there so he knows just what goes on. But don't forget—he's got to be both a damned good janitor and a damned good actor, too."

Oxford nodded in agreement. "No sweat. I can think of a dozen guys right here in the city who can do it perfect. And rig jumpers on the alarms if you need it."

"I suppose every one of these guys is colored?"

"Huh?"

"This janitor service happens to employ Negroes. I took it on a little while ago to swamp out my bar. The boss has a policy—no whites need apply."

"That makes it tougher. I can still find us one."

"Make sure it's a guy with no fingerprints on record anywhere, because he'll have to be bonded. Find more than one—I'll come up and we'll pick our boy together. While you're at it, scrounge around for a scavenger truck, one with a packer body, and a couple of guys to handle it. Also one who's willing to steal a car, sit in it for a couple of hours, then drive it like a bat out of hell and abandon it wherever we tell him to."

"You think I run an employment agency?"

"If hanging people was good business, you'd run a gallows. This thing has a better chance of coming off if I don't do the recruiting."

"That mean you expect syndicate trouble?"

"I guess you've heard of the Commissioner. We've had some words."

"A-a-a-h." Whispering Jim Oxford's eyes became guarded. "I see by the paper somebody's torpedo got cancelled out in your town last night."

"I just came from talking with the Commissioner. I think we understand each other. He doesn't want his tail twisted."

"He could make big trouble."

Denton Farr emptied his beer, slid the bottle across the bar. "Go in on something like this and you can damned well be sure of big trouble. You know that."

"I know it." Oxford was smiling the old knife-in-the-spinal-cord smile.

Denton Farr felt sorry for the man who tried to take Whispering Jim Oxford.

He rolled dice with Oxford for the price of the beers, lost, paid up and went out. He walked the rough waterfront street until he could hail a cruising cab.

The afternoon fog was heaped on the steel-gray surface of the bay, glinting like silver cotton candy.

Farr knew everything was going for him again.

CHAPTER 7

The colored man closed the door behind him and stood without moving, blinking into the sun-glare of the flood-lamps. The light was a blazing curtain around him; he could see nothing of the room but the stark outline of a chair placed so that no matter which direction its occupant faced, it would be looking directly into at least one flood-lamp. The whites of his eyes rolled and he felt behind him for the doorknob.

"You are Herman Gove?"

At the sound of Denton Farr's voice the man stopped reaching. He tugged at the lapels of his gray plaid jacket. "Yes, sir."

"Then sit down, Herman. I understand you're an actor of sorts, so bright lights should make you feel right at home. The lights are for protection—mine and yours. If you're accepted for the job we have open, you'll sleep better if you don't know who you're working with until the time comes. So will I. There's a small table on the other side of the chair. You'll find smokes and a pair of sunglasses on it. You may put the sunglasses on if your eyes hurt."

Herman Gove went to the chair. He sat carefully, grasped the arms, crossed and recrossed his ankles. He put the dark glasses on. "It's okay to smoke?"

"I said it was. Get what I say straight the first time. If something goes wrong later, I might not have a chance to repeat myself. Understand?"

Gove lit a cigarette. "Yes sir."

Denton Farr appraised him from the darkness. Gove looked right for the part; medium height, medium build, average Negroid features, nothing distinctive about the voice or the walk. The notebook in Farr's hand said Gove was thirty-two; he could have been twenty-five or forty.

"Smile at me, Herman."

Gove smiled.

"Wider."

The heavy lips spread until they were distorted. "Okay. Nice teeth. No gold caps for anyone to remember."

"I was born in San Francisco, mister." Gove scowled at the lights. "Maybe I've got just as good taste as you."

"One more thin-skinned remark and you can go home," Farr said. His voice was a knife slashing from the curtain of light. "This job requires you to be a second-class citizen for a while. Do it right and you'll come out with enough to be first-class just about anywhere. How about it?"

Another grin. "I'm your boy, boss."

"We'll see." Farr flipped the pages of the notebook. "You work days as a department-store porter. Two or three nights a week you beat skins in a so-so combo in a rathole nightclub. Occasional TV bit parts. No family. You pad with a high-yellow gal, shoot lousy craps and owe nearly four grand because of it. This worries you. Right?"

"You find out a lot, boss. Every bit's right on the nose."

"You on weed? Narcotics of any kind?"

Gove shook his head in a vigorous negative. "Not me. I got enough troubles with the bones."

"Good. Ever been arrested? Anywhere? For anything at all?"

"Nothin' but a few traffic tickets."

"Ever booked?"

"Uh-uh. If you're thinkin' 'bout fingerprints, nobody ever got mine but the Army. I wasn't in, but they took my prints when I went up for a draft physical."

"Damn it!" Farr slapped the notebook against his open palm. Grove had done fine up to this. He turned to Whispering Jim Oxford. Oxford leaned against the wall behind them, a cigarette dangling from his mouth. "You better go find some more candidates."

Oxford frowned. "That draft thing makes it tough, unless you can use somebody under seventeen or over seventy. Hell, it's his neck. If you think he's right for the job, tell him the odds and let him decide."

Farr swung around, studied Gove a moment. "Okay, Herman. I'll put it on the line. You'll have to be bonded to get in where we need you. This gives you two choices. Stick around afterwards like you had nothing to do with it and try to come up with the right answers for some federal boys. We'll cover you the best we can. Or you can take off and hope to hell you're never caught. It'll be up to you, and you won't have to decide until we're ready to work the job."

Gove looked doubtful. "Boss, how big a piece of this melon do I cut?"

"Ten per cent of the net," Farr replied.

"Just what you have in mind for a net?"

"One million dollars."

Gove whistled. "That's good wages. When do I start?"

"In a few days. You know Peninsula City?"

"Uh-uh. Never been there."

"You'll get word pretty soon. You'll go ask for a janitor job with a cleaning outfit. It'll all be arranged. From time to time you'll get instructions. You'll have something over a month on the job before we go to work. How about your girl—will she raise a fuss if you check out?"

Gove chuckled. "Not that one. The fellas I owe the loot to might get disturbed."

"We'll take care of that. You'll be paid up this afternoon. One thing— you don't do any gambling of any kind from now on. You don't take a drink of any kind. You don't do a single damned thing unless we tell you it's all right. We'll do all we can to protect you. We'll protect ourselves even more. If this means we have to kill you, you're dead. Got it?"

Gove's tongue flicked over his lips and he swallowed. "I dunno know nothin', boss. I just sweeps out here."

"All right, Herman. You can go. You'll hear from us."

Herman Gove stood, wiped perspiration from his dark face with a handkerchief. He removed the glasses, put them on the table and left the room.

Farr turned the floodlights off. He went to the window, ran the shade up and looked down over the rooftops of the city.

"The end of the month is two days off." Farr lit a cigarette. "You've seen the movies. Now it's time to see it live."

Whispering Jim Oxford came and stood beside him. On the corner below, they watched Herman Gove getting on a bus. "I think he'll do all right. The other guys and stuff we need should be lined up in a few more days."

"Any trouble?"

"Nothing big so far. The trash wagon was tough on account of the packer body. Finally turned up a town down south that was turning one in and made a better offer. It's nice and beat up and the paint job's the right color, even. I got it stashed and a guy's going over the motor."

"What about a crew?"

"Set. A pair of Mexican boys. Happens they drive a rig just like it for a living. I promised them a grand each. They think I'm smuggling H."

Farr smiled. Whispering Jim Oxford was worth ten men. "This would have been so much easier if the Commissioner was for us."

"Just as good he isn't," Oxford said. "If he hired the help, there'd be too many guys know who we are. This thing's too big. Somebody's sure to get picked up. Hell, maybe we all will. At least, the way it's going nobody'll be able to finger us because they won't know who we are."

"The Commissioner will know."

"I thought you were taking care of that."

Farr blew smoke against the glass. "I hope I am."

CHAPTER 8

Farr's fingers riffled quickly through the stack of bills. He put the deposit slip on top and snapped an elastic band around it before shoving it into the small canvas sack. He dropped the sack into his jacket pocket and considered the image of Bette Vout in the bar mirror. The hazel eyes were narrowed, the mouth pursed in a sulky pout. The clock over the cash register read one-thirty as he shoved the cash drawer shut and turned quickly.

"Just what the hell's chewing you?" he demanded.

She glared, mashed her half-smoked cigarette into an ashtray, drank from the glass in front of her and got another cigarette out. "I think you know. It's been quite a long time, lover."

"So?" Farr iced an Old-Fashioned glass, poured Pinch Bottle.

"I'm not accustomed to being dropped without an explanation."

"All right. My wife and I get along now. That enough?"

She curled the full lips, tossed the pale-blonde hair. "If I believed you, it might be. But I don't. You're not with me. But you're with someone four or five nights a week. I know when your car leaves the Inside Garage because I stay awake and wait for it to go down the alley, goddamn you! Four, five, six o'clock in the morning. She must be good, Dent."

Farr chuckled. He was covering himself better than he had hoped. The night people, knowing how late his car was at the Inside, believed he was bedding down with Bette. Mary Jean knew he wasn't because he would wake her in the way she liked to be waked when dawn was gray in the sky over the ridge; she did not question him. If he said he played poker, he had played poker. If he said he was checking cash-register tapes, trying to find a barkeep who was tapping the till, he was doing just that. If he said he just felt like staying up all night, it was accepted. And Bette thought he had another playmate. Fine. She would burn, but she would never admit to anyone that a man could get away from her.

"Never went back twice for any that wasn't." Farr walked around the end of the bar, brought his drink, took the stool beside her. Bette Vout was a lot of woman. Expert in the hay. Out of it, nothing much. Just another broad. Decorative, reasonably intelligent, but still a broad.

"I suppose you'd like me to take inventory tonight so you can make out," Bette accused.

Farr sipped the Scotch. "It's mostly done. All the stuff in the storeroom I got earlier. I'll be back after closing and check the back bar."

"You used to come upstairs after you did that."

"I used to do a lot of things. Now shut up."

"Well to hell with you. Dent—I promise you something. The next guy who walks in that door—I'm going to get him to dance with me. I'm going to get him to come upstairs after we close. You count the bottles. I'll be getting some sack time."

Farr finished his drink, rapped the glass on the bar for a refill. "You do that."

Whispering Jim Oxford was the next man to walk through the door.

This was wrong; Oxford was supposed to avoid all contact with Farr in Peninsula City. When the job was pulled, the law would be looking for two men who had mugged a couple of doorshakers. Their faces would be different, but their builds would be about those of Oxford and Farr; enough for at least a routine FBI check.

Oxford knew what *security* meant; there would be a reason for this.

Farr swirled the ice cubes in the new drink. "There's your stud, baby. Sic him."

He watched Bette cut Oxford off as he walked to the far end of the bar. Oxford was smiling easily at her, nodding. She went to the juke box, fed it a quarter and pushed buttons while he got a straight shot from a bartender and drank it without a chaser.

The record was rock 'n' roll. Fats Domino. Gutty, with a lot of beat. Oxford was a good dancer. Bette Vout's skirt flared up over the tanned legs and her breasts shook under the loose peasant blouse. Farr took his time with the drink, waiting until the third record was nearly finished. Then he pushed the glass away and walked back to the men's room. Oxford came in before he had a cigarette half-smoked.

Oxford held a finger to his lips, leaned down to look under the doors of the two cubicles. There was an electric blower for drying hands beside the wash basin. Oxford turned it on. As the machine whined, muffling the sound of the juke box in the bar, he put his mouth close to Farr's ear.

"That's your gray Thunderbird in the garage, isn't it?"

"Yeah. Why?"

"I got lucky. Walked in just in time to watch a guy put an ear in it. He didn't see me."

"My great and good friend the Commissioner again. See where the guy who planted it went?"

"Drove off in a car parked in the alley. I got the number."

"Good. If they're bugging me, they have to have a listening post someplace close. I'll get an eye on the ear." Farr took a key from his pocket. "Here. This fits the doors across the street. Our pigeons won't be around for another hour and a half or so. You can take your time. Just make sure nobody sees you go up."

"Check." Whispering Jim Oxford started for the door. "Hey—what about this bimbo out here?"

"She's hot to trot and mad at me. You might as well tell her you'll come back to see her about four o'clock. We'll be through by then."

"You sure this isn't your private stock?"

"No. Get her the hell off my neck."

"A pleasure. How many routes will she go?"

"Try her and find out."

The cocktail girls were going around, making the last call before closing. Farr went behind the bar, helped mix the final batch of drinks and began washing glasses. Whispering Jim Oxford was dancing with Bette again. The music was slow and sweet now and Oxford had his big hands cupped over her buttocks, pulling her hard against him in the darkness. Bette's arms were around his neck and Farr could see her teeth working on his ear.

Whispering Jim would keep Bette off his neck.

He was worth ten men. In a fight, a caper, a bed. Anywhere.

They sat in the darkness, a bottle of Scotch on the long table between them. Tilted back in the chairs, with the earphones clamped on, they were listening to the sounds from the bank downstairs. They watched through the window as the two merchant patrolmen were admitted; listened to their casual conversation with the man from the bank as they waited for the time lock to open. They went into the other room when the service door was opened to allow the janitors to carry the trash to the bin in the alley and saw one of the guards, pistol in hand, standing by near the open door until the stuff was dumped. The other would be just inside, gun ready, too.

"Same guards each time?" Oxford asked.

"No. They must change watches or something. These two I haven't seen before. The outfit they work for has a couple of dozen guys."

"Good and bad both. The bank character won't smell anything when a couple of strange ones show up. But we've got to be sure about which ones to clobber. Wouldn't do to have a real one show up."

"Not at all. We'll worry about that later." Farr tensed, leaned forward over the table. "Time lock just let go."

He switched the recorder on and listened to the tape hissing through the reels at top speed while the bank man worked the combination for the inner vault door.

Oxford adjusted the earphones. "Is this as close as you can come to the combo?"

"Without looking over the guy's shoulder it is. This part we don't have to sweat about. He dials it as soon as the guards show. Holds back two numbers waiting for the Army."

"And we've got to take a chance on getting those two numbers just right the first time, I guess," Oxford said. "I don't like it. Make a mistake and as soon as you pull that handle, bells ring, lights flash and we've got more cops than we want to see pointing guns at us. If we don't put the banker to sleep, make him do it for us, he'll probably be so shook he'll miss a number and it'll be the same thing."

Farr tried the bottle. "That's one of the parts we sweat out. Unless you have a better idea."

"I have, if we can take five minutes longer to get the vault open."

"Talk-juice?"

"Works better than a gun in the short ribs."

"Plan on it." Farr checked his watch. It was almost time for the Army convoy to arrive; they could leave now, with the tape recorder set to pick up the final clicks of the dial when the lock was opened. "Any other ideas?"

Whispering Jim Oxford fingered the headset wires. "I guess you'll be pulling the mikes out after tonight."

Farr chewed his lip. "I thought about it. But it might be good to have a way of tapping in on downstairs right up to the minute we're ready to go in."

"And right after the job's pulled, maybe before we've got the loot stashed, the FBI chaps will be swarmed around. They'll find this setup and put out enough heat to tie you up to it, Dent. No bookie or front man is going to cover you."

"I guess you're right. We'll pull the ears."

"No. No need to. The mikes and wires, yes. Leave it looking like a horse parlor—that can't hurt." Oxford slipped the headset off, walked slowly across the floor, scuffing his feet on the tiles. "I can get us some baby transmitters that'll work long enough on batteries to do what we want. They'll go right in under the tiles where you've got the mikes. We can be a mile away and hear as much as we are right now. The Washington crew can trace wires easy. They're not about to rip up a whole building looking for what I'll use."

"Work on it. Let's take off."

They walked down the stairs. Farr locked the outer door behind them and saw the first cars of the convoy moving down the street as they rounded the corner. Oxford paused and looked back toward the Loving Cup.

"She's waiting," Farr said.

"You sure you don't mind?"

"I meant it about wanting her off my back. She give you a key?"

"Yeah."

"So what're you waiting for?"

Farr watched Whispering Jim Oxford hurry across the street, cutting between the Army cars, striding down the alley toward the back door of the Cup. He lit a cigarette, then walked down to an all-night lunchroom. He took his time over a hamburger and two cups of coffee, smoked a cigarette.

He used the front door of the Loving Cup, turned on the lights over the bar, got the inventory book out and began listing bar stock to within a tenth of the contents of each bottle.

One of the legs on the Hollywood bed upstairs was a fraction of an inch shorter than the others. After nearly a half-hour he heard it begin to thump steadily against the ceiling. The thumping kept up until he was finished with the inventory, and as he let himself out he listened to the faint, throbbing, near-scream from Bette's throat.

The sound stayed with him as he drove the T-bird from its parking space. He thought about Mary Jean and his foot pressed harder on the accelerator.

CHAPTER 9

The floodlights centered on two chairs now. The men who sat in them were much alike; each about five feet six, possibly an inch taller, dark of skin, with Indian cheekbones and eyes. The eyes, however, were softened by the Latin blood. Phil Alvarado was on the left; his brother-in-law Angel Sanchez on the right. They wore stained coveralls, heavy, ankle-high work shoes with the tops of discolored sox showing. Equally stained work caps were crumpled in their laps. They picked at the caps with grime-encrusted fingers.

"Sure we still wanta do it," Alvarado said to the lights.

"We just want you to know you'll be breaking a law. If you are caught you can expect to do some time."

The brothers-in-law exchanged glances and their lips curled back over the white teeth. "We're not stupid, mister," Alvarado said. "If you weren't a crook, you wouldn't be paying us a thousand dollars apiece to drive a truck for an hour. You wouldn't be hiding back of the lights."

"You've seen the truck. Think it'll give you any trouble?"

"We have no troubles with such trucks. And this truck you have is a very good one. With one like it we would go into business for ourselves and inform Sorri, the *burrero*, who now works us like dogs, of several things he could do to himself," Alvarado replied. He dug a cigarette from a bent-up pack and lit it with a kitchen match.

Sanchez nodded, smiling to himself at the prospect of putting the fat slug Sorri in his place. Sorri, whose skin was lighter than his own or Alvarado's, but dirtier. Before each dawn Sanchez and Alvarado and their truck would be moving through the alleyways of the city, collecting its leavings, performing an unpleasant, but necessary and therefore honorable, service. At the end of the day they would reek of the slop which had spilled from the heavy cans on their shoulders, but they would clean themselves, make themselves presentable to the eyes and noses of others, even before they went for a bottle of beer or a few glasses of port. Alvarado and Sanchez kept themselves as clean as circumstances permitted; when they were filthy, it was with good cause. But Sorri, who drove a lavender Cadillac convertible which was paid for, his fat neck was like that of a coal miner more often than not. Sorri, who had changed his name from Serrano because it was better to be a Dago in this city than a Mex.

In a few weeks, they would have two thousand dollars between them. Never before, at one time, except perhaps when they had been mustered out of the Army, had they had so much as a hundred dollars to spend. And for a long time it had been necessary to take every last cent of their paychecks into consideration; try to spread what was there as far as it would go and then placate those creditors who got nothing. The rental agent, the utility company, these could not be put off for long. The furniture store was given to writing degrading letters but so far had not come for the televisions and the beds. The doctor was an understanding man, content if something was paid on the last baby before the wives began making new ones.

Angel Sanchez began to worry about what would happen to their families if the police arrested them. This man behind the flaring lights, this man with a cold, precise voice, was going to do something against the law. A man with a voice like that would be sure he would not be caught. And a man with such a voice, such a way of speaking, would not care if the police put his brother-in-law and himself behind bars for the rest of their lives.

Two thousand dollars would not do much for their families if they rotted in an Anglo jail; in time there would be the humiliation of knowing their wives and children were living on the Anglo dole.

But with two thousand dollars they could make a down payment on a packer truck of their own. They could give a better service than the slob, Sorri, was willing to give. It was not beyond reason to think that in time they might buy other trucks, do well enough to buy new cars. Not lavender Cadillacs. Such machines are for the Sorris and *pachucos*. Station wagons, perhaps; machines with enough room to take a man and his brood out of the city, to the pleasant places in the California hills, or the sun-bright beaches.

They would be taking a chance. But this unknown man who was offering the chance, for his own protection, would have to do whatever he could to protect them.

Sanchez knew they would take this chance. It was the only one ever offered to them.

"Tell us what we are to do with this truck," he said.

"You will wait until we tell you to come. When we get in touch with you, you will drive the truck to a city some distance from here. You will be shown a route, which is the same as one taken by scavengers who work there. It will begin at a row of warehouses along the waterfront. Seven blocks away there is an all-night garage. When you are given a signal, you will drive to that garage through a certain alleyway, still picking up whatever trash is waiting. You will park at a certain point inside the garage and leave the truck," Farr said.

"You will go to a restaurant nearby and spend not less than twenty nor more than thirty minutes having coffee or whatever you want. You will then return to the truck and drive it away. By that time there may be some policemen around. If there are, act like anyone else would—hang around and watch the excitement until they run you off. Understand?"

Phil Alvarado and Angel Sanchez held a conference with their eyes.

"And what if the police don't order us to leave? What if they order us to come with them, and search the truck?" Alvarado said warily.

"They won't. The last thing on which the police will want to waste time is a pair of Mex garbagemen," Farr snapped. "And they would find nothing if they did look through the truck. What you will pick up for us will be removed as soon as you are in the diner. There'll be nothing to connect you with any trouble."

"And the truck?" Sanchez asked slyly. "What do we do with the truck?"

"You'll drive it to a spot on the coast a few miles from the city. The cliffs are high and sheer and the water beneath them is deep. One of you will drive the truck; the other will follow in a car. The truck goes into the ocean. You two get back to Frisco and forget about what you've done."

Angel Sanchez considered his fingers. Strong fingers, lumped with calluses. "It is a shame to dispose of such a truck. Perhaps foolish also."

Denton Farr scowled at the two Mexicans. They had a stubborn look to them; Christ, they might be fools enough to try keeping the rig. He controlled his impulse to cut them down to size; better to let them say what they were thinking and get it out in the open. "If that truck is found, the police may figure out how the job was done. That's why it must be disposed of. Tell me why this is foolish."

Angel Sanchez squirmed in the chair and looked to his brother-in-law for support. He scratched at his moustache for a moment before speaking.

"The truck might be found even in the water, mister. You never know if someone is maybe camping out and sees it being driven over a cliff. Or a boat could be passing, or maybe a skindiver will find it when hunting abalone. The police would surely make a connection in such a case."

"That's been considered," Farr told him. "There are always some risks. That is one of them. What would you do?"

Angel Sanchez tightened his control of the excitement that threatened to tangle the words his tongue would speak. The brown eyes were bright now. "Let us keep the truck."

"Impossible." Farr got a thin cigar going, caught Whispering Jim Oxford's nod of agreement with the corner of his eye.

"Let me tell you," Sanchez blurted. "A truck of just the same make and model was wrecked here in the city not long ago. It will never be the same again, but it has number plates and we can buy it for a few hundred dollars. If we were to buy it, take it away somewhere and pretend to fix it up, we could later register your truck as the wrecked one. There would never be a question, because everyone would know our truck was being fixed when the crime was committed. Do you understand ..."

Farr's teeth tightened on the cigar and he motioned Oxford to the far corner of the room. "How's it sound, Jim?"

Oxford rocked up on the balls of his feet, let his weight down slowly. "It could be good. Deep-sixing the honey-wagon has bothered me. The Mex boy is right—it could be found, and if it is, the law's that much closer. He's got an angle all right."

"Can we trust them?"

Oxford grinned. "We're trusting them to haul the loot off for us. Hell, Dent, I've checked both these guys out. They got families and they go to Mass regular. Now they're just garbage collectors. With that truck they can be businessmen. That can be a hell of a big thing to guys who've never had anything and don't have prospects. I'd say yes."

"You just check and make damn sure there is a wrecked wagon."

Alvarado and Sanchez looked worried now. Sanchez shifted nervously on the hard seat of the chair, as if sure his mouth had got him in trouble, as it often did. Farr blew smoke at them from between the lights. "What you say sounds all right. If the cops do find that truck, you boys are stuck with it. Okay?"

Sanchez grinned. "It won't be found." He glanced at Alvarado, then turned back to the point from which the voice had come. "We will need some money to buy the other truck."

"You'll get a thousand dollars in the mail in a day or two. Half of what you'll be making for the job. The other half after it's finished. You can go now."

The two men stood, saying their thanks to the lights. They hurried to the door, hardly smelling the odors the heat brought out from their clothes. A few more weeks and Sorri would be put in his place. It was a great shame to keep such a thing a secret. It would be a much greater shame to let a hint of it out and perhaps be killed by the man with the voice.

It was a voice of a man who could kill if there was a need. And somewhere behind those lights had been another man, one who never spoke to them. This man could be even more dangerous.

They left the building, hurried to the public bathhouse for their showers and a change of clothes. Today they would drink more beer than usual at Juan's Place; slap the ripe hams of the bar girl with new enjoyment. Later their wives might find themselves starting on new babies, if they weren't that way already. It seemed they always were.

Farr extinguished the lights, dismantled the stands and fitted them into the carrying cases before opening the drapes. Unless something went wrong, the robbery would take place in twenty-six days. It had become a living thing inside him. Several times each day he thought about how it should go, about all the foreseeable and unforeseeable things which might bitch it up.

The Army, that routine-dominated monster, could change its routine and the uniformed men with their carbines and water-cooled machine guns could arrive ahead of schedule. Herman Gove could be taken down with appendicitis and they'd have to improvise on the spot, maybe stick a gun in the other guy's back and make him pack the loot out. But no, that wouldn't work because it'd be a straight link with the trash wagon. Damn it. The Peninsula City cops didn't keep any particular schedule with their cruiser cars; one might come creeping through the alley at the wrong time. And all this depended on getting into the vault with no strain in the first place. Well, they could make the cashier spill the rest of the combination with a needle full of talk-juice, and if that didn't work out he still had his own idea of the combination from the tapes.

Whatever happened, phase one would be ended when Alvarado and Sanchez picked the money sacks from the trash bin, fed them to the hopper of the packer truck, drove into the Inside Garage and parked it. By this time Farr and Oxford would have shed the doorshaker uniforms and be ready to grab the stuff from the truck. Where it and they went from there would depend on how the action developed. Farr had arranged three possible places to stash the take for several days at least. Two days would more than likely be enough. Within forty-eight hours, they would know whether it was a clean caper or not. If it wasn't, they might not be alive to care.

Farr watched the whitecaps of San Francisco Bay from the window. He hoped they came out clean. The central California coast was a hell of a fine place to be when you had better than a million dollars behind you. Much finer than some Mex village or being holed up in South America with the local cops knowing who you are and what you did and how much you'll pay to keep from going back.

Whispering Jim Oxford lifted a suitcase to the bed and opened the snaps. "You better take a look at the radio gear."

Farr sat on the bed and his eyes inventoried the equipment. "This is all of it?"

"Better than five thousand bucks worth."

Farr whistled softly through his teeth. "Your guy is a goddamn crook."

"Sure. Otherwise he wouldn't have built it."

Oxford handled and explained each piece. One looked like a standard Motorola walkie-talkie of the type used by many police departments. It had a battery and transmitter-housing not much larger than two cigar boxes, a three-foot antenna and a hand phone for transmitting and receiving.

"This is the real gem. We carry it in with us and it picks up everything on the cops' band. If they're sending a cruiser by the bank, we know about it. We can send on it and call the boys in the truck when we want them. When we pull out, we leave it behind and flip a switch. Guy who built it says then it'll jam the band every time the cop shop or one of the cars tries to transmit. It stops when they do, so they can't pick it up with a direction finder very quick." Oxford put it aside and picked up a lunchbox. "This is the receiver for Alvarado and Sanchez. It's even got room for sandwiches. If they should get checked out, no cop will look twice at the thing. They'll have to remember to chuck it in the bay."

"For damn sure. Any chance this stuff could go haywire?"

Oxford fingered a box the size of a king-size pack of cigarettes. "If it gets hit by lightning. Otherwise, no. This toy is the ear we plant upstairs. For a double check on what goes on inside before we get there, Gove will bring in one just like it and put it in a good place. You'll monitor through the hearing-aid glasses."

Farr slipped the glasses on. They were a heavy, unfamiliar weight on the bridge of his nose and his ears. The speaker pressed snug against his skull just above the right ear. The lenses were thick, distorting his eyes. "Try it."

Oxford crossed to the far corner of the room and stood with his back to Denton Farr. Farr heard a flat, crackling sound which bypassed his outer ear, reaching him through the bone structure of his head. There was some distortion but what he heard was louder than Whispering Jim Oxford normally talked.

"Good enough."

Oxford stopped the tiny transmitter. He began replacing the instruments in the suitcase. "This gear is worth the five grand. Shame we'll just use it once."

"Yeah. Think you can get hold of some thermal pencils?"

"I guess. Why?"

"When we're finished with these boys, I want them melted down. All but the one planted in the ceiling over the vault—we'll set it so it stops transmitting when we go into the bank. Washington's got some smart boys. No sense in letting one of them get hold of these. They'd look it over good and figure out who built it from the way it's put together."

Oxford rubbed his chin. "It wouldn't hurt. But I know this guy and I got the things built through a front man. Hell, you're worrying about things that're way out in left field."

Denton Farr stood quickly. There was a taut line of muscle ridged along his jaw and the flesh at the corners of his mouth. His words were sharp. "This is not Italy in the late Forties. It's California in the late Fifties. We don't have a couple of hundred partisans helping us steal and no law to stop us. We've got one guy on the inside, a colored boy who won't know what he's supposed to do until it happens. Plus a couple of Mex garbagemen who'll be more worried about getting off with a secondhand truck than about what happens to us. And that's all, chumly. Five guys involved in pulling something that could be bigger than the Brink's job. Only two of the five knowing what's really going on. You. And me. We rig a fake getaway car and an airplane and try to throw J. Edgar's pack off. But the car and the plane won't be worth a damn if we leave behind anything that could be tied up with us. And the radio gear sure as hell could.—You're damned right I'm a worry wart."

Oxford was grinning at him, closing the suitcase again. "Okay. Don't flip. This is your show."

"And it's one hell of a big one. If something screws up, you know who gets to play boulder polo on The Rock."

"Christ, but you're cheerful. You need to get laid."

Farr flipped the butt of his cigar at a wastebasket.

"Seems a shame to come all the way up here and not get some. Know a place?"

"A couple. I haven't been around there much since I got next to that Bette."

"Don't make too much of a thing out of it," Farr said curtly.

"I thought you didn't care."

"You got the right idea. I just don't want you distracted."

"She's just another broad. One that loves you not, by the way."

"It figures. What's she tell you about me?"

Oxford fingered a cigarette pack and found it empty. He carefully stripped the cellophane from a fresh one, peeled the foil open with his thumbnail and lit a smoke before answering.

"She tells me you're a bastard. And that you're going to heist the Army payroll."

Farr caught his breath. His fists were knotted; the knuckles lumps of white. They'd had it. The bitch would sit back and wait for him to pull it off, then tell the cops. Or maybe not. She liked money—hell, she worshipped the stuff. Give her enough money and enough sack time and she was one happy kid.

Bette Vout knew her way around. She knew who the Commissioner was, knew how to reach him. She would know the Commissioner was a man who would take a great interest in a couple million dollars. Farr wet his lips.

"She's dead, Jim."

"I guess so."

"No guesses. She's dead. Or we call it off. Take your pick."

"Christ! Maybe we could cut—"

"No! Goddamn you, I know that bitch! She'll drink my blood and wash it down with yours." Farr was deep in rage. "Which is it? And no second thoughts!"

Whispering Jim Oxford opened a nail clipper and touched up his manicure. "She's dead. How soon, Dent?"

"We'll talk about it."

CHAPTER 10

"Tell me about it. Every damn word she said."

"Sure, Dent." There was a suggestion of mockery in the way Whispering Jim Oxford answered. "Let's pack up and get out of here first. I could use a drink."

They carried the cases containing the floodlights and radio gear to the Chevy sedan Farr had rented. Farr parked in front of the first bar they came to. It was a neighborhood place. Men in shirtsleeves watched the ball game on TV from the bar. The TV and a juke box tried to drown each other out. There were several booths, empty, and they took one near the juke. The barkeep brought their drinks without missing a pitch. Farr waited. His hand trembled as he picked up his glass.

"Bette's not dumb, Dent. She sees everything that goes on around the Cup, and she hears everything that's said sooner or later."

"Skip the preliminaries. I know the pig."

"You just think you do. She sold you half the Cup because she knew it was too much for her to handle by herself and you're good in the booze business. She never trusted you. The girl has a lot of good contacts and she did some checking. I guess she knows about most of the jobs you've pulled. She saw you walk Perisi out of the bar that night, saw you come back alone and heard the guns going off a few minutes later. Perisi had talked to her earlier and she knew he was from the Commissioner. She spotted you going to the office over the bank and she found the films you made of the payday operation and ran them off. And she saw me coming out of the place with you the first night I came down. That's about it."

Farr's stomach churned. Something was wrong; always before he would have sensed something like this. He had the feeling that he'd been chucking rocks at a jug of nitro. He had concentrated so hard on setting up a perfect caper and keeping the Commissioner out that he hadn't thought about Bette Vout. He considered what Whispering Jim Oxford had said for several minutes before speaking.

"Something smells, chumly. She has this all figured, knows you're in it. So why does she spill her guts to you? It can't be she trusts you. I can see her running off at the mouth if she thought you weren't with me. Maybe. But not this way."

Oxford spun the ice cubes in his highball with the tip of a finger. "It smells until you consider it from the angle that she wants to buy in and thought you might break her neck first and listen second if she hit you with a proposition herself."

"The sly bitch," Farr growled. "The first night you came down she tore into me, accused me of dumping her for another broad. I swallowed it."

He rubbed his knuckles hard against his forehead. "Okay. Give me the rest of it. Tell me she's got it all written down somewhere just in case and all that crap."

"That's what she claims. The same gimmick you used on the Commissioner."

Farr banged his glass on the table for a refill. "She think some lawyer reading a letter can bring her back to life? If she's so damned smart she should figure I'd cover myself."

Oxford shook his head, waited until the barkeep brought another round before replying. "Go on. Bitch. Get it out of your system. You couldn't take the heat and you know it."

Farr bit down hard on his underlip and stared at the bubbles around the rim of his glass. "Okay. We can't put her on a slab. Instead we worry about keeping her healthy. I've put close to twenty thousand into setting this thing up. I won't be broke if we write it off. What do you think?"

"I think it'd be dumb as hell to let one blonde stand between us and a couple million bucks. The more I see of this the more it looks like an easy heist."

"How big a slice?"

"I guess she'll go along for ten per cent."

Anger stirred through Farr again. "The chiseling little—"

"She can earn it," Oxford cut in.

"How?"

"We could use a lookout. From the pad over the Cup she could watch up and down both streets. I could get another radio."

It was true. Farr had been concerned about the things that could happen on the street to foul them up. Anything from a prowl-car cop pulling into the alley for a smoke at the wrong time to the Army rolling in early. He had weighed the possibilities and had decided it was better to take the chance than to bring in another partner. They had set it up so only Herman Gove would know what was going on. He would not know exactly what was going to happen until the moment it began, and he would not be able to recognize them. Phil Alvarado and Angel Sanchez would not know what part they were playing until the show was over, and they would never see Oxford or Farr.

There would be nothing to lose by cutting Bette Vout in. She knew the score already and she was hungry for money.

"We'll talk to her. It's got possibilities," Farr said. He remembered the ear the Commissioner's boy had hidden in the Thunderbird; he was sure there was one, maybe more, in the Loving Cup. "Where were you two when she mouthed off about this? In the hay?"

"It started there. As soon as I got the drift I hustled her out and we sat in the park. No wrong ears around."

"Good." Farr slid from the booth. "I'll make the deal with the girl. You get your boy to build another transmitter."

"Check. Anything else?"

Farr paused in his walk toward the door. "Not unless you think lighting a candle in the chapel would help."

"This calls for a Black Mass, buster."

"You don't have to go home but you can't stay here." Farr held the door open for the last of the night's trade while the combo packed its instruments. A girl with a too-tight sweater was smiling at him while she stopped just outside the door and dug a ring of keys from her purse. Farr grinned and said, "Motel time?"

The girl arched her back and he could see there was nothing between the sweater and her skin. She made a chuckling sound, reached for his arm, pulled it into the light and looked at his wrist watch. "You could be right."

"If I didn't have another hour's work ahead of me I'd prove it."

She let his hand drop. Her eyes said that maybe he'd be through earlier another night. He watched her walk to the hardtop coupe a short distance down the street. She had fine legs. Farr shook his head. Damn shame what a bartender has to pass up at times. He locked the door behind the musicians. Bette Vout was on a barstool. She had been watching and listening.

"Some guys just can't help but make out," she said. "You want to talk?"

"You know it."

Herman Gove came from the kitchen, where he'd been swamping out. He began stacking chairs on the empty tables. Bette went to the juke box, fed it two quarters, pushed buttons and turned the volume up loud. She went behind the bar, fixed them two drinks and came out to sit with Farr. Gove was using a push broom, sweeping in time to the beat of the juke. Farr had watched him closely. Gove worked hard at being a colored boy who swamped out whatever he was told to swamp out, from the women's john at the Loving Cup to the office of the bank president. If a bartender offered him a drink he refused politely, and he did not go out with women.

Herman Gove was working out just fine. Farr had brought him to town, set him up in his job with ease. One of the janitors who regularly worked the bank had been hired away by the Tack Room, which needed a bus boy. Following instructions, Gove had applied for the janitor's job. He got it after one interview which left his new boss slightly amazed at his good fortune. Hardly ever did a man of any apparent intelligence *ask* for a job as a broom jockey; most of his recruiting was done in pool halls and beer parlors inhabited by people who considered working a hell of a way to pass time.

At the same time, Denton Farr had arranged for janitor service at the Loving Cup. For obvious reasons, he demanded a man who did not drink. In his application for work, Herman Gove had listed himself as a strict teetotaler.

Now Denton Farr tasted his drink. He leaned across the bar, grabbed soda from the well and diluted the Scotch. His eyes pinned the girl as he said, "Understand you want to go into the bank-robbing business."

Bette Vout smiled. There was some malice in it. "With a good businessman like you I might, Dent."

"The firm might never open up for business."

"That would surprise me."

"Things have a way of going wrong. What did you have in mind?"

She took her time with a cigarette and grinned impishly. "What do you think the profit might come to? And level with me, because it'll be in the papers, down to the last penny."

Farr did some fast mental calculation. Even with putting twenty-five per cent aside to make peace with the Commissioner, if that was possible, the amount involved was immense.

"At least a million and a quarter in the payroll, maybe a million and a half. Plus whatever else in fives or higher there is in the box. Rough guess, two million in all. Take a quarter off the top for protection, a little more for expenses. Million and a half to cut up. Or maybe nothing except a gut full of lead if it goes wrong."

"You don't think it'll go wrong. Or you wouldn't try it."

"There's always a chance."

"You take a chance when you walk across the street." She made a smoke ring, sent a second one after it. "Twenty per cent sounds like a nice, round figure."

Farr's eyes narrowed to slits. "I don't want it bad enough to give you a fifth, you chiseling bitch."

She made a slight shrugging motion with her shoulders and knocked the ash from the cigarette. "I expected you to scream like a wounded eagle. I figure you and Jim have guys who'll *really* be sticking their necks out— doing it for shells without peanuts under them. You and that lanky tiger are a pair of weasels."

"I told him you'd drink my blood and use his for a chaser."

Bette Vout made a clucking sound with her tongue. Denton Farr stood on the rungs of the stool and reached across the bar for a bottle. It was the rough bar Scotch but he didn't care.

"Ten per cent, and you do something to earn it. Take it or leave it."

She emptied her glass, poured a straight shot from the bottle and drank it neat, twisting her mouth at the taste. She thought about haggling. If Jim Oxford was sitting in on this it might be worthwhile. Oxford was hot to make a big strike; he needed money the way she did. Farr, the bastard, was already loaded with legit money. And he was an obstinate sonofabitch, fully capable of saying to hell with the whole deal. If that happened, she would be punished. Probably not killed, because Denton Farr would not want the letter she'd put in a safety-deposit box turning up. But there were worse things than being dead. Farr could and would make her wish she were dead.

"If I take ten, what do I do to earn it?"

"Sit on your butt upstairs and watch the street. You'll have a radio to keep us in touch with what goes on."

"And that's all?"

"Yeah. You stay out of sight. No matter what happens, you don't show your face."

"Don't worry."

"Deal?"

"Deal." She poured from the bottle, touching up their drinks. They raised the glasses, clicking them together, winking. "Is there anything I should know?"

"Just that some big-time people think this shouldn't happen and may try to take us over when it does. They've got my car bugged, probably this place, too. Don't even talk in your sleep."

Her eyes darkened and she wet her lips with the tip of her tongue. "I think I know who you mean. Does it frighten you?"

Farr lit one of the small cigars. "If I was frightened, I'd quit. It just makes me careful as hell."

"All right. I'll take a chance on you." Her eyes were wide and heavy-lidded now. The thought of the money, of being involved with something as big as this, and with Denton Farr, excited her. "You're an easy guy to hate."

He met her eyes, grinning. "Probably."

"Damn you."

"If you want something, you're big enough to ask for it."

"God damn you." She poured whisky with an unsteady hand, drank it in a single gulp.

Farr laughed, teeth tight on the cigar. "That's no way to ask for something. Particularly when you want it real bad."

She threw her glass. It shattered against the keys of the cash register. "All right! I want you."

Farr slipped off the barstool. He picked her up in his arms, and her hair tickled his neck. He carried her toward the stairway. She tried to break loose, kicking at him.

"Baby! Doesn't Jim keep you happy?" She tried to bite him and he jammed his mouth on hers as he climbed the stairs.

Herman Gove leaned on his push broom, grinning.

Farr sat on the edge of the bed as he had that first morning, watching the bank building. Bette was close beside him, her back propped up against the pillows, the warm line of her leg pressing lightly against his back. The ashtray on the nightstand was beginning to fill with half-smoked butts.

"It's awful big, Dent," she whispered. "I feel funny."

He got up, put some records on the small phonograph, turned the volume up high enough to cover their voices and went back to bed. "If you decide you want out, it's okay. Right up to when it happens. Not later."

She forced a grin. "I'm a coward, I guess. But I'll never have a chance like this again. I wish I could be like you."

"How come?"

"I've watched you. Ever since I figured out something was up. It doesn't show a bit on you. You must be dry ice inside."

He shook his head, crushed his cigarette in with the others and stretched out beside her. "What you're seeing is discipline. Walking the post in a military manner and that sort of thing, kid. I'm nervous as a tomcat with his head stuffed into a boot. Until Jim turned up I had to carry this whole deal by myself. I stayed awake thinking of all the things that could possibly go wrong, and what to do if they did, and you never know until it's over whether you guessed right or not. The job itself shapes up easy. But there's no way to be sure what'll happen later. Hell, it's tough to even make a good guess."

"It'll mean an awful lot of cops, Dent."

Farr snorted. "The cops don't worry me. The way it's set up they'll figure the guys involved scattered like quail right after. And we'll be sitting tight right here. At least I will, because they'll take a lot of interest in anybody that lives here and leaves. Jim could wander off without getting much more than a casual glance because he's not local. The outside guys on the job don't count. They're just working for wages and don't know anything. The guy that makes me sweat is the Commissioner."

"What's the real problem with him?"

Farr briefed her. "So I've offered him a quarter share but I don't think he'll go for it. We're thumbing our noses at him and the organization. If they weren't afraid to kill me I'd be dead already. But there's nothing to stop him from trying for the whole pot. If he can pull it off, it puts him in solid with the really big cats again. He was supposed to block me on this and he couldn't, so now they're thinking maybe it's time for a new Commissioner in the territory. If he finds out you're in it, he'll go for you just as hard as for me."

He felt the involuntary trembling through the length of her body, smelled the sharp odor of fear. "I guess I'm on my own there, huh, Dent?"

He squeezed her hand. "There we're all on our own. We're going to have to stand and fight because there's no place to run to."

She turned on her side, pressing closer against him. "Why? Couldn't we go to Mexico? Or even farther. South America or some place in Europe. We'd have plenty of money to fix it up."

"No!" He shook another cigarette from the pack, scratched a match, got it going. "First, there's no fast way to get the money out of the country. And be sure of keeping it, that is. Plenty of airplane drivers would fly us and it out—and sell us out, too. We just wouldn't have the time to do it right. And if we did, don't forget this is Uncle's dough. Practically any country we'd hole up in owes Uncle plenty and the handouts are still going strong. So Washington asks for a little cooperation and we've had it. For the three of us, that wouldn't be too rough. We know what we're doing and we can take our chances. But what about Mary Jean?"

She took the cigarette from his fingers and puffed on it before answering. "You surprise me. I didn't think you'd worry about her."

"Well, I do."

"Love her?"

"Hell—I don't know. Some ways, yes, I suppose. She's a good gal. Never have any part of something like this, and probably holler copper on me if she found out in time. Get me in a little trouble to keep me out of something big. If we ran, I couldn't take her with me."

"And you wouldn't leave her?"

"Not for money. For other reasons, maybe. Like nagging, or if she insisted on running around with people I didn't like, or was drunk all the time. But not for dollars. I don't really care too much about money."

Bette Vout chuckled. "Just enough to work twenty hours a day making the stuff, and enough to try stealing a fortune."

"So I'm psycho." He ran his fingers through the blonde hair and got up, reached for his clothes on the chair. "Talk you into staying a little longer?"

There was none of the earlier animal wanting in the words. When he carried her up the stairs she had been furious, and that fury had spent itself on the sheets that were still damp with the sweat of their bodies. A few weeks ago she might have tried to keep him with her in the hope that he'd come to want her enough to leave Mary Jean. Bette Vout had conceded this wasn't likely; had acknowledged the fact without animosity. Now she was offering herself with no more emotion than she would offer a friend a drink. If the offer was accepted, the result would be enjoyable; there would be nothing personal in a refusal.

Denton Farr stuffed his shirt into his slacks and tightened his belt. He leaned down, kissed her lightly. "Better not, partner. I want to get home before the sun's on the morning side of the mountain."

She drew the sheet over her. "Better take a shower. You smell sexy."

CHAPTER 11

Johnny Emery headed him off as he walked through the dark, grimy barn that was the Inside Garage. Farr decided Emery was almost sober, which meant something was up.

"Thomaston find you?"

Farr leaned against a post. He had not thought about Burt Thomaston since the night at the Tack Room. Thomaston was no longer important to him. "No. When was he looking and what's he want?"

"What he wants I dunno, but he came through three times tonight. I told him you were workin' the Cup but it looks like he didn't want to see you there. He said have you call him at home no matter what time you showed. Sounded like he meant it."

Farr scowled. He did not want to talk to Burt Thomaston. He decided he couldn't take a chance on ignoring the summons. He looked up Thomaston's number in the book, dialed it on the office phone. Thomaston answered on the second ring. It was four in the morning but he didn't sound like he'd been sleeping.

"Come out here, Farr. I want to talk to you." He was using the sword's-edge Grand Inquisitor tone.

"Suppose you say what the hell for first," Farr countered.

"Not on the phone. Be smart and come."

"It better be worthwhile." Farr slammed the phone into the cradle.

The house was big, with fieldstone walls, a gabled roof with a lot of overhang. Farr drove the Thunderbird past a kidney-shaped swimming pool set in the middle of half an acre of lawn. He parked near the front door. The graveled drive was light in the pale glow of the moon and it crunched underfoot. A line of poles to his left carried a set of heavy cables to a small wing of the house. He supposed that wing would house the studios from which Burt Thomaston did his West Coast Grand Inquisitor shows. The door opened.

The girl who opened it was not quite tall; a willowy ash-blonde. As Farr went in he looked her over quickly. Good figure showing through the wine-colored lounging pajamas. Fine bone structure and eyes that were a violet-blue. She said nothing as she closed the door behind him.

It was a large room, with heavy, dark ceiling beams, a fireplace about half the size of a boxcar and a lot of leather around. The books which filled one wall were leather-bound. The chairs and sofas and even the tables were leather-covered and there was a faint odor of saddle soap in the air.

Burt Thomaston sat on the broad raised hearth, his back against the rock-work of the fireplace. He wore a polo shirt, wrinkled denims and sandals and he held a drink. He did not get up as Farr came in.

"Okay, babe. Shove the bar cart over here and go hit the sack."

Without replying the girl trundled a small bar on wheels toward the fireplace. She smiled at Thomaston, nodded to Denton Farr and went out, closing the door behind her.

"Build yourself a drink," Thomaston said. "And get comfortable. This could take some time."

Farr almost refused. He did not want to drink with Burt Thomaston. But hell, there was a difference between drinking with a guy and just putting some of his liquor down. And he could use a drink. He found a bottle of Scotch, dropped ice cubes from the leather-covered bucket into a tall glass and poured a big one. He made himself comfortable on the other side of the fireplace, took a pull at the drink and said, "Let's hear it."

"Okay, Dent, I'll lay it out fast. We hate each other's guts. I gave you a screwing a long time ago and figured the books were even when you got Mary Jean away from me. But—"

"Leave Mary Jean out of this," Farr snapped.

"Sure. Let me finish. I just want you to know I really liked the girl, and I thought you were satisfied. You weren't. You scared hell out of my gutless producer and a whole wad of gutless network lawyers and wound up with a hunk of my contract. And then when I'm having my big night a couple of months back you belt me in the face with this. On top of making me look like some goddamned hick over a lousy jug of wine. So you're a couple up on me."

"You don't want sympathy. So what the hell do you want?"

"My contract back. And a peace treaty."

Farr laughed. He took a drink and laughed some more. "I like my piece of you, buster. A nice profit. But you're not important enough for me to kick your tail unless you get in my way. Stay clear and it'll be peaceful. That's a promise."

"I thought you'd be hard-nosed." Thomaston's face was dark with anger and he almost shouted. "You better listen to the rest of it. I'm willing to give you something in return."

"How much?" Denton Farr did not really care what Thomaston might offer. The money represented by his quarter-share of the contract was insignificant at the moment. But Thomaston had some reason to think he could muscle him. This was bad.

"One dollar. Plus some information I happen to have."

Farr threw his head back and laughed. He finished the drink and held the empty glass in his hand.

"You think it's funny?" Thomaston bounced to his feet, stalked to the bar and made himself a new drink. "Well you listen, you smart bastard: A guy named Nicholls was around to see me a little while back. The captain of inspectors, no less. He had a lot of questions. About how I got onto that race dodge of yours, who my sources were, how much more I might know. And right after him there was some private cop from a big agency that does a lot of insurance work. The same thing. And you know what I did? I told them nothing. Said I got suckered in on the thing, that you came out of it clean enough to take a bite out of my hide where it hurts, with that contract. So—you see how it goes. For one buck and a lot of quiet, you sell out. Or take what comes." Thomaston gulped the fresh drink, poured more liquor in the glass. When he tried to put the bottle into its well, it dropped and spilled over the thick carpet, gurgling to itself. He kicked it toward the fireplace, and it shattered against the stone.

Thomaston glowered at Denton Farr and sat down again. Farr kept his face under control. It showed nothing. So Gene Nicholls was digging. It looked like somebody had enough interest in the Jamesburg Club thing to keep him at it—it wouldn't be the Perisi thing because Nicholls didn't care how a hood got dead as long as he got dead. And an insurance company dick spelled Jamesburg for sure. What the hell. He had come out clean on that one a long time ago. But anybody looking cross-eyed at him could queer the payroll job. He concentrated on the blocky face of Burt Thomaston.

"As a blackmailer, you stink, Burt. How much you know about me I don't know, and I care less. If there was anything at all you'd have used it a long time ago. And you wouldn't be spilling it to the cops, so don't give me that crud. I should beat hell out of you but it's not worth it." Farr went to the bar cart, tilted a bottle and let Scotch drain into his glass. "You finished mouthing off?"

Thomaston leaned forward, one elbow on his knees. He fixed his eyes on Denton Farr and said, "You might think a little about Mary Jean. Or maybe—"

Farr's hand shot out and the liquor sprayed from his glass into Burt Thomaston's eyes. "Now it's worth it to whip you."

Thomaston yelled, rubbed his knuckles into his eyes, trying to scrub the fire away. His glass bounced on the hearth and shattered. He got up into a crouch and pawed the air.

Farr took his time and kicked him in the belly. Thomaston screamed and doubled over, gagging. Farr waited until he was able to straighten up. He hooked a right to the nose and followed up with a left that mashed the tight-lipped mouth. There was blood on his knuckles. Thomaston stumbled backward, fell against the fireplace and slid to the floor. Farr began to use his feet. Kidneys, ribs, groin, face. The blood stained his shoes.

Thomaston's face was pulp but he was still conscious. Farr took a pitcher of water from the bar cart and poured it over the Grand Inquisitor. Then he stuck a bottle to the torn mouth and tilted it until Thomaston coughed and rolled on his back. The flesh around his eyes was turning a yellowish-purple but the eyes were more or less steady when they found Farr.

"You just think about Mary Jean and you're dead. You see her coming along the street, you cross it to miss her, Thomaston. If I even think you're messing with her, there's not enough cops in this state to keep you alive." Farr waited until he was sure the message got through. Then he turned away, toward the door. He passed the bar cart and grabbed the Scotch as he went. He passed the girl at the far end of the room. She had changed from the lounging pajamas to a sheer, smoke-colored thing that showed off her figure. She was looking at Burt Thomaston as he lifted himself up on his elbows and finally got his hands underneath him.

There was gut-deep fright in her eyes and Farr thought she might scream.

He wished this woman meant something to Thomaston. If she did, he would have carried her to the sofa, peeled the smoky cloth off her and taken her with Thomaston watching. There was leashed passion showing in the violet eyes and she looked like she'd be good. But from the way Thomaston had ordered her around he knew she was a tramp and wouldn't give a damn what anybody did with her.

Farr thought this was a shame. She looked like she could be a good kid.

He drank from the bottle, swallowed, blinked his eyes and gasped at the burn of the straight whisky in his throat. It hit his stomach hard. He exhaled noisily, wiped his mouth on the back of his hand and handed the bottle to the girl.

"You better take care of him."

The girl looked helplessly at Burt Thomaston. He had made it to the big couch and lay across it, head hanging loosely as he tried to watch Denton Farr. Farr walked out the front door into the light of a new day.

There was a cloth in the glove compartment of the car. He took it to the edge of the swimming pool, dipped it in the chill water and carefully wiped the blood from his shoes. He rinsed the cloth out and shuddered a little.

He'd come close to killing Burt Thomaston. Close to being a fool. Right now would be a hell of a time to kill anybody.

The new sun was turning the hills which framed either side of the valley green and gold, but the sight did nothing to improve Denton Farr's mood. He scattered gravel pulling the Thunderbird into the carport and stalked into the house, wondering just what Burt Thomaston had really turned up. There had to be more than Nicholls and some private cop nosing around with some vague questions. Farr went into the shower, stripped, got the water running hot and soaped his lean body, massaging the ache from his knuckles. He tried to think of some way Thomaston could have tumbled to the payroll job. It just didn't figure—a leak at this point seemed out of the question, with just himself and Whispering Jim Oxford and Bette Vout really knowing the deal. Would Bette talk? No. Not unless she'd been unable to cut herself in.

Farr gave up. He stepped out of the shower, toweled himself dry and put on fresh shorts before going into the bedroom. Mary Jean was waking, lifting up on an elbow, looking from him to the shafts of sunlight coming through the open window.

"I could say 'where were you all night.' But I won't. You look too tired to tell me." She was smiling, moving over to make room for him in the bed.

Farr lay down, drew the sheet up across his chest and took one of the cigarettes from her pack. He lit it, inspected the glowing tip. "I'm a little beat. Feel like I was rode hard and put away wet." He blew smoke at the ceiling. "Would you do something and not ask questions? Just because I ask you to?"

She reached for his hand, her fingers closing on his knuckles. They pressed against the swelling. She caught her breath and said, "You've been in some trouble again."

"No. Not really. But answer my question. Would you?"

She took time to get a cigarette of her own going. "I might say yes, ordinarily, Dent. But I've got a feeling, female hunch or something. I'd like to hear what it is first."

"Take a trip." Farr forced himself to speak casually. "By yourself for about six weeks, and I don't mean Reno, so relax. A Caribbean cruise, or Europe, whatever you like. I'd catch up with you in two months at the longest. We've got it coming, babe. A little time together, forget business, just live."

She was shaking her head, and the blue eyes were steady. "No. Dent, you're a big boy and I know you can take care of yourself. But I'm not going to sail off somewhere and leave you in the middle of some trouble or other. I wouldn't be able to relax a minute, worrying about you, wondering what it is. I'm not being the noble wife standing by her man. You don't want that. I wish you did, but you want to twist the world's tail by yourself. And I have to admit so far you've done pretty well. But the strain would be too much. You understand—?"

He sighed, made himself grin as he said, "Sure, babe, I understand. Look—I'll put it on the line. I've stepped on some big toes, and there are more where I'm going to walk for a while. We've all got each other where the hair is short and I'm not afraid of anyone getting rough with me. But they might decide you'd make a good lever. I don't want to have to kill somebody. I'd rather have you out of the way."

She compressed her lips, accused him with her eyes. "I can't think of anything important enough for you to go ahead with if it could mean killing, Dent. For once in your life, couldn't you back down?" She watched his face for a moment, then sighed and muttered. "No—Denton Farr could never do that."

Farr took a deep drag on his cigarette and said nothing.

She looked closely at his knuckles. "Who was it?"

"Your great and good friend Thomaston. He's one of the boys trying to muscle me. He brought you into it and I got mad."

"Oh."

"Not just because I don't like the guy," Farr snapped. "For a damned good reason. I told him I'd kill him if he so much as spoke to you, and I meant it. Someday I'll explain it all, but for now just believe me when I say it's for real. Okay?"

He could see from the set of her jaw and the way her mouth tightened that it wasn't okay.

"Put it this way, then," he added. "I've never laid a hand on you, Mary Jean. But if I hear of you being seen with him, I'll whale hell out of him and you both!"

There was a flash of sun-bronzed thighs as she swung her legs out of bed. She was pulling a robe around her shoulders as she went out of the bedroom. The door banged viciously behind her and in a moment he heard the rap of a glass on the bar in the front room and the slam of the refrigerator door as she got a tray of ice cubes out.

Denton Farr pulled a pillow over his head, shut his eyes against the sun and tried to sleep.

What the hell. He cursed the stubborn ways of women. At least he'd tried.

CHAPTER 12

The unshaded bulbs set in the frame of the cracked mirror created an eye-burning glare, giving Denton Farr's face an unnatural pallor, showing up the small wrinkles around the eyes and the corners of his mouth which were the only real indication that he was in his middle thirties instead of late twenties. It was a dressing room which would be used later in the day by the chorus ponies of this second-rate nightclub; the air carried the stale odors of their bodies, merged with the old smell of thousands of cigarettes. Whispering Jim Oxford watched over Farr's shoulders as Farr's fingers worked with the materials spread out on the table.

"Guess that should about do it," Farr said when he pushed the flimsy chair back and stood, turning to Oxford for a critical inspection. The voice had a nasal, faintly lisping tone.

Oxford looked at the face of a stranger. The pale-blue eyes were, in this light at least, black behind the tinted contact lenses. The nostrils were flared wide, flattened, the upper lip flared out, elongated, and when the mouth opened a gold-crowned upper left canine tooth was visible. The teeth were discolored and heavy wires of the type used to anchor bridgework in place were prominent. The right corner of the mouth was pulled down a little by a scar which angled across the cheek. Farr stood two inches taller than normal and walked with a pronounced limp. The hair was an indiscriminate shade of gray, the eyebrows darker, growing together above the nose.

"Your own wife wouldn't know you," Oxford said finally. "You look like every broken-down special cop there ever was."

"Too bad you're so long and lanky," Farr replied. "We can't shorten you down or do a hell of a lot with that face. Moustache and eye caps and propping your ears out—that's about it."

Oxford shrugged. "It'll be enough. I'll look kind of like every other cop until it's too late, and I'm a stranger in town."

Farr nodded in agreement. He was removing the chunks of cotton from his mouth, slipping the contact lenses into their tiny case, peeling the scar loose, brushing the silver-gray powder from his hair. He had spent hours studying his face, concentrating on the bone structure, on ways to alter the natural planes. He had been satisfied only when the result convinced him no one looking at the face he built would be even vaguely reminded of his own. The boots with the built-in height and built-in limp would alter his walk to the same degree, and he would look maybe twenty pounds heavier in the uniform because of the plastic bulletproof vest that went under it. The vest wasn't much more uncomfortable than winter underwear, but it would stop a forty-five slug. The jarheads had stopped a lot of them with the same vests in Korea. He finished wiping the pancake makeup from his face and began to inspect the articles laid out on the tired studio couch.

He counted four hypodermic syringes, slender, not more than four inches long. There were two others, at least half again as large. They were placed neatly side-by-side, and next to them were the slender, gleaming needles, each in its own sterile glass tube. There was a bottle of powder which could have been light-brown sugar.

Farr picked up one of the syringes, pressed its plunger slowly. "This is your department, Doc. How's it work?"

The suggestion of a worried frown tightened Whispering Jim Oxford's mouth as he said, "I don't think it'll go just the way you had in mind. This business of slipping a shot to these two doorshakers we got to take is bad."

"How bad?" Farr said cautiously. They had a week to go. He didn't want to be pushed into changing plans now.

"Fatally bad. We don't want to knock anybody off just to be cute."

"Sure, sure. Tell it in words I can understand," Farr growled.

"Okay. Under controlled conditions, with a patient who isn't fighting us, I could name you dozens of drugs that would put him out and tell you within fifteen minutes of when he'd wake up. I would also know the guy's medical history, whether he was allergic to this or that and be able to tell just when to stop shooting the juice to him. I sure as hell couldn't hit a vein right in a dark alley and have a guy knocked out before he knew what was happening. Get it?"

Farr jammed his fists into his pockets and prowled the room. "If you say so. But look—I've seen movies where some guy is out in the jungle hunting baboons with a blowgun. He's got a dart smeared with something or other. He points it up in the air—phutt!—and he hits the ape in the butt or someplace and the damn thing comes banging down. He sure as hell doesn't hit a vein and the baboon lives because this guy sells them to zoos. That's what I had in mind."

"I thought so," Oxford replied. "Sure, something like that will put a guy out—but for how long? Dent, this has to be controlled anesthesia. We want these guys out of action for X-minutes or hours or whatever. Not up and walking around fifteen minutes later, and sure as hell not dead."

"Like I said, this is your department. What do we do?"

"Slug them, truss them up someplace."

"Yeah," Farr conceded. "Now how about the cashier. You having any second thoughts about giving him a needle and making him talk?"

Oxford smiled. "No strain. I take him from behind, put a sleeper on him. Before he wakes up I've got a needle in him. The big syringe, loaded with about 40 cc's of Sodium Pentothal. Twenty cc's and he should be ready to tell us whether he ever humped his sister. I'll ask the questions."

"How long?"

"Maybe five minutes."

"Good enough." Farr began turning lights off. "Let's get out of here."

They stepped out onto a street that was dank and cold with the fog that had hung tight to the city that day. They stood on a corner, waiting for a cruising cab.

Oxford lit a cigarette, flipped the match into the gutter and asked, "Any loose ends at all now? How about the plane?"

"Set. A twin-engine Grumman amphibian. The airport is just over three miles from the Inside Garage. The pilot will be sitting out there three nights before it happens. No point to having him there just one night and pinpointing this thing."

"The hell," Oxford countered. "We aren't exactly going to take that bird, are we?"

"I sure hope not," Farr said. "But just in case."

A cab angled in to the curb. Whispering Jim Oxford got in, carrying the leather case which contained the needles and drugs. Denton Farr watched it dissolve in the fog before walking down the street to where the rented car was parked.

The room was totally dark, except for a faint rectangle of window. Denton Farr watched the man outlined against the window hunch his shoulders as he sat leaning forward in the chair, elbows on knees, fingers lacing and unlacing.

Herman Gove shuffled his feet nervously and muttered, "Boss, I wish you'd tell me just what I'm gonna have to do."

"I want you to do exactly what you're told to do. Nothing more and not one bit less."

"Sure—but by who?"

"You'll know by who when you get a gun pointed at you," Farr said curtly. "You get the position of all the alarm buttons marked on that layout of the place?"

"Sure did, Boss. That cashier guy got worried for fear I'd bump one with the broom so he showed me where they are. I got it right here. What you want me to do with it?"

"Hold it out in front of you, arm's length," Farr ordered.

He spotted the faint blob of white, stepped forward and took it, folded it into his pocket. "You decided whether you want to bug out when it's over or take a knot on the head and play it innocent when the law comes in?"

"You don' care which I do?"

"No. You can scram and take a chance on not getting picked up later or stick and take a chance on having them break your story. Either way you won't know who I am—you won't be able to finger me."

"Yeah. Boss, the less I know, the better I like it. What happens to my cut if I get put away?"

"Same as happens if we all come out clean, Herman. I guess you've figured we're not about to stand around on the sidewalk splitting it up. That payroll is going someplace where nobody'll find it. I've got some number bank accounts in Switzerland. It's against their law to reveal to anyone who has those accounts. I can bank it there for you. Or any place in this country you want, in small amounts. Whatever you like."

"Sounds like I gotta trust you, mister."

"Herman—If you don't trust me, I suggest you pull out now. I'm trusting you to do your part and you're trusting me to pay you off your ten per cent. So?" Farr said coldly.

"Okay, Bess, I was just talkin'." Gove cleared his throat nervously. "If it's all the same to you I guess I'll take a whack on the head and lie my way out."

"Good enough. I think you're smart. The bonding outfit has your fingerprints and you'd have this over your head the rest of your life." Farr stood. "See you on the thirtieth. Early in the morning. Now you sit here in this room with your face to the wall a good five minutes while I go."

He waited until Herman Gove stood in the corner, then slipped through the door into the hallway, hurried down a short flight of stairs and mingled with the crowd on the sidewalk. He did not look back at the building.

Farr went into a bar, ordered a beer and lit one of his thin cigars. He drank the beer slowly, thinking over everything that had happened in these past weeks.

It wasn't perfect, but there wasn't enough going against him to make him think about the panic button. As far as the job went, everything was right on schedule. Phil Alvarado and Angel Sanchez had been over the route they would take. They would do exactly what they were supposed to do when they were supposed to do it, and they had mastered the short-wave radio built into the lunch box. They did not care a damn about why they were in this. They cared only about that big truck with which they could work their way out of peonage.

Whispering Jim Oxford had lined up two men to drive a car from the vicinity of the bank to the airport at the proper time. They had talked it over and decided it would be better to rent a car under a phony name than steal one.

Oxford was confident his needle would bring the combination of the vault from the cashier with no strain. If it didn't, they still had the numbers worked out from the recordings. Oxford had also decided where he would mug each of the two merchant patrolmen whose places they would be taking.

Denton Farr had figured out not one but three places to put the money once they had their hands on it. If luck was with them, it would move less than two hundred yards from the bank vault. It might be years before they could touch it, but it would be there, waiting.

As close as Farr could figure it, within ten minutes after they left the bank, the money would be stashed and they would be back on their alibi jobs. Whispering Jim in the pad with Bette Vout, so she wouldn't be alone when the cops showed. Farr would be in the Tack Room, finishing the inventory for the end of the month.

All these things were going for them.

Against them—not too much, at least until the papers and radio-TV commentators got hold of the deal. Then there would be the Commissioner and whatever he could work.

Also Burt Thomaston.

Farr emptied his beer and rapped the bottle on the bar for another. He raised the fresh bottle to his lips and drank while it was still foaming, thinking about Thomaston. He had vaguely expected trouble over kicking hell out of the Grand Inquisitor, but nothing had happened. An assistant named Jack Gardner had taken over the show with the explanation that Thomaston had injured himself in an accident in his swimming pool. Farr tried to cancel Thomaston out but his instinct wouldn't let him.

Thomaston had said Captain of Inspectors Gene Nicholls had been around asking questions. Also a private cop from an insurance company. Through a contact in the records division at police headquarters, Farr had learned Nicholls questioned Thomaston on orders of the deputy chief. The detail report said Thomaston had been unable to add anything to an anonymous and unsubstantiated tip and recommended the investigation be placed on file.

But Farr was still cautious. Gene Nicholls was not the type of cop to put everything he knew on a detail report that could be leaked to a suspect.

So what the hell—there wasn't much chance of Nicholls making him in connection with the Jamesburg Club now. Sooner or later the Washington boys would talk to him about the payroll. Hell, they would talk to every guy in Peninsula City who ever got a ticket for overtime parking.

Farr finished his beer. He was glad he was not a cop.

CHAPTER 13

"You don't have to go home but you can't stay here."

Farr watched the customers file out, his hand on the door, keys hanging from the lock. The girl with the sweater was one of them and he winked at her, remembering the time before, and said, "Motel time?"

Tonight she was wearing a thin blouse instead of the sweater. She stopped, appraising him. "You said that once before, Dent. Nothing happened."

Farr chuckled. "And nothing's about to happen tonight, doll. I've got to take inventory here and out at the Tack Room. Stop in tomorrow."

Her eyes were intense. "Why should I?"

"Because I'll let the bartender close up and we'll make the rounds like a couple of big spenders."

The girl looked at him a moment, then turned and walked to her car without replying. Farr studied the walk and knew she would be back. He locked the door, walked the length of the bar and went behind it, reaching for the Cutty Sark and a glass.

Bette Vout looked up from the cash register, where she was counting bills. "Think you should touch anything—tonight?"

Farr felt like he was walking two feet off the ground. It was always this way when the planning was over, when the action was ready to start. He poured the Scotch.

"Kid—if I don't, I'll walk right off the end of the world. Tonight I live. Tonight I do something a lot of smug bastards think can't be done. I slip it to them easy and then wait to hear the screams of *rape*." He checked his watch. "In two hours I'll either have close to a couple of million bucks stashed or I'll be dead. And you know something?"

Bette folded the cash-register tape, slipped it into the account book. "What?"

"I don't give a damn about having two million bucks. I don't even know if I care about maybe being dead."

"You're crazy. Like a matched pair of barn owls." She shook her head, went to the front window and parted the drapes. "The colored guy is in there okay. He's getting started on the windows now." She whirled, reached for the bottle, took a glass from the tray by the beer taps and poured. She tossed off a shot and poured another before saying, "You know, I believe you don't give a damn about the money. But understand this—I do. I want it real bad, Dent."

Farr grinned. "Why?"

"*Why?*" She pointed around the interior of the Loving Cup. "You think I want to spend the rest of my life in this dump? You could quit work today and never have to worry about a thing. Me, I'm just a dumb blonde. Everything I touch doesn't necessarily turn to gold. My name isn't Denton Farr—"

Farr blew smoke at her. "Cool off. Jim should be along pretty quick."

"And I'm supposed to bed down with him as soon as it's over? Just like nothing had happened?"

"Has to be. We won't have more than half an hour before this is discovered. After that, a mole won't be able to dig his way off the peninsula."

There was a brief draft as the rear door opened, a click as it shut and locked again. Then Whispering Jim Oxford was in the shadows at the back of the room, saying, "Bring the jug."

They went upstairs. Oxford led the way and Farr wondered how a man so big could move so lightly. They went into the apartment. Oxford and Bette Vout sat on the bed, the bottle between them. Farr took the only chair, propping his feet up on the foot of the bed. With his eyes he asked Oxford how it had gone.

"Like Italy all over again," Oxford said. "Both out without a sound. Gove's got the ear planted and it's sending five-by-five. The honeywagon's ready to roll. So's the car. How about your end?"

"Fine," Farr replied. "There are six moneybags, and they're fat." He got up, went to the window for a moment, then settled in the chair again. "Gove's got cleaner smeared on all the important windows. Nobody on the street'll be looking in. That about covers it."

"The hell," Oxford said. "What about the guy in the Inside Garage?"

Farr yanked a bureau drawer open, pulled out a fifth of rye. "He'll sleep like he's never slept before."

"I thought you'd have slipped that to him a long time ago," Oxford retorted.

Farr scowled. "Oh, yeah. I just walk in, say, 'Johnny, here's a crock, kindly take a drink and pass out.' So what happens? He passes too soon and somebody comes in and finds him and by the time we get there there's a face we never saw before looking at us. I'll slip it to him just before we get ready to go."

"Okay, okay. Let's have one for luck." Whispering Jim Oxford twisted the cap from the bottle and passed it to Bette Vout.

They drank from the bottle. Between drinks, Oxford went downstairs and brought back the short-wave radio set Bette would use.

"I showed you how to use this thing before," he said to Bette. He pressed a switch. The radio stuttered for a moment and then they heard the voice of Herman Gove talking to another man, and, in the background, the chatter of an adding machine. Through the window they could see the assistant cashier in the bank across the street. He was fingering the keys of an adding machine. "Remember, honey, no names. You're 'Radio' if we call you and we're 'Car Five.' The trash wagon is 'Car Six.' Any police car you see you call it 'Checker' and let us know which way it's coming. Nobody's supposed to be on this band but if a ham tunes us in he'll think he's listening to some taxi outfit and won't get shook. Got it?"

"Sure," she said. "I got it the first time you told me."

"Okay. Might as well start making up and get dressed," Oxford said. "Ready, Dent?"

"You first. I'll deliver the jug." Farr went to a closet, picked a topcoat from a hanger and draped it over his arm. Under it he held the bottle of rye. He let himself out of the apartment, walked lightly down the steps, out of the Loving Cup and across the alley to the Inside Garage.

Johnny Emery was gassing a car. Farr slipped into the office, slid the lower drawer of the desk open. The bottle in it was nearly full, close enough to the level of liquor in the one he carried to make a switch without pouring some off. He traded bottles, stepped into the adjoining toilet, emptied

Emery's rye in the washbasin and stuffed the bottle into a big box nearly full of used paper towels and trash. He walked back into the office as Johnny Emery came back from the beat-up gas pumps and shoved a dollar into the till with a grimace.

"Christ, what a place," Emery growled. "A man can work his ass off twenty hours a day here and still go broke."

Farr peeled the cellophane from a cigar and lit it. "I thought you did pretty well. You know, guys pay up old bills when you don't expect it, that sort of thing."

Emery shoved the door closed. He was slack-mouthed but his eyes were alert. "Sometimes. Like I got five bills in the mail the day after that guy was shot in here."

"Pretty big bill," Farr said quietly.

Johnny Emery yanked the lower drawer open. He did not reach for the bottle. Instead he dropped into the old wooden chair back of the desk and put his feet up. "The guy that paid it got all the credit he wants. Anytime."

Farr smiled and asked quietly, "Who is he? I'd like to get him drinking at my bar."

Emery's face was a blank. "You know, Dent, I can't remember. I just can't remember."

"Lay off the rye for half an hour. Maybe it'll come to you."

Farr winked at Johnny Emery and went out. Climbing the stairs to Bette Vout's apartment, he thought again that Emery was a good guy to have on your side. Whatever happened in Peninsula City, sooner or later it got to the Inside Garage. And Johnny Emery had just taken the trouble to reassure him of something. He had no memory where Denton Farr was concerned. And he would go along with anything Denton Farr wanted to do without asking questions.

It was pleasant, having unlimited credit.

Whispering Jim Oxford was dressed. The uniform looked half-way worn out, as it was supposed to, and in spite of his height Oxford was a stranger. Cased handcuffs and a holstered thirty-eight hung from the heavy belt around his narrow waist. He shut the door and said, "You took long enough."

"Talking to Emery," Farr snapped. "I don't think we have to sweat him out anyway. The guy can keep shut." He peeled his jacket off and began working on the buttons of his shirt.

He spent five minutes on his face before he was satisfied with it, then worked the powder into his hair and carefully fitted the tinted contact lenses under his eyelids. He dressed without speaking, feeling slightly strange with the boots adding a couple of inches to his height and making him walk lopsided. He nipped at the bottle, smacked the cork back with the palm of his hand and looked at them.

"It's time," he said, his voice soft, the words measured. From a pocket he took a small bottle of clear liquid. He tossed it to Whispering Jim Oxford. "Smear it on your hands."

Oxford removed the cap and poured. "How come?"

"We can't go in wearing gloves. This synthetic goop will take care of fingerprints. Ready?"

"Grab the radio out of the car when we go."

The two men went down the narrow stairway, with the holstered guns slapping against their hips.

Bette Vout watched until the door closed behind them. She turned the lights off, resolutely put the bottle in the bureau, and pulled the chair over by the window. She made herself comfortable, with the miniature radio in her hand.

She watched as two men with guns on their hips and gold stars on the front of their jackets walked up to the glass doors of the bank. The shorter one rapped at the glass with a flashlight.

CHAPTER 14

The assistant cashier's name was Charles Rouse. He was a slender man, about medium height, with thin features and pale eyes behind rimless spectacles. He was forty-five years old, married, with three children, one in college and already married. He had worked for this bank twenty-five of his years, had a take-home pay of just under five thousand dollars annually and never once had any cause to feel apprehension when the bank examiners arrived. He was an Elk, a member of the Kiwanis, the PTA, and each year he served on committees of various charity drives. It was through Charles Rouse that Denton Farr had opened his accounts in this bank.

Denton Farr raised a finger to his cap in respectful salute as Rouse approached the door. The cashier peered at them briefly, then fitted a key to the lock. They stepped inside and waited while the door was secured again. Rouse pocketed his keys and the pale eyes studied them again.

"Good morning," he said. There was a thin banker-type smile. "Do you fellows draw lots for this assignment? We never seem to have the same guards twice."

Farr grinned, showing the discolored teeth. "I'm Bishop and this is Officer Latham. The agency is shorthanded and the supervisor has to shift us around to cover as well as he can. Would you like to show us exactly what we're to do?"

"Certainly. Let's go back and sit down first." He led the way toward the

rear of the bank, to the area of the vault and the desks of the junior officers. To their right were the wide glass windows flanking the street. On the
left were the high counters with the tellers' cages. The bank was sleekly
modern. Beyond the end of the counter they came to the railed-off area of
desks. The polished tops were, with the exception of telephones, blotters
and writing materials, bare except for the one at which Rouse had been
sitting. On it were several neat stacks of bank forms, a calculating machine
and an ashtray well filled with cigarette butts. Rouse waved them to chairs.
"There is very little for you to do. Just stand by until the Army officers come
for the payroll in approximately an hour. The insurance underwriters re-
quire at least two guards in the building at any time when the vault is open
or can be opened. This does not take place until the Army arrives. There
is one other duty. The service door is opened for a few minutes while the
janitors take the trash out. When I open the door, you will stand by, one
inside the building and the other in the alleyway, with your pistols in hand.
We've never had any difficulty here. One time a drunk was in the alley, apparently became confused and tried to get in to buy a drink. He was sent
on his way."

Rouse's words suggested he was a fine, charitable person for not having
the drunk prosecuted for attempted bank robbery. Denton Farr and Whispering Jim Oxford smiled agreement. Farr looked around, saw Herman
Gove polishing a window some distance away. The other janitor used a
duster on the tellers' counters.

Farr adjusted the heavy glasses on the bridge of his nose. The tiny receiver
was working perfectly. He hadn't spotted the transmitter Herman Gove had
planted but it was someplace close because their conversation was being
broadcast right back to him. He left the chair, carried the walkie-talkie set
to a counter and switched it on, with the volume low. The only traffic was
a time check from the dispatcher at police headquarters and acknowl-
edgement by several cruiser cars. Their location reports didn't put them any
closer than fifteen blocks to the bank, which would mean a two-minute
run at least. He turned his attention to Gove.

The man was showing a slight nervousness. Twice Farr had seen him
check his watch, and every few moments he would stop wiping the white
film of cleaner from the windows and watch the street, as if looking for
some sign of the men he expected. Farr began a search for the transmitter
Gove had planted. It had done its job and the time had come to shut it up
so it wouldn't cover Bette Vout's transmissions, if she had to come on the
air quickly. Carefully, standing a few feet from Gove, he let his eyes circle
the bank, looking for something which did not belong. It would have to
be in plain sight somewhere. He saw a clumsily-folded racing form on a
table. He walked toward it and the signal reaching his inner ear became

stronger. Casually he picked up the form sheet, felt the hard outline of the transmitter.

Herman Gove's eyes were round, the whites showing like those of a nervous horse. He wet his lips.

Farr met the stare, saw the sudden awareness and understanding in the dark eyes as he slipped the transmitter into his pocket and switched it off. He glanced at the paper momentarily before strolling past Gove.

"You're doing fine," he whispered without moving his lips. "Work down toward the banker in another five minutes or so."

Gove gave no indication that he had heard. Farr went on, past the ell of the banking windows. The other janitor was out of sight but Farr could hear the sounds of a mop being used and then he saw the door of a lavatory propped halfway open by a bucket. He glanced at his watch, and for an instant his eyes narrowed. Time was supercharged tonight, passing with strange speed. Or maybe it just seemed that way after the long months of waiting and planning, and with the tension of the moment.

Whatever it was, the firm of Farr & Oxford had just gone into business for sure.

The time lock had released the ponderous lock mechanism with a sound that hadn't carried this distance.

From the corner of his eye he watched Charles Rouse carefully press a blotter to a paper on his desk, stand and approach the burnished steel door of the vault. Some ten feet away from Rouse, Whispering Jim Oxford leaned against a table, arms crossed over his chest, watching as Herman Gove worked his way toward them. Farr knew Oxford would also be watching the reflection of Rouse in the heavy plate-glass window.

Farr's fingers slipped over the strap of the shot-loaded sap in his rear pocket. He moved soundlessly through the door of the lavatory.

The man was on his knees by the toilet. He wore rubber gloves and hummed to himself as he scrubbed at the bowl. The dark, balding head started to lift, turn toward him, as Farr swung. The load of shot struck an inch above and slightly behind the right ear. The janitor slumped forward. Farr jerked the man's head up, looked quickly at the eyes. He was out and probably would be for a while. He used the sap again to be sure, then backed from the room. He put the scrub bucket that had been against the door inside and pulled the panel to until the lock clicked. Then, with the slight limp which had already become natural to him, he walked back to the vault.

Charles Rouse was fingering the combination dial. Farr stood back several feet, but close enough to see three of the numbers which stopped under the pointer set into the steel at the top of the dial. He felt a little of the pressure go off. The numbers were among those he had worked out from the tape recordings. If they were right, it was an odds-on bet that it was right all the way.

Rouse, his lips moving silently, rotated the dial one more time, then, glancing at the wall clock, returned to his desk and lit a cigarette before sitting down and leaning back in his swivel chair.

"I thought you didn't unlock the vault until the Army got here," Farr said.

"I don't," Rouse replied. "It's still locked. But I become nervous with the Army people looking over my shoulder. It's a rather complicated combination, and once I found myself concentrating on a captain who had a machine gun instead of the dial and the next thing I knew I'd done it all wrong. So I had to go through a time-consuming procedure of pushing buttons and switches in just the right order before I could start again. Otherwise the vault would have thought it was being robbed and it would have defended itself. With a loud call for help and tear gas. Very unpleasant situation. And I would have had to make a report to the main office." He frowned at the memory. "Since then I've gone through most of the combination beforehand, leaving only two numbers."

Whispering Jim Oxford had moved quietly around until he was now standing directly behind Charles Rouse's chair. He questioned Denton Farr with his eyes. Farr dipped his head in an almost imperceptible nod.

Oxford moved with the speed of a striking snake. His left arm locked around Rouse's neck and the long fingers pried at nerve centers under the lower jaw, forcing the banker's head back and to the left. Oxford's right thumb knuckle sought a point below Rouse's ear, pressing, twisting as it dug in.

Rouse's mouth was open, his eyes wild. His feet flailed in the air for perhaps ten seconds before the sleeper hold had rendered him as unconscious as Farr's blackjack had the janitor. Oxford released the limp figure, dumped him forward out of the chair to the carpet.

"Strip his coat off and roll up his left sleeve," Oxford said curtly as he unzipped his leather jacket and took a flat case from an inner pocket. He saw Gove, statue-stiff, watching and he snapped, "Get back to the window and keep an eye out for cops, goddamnit. We'll call you when we want you."

"Yessuh," Gove muttered.

Oxford opened the case. There were a bottle of pale-green fluid, transparent; a fifty-cc syringe and two needles in their sterile tubes, a vial of colorless fluid and a small amount of cotton. Oxford poured some of the clear liquid on a tuft of cotton and swabbed a vein below Rouse's left elbow. The odor of medicinal alcohol was sharp in the air. With practiced skill Oxford poured the green fluid into the syringe, fitted a needle to the end and pressed the plunger until the air was expelled and a few drops of green sprayed out.

When he spoke, his tone was that of a surgeon ready to make his initial decision.

"Hold him down flat, make sure he can't move that arm. When he starts to come around I'll give him five cc's to start the ride, check?"

"Check." Farr glanced at the clock. The Army was due to arrive in twenty-five minutes, possibly less. "How much time?"

"Five minutes at the outside." Oxford thumbed the skin tight where it was damp with alcohol, thrust the needle into the vein. When Rouse groaned softly and his muscles tensed, Oxford's thumb pressed steadily on the plunger until the indicator showed five cc's had been injected.

When he spoke again, his words were a caress, a persuasive caress. Farr knelt at Rouse's head, leaning forward over the cashier, pressing the man's arms and hands flat against the soft nap of carpet. Watching Oxford work, Farr thought for a minute it was a damned shame they'd fired him from Harvard med school. He would have made a hell of a doctor.

"Easy ... try to relax ..." The words were spoken slowly, distinctly. "... you had a little attack, but you'll be all right now ..." The plunger moved slowly, precisely, pumping the Sodium Pentothal into Rouse's blood-stream. "How do you feel now?"

Rouse's eyes fluttered open, showing no comprehension. "All right ... weak ... like I was lost ..."

"Do you know who you are?"

A loose nodding motion. "Yes ... of course ..."

"Good. You're recovering very well. Now you must help us. I want you to count. Count backwards from one hundred. I'll count with you. Go ahead now ... one hundred ..."

"... One hundred ..."

Whispering Jim Oxford flashed Denton Farr a look that said it was going perfectly so far. "Ninety-nine."

"... Ninety-nine ..."

"Fine. Continue. Ninety-eight."

"Ninety-eight ... ninety-seven ... ninety-six ... ninety-five ..."

The plunger had passed the thirteen-cc mark and the words were coming slower now, blurring. Oxford said, "Ninety-four ..."

"... Ninety-four ... ninety-thr—" The word ended in a sound like a yawn.

Oxford's thumb released its pressure on the hypodermic plunger. "This is it. The patient is ready." He watched the wall clock while the sweep of the second hand counted off thirty seconds, and he put his mouth close to Charles Rouse's ear when he spoke again.

"Can you hear me?"

"Yes ..."

"Who are you ... do you know your name?"

"... I'm Mister ... Rouse ..."

"Fine, Mister Rouse. And what is your profession?"

"... Banker ... I'm cashier at the County Bank ... all my life ..."

"Good ... Mister Rouse, the president of the bank must trust you completely to make you a cashier. Isn't that so?"

"... Certainly so ..." There was a stirring of his muscles and Oxford reached for the plunger, pressed it a small fraction of an inch, until Rouse relaxed.

"Then of course you know the combination of the vault, Mister Rouse. Do you know the combination?"

"... I—known it years ... many years ..."

Farr wiped a sheen of sweat from his forehead. The slowness of the replies, the gentle, leisurely probing of Oxford's questions, were eating into their time. Perhaps they had only twenty minutes left. Twenty minutes to get into that vault, get the stuff out of the building, have Alvarado and Sanchez pick it up and then dispose of it. Too close. Too damned close.

"Can you remember it now? If you can, repeat the numbers."

"Yes ... two turns right to twenty-three ... left to forty-seven ... right to thirty—"

Farr checked the numbers off mentally. Hell, they could have skipped this truth-serum gag. He'd had it figured right all the way. By this time they could have been inside, grabbing the whole load.... He scowled as Rouse's voice droned slowly on. As the last two numbers came up he listened with impatience.

"... left thirty-eight ..."

Fine. Now say right sixty-one and drop dead, you prissy bastard, he thought angrily.

"... and finally right to sixty-two ... that's it ..."

Farr looked up, caught Oxford's eye, shook his head and soundlessly mouthed "sixty-one".

Whispering Jim Oxford looked doubtful. He didn't believe it was possible for Charles Rouse to lie about one number of the series. He injected another cc of the serum and asked Rouse to repeat the final numbers again. The reply was again "... sixty-two ..."

Farr went over the calculations he had made many times before, finally isolated his error. On the last turn of the dial, the tumblers had always released after the sixty-first click. What he had not realized was that they dropped on the sixty-second, their sound drowning out that of the dial sliding past the pointer. He thought of what would have happened if he'd tried to spin the heavy locking wheel one number away from the right combination and shuddered.

Oxford thumbed the plunger until nearly thirty-three cc's of Sodium Pentothal had been injected. He pulled the needle out and dumped the remaining fluid before replacing it in its case. "You check the radio and get Gove here with the hamper. I'll open the box."

Moving quickly, aware of the few minutes left to them, Farr called Gove, told him what to do. While the colored man trundled the wheeled hamper up to the vault door, Farr used the walkie-talkie.

"Car Five to Radio. Have a fare aboard. You see anything of Car Six?"

The reply cracked through the frames of his glasses. Bette Vout sounded strangely cool and detached. "Check, Car Five. I just saw Six turning up the street. No Checkers in sight."

"Roger and out." Farr turned up the volume on the police monitor and crossed to the vault. Whispering Jim Oxford's fingers were spinning the dial smoothly, and it was stopping on all the right numbers. Farr held his breath. Sixty-one ... or sixty-two?

Oxford edged the sixty-one past the pointer, stopped with sixty-two squarely under it.

Farr's fingers were wet under their plastic coating as he gripped the gleaming steel wheel which would roll the heavy dogs back from the edges of the door.

He sensed a moment's hesitation before it turned with the solid slowness of ponderous machinery. When it halted, he caught his breath and pulled steadily outward on it.

It swung outward without a sound, perfectly balanced. The door was nearly two feet thick, its works exposed from the rear through a sheet of bulletproof glass. Bank customers seeing the door open would be impressed by such an obviously impregnable piece of machinery.

Farr checked to be sure the electric eye which was just one more precaution, standing guard a scant inch above the floor of the vault, was switched off. Then he stepped into the vault.

The bags they wanted were ranged neatly on a steel shelf along the left wall, with a sheaf of receipt forms beside them. Farr motioned to Oxford to take them while he studied the interior of the vault. There were no other money bags in sight, but a stack of empties was on another shelf. The bank's own currency would be stored in the row of bins under the shelf. Each bin was equipped with a substantial double lock. Farr pushed past Oxford and quickly went through Rouse's pockets until he found a key case.

He compared the keys with the bin locks, selected the only two that were cut to the right blanks. He opened the first bin, then slammed it shut and went on to the second.

"Nothing there?" Oxford asked.

"Lousy singles. We won't have room for anything smaller than tens." The second bin was sliding open now. Farr's heart drummed blood through his head in increased rhythm as he saw the neatly-packaged bills. Tens, a hundred of them to a pack. This one drawer, he guessed, held at least a hundred thousand dollars. "Grab a sack and clean it," he ordered, and went on to the next bin.

Working without waste motion, Whispering Jim Oxford filled the heavy cloth bags and handed them to Herman Gove, who looped the drawstrings tight around the tops. Gove's eyes were immense. They took nothing larger than hundreds, nothing smaller than tens. The job was complete within four minutes, the sacks piled in the hamper.

Denton Farr felt as though he was raining sweat. The heavy glasses were slippery over his nose and ears and the guard's uniform was suddenly unbearably hot. He stepped from the vault, swinging the heavy door shut behind them. "Get the stuff out," he snapped.

Gove pushed the hamper toward the service door while Whispering Jim Oxford manipulated the alarm switches that were on their diagram and used one of Rouse's keys. Denton Farr used the walkie-talkie handset.

"Radio—where's Six? We've got a fare for him."

"Roger. I'll send him right along."

"Thanks and good night."

Farr snapped the walkie-talkie's jammer switch. He opened the top of the housing, slipped a thermal pencil inside and closed it again. For about an hour, every broadcast on the Peninsula City police band would be jammed. After the hour, there would be an intense fire inside the walkie-talkie, melting its components so nobody would get a lead on the builder from inspecting it. He hurried toward the service door.

Herman Gove was pushing the empty hamper inside as Oxford held the door open. The door closed and they could not be seen from the street or alley.

"Your job's done, Herman," Farr said. "Still want to lie your way out?"

Herman Gove managed to say yes in the instant before Whispering Jim Oxford hit him behind the ear with a blackjack. He fell without a sound. Oxford knelt beside him long enough to finger his pulse and nod. Then he and Denton Farr went through the rear door, setting the lock behind them.

They stepped into deep shadow, breathing the clean, fog-damp air just as headlights flashed along the alley and a heavy truck growled its way toward the small wooden shed, open on one side, in which the bank kept its discarded trash until it could be picked up.

Farr grinned in the darkness and muttered, "Perfect—just per—"

He was interrupted by the near-hysteria of Bette Vout's voice crashing through his skull.

"One Checker right behind Car Six," she said. "I don't think he's caught on, but he's there—"

Farr cursed. Of all the shitty luck: Everything perfect and then some stupid harness cop has to decide it's time to swing through the Inside Garage. The picture of what would happen horrified him.

Phil Alvarado and Angel Sanchez, those happy men with a honeywagon, would make their stop and innocently start dumping a couple of million dollars into the hopper at the rear of the truck.

The cop, unable to pass in the narrow alley, would have to pull up behind until they were finished. Only they would never finish, because his headlights would be bright on the money sacks as they cascaded from the big containers.

Peninsula City cops rode with automatic shotguns loaded with doubleaught buck secured to the instrument panel. One sight of a money sack and that cop would be out of his car with those two poor bastards under the gun. His radio wouldn't be worth a damn, but in the heart of a city like this he could get plenty of help just by blowing his whistle.

"That's a cop," Farr snapped. He loosened the thirty-eight in its holster and turned down the alley, walking toward the truck. "We'll have to take him."

CHAPTER 15

They hugged the rough surface of a weathered brick wall as the packer truck crept past them. Alvarado was behind the wheel, Sanchez riding a step at the rear, beside the hydraulic mechanism which pressed material from the hopper up into the body of the truck. Sanchez was looking backward at the headlights of the police car.

Farr could see the red flashers mounted on the roof of the car. They looked like the ears of a hippopotamus in silhouette. The headlights gleamed on the badges Farr and Oxford wore. The red lights flashed twice and went dark again.

"Wants to talk to us," Farr said. "Probably some guy got beat up and he thinks we might have seen who did it. Let me take him."

"Be my guest," Oxford replied.

The truck was stopping now, and the prowl car braked about ten feet behind it as Alvarado swung down from the cab and walked slowly toward the rear end. He was sure to have seen the red lights flash in his mirror. He waved lazily toward the police car, grinning.

Denton Farr, with Oxford a couple of paces behind and to his left, stepped up to the police car. He leaned down, resting his elbows on the door, looking in the open window at the cop. "Hi—anything doing?"

The cop grunted in disgust. "Nah! Bunch of punks come over from Seaside, got a rumble going at Cookie's drive-in. Thought you might have seen them. They're rolling in an old Chev with pipes."

"Not a sign." As Farr spoke, he eased the revolver from its holster. He laid the muzzle across the top of the open window. "And don't be a hero. Just keep the hands on the wheel."

The cop's head swiveled with an awareness that came too late. He kept his hands in sight on the steering wheel. Whispering Jim Oxford strolled in front of the headlights, went around and opened the passenger-side door and got in. As he did he swung his sap twice against the cop's head. The uniform cap fell to the floor. Oxford retrieved it and switched the headlights off with the same motion.

Farr opened the driver's door and said curtly, "You guys make your pickup and get the hell on your way."

He got behind the wheel, with the cop slumped between himself and Oxford. Once there was a burst of static from the short-wave set. A portion of a syllable came through but the rest was hash. The jammer was on the job.

Alvarado and Sanchez finished their work. The truck inched forward, turned toward the Inside Garage.

"What now?" Oxford said nervously.

"Business as usual. Hit him again." Farr put the prowl car in gear and drove into the Inside Garage. Running into the cop was bad but they'd handled it well. He passed the office, saw Johnny Emery slumped back in his chair, arms hanging loose. The truck was parked in exactly the right place, beyond view of any through traffic, in an area that was almost pitch black. He wheeled the car out the far door, cut it into a parking lot halffilled with cars and trucks which more than likely would never move again under their own power. There was an old van near a wall, with enough room beside it to squeeze the police car in. Farr parked, grabbed the ignition keys.

"Drag him out and we'll stash him in the trunk." Whispering Jim Oxford tugged the unconscious cop from the car and poured him into the trunk. Farr took the cop's gun and used it to prop the lid open enough to let air in. "Now back to work."

They hurried into the dark of the Inside Garage. The packer truck was a green and silver shape in the shadows.

From the trunk of a wrecked car, Farr lifted three stainless steel canisters, each about three feet long and nearly a foot in diameter. "Get the sacks, and be goddamn sure you don't miss one," he said curtly.

Oxford pawed through the hopper of the truck. In a moment he was back, dumping the heavy cloth bags at Farr's feet. There were thirteen in all. Farr jammed them into the canisters and secured the tops. He carried two to a grating in the floor, motioned for Oxford to bring the other. The grating lifted noisily. Farr let each can down into the hole carefully, then scuffed dirt over the grating. He heard a faint, heavy gurgling from the hole. He whipped off the heavy glasses, broke the thin wire between the miniature battery set in one side frame and the transistor radio in the other. They went between the iron bars. The contact lenses, faked bridgework and the rest of his disguise followed. Oxford was doing the same.

There was a nerve-eating urgency to their movements. There was no way of telling when somebody might wander through, using the Inside Garage as a short cut. In these fast seconds they were more exposed than they had been inside the bank. The last article Farr dropped through the grate was the special heel cap which had given him the limp. The trunk of the wrecked car held sport jackets and shirts.

Oxford, who'd had less disguise to shed, was already stripped to the waist, changing clothes. The uniform hats and jackets and shirts and gunbelts and the rest of the gear they rolled into bundles. Using a shaky ladder, Denton Farr climbed to the top of a huge stack of old tires that had been in this corner of the Inside Garage as long as he could remember. He dropped the bundles, heard them bounce down the stack and hit the floor.

Farr pulled his sports coat on and wiped the remaining makeup from his face with a towel. According to his watch, it was three minutes before four o'clock in the morning when he and Whispering Jim Oxford shook hands. "Inches to spare," he said. "How big?"

Oxford's grin was barely visible in the gloom. "I quit counting at two million."

"Better take off. Bette will probably need something to calm her down."

"I got just the thing." Oxford held to the shadows as he went through the big door and circled the block on a route that would bring him to the rear door of the Loving Cup.

Denton Farr felt no pressure for the moment. The big strike had been made; except for the cop showing up it had gone without a hitch. He was Denton Farr again; the critical moments of shedding his disguise had passed without incident. He started toward the parking area, had gone perhaps fifty feet before he remembered the radio in the packer truck.

He whirled, and in that instant heard footsteps somewhere in the vast, old building. He yanked the cab door open, grabbed the lunch bucket, opened it and pulled the tiny set out. He made sure it was turned off, then chucked it high over the pile of tires. He could hear it bounce off the wall, thump a couple of times, and make a solid, smashing sound as it struck concrete. The tires were not a perfect hiding place, but they would do.

Without a reason, police would not be likely to paw through the filthy mountain of old rubber. And if they did find the uniforms and the rest of the stuff, there would be no real harm done. They were inanimate objects, unable to point a finger of accusation at the men who had used them.

The old sump was even better. In years past, it had been a grease pit, until the Inside Garage installed a hoist. The pit had been closed in and was unused except as a place to dump oil drained from cars in for service. It would hold several thousand gallons, probably wasn't pumped out once in two years. And if it was, a suction hose wouldn't bring up the cans with the two-million-plus in them. They would stay on the bottom of the sump until Farr had a chance to fish them out. Only if the top was removed from the old pit was there any danger. And that wouldn't happen. Denton Farr had bought the Inside Garage.

Farr crossed a lighted area of the Inside Garage and the footsteps were louder now. Casually he turned toward the sound. He relaxed; the two men coming toward him were Phil Alvarado and Angel Sanchez. They looked once over their shoulders toward the door through which they had driven into the garage and eyed Farr furtively. They were walking quickly to the truck and as Farr came abreast of the Thunderbird he heard the truck motor start. It backed around, groaned to itself and rumbled out to the alleyway.

Johnny Emery was still sleeping. The drawer was open and the bottle of spiked rye was visible. On a workbench, Farr found a bottle of solvent. He carefully scrubbed the plastic coating from his fingers. Then he drove to the Tack Room, let himself in and built a tall drink before getting out the books to start taking inventory.

He sat for a long time in the quiet room that was illuminated only by the small light over the cash register. The ranked bottles of the bar glowed with myriad colors. He savored the minutes, knowing they would not last. Already the sharp awareness, the fine sense of living, was losing its edge. It was a natural reaction, something he had felt other times after a score was finished. The long months of planning, the slow suspense that lived inside him, building to the time that was almost like a sexual explosion when he was doing the job—these things were over. Now would come the anti-climax, the time of quiet waiting to see if he had gotten away with it.

The action was over.

Now he could expect suspense and anxiety, but from here on he could do only play-acting. Go about his business, act normal. If the law came around, parry the questions, put it on an intellectual rather than physical level.

He considered the way it had gone from the beginning and decided he could expect no more than routine questioning from the FBI and the Peninsula City police. Looking for leads, they would question everyone who had been anywhere near the bank across the street from the Loving Cup on this particular morning, hoping to turn up a lead. Denton Farr, barkeeper, would be among the first.

He turned his mind to the pressure play that was sure to come from the Commissioner. As soon as the word was out, the Commish would be on his way to Peninsula City.

To hold his place in the pecking order, he would have to get the loot away from Denton Farr. There would be nothing personal in it, and Farr accepted the situation without animosity. It looked like a situation which could be handled. Without him, they could never hope to find the money, any more than he could hope to buck the organization the rest of his life.

So—it would have to be a compromise. Farr was willing to offer a quarter of the take, possibly go as high as a third if they could make a deal on moving the bills out of the country.

He finished the drink, went behind the bar and began measuring the liquor in each bottle and writing in the book. The sun was up when he finished. He thought about going home, then decided to take a nap first.

He stretched out on the padded seat of a booth and let himself doze. In the distance he heard a plaintive chorus of sirens. The sound continued and Denton Farr fell asleep, smiling.

He awoke shortly before eight o'clock. In the washroom he splashed cold water on his face, dried with paper towels and let himself out. He turned the radio on as he warmed the T-bird's motor. On the way back to town he drove slowly, listening to the news flashes.

It was a beaut.

Two men disguised as bank guards had made off with a total of $2,148,725, nearly two million of which had been Army payroll. They had first slugged the regular guards. After gaining admittance to the bank, they had rendered one janitor unconscious and held the other prisoner until they were ready to make him carry the loot through a service door. One, evidently with considerable knowledge of medicine, had used a truth serum to extract the vault combination from a bank official. The second janitor had finally been clubbed insensible.

A police officer who had cruised through the alleyway behind the bank on routine patrol had been taken in by the uniforms and beaten. He was hospitalized with serious head injuries.

The daring robbery had evidently been timed to the minute. Authorities estimated it had been completed less than five minutes before an armed convoy set out from the training camp outside the city to pick up the payroll.

A potential witness, the proprietor of an all-night garage near the bank, had been drugged. The cashier, who had not recovered from the effects of the injection given him by the robbers, so far had not been able to describe them. The descriptions furnished by the janitors did not match those of any known thieves.

Authorities were frank in admitting the pair might have made good their escape from the area even before the robbery was discovered. A car had been seen speeding toward the airport and was later found abandoned there, near the point where an amphibious airplane had been parked for four nights. Attempts were being made to trace ownership of the car and plane.

Police had been hampered in establishing a network of roadblocks because an electronic device had jammed their radio. A portable transmitter, apparently used by the thieves, had been destroyed by an intense fire within its own mechanism.

FBI agents and local police were questioning scores of persons this morning, searching for any possible lead ...

An unadorned gray sedan occupied his usual parking space in the Inside Garage. Farr cut the T-bird into another slot. The garage was nearly full, unusual for this hour, and many of the cars were unfamiliar. He glanced through the window of the one in his usual parking space and saw a radio mike hung under the dashboard. He guessed there were probably twenty federal cars here. Two men in conservative suits were standing inside the office, talking to Johnny Emery. Farr started to walk past when Emery called him.

Farr turned back, smiling, shaking his head at the garageman. "You look like hell. Why don't you give these fellows the money and maybe they'll let you go back to sleep."

The men turned, looking at him curiously. They had polite, solid expressions. One took a small notebook from his pocket, poised a ball-point pen and said, "Your name, please?"

"You're officers?"

The second man displayed a leather folder with badge and identification card. Farr told them his name, that he was a partner in the bar around the corner and owned another outside the city limits.

"Could we infer from your remark to this gentleman that perhaps you have some information, Mr. Farr?" The one with the notebook was doing the talking for now.

Farr grinned. "Not that I know of. I heard the radio broadcast, that's all."

"You were working last night—in the early hours of the morning?"

"I was. We closed up at two, as usual. Counting cash, bringing up stock and that sort of thing usually takes at least another half-hour."

"Then you left perhaps at two-thirty, or a few minutes later?"

"No. Much later than that. End of the month and the State Liquor Commission requires a detailed inventory. I was tied up with that. An hour maybe. And I had a couple of drinks before heading out for the Tack Room."

"The Tack Room?"

"My other bar. I did the inventory there too, then took a nap. I live a long way out from town and I was pretty tired. A little canned too, and I don't drive when I'm stiff. Not with two liquor licenses to lose."

The FBI man nodded understandingly. He was no longer taking notes, but there was a slim leather briefcase at his feet. Farr was sure the conversation was being recorded.

"I'll be very honest with you, Mr. Farr. We can use every scrap of information you can give us. Something you may think is insignificant could be vital. To the best of your knowledge, when did you leave your bar down the street there?"

Farr pretended to think. This was an important question. A person with something to hide might be tempted to say he had left at three-fifteen, before the robbery took place, and offer to prove he was miles away if need be. Denton Farr rubbed his chin and said, "I guess about three-forty, maybe three forty-five."

"I see." The FBI man was obviously not pleased. At three-forty, the thieves had been inside the bank several minutes. "To the best of your recollection, where did you go and what did you do?"

Farr shrugged. "Nothing, really. Locked up, walked down the alley you see there, got in my car and drove out to the Tack Room."

"Did you see anyone, speak to anyone?"

"I saw Johnny here." Farr chuckled. "He was asleep in that chair. I yelled at him but he didn't look up. Radio said somebody slipped him a mickey."

"And no one else? No automobiles passing through?"

Farr almost said he had seen a police cruiser round the gas pumps and go out the back way. But if the cop they'd slugged happened to remember the trash wagon being in front of him in the alley and mentioned it to the FBI, the FBI might then wonder why Farr had not remembered the truck as well, and that would mean more questions later.

"No. I don't think I would have noticed a car unless I had to pull out to go around it or something. I'm sure I didn't see anyone."

The federal man exchanged glances with his partner, frowned slightly and slipped his notebook into a pocket. "All right. I guess you can't help us much. But Mr. Farr—were you alone?"

"Yes."

"From the time you closed the bar, came through here and went to your other place, you were alone?"

"Yes." Farr found a cigarette in a nearly-empty pack and lit it. "My partner has rooms upstairs over the Loving Cup. She was up there. Or I believe she was. I was alone at the Tack Room."

"I see. Do you think for any reason your partner might have been in company with anyone else?"

Farr tilted an eyebrow slightly. "I wouldn't know. A person could go to the apartment without passing through the bar. I don't know that anyone did."

"All right. Thank you, Mr. Farr."

Farr strode down the alley, stopped at a news rack on the street and picked up two newspapers. The San Fran sheets had put out honest-to-God extras—almost unheard of since TV came along—and the local paper had made over the front and back pages of the previous evening's edition to meet the competition. Jack Anderson was behind the bar at the Cup. Farr settled himself on a leatherette stool. He nodded to Anderson and the bartender slid a bottle, glass and tray of ice down to him. Farr built a drink, sipped it and began to read.

The papers carried more detail, more conjecture than the radio broadcast had. But no more facts. Nothing to indicate the police had a solid lead of any sort.

Jack Anderson leaned across the bar, reading the extra paper. The headline type was so big it was difficult to read. "Jesus, what a haul," he muttered. "With all these cops around, I put the dice boxes out of sight, Dent."

Farr chuckled. "You think they give a goddamn about rolling for booze? Bring 'em out and maybe we'll get some of this FBI money. Those boys are going to be real dry in the throat before the day's through."

"You know it. They get to you yet?"

"Caught me at the Inside."

"Christ, they were waiting at the door when I opened up. Had a hell of a time getting the floor swept. Those guys clobbered our swampers, you know. They got finished with me. Real disgusted because I was in San Fran last night and picked up a ticket from a highway cop eighty miles from here when they thought I was robbing a bank. They tried Bette then."

"Oh? They get anything?"

Anderson grinned. "How the hell do I know what mood she was in? All I know is Cap'n Nicholls and a couple of smooth types went up to try their luck. They left a little while ago. There was a guy with her."

"Is that so?" Farr said mildly.

"A long, lean, mean type. He came down for a jug later. Didn't ask me. Just came back of the bar and helped himself."

Farr guessed Bette and Whispering Jim Oxford had made it over the first hurdle. If their story was simple and plausible enough, there might not be a second interview. He hoped they admitted to nothing more than screwing mightily. Farr emptied his glass and poured a small amount of Scotch over the remaining ice. He was about to drink it when an old man pushed in through the swinging door.

Emilio's eyes passed over him, then returned suddenly. The old *vaquero* shoved his wide-brimmed hat back and scratched at the remains of his graying hair. He rocked on the high heels of his boots and said, "Hell, boss, you sure got fixed up quick."

Something in the voice cut at Denton Farr. He swung his feet down from the rungs of the stool and caught the Mexican's shirt. "What do you mean fixed up? Am I supposed to be hurt or something?"

"Well, sure. Where's Mary Jean?"

Denton Farr forced his fingers to release their grip. He grabbed the bottle, shoved it into Emilio's hand. "Here. Take a belt, you goddamn Indian and tell me what the hell's going on."

Emilio pushed his belly up against the bar. He poured liquor into the glass Farr had used and drank it neat. "Boss, all I know is that bastard from the television, Thomaston, come up to the ranch. Early, when I was fixin' the horses. He beat on Mary Jean's door and got her up. I know what you think about him so I got a pitchfork to run him off, but Mary Jean, she just told me to stay there. He told her you got drunk and came up to his place a couple hours before and wanted to beat him up again. He said you got hurt and they couldn't move you so he come to get her."

"*And she went with him?*"

Denton Farr shouted the question, knowing what the answer would be. He could see the way it was now. There were great gaps in the picture, but the principal figures were clear.

Burt Thomaston, the Grand Inquisitor, in the foreground. Behind him, the Commissioner.

He had known the Commissioner had a man on him in addition to Tony Perisi. There had been no reason to think that man was Burt Thomaston, whose guts he instinctively hated.

And Burt Thomaston had dared to come to the ranch high in the green hills over the valley one more time, to tell Mary Jean Farr her husband was hurt and she'd better come for him.

Now the Grand Inquisitor and the Commissioner had a lever that could pry $2,148,725 out of an old oil sump.

CHAPTER 16

The white-hot anger flared for only an instant before the rigid self-control reasserted itself. Blind fury wouldn't help; this was the pressure play. Bolder than he thought the Commissioner would attempt. Bolder and faster. "Emilio—Don't say a word about this to anyone. *Anyone*—understand? Same goes for you, Jack."

He looked into their eyes for a moment before walking at a normal pace to the back of the bar. He climbed the stairs and rapped lightly on Bette Vout's door. "Open up. It's Dent."

Whispering Jim Oxford opened the door. He only glanced at Farr's face before stepping into the narrow corridor and pulling the door shut behind him. "What's happened?"

Farr told him.

Oxford rubbed his chin. "Damned shame. Everything was going so sweet." He dropped a big hand on Farr's shoulder, grinned down at him. "Guess we better take a drive up there and pick your wife up."

"Thanks, Jim. We better not go together. Take your car and meet me at the turnoff to Thomaston's place."

"Check. I'll tell Bette some sort of thing. See you there."

Farr left the building. He could see MP's standing around in front of the bank. A half-dozen Army officers were talking earnestly with three men who were duplicates of the ones who'd questioned him earlier. He guessed the FBI was having its troubles getting any work done with the Army brass raising hell. He remembered the fat major who had wanted in anytime somebody figured a way to get at that payroll; wondered what that particular officer thought about the whole business. He went into the garage, waving to the two federal men who were still there. They showed no interest in him as he drove the T-bird out. He took his time on the drive to the wooded hill area where Burt Thomaston lived, trying to figure the strong and weak points of both sides.

The Commissioner and Thomaston had two things going for them. They knew Denton Farr had heisted $2,148,725 and they could finger him for the job. They had Mary Jean Farr. Fingering him would get them nothing and laying a rough hand on Mary Jean would get them dead.

Going for him, Farr had the money. He could not touch it for a long time if they didn't make some kind of a deal, but he had it and wasn't about to give it away. He had whispering Jim Oxford, who had not hesitated, had not blinked an eye before telling, 'Guess we better take a drive up there and pick your wife up,' and he had himself.

Without conceit, Denton Farr decided the Commissioner and Burt Thomaston didn't stand a chance. Not when you took the long view. He parked, waiting for Oxford.

When a two-toned hardtop pulled off the road behind him, Farr walked back to it and got in. Oxford reached under the seat and pulled out three pistols, a Walther automatic and two stubby revolvers. "Take your pick."

Farr shook his head. "I'm going in clean. They'd only take it away from me, and what's the point in giving them another gun?"

"Well, hell, Dent—"

"They're waiting," Farr interrupted. "They know I'll be along. There's only one way to get close to that damned place and that's drive up like you owned it. So that's what I do. I go in and try to make a deal. Clean. They'll be busy with me. You try to bust in quietly after about ten minutes. If I haven't settled it by then, it won't get settled quietly. Not at all."

"Yeah. How many do you think there'll be?"

"Half a dozen guys, probably. With a place that big, Thomaston has to have at least a houseboy. The Commissioner packs at least two torpedoes."

"Plenty of firepower," Oxford agreed. "Look—how do I get in there? They'll figure you covered yourself."

"You'll think of something." Farr lit a cigarette and watched a milk truck turn a corner down the hill and angle in toward the curb. He watched the milkman jump out and trot up the flagstoned walk of a house, carrying his wire basket of bottles. When the man returned to the truck, Farr looked at him more carefully. The truck was moving up the grade toward them now.

"Maybe you won't have to at that."

Farr got out and waved the truck down. He put his foot on the running board as the driver yanked the brake on. He smiled and said, "Hi, Mickey. How's the route going?"

"Well, hello, Mr. Farr. What brings you 'way up here?" The milkman was missing a couple of teeth at the left side of his mouth. He was tall, lanky, pleasant-faced. "Route's doing fine. You won't have to hold the note as long as I expected. Might have you paid off by summer."

"No hurry, Mickey," Farr said. He blessed his luck. The policy of giving a guy a hand when you could was about to pay off again. Until he saw Mickey Hart walking up that driveway, he had forgotten the day, months before, when he had advanced several hundred dollars so Mickey could make a down payment on the truck and buy the route franchise. Mickey was a hustler. He would do all right. Denton Farr got a cigarette going and pitched his voice low as he said, "Mick, I need some help. Right now, bad, and without any questions."

Mickey Hart's face became long, serious. "Sure, Mr. Farr. You just tell me what it is. I'm your boy."

"Good. Take off your leather jacket and cap. Leave them on the seat. Take a walk or something. You deliver up to Thomaston's?"

"Yeah. Two quarts homo-VD, butter, heavy cream sometimes." He tossed his cap on the seat and unzipped the jacket. "What about the rest of the route?"

"This shouldn't take too long. Another guy's going to borrow this truck. He'll ditch it around here in maybe a half-hour. If anyone should ask you, the truck went walking while you were making a delivery. Right?"

Mickey Hart's bewilderment showed plainly. He reached for the door handle. "Sure. Sure, Mr. Farr."

"Good. Give me your pen and something to write on." Hart handed him a pad of invoice blanks. Farr tore one off and on the reverse side wrote, *Received from Mickey Hart full payment for all loans made to him.* He dated it three days previously, signed it and gave it to the milkman. "Now scram."

Hart read the note, said, "Gosh, Mr. Farr, you don't—" then stopped talking and scrambled from the cab when he looked closely at Farr's eyes. He hurried down the hill.

Farr went back to the hardtop. "You're now a milkman, chum. Two quarts of something called homo-VD, some butter. Give me ten minutes and use the service entrance."

Oxford chuckled. "Christ! From bank robber to butter-and-egg man in one day. Luck, Dent."

Farr nodded. He walked to the T-bird, got in and drove up the curving path to Burt Thomaston's house at a normal pace. A Jaguar sedan was parked off to one side, near a green MG roadster. He left the motor idling and walked casually up the steps. He could feel the eyes, and he knew that more than one gun was centered on his belly at this moment.

He breathed deep and leaned on the button beside the latch of the immense door. The air was sweet, sharp. He was living again.

The man who opened the door was small; much too small to keep from bouncing around with the recoil if he ever fired the gun that was in his right hand. A .44 Magnum, a field piece without wheels. The torpedo had ferret eyes that did not blink.

"I'm clean," Farr said as he took a slow step into the house. The door swung shut and a slightly taller version of the man with the Magnum shook him down. The big room looked about as it had the first time he had come here, the night he worked Burt Thomaston over. The aroma of leather was still heavy in the air. The Commissioner was settled comfortably in one of the deep leather chairs, a drink close to hand on a table. He was smiling around the stub of a cigar.

Burt Thomaston lounged against the wall near the fireplace. When Farr's eyes found him his hand edged close to the handle of a brass poker that was racked with other fireplace tools. Thomaston's nose had not set properly; it was a lump in the otherwise sharp profile. The face was scored with worry lines and the black eyes shifted away.

"You're dead," Farr said softly. The hood who had the Magnum started to edge his hand toward his belt but let it drop after a glance from the Commissioner. "They can't protect you the rest of your life, Thomaston," he continued. "I don't think they'd bother."

"It was a sweet job, Dent," the Commissioner said quietly. "You ready to make a deal now?"

"Sure." He looked around for the bar cart, went to it and plopped ice cubes into a glass, added Scotch and tasted it. "I offered you a quarter of the take before, old chum. It's still good. I want my wife out of here in five minutes. And I want Thomaston."

"You want a lot," the Commissioner said mildly. "Thomaston's not doing much for us lately. He couldn't even let us know where you were going to hit. I guess I could give you that much for old time's sake. But your price has to be better."

Farr shook his head. "You've known me enough years to know you can't push, Commish. Where's Mary Jean?"

"She's all right," Thomaston blurted.

Denton Farr saw the thick, solid line of the man's throat and his fingers curled. "What's that mean?"

The Commissioner cleared his throat, crossed and recrossed his ankles. He looked at the carpet near Denton Farr's feet. "She's upstairs, lying down, Dent, and she's all right. Just a bruise on her forehead from the door."

Farr went for him then. The second hood had a .44 Magnum, too. He reached out and slapped the length of the barrel against the side of Farr's head. Farr dropped to his knees on the rug, feeling a drop of blood tickling its way down his forehead. He got his feet under him, shaking the pain off. There were two guns on him now so he just stood there, waiting.

"Relax, Dent. Your wife's not hurt," the Commissioner said. "She's a smart girl, though. The minute she walked into this room with Thomaston she knew something was queer. She tried to run out and walloped her head against the door. She came out of it in a few minutes. We gave her a sedative. Thomaston's broad is upstairs with her."

Denton Farr looked at each of the faces, burning them into his memory, promising himself he would see them as dead faces some day. He saw a stairway and walked toward it.

"Farr—get the hell back here!"

Thomaston had shouted the words at him. Farr paused, looked at him and at the others contemptuously. "Kill me. Then try finding the money. Try explaining the letters I'd leave behind."

He climbed the stairs. The buzzing in his head became a sharp pain with the effort and he wondered if he had a concussion. He was in a long, carpeted hallway. The walls were paneled in dark, gleaming wood. He walked until he found an open door. It was a bedroom. He wiped the streaked blood from his face and went in.

Mary Jean was on the bed, not moving. The bed was made but a comforter had been drawn over her. The willowy blonde with the violet eyes was in a chair by a large window. Her face tightened in alarm and she fumbled at a pocket in the quilted robe she wore, found a gun and pointed it at Farr.

"Put it down," he said quietly. "This is my wife." he crossed to the bed, eased his weight down on it and bent over Mary Jean, lightly fingering the dark bruise high on the right side of her forehead. Her pulse was slow but steady.

When he made no move toward her, the blonde lowered the gun. But the violet eyes remained on him. He brushed the soft dark curls back from the bruise, thinking, *Those bastards. They will pay for this, pay for touching you. They know they can't break me so they use you for a weapon. Dirty pool. This was my score. I set it up and if I got denutted it would have been all right. Bringing you into it was not all right. Not by a goddamn sight.* He peeled the comforter back, tugged Mary Jean's skirt down over the rounded knees. He looked at the blonde girl and said, "I'm taking her with me. You can do whatever the hell you want to do."

He lifted Mary Jean from the bed, walked around it toward the door. The girl was standing now, uncertain. She dropped the gun in her pocket. Through the window behind her Farr saw a milk truck coming around, stopping behind the house.

Denton Farr carried his wife downstairs.

They were waiting, watching to see what he would do. Farr crossed the big room, eased Mary Jean down on the cushions of the sofa, feeling the leather soft and cool under his hands.

This was about as far as he could go. The rest of it would be up to Whispering Jim Oxford.

The Commissioner would let him carry his wife downstairs. He was not about to let him carry her through the heavy, studded door. Not until Farr kicked in $2,148,725—or however much the Commissioner demanded. Farr looked around, saw where he had left his drink and retrieved it. There was one thing he had to know before the haggling began.

"How much does she know?"

"Nothing," the Commissioner said. "It's the truth, Dent. She cold-conked herself before anything was said. Later she might start adding things up and figure it all out, but so far she knows nothing."

"Good." Farr prowled the carpet. The fury was still eating at him. If it was just the Commissioner he wouldn't have minded a deal. You had to get along with the big boys, and the Commish was their ambassador. He'd goofed this one and if he didn't manage to turn what the organization felt was a good profit, enough to make the federal heat worthwhile, it would be his ass. The Commish had his ethics. He would give you a yes or no answer and stick with it. Thomaston and these others were punks. Farr nodded toward Thomaston. "I've been trying to figure this guy. He's a bum. A bum with nothing going for him but a muckraking TV program. What good could he do you, Commish?"

The Commissioner beetled his brows and took a pull at his drink. "If you remember, he raised hell with one of your operations once. He's done the same for a lot of reform characters who could have given us a bad time. Some congressman gets too nosy, a little digging and half an hour of the Grand Inquisitor and he'd be out of the congressman business. Just insurance, Dent. Just insurance."

Denton Farr watched a doorknob turn slowly, saw the panel ease open a fraction of an inch, then enough to allow the barrel of a gun to slide through.

CHAPTER 17

Denton Farr put his glass down and strolled toward the wall, where he would be out of the line of fire. "I want you all to listen to what I'm going to say now. Every damned one of you. You listening?"

They were looking at him strangely. The Commissioner shifted his weight in his chair. He had heard Denton Farr say things like that before; always something unexpected and usually violent had followed.

"I want every damn gun in this room tossed out in the middle of the carpet. Then you all go climb the wall," Farr said curtly.

The two gunmen who had come with the Commissioner flipped their jackets back. The one who had let Farr in narrowed his eyes. "Now just why in hell should we do something like that, you crazy son of a bitch?"

They were watching Denton Farr now, waiting. Farr grinned.

Whispering Jim Oxford rammed the door open with his foot. He held an automatic shotgun waist high, swiveling the muzzle from one side of the group to the other.

"Be hell to pay if you don't, fella," Oxford said in a cold, soft voice.

Oxford let the door shut behind him. He wore the milkman's cap and jacket. It was open and there were two pistols stuffed into the waistband of his slacks. Motioning with the shotgun, he herded them into a line at the far side of the room. "Now, one at a time, left to right, reach real slow and toss the artillery out. Don't expect help from the boy you left out back. He's taking some time off. Check 'em, Dent."

One by one they dropped their weapons and turned, leaning forward against the wall, arms and legs apart. Farr patted each one swiftly without turning up any hideout guns. The chubby hood had a switchblade knife. Farr emptied the guns, except for a thirty-eight automatic which he thrust into a hip pocket. He carried the others to the fireplace, pried the little trap door set in the stonework for disposal of ashes open and dropped the guns into it. He crossed the room, with the automatic in his fist.

"All right, tough people. Relax but stay down this end of the room." He watched them carefully as they turned away from the wall. The Commissioner and his two gunmen were taking it like pros. The Commissioner was smart enough to figure Farr couldn't kill them here if he wanted to, not and come out of it clean with the law. And there were too many of them to take off somewhere. The gunsels would do what their boss did. Thomaston was sweating it, pushing the blonde girl away as she tried to come close to him. "I'll hold them. Take a look, see how Mary Jean's head looks, chum."

Oxford circled behind Farr, lay the shotgun on the floor by the sofa and bent over the unconscious woman. He raised her eyelids, nodding to himself, fingered the bruised area and took her pulse. He straightened, scooped the shotgun up and said, "Seems all right. Maybe under sedation. She'll have a sore head for a few days."

Farr pocketed the automatic again. He picked his wife up, wondering how he would explain all this to her when the time came, and started toward the door, then turned and looked directly at the Commissioner.

"If you're smart, you'll go home and forget any of this happened. I'd like to take Thomaston with me, but I can't now. He could get chicken and spill to the cops before I do get to him. If that happens, everybody's hurt." He jerked his head toward the door and told Oxford, "See if it's clear."

"Better dump this first." Oxford leaned the shotgun in a niche behind the door, twisted the knob and stepped out, pulling the door nearly shut behind him. "Looks good," he called back to them. "Bring the cannon and let's go."

Denton Farr turned away from the people in the room for an instant, starting to hoist his wife to his left shoulder so he could carry her with one arm. At the same time he bent forward, reaching for the shotgun.

Two bullets struck him in the back.

The first went in near the left shoulder blade, following a generally straight course until it passed almost through his body. It broke into ragged chunks against the collarbone. He felt the impact long before he heard the sound of the small-caliber gun firing. He began to fall then, and the second bullet took him lower, almost in the small of the back, close by the spine.

Mary Jean spilled from his shoulder, falling heavily. She rolled as she fell and the skirt she wore whipped up, exposing the sleek roundness of her thighs.

From the hips down, there was no sensation in Denton Farr's body. There was no pain yet, but there was a dulling numbness and his legs were twisted grotesquely, incapable of movement. The shotgun was beyond reach. He pawed for the automatic and his fingers clamped around the smooth, solid butt.

Only a second or two had passed. The echoes of the second shot were still in the room when the door slammed open again. The shotgun was behind it but Whispering Jim Oxford had a gun in each hand and the hammers were dropping even as Farr, flat on his belly now, picked his target.

He tried to call out to Whispering Jim Oxford to hold it up but his voice was lost in the bark of three guns.

Denton Farr shot Burt Thomaston three times in the belly. The chunky man pitched face-down on the floor and the little sleeve Derringer, its two barrels spent now, skidded on the rug.

He shouted at Oxford again to for Chrissakes stop, and he knew, even in that instant, when the murderous fire would end. Not until the bucking, barking, flame-spitting guns were empty. It would be like the night a four-man Nazi patrol had jumped them up in the last days of the war, when the Germans were trying to do nothing but get the hell out of Italy. Whispering Jim Oxford had used up a whole magazine from a tommygun, a fifteen-shot clip in a carbine and a full clip in a .45, pumping lead at anything that moved. The Germans had been dead after the first burst of fire.

The Commissioner was on his knees, hands grabbing at the place where his throat and jaw had been. The blood gushed for a few seconds, then slowed to a steady seeping as the great arteries drained themselves. The girl with the violet eyes and ash-blonde hair died quietly, with one spreading patch of red between her breasts. The Commissioner's hoods dropped with lead burrowing into their brains from the rear as they tried to run.

Whispering Jim Oxford's guns made futile clicking noises and he tossed them away. He slammed the door shut tight behind him and knelt beside Denton Farr.

The pain was beginning now, welling up inside his chest, throbbing. He tasted blood in his mouth. Oxford had a knife out, was slitting through his jacket and shirt, looking closely at the holes.

"Own goddamn fault," Farr muttered. He could feel sweat beading on his forehead. "Sleeve gun. Missed it. Feels like I'm leaking inside. Can't move my goddamn legs at all." He swallowed the salt taste of blood, managed to grin. "Christ but it was sweet while it lasted. How bad is it, ole doc?"

Whispering Jim Oxford's face told him even before the lean man spoke. "You want it straight."

Farr felt a wave of dizziness surge through him. "Hell, yes."

"The top one got a big artery somewhere. Damn little twenty-twos will kill a man when a Magnum goes right through him, leaves a nice clean hole you can plug with a bottle stopper. The other one buggered your spinal cord, from the looks of it."

"Well God damn," Farr muttered. This was a hell of a way and a hell of a time to get it. He thought about dying, and was not much impressed with the prospect. There was no point to wheeling around the rest of your life instead of walking. He reached until his fingers touched Mary Jean's outstretched hand. He drew it to him and pressed his lips against it, then stared at the ragged imprint of blood on the golden tan. He raised his head, looked at the dead people. "Massacre. You better get the hell out, Jim."

Oxford said nothing. He looked at Denton Farr and shook his head slowly.

Farr clenched his teeth and raised his head enough to spit. "Don't be a damn fool. Get out. Probably nobody heard the shots, with these stone walls and no houses close. For Christ's sake, get out and take care of my wife. You'll have to tell her some kind of story. And rig some way so she gets my cut of the payroll without knowing it, hear?"

"Dent—I ..."

"I'm dead, chumly. Do this for me. And take care of the other guys in it. You can all—get out clean ..." He choked, coughed, spat again. The pain was growing steadier now. "When the cops find that crew there they'll—think they got their birds. Now get the hell out ..."

Farr's head rolled as he tried to escape the pain. He felt Oxford's hand on his. Then the big man was standing over him, Mary Jean looking small and incredibly beautiful in his arms.

Denton Farr winked, and without sound his lips framed the words, "Luck, Jim."

He shut his eyes before the door had entirely closed. He did not mind dying alone, but he didn't see why it had to take so long.

He began to be afraid the law would get here, find life still in his body, patch him up, make him talk. Get him healthy again so they could put him in the gas chamber at San Quentin. He heard a scratching sound and turned his head.

Burt Thomaston's eyes were open; still black and bright and knowing through the pain.

Denton Farr swallowed a little more blood as he cursed a coward who would shoot a man in the back.

"Screw you," Thomaston said raggedly. "You gutshot me, you bastard. I'll take a long time dying. They'll find us before that happens. I'll make it real sweet for your Mary Jean. And your buddy ..."

Denton Farr tested himself. The powerful, disciplined muscles of his arms and shoulders responded. The pain was great now, a living, clutching being. He raised himself on his elbows, fingers grabbing at the carpet, and dragged himself forward.

"... you're dead, Thomaston ..."

His legs dragged heavily behind him. Before he had moved the gross weight of his body a foot he had been forced to stop and rest twice. He listened to the gurgle of blood in his lungs and tried again.

Burt Thomaston tried to crawl away. The effort was too great, and he knew somehow he could never crawl far enough. Finally he lay there on his belly, face turned sideways toward the grotesque, pain-distorted countenance of Denton Farr.

He tried to break away when the fingers reached his throat.

Denton Farr felt reality slipping away from him. Nothing had substance. He was aware of only two things in the final seconds—the rising throb of sirens, still far away but coming fast, and the neck of an enemy in his hands.

THE END

Terror Tournament

BY JAY FLYNN

Writing as J. M. Flynn

CHAPTER 1

By the time the count reached three hundred and fifty thousand dollars, the money had become both an abstraction and a source of concern and irritation to Stannard. He walked away from the table with the weight of the Thompson gun heavy and uncomfortable against his right arm. He stared out the big window, past the eighteenth green, frowning at the orange ball of sun as it floated toward the rim of the bay. The shadows were long under the cypresses and pines and oaks, and the September wind was damp and heavy with the smell of the Pacific.

The pro-amateur golf tournament had brought better than fifteen thousand cars a day through the Forest gates for three days. It would have been big even with a blizzard, but the weather had been crisp and clear and cool, and the San Francisco papers figured the total attendance had topped the hundred thousand mark. Burl Stannard's guess was closer to seventy-five.

Altogether too many, when you were responsible for security.

He wished it had rained. The tournament committee had expected about fifty thousand and allowed just enough money to police a crowd of that size. It would have been a breeze.

The monotonous voices of the two other men in the office ate at him.

"Hill gate, $11,341," Husted muttered.

"Check," Bacher agreed.

"Programs, Hill gate, $4,853."

"Check."

Stannard swung away from the window, scowling. There wasn't much daylight left.

Major Harry Bacher fumbled a thick rubber band around a stack of currency. He was a heavy-set man with thinning, sandy-colored hair and restless eyes. Better than twenty-five years in the Army before a Jeep flipped and they retired him with a hundred per cent disability. It didn't keep him from at least one round of golf a day or slow him down when it came to selling staggeringly expensive homes and building sites in the Forest. Bacher's face was flushed again. Stannard couldn't decide whether it came from nips at the flask or the financial success of the tournament. Major Bacher was finance chairman. He played the officer-and-gentleman bit too hard but could be tolerated.

Stannard had given up trying to tolerate Dick Husted. Husted was too chubby, his bright little eyes set too close together behind the rimless glasses, his mouth too petulant. But he worked for Bacher, which meant he worked the tournament free. Now he pouted at the figures on the tape, then sucked the eraser on the end of his pencil.

"How much longer?" Stannard demanded curtly. "Wrap it up quick, or I'll call the sheriff's men in for an escort."

"A few minutes, Stannard," Bacher said. He worked the stub of a cigar across his mouth and studied the figures. He nodded slowly, smiled. "Four hundred and three thousand even. Check, Dick?"

"Check, Major." Husted stacked the bills in a strongbox. "Amazing, sir. Amazing to know there's money like this in golf."

Stannard leaned across the desk and slammed the strongbox lid down. "Now you know, buster. Now it goes to the bank. Coming?"

Bacher paused as he reached for a suede sports jacket hanging over the back of a chair. He removed the cigar from his mouth.

"Mr. Stannard. Your attention to your duties is admirable. Your arrogance is unjustified. I'm sure other members of the tournament committee—"

"Feel the same," Stannard interrupted, eyes narrowing. "They can tell me so if they feel like it. Let's go."

Husted cleared the desk. Bacher inspected the ash of his cigar. "You're efficient," Bacher said. "But you've given the Forest and the tournament some bad publicity. There was a picture of you with that Tommy-gun in all the papers yesterday. No justification for it. None whatever."

"I was hired to protect this operation. I didn't know about the picture until I saw it in the papers, and if you must know, I don't give a damn. Now grab that money and let's get out of here."

Stannard went to the window. The Caddy limousine was waiting on the drive below, and the area had been cleared of cars and foot traffic. He worked the machine gun's bolt, then rechecked the safety. His head ached and he wanted a drink. He had wanted one for three days. He intended to have one in front of him within a minute of the time the money was banked.

Husted tucked the strongbox under his arm and started for the door without looking at Stannard.

Stannard shouldered him aside, yielded to temptation, and brought his foot down on Husted's instep. The yelp of pain was a satisfying sound.

"I go first, remember?" Stannard unbolted the door, stepped into the hallway, where a uniformed guard waited at the top of the stairs.

The guard slid his revolver from its holster. "All clear, Burl."

Stannard poked his head back into the room. "You can come out now. Stick behind me; wait for me to check the grounds before you go to the car. Don't waste any time."

Husted chewed his lip and glared. Stannard led the way as the four men went down the steps. He checked the area, then crossed the brick sidewalk

to the limousine. Norm Keyes, the Peninsula City cop who had the driving assignment, held the door open.

"OK," Stannard called. "Lock the doors from inside."

Husted limped to the car, bumped Stannard aside as he tossed the box
on the floor, and climbed into the rear seat. Bacher followed. Stannard tried
the door handles, circled the car, and rolled the front window down before sliding into the seat beside Keyes.

The upstairs guard holstered his gun as he told Stannard, "The sheriff's
car is standing by at the Hill gate. I'll phone ahead that you're on the way."

Stannard nodded and slipped the Tommy-gun between his knees. His eyes
searched the curving road. It was deserted now except for a few people
crossing between the clubhouse and the Lodge. Lights showed through the
curtained windows of the small bar at the far corner of the Lodge and in
the clubhouse. Stannard knew there'd be plenty of action around the Forest that night. The formal victory dinner in the Lodge banquet hall would
rate the big space in the papers, with the sports writers and society reporters
squeezing every inch of copy from it. But the stuff of which locker-room
stories and divorce suits are fashioned would take place in the half-dozen
bars in the Forest and in the private soirees that would be rolling merrily
in another hour or so.

Stannard thought in passing that he might try some of the action himself. There was a gorgeous doll with a poodle to match her platinum-blond
hair and Thunderbird convertible who'd shown some interest.

He smiled at the thought. Fat chance. He looked at Bacher and Husted
settled in the rear seat. "Roll it, Norm," he said.

The sun was half down, muddling into the purple of the false horizon,
as the heavy car pulled away smoothly, leaning into the turn. Burl Stannard watched the ribbon of pavement unwind through the dark groves that
were shrouded in Spanish moss. Houses huddled in their expensive seclu-
sion on the uphill side. To the right, between the road and rockedged shore
of the bay, were the manicured fairways of the beach course. A scattering
of die-hard golfers hacked away in the purpling dusk.

Stannard decided a *concours d'élégance* could be organized in fifteen minutes by grabbing cars at random from the driveways they passed. It was
an occasion for Jags, Aston Martins, diffident Bentleys, undiffident Rolls
Royces, Mercedes, MG's, Ferraris, and crass Cadillacs. There were people around the cars and the houses; the people appeared to be getting a
good start on some serious drinking. Through experience Stannard knew
a certain percentage of guests would fall, jump or be pushed into swimming pools. The horse set would raid the stables and get a moonlight polo
match going on the sixteenth fairway. There would be fistfights, flirtations,
propositions, adulteries—and sly items in the San Francisco gossip columns

for some weeks.

He lit a cigarette, thankful that such goings-on were no direct concern of his. There had been enough to sweat out without them—enough to convince him that the tournament directors had been crazy to offer the security job to a new one-man agency. And that he had been crazier to accept.

A wry grin twisted his mouth as he thought of himself passing the job up. It would have meant passing up eating, paying rent, getting laundry done, and a few other things which had been possible when he was Lieutenant Burl Stannard of the Peninsula City police department. The pay had been steady, if not good, until the beef with Captain Jim Moss, night watch commander, four months ago. Since then, income had been neither steady nor good.

And the agency fee on this one job would be enough to at least pay the office rent a couple of months, take care of some bar tabs, pay Lee Ellen the back salary she had coming, and temporarily tranquilize the credit-bureau bird dogs. A clean, smooth operation would mean the start of a good name for the agency and more work. And to hell with Major Bacher and his Chamber of Commerce attitude about bad publicity.

It had required careful organization plus discretion. The organization had involved hiring off-duty cops from the sheriff's office and police force and bringing in some agents, male and female, from other detective agencies. Receipts needed guarding; the roads of the private barony that was the Forest needed patrolling; traffic needed directing. The tournament brought big money, and big money brought thieves.

In three days they'd jailed eight burglars, a car clout ring, three bartenders who were tapping the till, and a pair of lads who came up from LA with dice to fit any and all situations.

A flying squad of call girls had been rousted, which came under the heading of *Organization*, but allowed to set up shop in a motel outside the Forest, which was classified as *Discretion*.

All hands had been reasonably happy, with the exception of Major Harry Bacher. Bacher had remarked more than once that Stannard was a roughneck who had resigned his police department job after being accused of brutality and sadism. Stannard had retorted that if anyone should know about such things, it would be a guy who'd spent most of his life as a Military Police officer.

Now Stannard adjusted his rear-view mirror and watched Bacher nip at his silver flask. He restrained an urge to point the chopper's muzzle at the sky, let off a burst, and see what happened to the rear-seat upholstery.

The trees were thinning out on the right now, and the road swung along the edge of the fifteenth fairway. The sun was well below the horizon, but three golfers were still poking through the rough along the edge of the road a hundred yards ahead. They wore casual, loose-fitting clothes, big, floppy caps, and dark glasses. As Stannard watched, they glanced toward the car, tossed their clubs into an electric caddy cart, and climbed aboard. The three-wheeler bumped slowly over the turf, angling down a narrow slope toward the road.

"Golf nuts," Norm Keyes muttered as he flipped the headlight dimmer and tapped the horn ring lightly. "They won't have enough light to get that rig back to the clubhouse."

Shallow frown lines ridged Stannard's forehead, and he raised the Tommy-gun to his lap. He stared at the golfers, trying to pin down something that had alerted him for an instant and then dissolved in his mind before it could be identified. He slipped the safety off and poked the muzzle through the window. The machine gun was awkwardly long even without the shoulder stock mounted, and he realized he'd have to be out of the car to use it.

And he was suddenly sure he'd have to use it. He let the barrel rest against the bottom of the window and dug with his left hand for the stubby .38 holstered on his left hip.

The three-wheeler was close now, too close. It rode up the berm of the road and cut onto the blacktop in front of the speeding Cadillac. He heard Keyes swear as he braked the limousine and spun the wheel to the left. Tires howled, and Stannard could see the man who drove the cart look over his shoulder, then flip the tiller.

In that instant, Stannard spotted the thing that was wrong: with the sun long gone, the three men still wore heavy dark goggles that effectively covered the upper parts of their faces. And scarves had been twisted up to conceal their chins.

"Gun it, Norm!" He tried to bring the Thompson up as he shouted. The front sight hung up on the windwing, and the stock jammed against his chest.

The limousine went into a skid. Stannard saw the right front fender brush the caddy cart. The cart tilted, hesitated, then rolled up sluggishly on two wheels and spilled on its side. The three men had jumped just before the impact.

Keyes had his foot down hard on the gas. He was fighting the wheel as the big car left the road and crunched its grille against a wind-twisted cypress. Stannard felt the windshield come up and rap him hard across the forehead. Then he was fighting the door handle, trying to get out. The door swung open a couple of inches and stuck. He swore, wrestled the chopper around, and drove his shoulder hard against the door. The twisted metal refused to move.

The headlights, bent cockeyed, still worked. Stannard saw the three men moving fast toward the Caddy. One ran around the front with a sawed-off shotgun held across his chest. The others had pistols. They fanned out to the front and right. Major Bacher was shouting something from the rear seat, and Keyes had his service revolver out. He triggered a shot through the windshield, the sound deafening in the confines of the car.

Then the one on the right ran across the sights of Stannard's Thompson. Stannard fingered the trigger. The gun bucked against him, its muzzle spitting flame and smoke. The man stopped running, his body jerking as the heavy slugs drilled through his chest. His mouth opened in a scream that was covered by the chattering shots. He fell on his back, blood welling from the torn flesh.

From the left side of the car, the twin barrels of the shotgun erupted. The windshield disintegrated, and shards of glass chewed at Stannard's face and head.

Norm Keyes slumped over the wheel without a sound. The top of his head was torn away.

Stannard tried to swing the chopper around, but there was no room. It wedged against the door. He swore and went for the .38 again. The one he had shot was motionless on the ground, but the thug with the shotgun was pulling at the door on the driver's side, and the other one was trying a couple of shots from the right. Stannard heard a bullet tear through metal and bury itself in the instrument panel inches away from his face.

He wanted the scatter-gun man. Wanted him for Norm Keyes. He had the .38 out of its holster now and tried to bring it around behind Keyes's body for a snap shot at the gunman. The double was worse than useless until it could be reloaded after its first two shells.

Stannard shot once but knew even as he pulled the trigger that his man had ducked to safety. Another bullet chewed its way through the car, tugging at the shoulder of Stannard's jacket as it went by.

Dick Husted's voice was shrill in his ears. Stannard twisted on the seat and saw Husted swing a .45 automatic in a wide arc toward the right side of the car. His lips were stretched tight over his teeth, his eyes bright.

"I got this one! I got him!"

Stannard tried to duck down on the seat as the heavy gun fired. The top of his head exploded, and where it had been became a black and red ball of pain. He heard the .45 go off again, and then he was vaguely aware of pitching forward, slumping across the floor of the car. Then there was no more pain, no awareness.

There was nothing but blackness.

CHAPTER 2

The grass was cool and damp, and there were diamond-sharp stars swirling in a sky that wasn't yet completely night-black. Stannard tried to sit up, but fresh pain lanced through his skull. A strip above his left temple seemed to be on fire.

"Lie still, buddy. Doctor'll be here pretty quick." The man who bent over him wore white. He swabbed more fire on Stannard's head and taped a bandage on.

Stannard let his weight down on his elbows. There was a delicate operation involved in turning his head, focusing his eyes.

The Caddy was still nosed into the tree. A white ambulance waited nearby, flashing its red lights. He saw several sheriff cars and a blanket-covered form on a stretcher by the ambulance. Blood had darkened the blanket at the head end. He remembered it all then and tried to get up.

The man in white held him. "Better lie still, buddy. Looks like the slug just grazed you, but we better see if there's a fracture or concussion."

Stannard knocked the hands away and rolled up to a sitting position. His head seemed to fall apart, and he pushed it back together with shaking fingers. He made it to his knees, then managed to stand. Then he put one foot in front of the other and made it to the car.

The rear doors yawned open. The chopper lay across the front seat. Somebody had yanked the drum of ammunition from it and opened the bolt. The seat was blood-soaked, littered with fragments of glass. Stannard picked up the machine gun, hefted it, scowling. Hell of a good weapon. Just remember you got to have room to use it, he thought. A flashbulb flared in his eyes, and he saw one of the men from the local paper flip the film holder of a Speed Graphic. Stannard tossed the gun back into the car and glared.

The photographer approached. Stannard fixed him with his eyes and said, "Scram. Damn you, get away."

Someone got out of one of the police cars and crossed the patch of light. Stannard blinked at the bony, bitter face of Captain Jim Moss. Without speaking, Moss handed him something small and heavy.

Stannard looked at his .38, saw it was loaded except for one spent shell. He shoved it into the holster and met Moss's eyes. "OK. Say it."

"What, Burl," Moss replied mildly.

"Tell me I screwed up. Save me the trouble of reading it."

Moss shook his head. "A hell of a thing. But I can't see it was your fault."

"That bad, huh?" Stannard shook his head in weariness, fumbled a cigarette from the crushed pack in his shirt, and got it going. "I look bad enough so it doesn't need any help."

Moss lit a cigarette himself. "Why don't you save it? You got plenty of time to scrap with me right now?"

Stannard studied the older man's face a moment without finding malice. "Sorry, Jim. I'm shook. They get away?"

"Clean," Moss said. "You were out about three-quarters of an hour. Norm's dead. Major Bacher got roughed up a little. He and Husted told us what happened, and we ran them back to the Lodge. Both of them seemed to need a quick one."

"Yeah. I remember Norm getting it. I scragged one with the chopper, and then Husted started banging away with a cannon I didn't even know he had. Stupid bastard almost took my head off. What happened then?"

"They made the two of them get out of the car, took Husted's gun. Bacher must have been a little slow, because one of them fattened his lip with it. They grabbed the money box and scrammed."

Stannard looked at the ground. "Just how in the hell did they get through the gate? Past the sheriff's car?"

"They didn't. They used the caddy cart again. Scooted right across the fairway, into the trees on the other side, and went over the wall to a car they had stashed."

"I'll be damned. Get a make on the one I burned yet?"

Moss shook his head. "They took him along."

"The hell they did. He was dead!"

"If you say so. But they took him anyway. Made the Major and Husted put his body on the back of the cart."

"Crazy."

"Like little foxes." Moss sucked on his cigarette. "See much of them?"

"Nothing that counts." Stannard jammed his hands in his pockets. "Just three guys, about average size. Loose clothes, dark glasses, scarves, and floppy hats. Nothing to pin a make on."

"Real pros."

"They knew what they were doing."

"Wonder if they knew what they were doing when they killed a cop, Burl."

"I want them first," Stannard said in a tight voice. "You can have what's left."

"Uh-uh. You were too good a cop to expect that. You know how it has to be."

"I was a good cop?" Stannard retorted bitterly. "I was a brutal, sadistic bastard. So the chief said. You agreed."

"Don't dig that up again," Moss snapped. "Why not admit you just got all teed off and took everything—"

"Save it!" Stannard yanked the .38 out and emptied the cartridges in the palm of his hand. He tossed away the fired shell and replaced it with a new one from his belt. He took a small knife from his pocket and carefully cut a cross in the nose of each slug. "I want that pair."

Moss grabbed for the bullets. Stannard pushed him away, reloaded the gun, and rammed it into the holster.

"Burl—I think the one you took on the head hurt you," Moss argued. "Look—work along with us and—"

"Sure," Stannard interrupted. "I'd like to. A one-man gang hasn't much chance, but I could get lucky." He flipped his cigarette away. "Remember something, Jim. Norm was one of your cops. But he was working for me when he got it. I liked Norm."

"Well, sure. But—"

"Murder trials bore me," Stannard said, patting the bulge on his hip.

Stannard bummed a ride to the Lodge with a deputy sheriff. He went directly into the Fiesta bar, pushed his way through the crowd of drinkers, and called for a double shot of brandy. The bartender eyed his torn clothes, the face chewed by flying glass, the strip of bandage. He brought the drink and quickly went away. Stannard saw him lean over the bar and whisper to a group of men. In a matter of seconds the barroom talk died, and he could feel an almost physical impact from the stares. He turned, glaring at the blank, curious faces, and sipped the brandy. It burned pleasantly in his throat. He turned back to the bar and considered his reflection in the tinted mirror.

The face that stared back at him was squarish, with black eyes wide-set above prominent cheekbones. An old scar tilted the right eye and brow in a doubting curl. The bandage was starkly white against the black hair. The mouth, ordinarily pleasant, was a tight, almost colorless line now, the jaw beneath it rigid, jutting. He fingered the tape, decided the bleeding had stopped, and ripped the bandage off. He wadded it in his fist and tossed it onto the floor. The barkeep frowned.

A tall, lean man in a dark suit moved to the vacant space beside him. Stannard met the eyes in the mirror and nodded a silent greeting.

Bob Custer was an agency man from San Francisco, in charge of the agents assigned to the Lodge building proper.

"Feel OK, Burl?"

"It'll scab and heal over. Anybody hear anything solid?"

Custer shook his head and called for a bourbon. "Just talk."

"Nobody claiming to be able to identify them?" Stannard said in mild disbelief. "Nobody saw a thing?"

"Just the two who were with you in the car. They're over in the pressroom trying to tell their yarn to the reporters."

"Shouldn't be hard," Stannard said sourly. He rapped on the bar for another brandy.

Custer chuckled. "Your Girl Friday pitched in to create distractions."

"She's got the build for it." Stannard worked up a grin, tossed a couple of dollars on the bar, and went out, ignoring the stares. He crossed a graveled walk to the clubhouse, which rambled along a grassy slope. A half-dozen of the sports writers who had covered the tournament sprawled on the steps leading to the pressroom. They groused among themselves and eyed the closed door balefully. Stannard picked his way through them, muttering hellos.

"Protect yourselves at all times, pal. That Holy of Holies reeks of crime writers." The man who had spoken ended with a brittle laugh.

Stannard shouldered the door open. A photographer swung his camera to eye level and popped a flashbulb. The room was brightly lighted, and Stannard was suddenly conscious of the wrinkles, stains, and tears in his clothes. He pushed through the knot of reporters that formed around him and growled, "See you all in a minute, OK?"

Lee Ellen was swinging down from a perch on a long table that was littered with discarded newspapers, score cards, copy paper, cigarette ashes, paper cups, pencils, and battered typewriters. She wore a fawn-colored sheath that rode up over her knees as she toed for the floor.

Stannard conceded she had magnificent legs, without being sure whether this was good or bad at the moment. She was tall, curved, graceful. Her pale blond hair was shoulder-length.

"Burl—" There was something in the way she spoke his name that made it good to hear. She came to him, fingers reaching for the bullet furrow. More flashbulbs popped.

"Damn it, can't you guys wait a little!" Stannard checked his urge to toss a couple of newspapermen on their ears.

"We've waited. We've got deadlines," one retorted.

"Yeah, I know." Stannard tried to make his words sound pleasant. "Look, I haven't even had a chance to talk with the people I'm working for. Let me do that; then we'll see what we can spill."

"Mean you're still working here?"

Stannard's face darkened, and he looked for the man who had spoken. Nobody said anything.

A photographer fed a fresh roll of film into his Rollei. "How about a shot of you and your girl?"

The prospect made Stannard wince. It would look great in the tabloids. Private eye with Tommy-gun under one arm and leggy blond under the other. Charging out to blast a pair of killers and recover four hundred grand. Sweet. The agency was as good as dead already.

"Maybe." He sighed and walked Lee Ellen to a corner. Through an open door he saw Major Bacher and Dick Husted holding down a battered sofa in an adjoining room. They had their heads together.

"How bad is it?"

She shrugged, the motion drawing the dress taut across her bosom. "Who knows? I was on my way out to where it happened when Jim Moss headed me off. He said you were all right and somebody'd better stall the newspaper gang. They're getting the fidgets."

"How about Bacher and Husted?"

"They're in a snit. The boys dragged them in here for an interview, but so far nobody's asked them any questions."

Stannard grinned. "Cheesecake's got its value."

Lee Ellen reddened a little. "You'll still have to tell them something."

"Yeah. Pacify them a little longer." He patted her shoulder and went into the next room, hoisted himself onto a scarred table, lit a cigarette, and fixed Major Bacher and Husted with his eyes. "You're about to be interviewed. Understand something—this is a police matter. I've got no official standing whatever. And I don't give a damn what you say about me. But first I want you to tell me everything you remember about the stickup."

Bacher flushed. He cut the end from a cigar and lit it.

Husted crossed and recrossed his ankles, blinking his little myopic eyes. "It looks as though you fell down badly on your job, Stannard. And we've already talked to the police."

Stannard boosted himself off the table, crossed the room in two strides, grabbed an ankle, and jerked Husted from the sofa. The chubby man thumped hard on his behind onto the wood floor. He yelped and scrambled back to the sofa, rubbing himself.

"Next time I'll kick it," Stannard said.

"Now listen here, you—" Bacher began.

"Shut up, Major," Stannard barked. "If you'd let me have the armored car, none of this would have happened. Let's hear it. Start with the men themselves."

"What about them?" Husted muttered.

"I want anything that can help us identify them," Stannard said wearily. "Any distinguishing marks or characteristics, anything that sticks in your minds about their clothes or voices."

"You were up front. You saw them before we did," Husted said peevishly. "It was getting dark, and I didn't notice them until we hit the cart. Then it was too exciting to remember much."

Stannard fingered his wound. "Yeah. You sure did get excited, buster. OK. Neither of you remember anything offhand. Take it step-by-step from where I shot one and you started blazing away. What happened next?"

Bacher gnawed the cigar. "Stannard, we've been over all of it with the police. And I don't believe the tournament committee intends to retain you any longer." The left side of his face was bruised and swollen where the hood had hit him.

"So talk to me anyway."

Their eyes locked. Bacher's mouth twisted into a clear expression of distaste before he spoke.

"The one with the shotgun pointed it in the window at us and made Dick drop his gun. By that time the second one was at the other door, on the right-hand side. They made us get out and carry the money box to the golf cart. I tried to refuse when they ordered us to tip it up on its wheels again. The one with the pistol slapped the barrel across my face. I was tempted to try for his gun—" His face darkened in remembered anger.

"Just as good you didn't. They'd killed one man already," Stannard said.

"I could have easily enough," Bacher retorted. "I'm not soft, Stannard. I was a professional soldier more than a quarter of a century and I know how to take a gun away from somebody. But there was still the one with the shotgun—"

"Good thing you remembered. What happened then?"

"We turned the three-wheeler up. The one with the shotgun had disarmed the Tommy-gun. They used the driver's handcuffs to secure us to the car, picked up the one you shot, put him and the money in the golf cart, and drove off."

"Uh-huh." Stannard rubbed his forehead. His head was throbbing steadily now. "How long did all this take?"

"Perhaps a minute or two," Bacher replied. "No longer."

"Who did the talking? Hear any names?"

"The one with the shotgun did most of it," Bacher said. "He didn't use any name. Except mine."

"Yours, huh? How, just 'Bacher'?"

Bacher chewed his lip in thought. "No—no, I think he just called me Major. Remember, Dick?"

Husted shook his head. "I don't know."

"OK," Stannard said. "How about the voice. Any accent?"

"None that I could identify. He spoke in a positive way. As though he knew just what he was about."

"And that's all of it?"

"It is," Bacher told him.

"One more thing. The one I hit with the chopper. He looked dead. Was he?"

Bacher nodded. "I'd say he was dead before he hit the ground."

"Funny. Hoods generally leave their dead behind. OK. Come on out and get your names in the papers."

Stannard allowed himself ten minutes with the reporters. He knew a few from his years on the police force. The questions were pointed but not unfriendly. He made it clear the case was in the hands of the police, that he was on his own. He denied being fired from the cops for brutality and grinned as he refused to pose with drawn gun and arm around Lee Ellen. When the reporters started concentrating on Bacher and Husted, Stannard hurried Lee Ellen out the door.

They crossed a lawn dappled with the shadows of live oaks to the parking lot where Stannard had left his Ford. He burrowed through the litter of the dash compartment until he found a bottle of bourbon.

"No cups," he said.

"That's OK, boss."

The bottle passed back and forth twice before it was capped. Stannard's head was on fire, and he laughed without humor. "Guess you might as well hit the office and make out payroll vouchers. Just day wages for the crew. When you send them down for payment, put in a note saying they don't owe me anything personally until I get their dough back." He sighed, then got a smoke going. "Hell, that can wait for tomorrow. And you can start shopping for a new job."

She turned to him, and her eyes were dark in the reflected light of the moon. "I'm fired?"

He found her hand, squeezed it lightly, then swigged the bourbon. "Kid, if I don't get those guys before the police do, it is a sad fact of life that in a week or so there will be no job. And you know the odds. If it's broken at all, it's a thousand to one the cops do it. One guy can cover only so much ground. After that it's luck. Understand?"

"Understand—one of your favorite words." She put a cigarette between her lips and used a lighter. "You make a decision about something, anything at all will do, and it's supposed to be immediately accepted by everyone. Understand. You leave nothing for them to understand except that you've spoken and that's that. No right of appeal." She reached for the bottle, drank quickly. "You call me 'kid', but I'm twenty-three. Old enough to see you may never get anywhere if you stick with this I-complex of yours. I work for you. I want to help. So do a lot of others, if you'll accept it. *Understand?*"

"I'm thirty-three, and so I've got talent for aggravating hell out of people. Lee, when I pay you, which hasn't been lately, it's for typing, answering the phone, decorating the office, and keeping people off my back. And if you mean I should buddy up with Jim Moss, I'm not about to crawl to him."

"Would it have to be crawling?"

"I'd call it that."

She moved away and leaned against the right-hand door, stretching her legs, her eyes angry as she looked straight ahead.

"Burl Stannard, Boy Detective," she said furiously. "He's thirty-three. He has a birth certificate to prove it." The tip of her cigarette flared red. "If you'll drop me at the office, I'll get that payroll out."

"Sure. Anything you say." He ground the gears, and the Ford fishtailed from the parking lot. He didn't look at her when he braked the car sharply in front of the office on Alvarado Street in Peninsula City. He stared moodily through the windshield as the door slammed and her spike heels beat an angry rhythm on the sidewalk.

He shrugged, wished his head would subside, ground his teeth in frustration, and drove to police headquarters. He argued with himself that a dead cop was justification for a truce with Captain Moss.

CHAPTER 3

Stannard read the bitterness and anger in the veteran cop's face. It was eroded, with the eyes sinking deep into the skull. A paper cup, half filled with coffee yellowed by curdling cream, sat beside a hamburger with only a single bite gone. The big mouth that had smiled through their hottest scraps over department matters was thin, mean. Moss nodded toward a chair, and Stannard dropped into it.

"About time you came by."

Stannard's knuckles whitened on the arms of the chair. "Oh? Was I supposed to be here earlier?"

"Cool it. I just want to go over it with you."

"So let's." Stannard crossed his ankles, slouched down in the chair, and went over it carefully—what he had seen and done and what Bacher and Husted had told him.

Jim Moss was frowning when he finished. "No help, Burl. How come no armored car?"

"Because they were too cheap to pay for overtime and mileage," Stannard retorted. "Said they were paying for protection and expected to get it. So they lost."

"And the department lost a good cop."

"Don't tell me. Jim, I was there. Sitting right beside Norm when they blew his brains all over the inside of that car. Don't try to tell me a goddamn thing about it."

"So what do you plan to do about it?"

"Get them. Get the dough back. Earn my fee." He stuck a cigarette in his mouth and scratched a match. "Do I get help?"

Jim Moss rubbed his stubbled jaw. "Cooperate?"

"Meaning?"

"If you get to them first, try to take them alive."

Stannard snorted. "Sure. Sure, I'll try. But those birds were pros, and they killed a cop. Think they'll let themselves be taken alive?"

Moss sighed. "Probably not."

"OK. Now that's settled. I haven't got a damned thing so far. How about you?"

"A big wad of nothing." Moss shuffled papers on the desk. "No make on the guys. No prints on the cart worth anything. We're looking for people who might have seen them before it happened, but no luck yet. They had a car stashed on the other side of the Forest wall. Stolen in San Fran. A Highway Patrol cop found it a little while ago about six miles from there, in a vacant garage. Nobody at the pro shop recalls renting out the go-cart, let alone what the guys looked like. Smooth deal, except you got one with the chopper. Even their timing was perfect."

"Yeah. The guy who was running it kissed the Caddy just perfect."

"More than that. Quite a few people saw them out there on the fairway. Not close enough to do us any good, but they at least remember them. And everyone says those birds showed up not more than fifteen minutes before you came through."

"Luck. Had to be." Stannard ran a hand through his hair and felt the hardening scab over the wound. "There was no way to tell when we'd finish the cash count and move out."

Moss raised an eyebrow. "You sure?"

"If there was, you tell me. Bacher and Husted and I were the only ones in that room. We all stayed there. No phone calls, in or out. There's just one window, and I was in front of it most of the time."

"How about from the outside?"

"I had a guard on the stairs with instructions to keep everyone out."

"Who?"

"Dave Cunningham."

"Oh. Scratch that. Cunningham was a department veteran when I was a rookie. Well, maybe someone bugged the place. I'll have a crew shake it down."

"Might as well. Anything on what kind of car they might have switched to?"

"Not yet. They carried the guy you shot in the trunk of the hot one. We found blood but no body."

"There's the gimmick," Stannard said positively. "The body."

"What about it?"

"It just doesn't figure. Look it over. Those birds got out clean. Nobody saw their faces. They would have had a change of clothes waiting, and nobody knew right off what kind of car they were using. So they'd have an even chance of getting past a roadblock if they did hit one. The cadaver would be a sure ticket to the gashouse if they got caught. So why pack it around with them? They've sure got to get rid of it sometime."

"Uh-huh." Moss rocked back in his chair. "Maybe if we found it, we'd have been able to finger them. Could be they all took a fall together before."

"Good as any other guess." Stannard stood; he felt the blood surge painfully through his skull. "Lab crew turn up anything?"

"They're looking the car over now. The go-cart's downstairs."

"OK to take a look?"

"Be clean about it. They dusted for prints, but there wasn't time to do any more."

Stannard left the watch commander's office and went downstairs to the garage. It felt good to be back in the building he'd worked out of for eleven years. Not the same as being patrol commander on the early night watch, but good.

Even the session with Moss hadn't been bad.

The cart had been ringed by a set of photographer's floodlamps. Stannard turned them on, squinted against the glare, and moved in close to study the three-wheeler. He smoked a cigarette before finishing with the exterior. There was nothing to note except the dent inflicted by the Cadillac and the scratches from normal wear and tear. Working carefully so that he wouldn't disturb any minute bits of evidence the crime lab crew might turn up later, he checked the motor and battery compartments and the bag rack behind the single seat. There were some bloodstains, brown and dry. In the narrow space behind the seat was the usual collection of debris. Cigarette packs, empty and twisted, without any stamps to indicate they'd been bought out of state or in a city that imposed a tax. Several stubby pencils of the type given out by the pro shop were dusty and could have been there a long time. So could several score cards. The cards at least had been there before the stickup; blood had seeped through them. With the tip of a pencil, Stannard poked through some discarded paper match covers. Most were empty or held only a few matches. Some had come from bars around Peninsula City, others from the expensive taverns of the Forest. He flipped them over.

His mouth puckered in a silent whistle at the sight of the fourth one. There was congealed blood beneath it, but the powerful lamps didn't show any on the cover itself. It was the double-width type with advertising on the matches as well as the cover. Only two had been used. And it had come from the Round Table, a small, discreet, and prohibitively expensive bar in the Lodge.

And the matches had been dropped after the blood had run behind the seat. Stannard replaced the book. It was a thin lead but at least worth a trip to the Round Table.

He went upstairs to the squadroom, washed his hands in the chipped basin, and peered into the mirror, inspecting the gouge over his ear. It didn't seem likely hair would grow there for a while. He thought of Dick Husted and that damned .45 he'd come up with and cursed all civilians who get their hands on guns and then panic when the time comes to use them. A quarter-inch to the left and the slug would have ripped the side off his skull.

Stannard left headquarters, glad it wasn't time for a change of watches and that he wouldn't have to see the guys and talk about what had happened. He started to drive to the Forest, then detoured down Alvarado to his office.

Lee Ellen was typing with fast, angry fingers. She looked up momentarily when he came in, then went back to the page in the machine without a break in the rhythm.

He smiled. "Cancel the sulk. I made peace with Jim."

She typed two more lines, yanked the paper from the roller, and shook out the carbons. She stood, smoothing her hair. "Feel dishonored?"

"No. He was pretty good." He told her about finding the match cover. "How about a drink at the Table?"

"Can we afford it?"

"Of course not. We'll charge it to the golf people." He considered his torn and stained suit. "Wait a sec. I've got some clothes in the other office."

He found a sports shirt and hound's-tooth jacket and decided his wrinkled slacks would have to do because there weren't any others. When he had finished changing, Lee Ellen took his arm, and they went down the creaking stairs together. He could feel the easy grace of her walk. He enjoyed walking with her, even if with heels she was as tall as he was. Stannard thought it was too bad a murder and robbery had to come up to get him to ask her to have a drink with him.

The walls and ceiling of the bar were heavy-timbered, hung with swords, shields, banners, and coats of arms. The Round Table itself was a bar, table-high, with chairs instead of stools. In spite of the King Arthur influence, it managed to be comfortable. Lee Ellen hesitated as the door with its studs and heavy strap hinges shut them in. Her eyes searched the bar and the boxish booths which lined two walls. The house was full, and it was noisy. It hadn't been intended to take more than forty people at a time, but it seemed to have at least twice that many now. They stood, sat on the stone floor and at tables, or leaned against the booths, drinking, talking, shouting across the room, both men and women wearing everything from full evening dress to flagrantly mismatched sports outfits. They seemed to have nothing in common but money. Stannard was sure the barmen would have turned up their noses if they had to use his sports coat—$29.95 at J. C. Penney's—to mop up a drink.

He spotted a couple leaving the bar and shouldered his way through the press of people. He was glad Lee Ellen was along. A bartender took one look, expertly flipped a paper napkin in front of her, followed it up with a hammered copper ash tray and book of matches, before giving him the eye.

"Hi, Charlie. Mule for me. My pal will have a beer," she said.

Stannard paused in the act of igniting a cigarette and stared.

She caught the look and laughed. "I haven't been here before. Neither has Charlie. He works steady in a joint on Alvarado."

"So?"

"You glared. Jealous-like. Or did I annoy you by ordering?"

"I glare at everybody. No, beer's fine. It'll last through some questions."

"Charlie's a good Joe. Poured me into many a cab."

Charlie brought the Mule in its copper mug and a bottle of German beer. He poured it into a stein.

"Put these on a check," Stannard said. He reached for the matches in front of Lee Ellen. "You just working extra?"

"Nope." The barman grinned. "Lee Ellen works for some creep who won't pay her, so she's been out of circulation. I've been up here a month. Why?"

"To begin with, I'm the creep." Stannard shoved his identification across the bar. "Tell me about those matches you give out."

Charlie was a stubby, round man with rimless glasses and a receding hairline. "How you mean?"

"Like how new this design might be. Where you can pick them up except here."

Charlie fingered the matchbook and looked thoughtful. "Don't know when it was made up, but it was a special for the golf deal. We've only had them a few days, maybe a week. They're an odd size that won't fit machines, and each bar in the Forest has its own covers. Doubt you could get them anyplace but here. Course, lots of people come in and grab a handful; they could get spread around like that."

"OK. Got a phone I can use?"

"Right here?"

"Yeah."

The barman brought a phone. Stannard dialed the Lodge operator, identified himself, and asked her to call around, find the golf pro, and ring him back. He hung up, took a gulp of beer, and settled down to wait. This was the hell of working alone, he thought. The waiting. It's bad enough when you're on the cops and sweating out a break, but at least you're part of the nerve center, and when a deputy constable in the hills remembers seeing a car or guys on the wanted list, you know about it right away. You don't have to read the papers to find out.

He sighed and drank more beer.

Lee Ellen leaned over and brushed her mouth against his cheek. "Try not to let it tear you up," she whispered.

He lowered the stein to the bar and met her eyes. "Thanks. You're a good kid." He studied the full curve of her mouth. It was soft and red, and he wanted it under his—a wrong thing to want. A cop was dead and killers were loose with loot that was his responsibility, and he had no business thinking about Lee Ellen's lips. He made his words casual as he said, "I might just kiss you back sometime."

"Do it and you'll find out something," she said seriously.

"Oh?"

"I'm not a kid."

Stannard shook his head and told himself: This girl has to go; she is too much girl, and she is too close to home.... He dropped the thought as a group of people sitting to his right left the bar and their chairs were filled immediately.

"Hello, Burl Stannard."

The woman was sitting close to him, and he could feel the roundness of her breast press lightly against his arm as she leaned toward him. The way she slurred the words told him she was half loaded—not enough to show in her movements, but she was on the road. She had a lush figure that boiled over the top of a scarlet evening dress that matched her lips. In the dim lights of the Round Table her hair was jet black.

"Oh—uh, hello," Stannard said, trying to place her and at the same time feeling Lee Ellen's eyes on him from the other side. His eyes moved past the woman to the men she was with—Major Harry Bacher and Dick Husted.

He remembered Tam Bacher then; she'd been around during one of the talks about tournament security. He guessed she was somewhere in the early thirties, at least fifteen years younger than her husband. He'd heard she was a refugee from one of the Slavic countries and had married Bacher overseas right after World War II. Her face was fine-boned, the eyes deep-set and wide and inviting. She treated her husband with open scorn.

"Hi," Stannard said. He introduced the women. "Thought you'd be at the soup-and-fish affair."

She curled her upper lip. "I was able to convince the Major he'd have looked just too foolish if he got up and gave a report as finance chairman with things the way they are."

"We'll get the dough back," Stannard growled. "Promise."

"That wasn't a dig," she said urgently. "You had a tough break. Any luck so far?"

Stannard shrugged and turned his head long enough to wink at Lee Ellen. "Police work is more than luck. It's early yet."

Charlie brought a drink, and Tam Bacher raised it to her lips, meeting his eyes over the glass. "Well, luck anyway." She sipped the drink, then tossed her head. "You might know the Old Soldier would come out of it without a scratch. Well, it'll be a relief to listen to something newer than how he and his men beat the Russians to some rocket engineers."

Bacher was talking in a low voice to Husted. Stannard couldn't decide whether the Major wasn't listening to his wife or was listening and chose to ignore her. He eyed the phone, wishing it would ring. Bacher stopped talking and swiveled his head toward them. Stannard noted the watery eyes and slack mouth and decided Bacher had more of a load on than his wife.

Bacher peered at him and said, "Well?"

"Well, what?" Stannard growled.

"Anything to report?"

"Still working," Stannard said curtly. "The committee was too polite to fire me tonight, and I don't see much point to yapping about it." He looked past Bacher at the owl face of Dick Husted and made himself shut up. Bacher was on a spot, and it was really the sight of Husted that griped him, anyway. Stannard just plain did not like the real-estate man. The phone rang and he grabbed for it.

"Stannard here."

"Ray Keene. What 'n hell you want at this hour?" Keene was the Lodge golf pro. A lanky, sandy-haired, red-faced man not long off the big-time circuits. Steady drinker but a good enough golfer to hold down a choice slot.

"Busy, Ray? You over at the dinner?"

There was a drunken laugh. "I'm sure busy but not there. We got a li'l game in the locker room. Why? You want in? Private eyes don't make enough to last with this bunch."

"No lie. I just want some dope, if you're sober enough. When a guy comes in to rent clubs or buy something, what kind of record do you keep at the shop?"

"Damn good records. Have to. Got a bunch of thieves."

"Tell me."

"This important? If it isn't, the game is."

"Yeah, it's important. You can tell me over the phone, or I can come over there."

"Yeah, you bastard, you'd do it. OK. There's a cash register that keeps books on everything. What's bought or rented, green fees, equipment—you know. Even what dough a guy puts up and what deposit he's got coming back."

"I'd like a look at that register tape for today. How soon can I see it?"

There was silence for a moment, and Stannard could hear crap-game sounds in the background. Then Keene cleared his throat and said, "We'll be open at eight in the morning."

"No. Tonight. Inside half an hour."

"You hard-nosed son—OK. It'll take me about that long to go over and open the safe and dig it out. You at the Table?"

"I'll be here."

"OK. I'll send one of the boys down for it."

"Do it yourself."

"I'm busy. Dammit, there's a guy ready to bust into this game with tops, and I want to be on him when he does. I'll—"

Stannard cupped his hand around the mouthpiece. "You'll have no game at all if I have to come over. I don't want the whole Lodge to know about this. Get humping."

He cradled the phone without waiting for a reply, lit a cigarette, blew smoke at the bottles behind the bar, and turned to Lee Ellen. "Sure wish everybody wasn't drunk. Or that I was drunk. You can't get anywhere talking to people tonight."

She nodded. There were now three copper mule cups in front of her, and Stannard saw a fresh beer beside his mug. Husted was standing, saying something about seeing Tam later.

Tam nodded. Then she leaned on Stannard's shoulder, put her mouth close to his ear, and whispered, "How'd you like to go to a party?"

Stannard laughed in her face. "Funny. Ha ha. I'm busy tonight. Remember?"

Her fingers tightened on him. There was a trace of a central European accent. "I'm not being funny, Mr. Stannard. Dick and the Major were just talking about what might be done to help you get the people you're after. The Major feels the responsibility for what happened is his as well as yours. He knows one man can do only so much without help, and he plans to offer you help."

"God give me strength," Stannard muttered. "The best help he can give me is to just stay off my back. Believe it." He looked at Bacher. Bacher was concentrating on draining a tall glass.

"I know. But listen—the Major may be a bore but he isn't a fool. During the war he commanded a Criminal Investigation Department unit. It was probably the best in the European Theater. He had detectives who did all sorts of fabulous things, recovered Nazi loot, broke up black markets, screened out spies the Russians were trying to plant. Several of them are staying with us for the tournament. When they heard what had happened, they decided they should do something. When we left home, they had their heads together, talking of what it should be."

"Tell them they should go home," Stannard said firmly.

"I don't think they will."

"Then they'll go to jail if they get in the way. I mean it, and the cops will back me up."

"It wasn't my idea," she said defensively. "But you might at least talk with them."

"Tell the Major to do it," Stannard retorted. "He was their CO. I was just an enlisted swine."

Tam Bacher's face flushed. She popped her cigarettes into her purse, snapped it shut, and said something to Bacher that Stannard couldn't hear. They stood. Bacher signed a check, nodded briefly to Stannard and Lee Ellen, and followed Tam from the bar.

Stannard wondered where he got the talent for saying things in the crudest way. Most of his trouble on the department had come from what he said rather than what he did. The incident which had cost him his badge was typical. Three leather-jacket-and-long-sideburns types had given trouble when told to move on. One had swung a length of taped-up chain, and the others had been digging into their pockets when Stannard went to work on them with bare hands and booted feet.

The one with the chain died on the scene, his throat crushed by a single chop from the edge of Stannard's hand. The others went to the hospital with multiple broken bones and internal injuries.

The chief, Captain Moss, and the police commissioner had backed him without question until Stannard had posted an order to his patrol:

WHEN YOU RUN INTO A HARD HEAD—
BREAK IT!

He had been chewed out, not for issuing the order but for putting it where newspaper reporters could see it.

"I want the word out," he said flatly. "Let the tough guys know this is a tough town."

"But the papers—" the chief, who was appointed by the City Council, began.

"Damn it, are you running a police department or a popularity contest?" Stannard shouted.

"You want to know?" The chief's face was red. "Well, tomorrow you move to the traffic bureau!"

"That's a plain enough answer!" Stannard retorted.

"And you ride a desk until you cool down," Moss snapped.

"You can both go jump," Stannard told them.

"You're suspended!" the chief shouted, whacking his desk.

"So I quit until I get the night watch back."

Stannard remembered the clatter of his star as it bounced across the desk. He thought it probably symbolized something or other that the star had skidded into the waste basket.

There had been no thought of going back. The chief and Moss could not yield without losing control of the department. Stannard would not apologize so long as he felt he had been right, and he could not see where he had been wrong, except in losing his temper....

Now the taproom talk drummed in Stannard's ears. He drained his stein, then refilled it. He checked his watch and saw that nearly three quarters of an hour had passed since he'd called Keene. Too much time. He pushed his chair back.

"Stick here by the phone," he told Lee Ellen. "I'm going to take a walk."

He went out. The bar air was heavy with stale cigarette smoke, perspiration, and perfume, with an overlay of alcohol. He let the door shut behind him and stood breathing clean air that smelled only of pines and grass and salt water.

Ray Keene was not in the dice game at the clubhouse. Stannard went out again, down to the single-story building that housed the pro shop. He cupped his hand over his forehead and peered through a window at the darkened interior.

Display cases and racks of golfing gear showed faintly in the pale illumination of a single light turned on somewhere in the depths of the shop. Stannard moved on to the recessed entryway, banged the palm of his hand against the door. He called the pro's name.

There was no response. But the latch clicked and the door swung open.

Quickly, apprehensively, he went in. He was on a small landing, and there was enough light to make out three steps leading down to the salesroom. He stepped across it, felt with his foot for the first step, and hesitated. His left hand flipped his jacket open, fingers reaching for the .38.

He heard the soft whistling sound then and tried to jump back as something with the impact of an artillery shell slammed into his belly. The breath left his lungs in a tortured explosion.

He gagged, swallowed pain, and pinwheeled down the remaining steps. Time stopped. Then it started again as he crashed onto a hard, smooth, cold surface that bruised and numbed his body.

Something clattered near him. Feet scrambled, and there was the sound of a door slamming.

CHAPTER 4

Stannard tried to breathe; the effort brought grinding agony. His stomach heaved, and there was a sour, burning taste in his throat and a foulness spilling from his mouth. He gasped, heard himself groan. He clenched his jaws, held his breath, let it out, and tried again. This time it was a little better.

He forced himself to lie motionless while the drumming of his head thundered in his brain. He decided he had not been shot after all. But somebody had hit him a beautiful lick. He wondered how many internal organs had been ruptured or smashed. His fingers moved across the smooth coldness and found a straight line, a shallow ridge. It felt like the strip of cement between floor tiles. He managed to lift his head a couple of inches and blinked his eyes.

Dim objects swirled and took up more or less fixed positions. He made out glass cases which reflected slices of thin light, and a rack of golf clubs. He remembered where he was and supposed somebody had belted him with a six-iron or something similar. There had been that sudden whistling sound in the instant he had broken his stride and tried to jump back.

The thought didn't make him feel better. He maneuvered himself into a sitting position, feeling the twisting pain in his abdomen. When he could without bringing on fresh nausea, he crawled to the second step. From there he got his feet under him. He slumped against a friendly wall and dug through the pockets of his jacket until he found the pencil flashlight.

There were light switches nearby. He snapped them and blinked against the sudden brightness. He tried the door, found the latch had snapped, locking it. A slender, gleaming shaft with leather-wrapped handle was on the salesroom floor. A four-iron. Moving unsteadily, Stannard stepped around it and plunged toward the pro's office at the rear of the room. He found another light there.

Ray Keene sprawled on the floor in front of the safe. The door of the safe was open an inch or two. A little blood puddled on the floor by Keene's head. It dripped from a swelling wound on his forehead.

Stannard squatted, fingered the pro's wrist. There was a faint pulse, but it seemed regular. He used the phone on the gray metal desk to call for a doctor and ambulance, then spoke briefly with the dispatcher at police headquarters.

The Lodge house doctor arrived first. He used his stethoscope on Keene, fingered the wound gently, made clucking sounds with his tongue. "Did you move him?"

"No." Stannard put a cigarette in his mouth, scraped a match, choked on the first lungful of smoke. "How bad is it?"

The doctor took a small syringe from his bag, rolled Keene's right sleeve up, and injected a colorless fluid. "I can't tell until I see X-rays. There could be a skull fracture. At least a concussion."

"When will he be able to talk?"

"In a day or two—if he regains consciousness."

"Brother!" Stannard leaned heavily against the desk. The pain in his stomach was spreading.

The doctor stood and eyed him professionally. "What happened to you? And what are you doing here?"

"Same thing, but in a different place." Stannard heard a groan slide through his clenched teeth. "I'm supposed to protect people. God!"

"I'd better take a look." The doctor made Stannard sit on the edge of the desk while he opened his shirt. He peered and poked and pressed, and Stannard bit deep into his lower lip when the fingers touched him. "I think we better take you to the hospital, too. It doesn't feel like any ribs are broken, but there's no way to tell now what may have happened to your internal organs. Mind telling me what happened?"

"Sure. A killer protected himself," Stannard said in disgust and self-accusation. Thinking of what he had done, he found it inexcusable. If he were still on the force, he'd have blistered any cop who walked into a darkened building under the same circumstances. The book said to call for help first, wait for it to arrive, and cover all exits. Then go in with gun in hand.

The possibility that whoever had clobbered him might have slipped away while Stannard was doing this was no excuse.

His self-condemnation was interrupted by the arrival of the police ambulance. Jim Moss and a detective bureau team drove up before the ambulance crew had the stretcher ready. Stannard told what had happened.

They went through the safe. The register tape wasn't in it.

"Tough break, Burl." Moss rubbed his chin. "I don't see yet what you expected to get from the tape anyway."

"Maybe nothing. But the only place I can see where those guys had to make contact with anybody was here at the pro shop. They rented the electric wagon and supposedly paid green fees. Maybe they bought some balls or tees. With the tournament winding up, nobody but the finalists would have been allowed on the course until the last teams had started around. That couldn't have been more than a couple of hours before the stickup. Say twenty parties went out in that time. How many were threesomes? A couple, maybe. Narrow it down that much with the tape, find the guy who took care of them, and it might jog his memory."

"Guess somebody was worried," Moss agreed. "We'll try the pro shop crew again in the morning. Who knew Keene was coming down?"

Stannard scowled in thought. "Nobody on my end. I ran him down on the phone. He was in a crap game at the clubhouse and didn't much like the idea of leaving it. Anybody might have heard him on that end."

"Where'd you call from?"

"The Round Table."

"Well?"

"With the racket in there I could hardly hear myself."

"Somebody got onto it, at one end or the other. Unless the guy thought of it first and was inside when Keene showed up. Too bad it went this way, but it gives a little weight to something I was thinking about."

"Inside job?" Stannard found himself automatically on the defensive. "Jim, every man I had on this detail is either a regular police officer or a licensed private op. Believe it."

"No, no, no," Moss said. "Not inside in that way. But from inside the Forest somewhere. I think those hoods doubled back on us. Ditched that hot car and cut right back to the Forest, knowing we'd be looking for them to run the other way."

Stannard fingered the sore muscles of his belly. "Either they came back, or they had somebody here to cover them. Whoever it is sure swings a mean club."

The door was closing behind the ambulance crew and doctor. Stannard checked his watch and saw there was still an hour and a half until midnight. He phoned the Round Table and asked for Lee Ellen.

"Anybody looking for me?"

"No. How much longer will you be?"

"On the way now." He hung up and told Moss he'd see him later and went out. The effort of going up the steps to the door filled the soreness, and he could imagine a brute of a bruise by morning.

The Round Table crowd had thinned noticeably. Stannard supposed the customers were being siphoned off to private parties. He eased himself into the seat beside Lee Ellen.

She saw the pain twist his face. "You're hurt!"

"Not too bad." He looked up and down the bar. "Charlie," he yelled, "a double brandy and bring the check."

The first sip made him cough; he felt as though he'd been kicked by a mule.

He put his head in his hands, gazed unblinkingly at the amber liquid in the snifter and pommeled his brain. There were too many things to be done, none of which promised to be productive and most of which would have to wait for morning. He felt weakness and sickness spread through him, and he remembered he hadn't eaten anything since a bear's-claw at breakfast.

"You're looking bad, Burl. Really," Lee Ellen said. "Let me take you home."

"If I got in a bed now, I don't know when I'd be able to get out of it again." He lit another cigarette. The smoke was flat and bitter. "I'm hungry."

"Then for God's sake, let's go. I'll see you get fed."

He signed the check, and they left. The cold air freshened his brain. He gave her the Ford keys. "You drive. But stop at Bacher's. I just remembered his junior crime stoppers."

"Burl, you're in no shape to get involved with anything else tonight."

"I'm afraid to let it go until morning. I'll give them the word, and that'll be that."

It was a big house, built in the English country style, with haphazard floor levels, a gabled roof, leaded windows, and dark, high rooms.

Dick Husted opened the door. His eyes were puffy, and he swayed, clutching the knob. He held a half-empty champagne glass. He blinked and fingered his glasses into place on the bridge of his nose.

"I was afraid it might be you."

"If it ruins your night, consider suicide."

Stannard shoved him aside, and he and Lee Ellen went in. The living room looked like a Polish wedding reception and Irish wake had been held in it simultaneously. There were only a handful of people in sight, but he guessed better than a hundred glasses in assorted shapes and sizes were parked on anything available. Some had spilled on the wine-red carpet, which was now ready for a trip to the cleaner. Stannard looked at the faces and recognized most as Forest people. Nobody looked sober, but there were no passouts in sight, at least in this room.

Tam Bacher came through a curtained doorway. She carried a shakerful of something greenish which she was pouring into a champagne glass. Her eyes found Stannard, and she made for him, mouth sultry and triumphant. Stannard wasn't sure whether the loose-hipped walk should be charged off to alcohol or advertising.

"Well. The private eye and his blond." The strapless dress seemed to ride lower on her breasts than it had before. She arched her back, then stopped with a little thrusting motion of her hips. "Change your mind?"

"Uh-uh. Just want to get everything clear so nobody gets hurt. Where's the Major?"

Tam tossed her dark curls in the direction of a stairway. "Upstairs, going over everything with the boys. Come on. Tell him yourself." She grabbed his arm and pulled him toward the stairs. She swung around, laughing, and some of the green stuff spilled from her glass. She looked at Lee Ellen and said, "Bring him back in a minute, honey. Drinks in the kitchen."

Stannard saw Lee Ellen's mouth tighten, caught the imperceptible motion of her head that said he was a big enough boy to fight his own battles. He shrugged and allowed himself to be led.

There were three landings. After the first Stannard found himself using the banister to pull himself up. Tam chuckled and slid her arm around his waist. He winced at the pressure.

"Private Eye, you're loaded." They were at the second landing then, and he stopped. Tam swung around in front of him and put her hands on his shoulders. He could feel the soft, taunting heat of her against his chest. "You need to relax."

He pushed her aside and went on. He expected trouble with Bacher, and there was no percentage in including the Major's ripe-bodied wife. There was a long, carpeted hallway, with a single step down about halfway along it. Light showed under a door at the far end.

"Just knock and kick it in, shamus." She watched him a moment, then stepped through another doorway.

Stannard rapped on the door. It was opened by a slender man in a gray suit that hung without a wrinkle from his broad shoulders. Pale blond hair was brushed back from a high forehead, and he had mild, inquiring eyes.

Bacher lounged on a window seat on the far side of the room. It was large enough for a couch, a desk, a couple of upholstered chairs, and a cellarette. Bacher waved Stannard inside.

"Meet Will Deck, there at the door, and Jack Taggart. They're going to give us some help."

"Never happen," Stannard told them.

Taggart got up from a swivel chair at the desk. He was another Deck, but with darker hair and an Ivy League suit. Both might have been in their middle thirties. They were shaking his hand firmly, smiling polite smiles, studying him with cop eyes, speaking with quiet, precise voices.

"Hi," Stannard said. They reminded him of FBI and Intelligence. "Boys, let's get something straight. I understand you were Army detectives and now you want to help the Major in this thing. With all due respect, I've got to tell you to lay off. Understand?"

"Sure," Deck said easily. "But can you take a minute or two to listen?"

"No. If you want to know, I'm dead on my feet, and I've been pounded like an abalone. Argue with me, and I'll just get mad," Stannard said evenly.

Bacher boosted himself off the window seat. His eyes were puffy, and Stannard wouldn't have been surprised to see him cry. He plodded across the room and looked up at Stannard's battered face.

"You don't like me. I suppose you have reason, but I like people to like me," the Major said sorrowfully.

Drunk, Stannard thought. About to be crying drunk. Got to abase himself. He felt embarrassment and a little pity.

"I think you're a nice guy, Major. We just disagree."

"No, no," Bacher went on. "I didn't like your attitude, so I blocked you when I shouldn't have." He fumbled the wrapper from a cigar. "You can use some help. I think Will and Jack and a couple of others here can give you a lot of help. You could at least talk to them, Stannard."

"No."

Major Harry Bacher blinked his eyes. He tossed his shoulders in a shrug, turned quickly away and left the room.

Deck was pouring bourbon into a tumbler. He brought the glass to Stannard. "Better have a snort. You look like hell."

Stannard looked into the cool eyes, took the glass, swallowed. The bourbon slid into his stomach, spread itself around, and began to scrap with the brandy.

Deck took a billfold from his pocket and handed Stannard a card.

"We understand how you feel, Stannard. This would be just a matter of professional courtesy with us. And perhaps a favor to our old CO. We've got an agency in Terre Haute. Murders and robberies aren't our line, but we're tops at asking questions, finding people, and preparing evidence. Might save you some legwork, and you can check on us easily enough. Make a difference?"

Stannard considered it. He was a one-man gang, and even being on good terms for the moment with Jim Moss didn't change that. He was as good as without a client and didn't have a dime to hire a legman. And if he'd been working on a case with leads in Terre Haute, there was a good chance he'd have farmed that end of it out to this outfit as a routine matter.

"Maybe." Stannard was suspicious of gift horses. "If you're willing to hoof it around, ask a lot of tiresome questions, and waste your time for auld lang syne."

"I guess we could do that," Taggart said.

Stannard finished the whiskey and let Deck refill the glass. The pain had subsided to a swollen numbness through his middle, and his head was pleasantly light. He told himself he should see about eating. "OK," he said cautiously. "We can try it."

"Just tell us what you've got and what you want done."

They settled into chairs around the desk. On a map of the Forest, he showed them where he wanted a house-to-house canvass made for possible witnesses. He circled the part of the village outside the wall where the getaway car had been stashed and told them to check that neighborhood for anyone who might have seen the killers when they were driving in or out. He thought up several more time-consuming chores and told them as much as he wanted them to know about the mechanics of the robbery and what had happened since. He drank a lot of bourbon.

The door was elusive, but Stannard caught it and lurched down the hallway. He thought it would be a good idea to see if Major Harry Bacher had any food in the house. His foot struck the single step halfway down the hall, and he tumbled on his face. The volcano of pain erupted again, and he felt the bourbon coming up. It had tasted better going down.

Hands tugged at him, hoisted him weakly to his feet. Soft hair brushed his face, and he heard Tam Bacher saying, "Something hit you hard and quick, Private Eye."

"Things've been hitting me all day. Gotta sober up. Eat. Ate nothing all day—"

She was helping him along, half holding him up, steering him into a room. Dim lights came on, and he saw it was a bedroom. She let him fall across the bed, crossed the room, and opened a door. There was a bathroom. He watched her pull a shower curtain back and turn on the spray. Little splotches of water darkened the scarlet dress, glistened on the tan of her body. Then she was at the bed again, pulling his jacket off, unbuttoning his shirt.

"Hey," he mumbled, thinking of Lee Ellen. Lee Ellen would still be downstairs. He should get Lee Ellen, and they should get the hell out of this place. Even smelling as bad as he did, they should go and do it right now. Damned mistake to come here anyway.

His shirt was open. She drew her breath in sharply at the sight of his stomach. Her fingers moved lightly across the bruise and she whispered, "My God—!"

"Exactly," he agreed. "Rough day. I gotta split out."

"Not like this, chum. You tossed your cookies. You smell horrid." Her hands were sliding the shirt off him, working at his belt. "You finish this. I'll hunt you up something to wear while you take a shower. OK?"

Clouds of steam boiled from the bathroom. Stannard was sure he wouldn't be able to get his shirt back on anyway. He nodded in agreement.

She left, and he worked his shoes off and finished undressing.

He made the shower stall without bumping into anything. He let the hot water scald him. There was a clear imprint of the head of the golf club and a slice of the shaft just below his ribs. The colors were magnificent. He toweled himself carefully and decided Tam wasn't a bad egg. Without too much concentration, he was able to walk a straight line back to the bed. His clothes were gone. He sat on the bed and felt the warmth of exhaustion seep through him. He wondered when she would find him some clothes. He let himself fall back against the pillows. He fought sleep long enough to pull the quilt folded across the foot of the bed over his nakedness.

The room was dark now. He had half-awakened with the soft closing of a door, and he was aware of movement and breathing and the red glow of a cigarette. He tried to think where he was, but the effort was too much. He let his eyes close, then fought them open as the bed sank under new weight. He watched the cigarette flare and float to an ash tray on the night table.

There was a light rustle of cloth over flesh and the smooth firmness of a woman. The quilt was still over him. He reached, found a warm curve of hip with thin silk bunched above it.

"Who—?"

Lips came down on his, cutting the word short. He tried to rise on an elbow, fighting the weight.

"Wait—" The woman was moving. He felt a leg slide over him, and the mouth was lifted, whispering, "Quiet—try to be quiet—"

A pie-wedge of light spread over the bed. Stannard focused his eyes. Tam Bacher was kissing him again, muttering deep in her throat. And Lee Ellen was watching from the doorway.

Stannard broke away, tossing his head angrily, his eyes on the figure of Lee Ellen. Her eyes were shut, her face contorted. Then the wedge of light narrowed, vanished. Stannard heard the quick muffled beat of high heels on the hallway carpet.

Tam trembled, then threw herself across him. She was crying and sinking her teeth into the meat of his shoulder.

CHAPTER 5

Stannard twisted and pushed. The teeth slashed his flesh, and fingernails laid strips of fire across his skin. The woman gasped and slipped away, the bed rocking as she went over the edge. There was a solid thump and she was on the floor. He groped for the table lamp and switched it on.

Tam scrambled on the rug, then knelt back on her heels. The dress was twisted above her knees. She was combing the wild hair back with her fingers, and her eyes were narrowed in cold fury. She smoothed the dress, pressing it tight against her thighs, and she said something in a foreign language.

Stannard saw slacks, a white shirt, and sports coat folded on a chair. His gun and holster were on top. He pulled the sheet around him and snapped, "I want to get dressed."

"You bastard! All right, I'll get out. If you hustle, maybe you can catch her!"

Her mouth twisted in scorn as she spun away from the bed and left the room without another glance in his direction.

Stannard groaned. His muscles were turning stiff again. He forced himself to stand, bend, stretch.

The clothes were a passable fit. He checked the loads in the .38 and jammed it into the holster. Then he found his way downstairs. There were more people, new people. They had full glasses and loud voices, and they ignored him.

He wandered through the house until he found the kitchen. A houseboy in a white jacket was mixing drinks. Lee Ellen sat on a high stool, feet locked in the rungs. Her face was streaked with mascara, and her eyes stared at the tumbler of whiskey in her hands. She did not look up as Stannard went to the sink, found a clean glass, and filled it with tap water. He drank and felt the burning in his throat ease. Then he stood in front of her.

"Let's get out of here," he said quietly.

She did not lift her head. When she spoke, it was a flat, sullen whisper: "I called a cab."

"We'll go in the Ford. I want to talk to you."

"Why? You don't have to account to me. You're male; why shouldn't you act it?" She raised the glass to her lips and swallowed twice. "I didn't mean to spoil the party."

Stannard grabbed the glass and hurled it into the sink. It shattered with a brittle sound, and whiskey splashed on the tiles. He yanked Lee Ellen from the stool and pushed her ahead of him through an outside door.

Once outside, she swung around, smooth and quick. The palm of her hand cracked across his mouth, and she said fiercely, "Don't touch me, Burl. Don't touch me!"

Stannard let his hands drop. Then he rubbed at the sting in his mouth, shaking his head. "Lee Ellen—please. You're seeing it all wrong. I'd just been sick as a dog, and she went to get me some clothes while I took a shower. I was asleep when she came back. I guess she was drunk and fed up with her old man. It wasn't my idea, and I wasn't about to go along with it. Honest."

He could feel her eyes on him in the dark. "There's no reason for you to care what I believe about anything, Burl. To use one of your favorite words, understand? No reason at all." She moved away, along a flagstone path which curved toward the front of the grounds, circling the big house. "I don't think you're capable of driving right now. I'll run you home in the Ford."

It was a silent ride. Stannard tried to convince himself he would not have taken the Major's wife, tried to find words that would convince Lee Ellen. Finally he threw the effort away. He tried to go over the separate factors in the case but junked that project too. There were too many angles, and his mind wandered in exhaustion. When the car stopped at his apartment, he mumbled a good night and got out without waiting for an answer. The Ford stayed at the curb until he went in. He listened to tires burn against pavement as he turned the lights on.

The day bed was not made up. He shed the borrowed clothes, scowled at the reflection of his wounds in the bathroom mirror, tossed the electric blanket over the bed, and crawled under it without bothering about sheets.

The heat was sticky, persistent. Stannard struggled, but it reached for him, burning, smothering. He kicked the blanket off. There was raw, pounding sound; after a time, he realized the pounding was not in his head. He fought to open his eyes, then saw the door shaking against the night latch. He yelled to wait a minute, dragged the slacks on, and opened the door.

Captain Jim Moss stepped inside and shoved the door closed. He looked at Stannard and at the blanketed couch. "I'm glad somebody can get some sleep," he rumbled.

Stannard scowled. "Oh, shut up." He rubbed his eyes and scratched his head, yawning. "What the hell time is it?"

"Almost eleven. I'd have been around earlier except that your office girl kept stalling, claiming you were on the way in."

Stannard studied the older man. He went to the Pullman kitchen, dumped coffee into an electric maker, and muttered, "I can see you're going to chew me. Do it while I get cleaned up."

Moss leaned against the bathroom door while Stannard shaved. The older man looked as though he had slept in his clothes, if at all. Stannard scraped at his beard and said, "Well?"

"Where should I start?"

"Start anywhere. It'll all be bad news," Stannard said.

"The papers are having a field day with murder and robbery in the Forest. All cops are idiots."

"Of course."

"You're getting a hell of a ride. Some feature writer got into our files, read some of your cases, and did a wild thing on how a tough cop is made and broken. The wire services put out that shot of you prowling around with the Tommy-gun, and people from all walks of life know your big blond wears lace-edged scanties."

"News to me," Stannard grunted.

"You don't have a client any more. The tournament bosses tied a can to your tail."

"They can't fire me."

"Go tell them."

"All they can do is refuse to pay me. I couldn't care less at the moment." Stannard cleaned the razor and turned on the shower.

Moss raised his voice to carry over the sound of the water. "They don't blame you for what happened. But they're burned up by these guys you've got working on the thing. Which, as it happens, I don't like myself."

"What guys?" Stannard shouted.

"A pair named Deck and Taggart. I haven't seen them, but I hear they're friends of Bacher's. They've been ringing doorbells and tossing questions all over the Forest since seven this morning. Claim to be working for you."

"Oh," Stannard said, remembering. He turned the water off and began to dry himself. The muscles of his abdomen and back were stiff but usable. He explained the Deck-Taggart situation to Moss and said, "They seemed pretty smooth, not the kind to get people burning."

"They're smooth, all right, but they just won't take 'I don't remember' for an answer. They keep tossing questions, and they listen to the answers, and then they think of more questions. Forest people don't go for that."

"Annoying, I'm sure." Stannard wadded the towel and dropped it into a laundry bag. He walked naked into the front room, found fresh underwear, and picked clothes off hangers. He began to dress. "Murder, robbery, and assault are annoying, too. Anything turn up yet?"

"Nothing. Crime lab's working the go-cart over."

"No sign of the body?"

"No."

"That body begins to look pretty important."

"The killers think so, I guess." Moss lit a cigarette. "Burl, you going to make Bacher call his chums off?"

Stannard combed his hair, careful of the bullet burn on the side of his head. "Why? They might turn something up. And I can't make them quit. They can go around asking questions as private citizens, and you know it. If they get in the way, you can pinch them for interfering with an investigation."

"Suppose so," Moss grumbled. "Heading for the office?"

"After coffee. Pour yourself a mug."

Stannard watched the unmarked police car squeeze into the morning traffic, then he walked up the flight of stairs. He heard the insistent ringing on the phone before he was in the office. Lee Ellen was talking rapidly on one line while the other buzzed at steady intervals. Stannard lifted the other phone, waited a moment, depressed the cradle, and let it come up again. When he heard the dial tone, he let the phone drop on the desk blotter. Lee Ellen finished talking, and he did the same with the second phone.

"Anything important?"

She consulted a penciled list. "Some important people object to questions by Deck, Taggart, Bacher, and a couple of others whose names nobody seems to know. Newspaper reporters got their licks in. *Playboy* magazine sent me a wire."

"Sounds like a fine morning. Want to take a ride, playmate?"

Lee Ellen grinned, and he decided she was over her mad.

"Sure. Where?"

"The Forest. More routine digging. Bring a notebook in case we take any statements."

The Spanish tiles of the Lodge roof were a sun-burned orange. There was a casual, costly leisure about the place now that the tournament crowds were gone. The grounds crews had already removed all traces of the spectator debris from the oak-shadowed lawns, and the complement of tables set up on the terrace overlooking the eighteenth green had been reduced to its normal strength. Waiters in green jackets and black trousers served drinks. There was the usual jamup of golfers waiting their turn at the first tee. There was nothing to suggest murder and robbery had taken place here.

Stannard pulled the Ford into the parking lot behind the pro shop and left it beside an unmarked coupe with a tall radio aerial. It was the car used by Ken Atwood, a day-watch detective, and Stannard and Lee Ellen found him in the office with a small, thin, weathered man.

Atwood was in his middle fifties, a thick-set man with rimless glasses and remnants of white hair. He took a pipe from his mouth, nodded to Lee Ellen, and said, "Hi, Burl. Just about to go looking for you. Know Paul Wallace, the assistant pro?"

Stannard and Wallace shook hands. Wallace had the tight, hard hands of a man who has spent his life in golf. "Tough break you had, friend. And everybody was real pleased with the police setup. Smooth all the way."

"Not *all* the way," Stannard said grimly, looking around the office. "Pick up anything here, Ken?"

"Nothing that looks like it's going to do us much good," Atwood snorted. "We might do better if Keene could talk, but he's still in a coma. There's ten thousand fingerprints in the sales part of the shop and not a damn one that'll do us any good. The four-iron he used was clean. It looks like nothing is missing except the cash register tape you wanted."

"It figures," Stannard agreed. "Figured out how he got in?"

"Not for sure. When you got here, the door was open, right?"

"Not open. Unlatched. It swung back when I knocked."

"I think the lock got itself picked," Atwood told them. "Probably before Keene got here. Then the guy, whoever he was, hid out until the safe was open, snuck up behind Keene, let him have it with the club, grabbed the tape, and was on his way out when you showed."

Stannard thought back. He guessed he had been hit within five seconds of coming through the door. There had been no warning except the whistle of the shaft in the air, so the burglar had been waiting for him at the steps leading down to the sales floor. His fingers moved across his abdomen, gently pressing at the soreness.

"Must have been," he said. "Keene got it from behind, huh?"

"That's what the doc tells us," Atwood replied.

Stannard sat on the desk and stared at his knuckles. "Something doesn't fit," he said. "The character who belted us was a real coward."

"Aah, boloney!" Atwood retorted. "From one point of view you can say that all killers are cowards. They're afraid of apprehension or physical or emotional damage of some kind so they kill. So he hit Keene from behind. You expect him to walk up in front of the guy, say, 'Pardon me,' and let him have it?"

"Wrong angle, Ken," Stannard said. "He wouldn't expose himself if he didn't have to. But look at what happened with me. I was walking down a short flight of steps. I couldn't see him, but from where he must have been standing, I'd have been in perfect silhouette. He's holding a golf club, which is a mean thing to hit somebody with. Just swing it like a fly swatter at the right instant, and I've got no skull. Right?"

"So what?" Atwood sucked on his pipe. "You heard the thing whistle and were quick enough to jump back. So he hit you in the gut instead of where he was aiming."

Stannard pulled his shirt open, exposed the bruise. "Ken, my whole point is that this bird wasn't aiming at anything. He struck out in panic, in blind terror. I wasn't able to jump far. If I hadn't moved at all, the club would have taken me about the middle of the chest. Now who in hell would pick a target like that if he was able to think and control himself?"

"Well—" Atwood said doubtfully.

"Take a good look at this souvenir," Stannard continued. "It's horizontal, like the guy was taking a cut at a baseball. Just a wild, ineffective swing. And I didn't pass all the way out, Ken. I can remember the sound of him running up those steps. I think he was in high gear before I ever hit the floor. This character wasn't thinking about killing me. Right then he wasn't thinking about anything but getting a lot of distance between us."

"OK. You can be right, and I can be wrong; and what difference does it make?" Atwood said irritably.

"None, I guess. Just one more thing we know about this one particular man. And I just can't fit a guy who pushes the panic button like that into that holdup. Now those three hoods must have been under some considerable strain waiting for us to come through. But they worked together like the Cal backfield. They got shot at, and they shot back; and when one was killed, the other two got him out of there. Would the man who did the job here have been able to take part in an operation like that? Would he?"

Atwood shrugged. "Well, I've said all along there was an inside man. There had to be, to tip them off when you pulled out with the money. He knew what to look for and slipped them a signal. And he must have been hanging around the dice game last night when you phoned Keene. When Keene left the game, according to the guys who were around, he griped about you sending him on an idiot errand."

"I told him to keep his mouth shut," Stannard said wearily. "My own fault. I should have gone over there and dragged him out myself." He boosted himself off the desk and prowled the small room. His feet rapped sharply on the composition tile floor, and the sound nagged at him. He tried to walk without making an audible noise and found it was impossible.

"Our man was in here before Keene showed up," he said flatly. "He couldn't have sneaked up on him without Keene hearing something."

"Keene was packing a fair load," Atwood said doubtfully.

"Not enough to have trouble understanding me on the phone," Stannard retorted. He turned to Wallace. "What's the burglar alarm setup here?"

"Black light. It was checked this morning, and it works," Wallace replied.

"It sure didn't last night," Stannard said. "Where's the cut-off switch?"

"Just inside the door. Come on, I'll show you." He led the way across the shop. "Here. You open the door a couple of inches, enough to stick your hand through, and flip the switch. If the door opens five inches and the thing is still on, it breaks the beam and all hell breaks loose."

"Well, it looks like our man knew his way around the pro shop," Stannard muttered. "Any idea of how many people could know about that switch?"

Wallace frowned. "I'd say dozens. Maybe hundreds. Everyone who ever worked in here, and the type of help we get moves around a lot. Then there are the caddies, maintenance men, janitors."

"My God," Stannard muttered.

"We're on that angle, Burl," Atwood said. "We've got men looking for employees, past and present, who've been seen in strange company."

"Which could take until Christmas."

"Christmas of next year," Atwood amended.

Stannard shook his head in disgust. He caught Lee Ellen's eye and said, "Let's get a beer."

The Round Table was moderately busy. They sat at the bar, and Stannard buried his nose in a stone mug of German beer and kept it there until the mug was empty. Then he poured a second bottle and frowned at it. A copy of the Peninsula City *Herald* lay within reach. He spread it open between them and eyed it glumly.

The lead story on the robbery filled two columns before it was jumped to an inside page. It seemed to be reasonably accurate as to the mechanics of the robbery. The writer had put some wild quotes into the mouth of "the Tommy-gun-toting private eye" who had cut dumdum crosses in his bullets and was out to square accounts. Stannard thought grimly it would be pleasant to square accounts with the photographer who had snapped the infamous picture of him with the chopper. Pictures were splashed all over the page. Robbery scene, golf cart, Bacher, Husted, Norm Keyes, the room where the money had been counted, Lee Ellen Underwood perched on the edge of a desk, phone to ear, bust in profile, skirt rucked up halfway to hips.

Stannard scowled at the picture. "Girl, what possessed you?" he muttered.

"The desire to keep the press away from Bacher and Husted until you could get there," she said defensively.

"Like something off the front of a paperback novel."

"I was tricked. With half a dozen photographers climbing around, telling me to do this, turn that way, say 'cheese,' when one of them asked me to pull my dress up a little, I said, 'How far?' and a little bald man with a mustache jumped up, gave it one deft tug, and said, 'Right about there, doll,' and before I could yank it down again, I was had. I let it go because I thought it was important to be nice to them. I'm sorry, Burl."

"It's OK. I appreciate it." He turned the pages of the paper. There was a map of the Forest and surrounding area showing the location of the robbery, the route of the getaway car as police reconstructed it, and the point where the car had been found abandoned.

It led from the stone wall that bordered the Forest, through a medium-sized village populated by artists, writers, tourists, and motel keepers, fol-

lowed a secondary road that skirted the rocky, spectacular coast line for
a couple of miles, then cut inland and uphill across the Coast Highway and
ended in a sparsely populated canyon. The second car used in the getaway
had apparently been hidden in the garage of a summer home. The place
was owned by a wealthy cotton farmer from Bakersfield. The cotton farmer
and his wife were in their seventies. They were at the moment on an ex-
tended trip through South America and obviously had no connection with
the case, police said flatly.

And that was that.

Stannard finished his beer and signaled for the check.

The bartender cleared his throat uneasily and wiped his fingers on the
bar towel.

"Well," Stannard said impatiently.

"Mr. Stannard, I—we had a notice from the front office today. You
understand that I—"

"Never mind," Stannard said in a quiet voice. "I already heard secondhand that I was fired. And nobody in his right mind would let me run a
tab with my bank account." He took a five-dollar bill from his wallet and
put it on the bar.

The barman chewed his lip. He wiped his fingers again and said, "We
have a chit which you signed last night, sir. I believe it comes to twelve dollars."

"About right for a couple of beers, a Mule or two, and a slug of brandy
at the Round Table," he said in exasperation. He searched his wallet.
"Friend, I haven't got twelve dollars. I've got three dollars. But now I can
go down and sell a pint of blood for ten, and with what's in front of me
that should about make it. Leave a little tip money too."

The barman's mouth pinched in a little at the corners; he seemed to be
trying to decide whether this would be a satisfactory arrangement.

"Burl, here." Lee Ellen passed him a bill under the bar. Stannard put it
beside the check and saw it was a twenty. When the change came back he
started to pass it to her, but she told him *no* with her eyes. He stuffed the
money into his wallet and walked her out.

"Thanks, banker. You've got a steak coming when I sell that pint."

She laughed and slipped her arm through his. He felt her firm, sleek body
brush against him as they went through the door. He stopped, turned,
looked back at the Round Table.

"Well, I guess that will go for partial payment of my account with him.
He'll have to write the rest of it off, because I don't intend to go back."

"What, Burl?"

"Just muttering in rage," he said. "That bird's been dipping into the till
for years. One of the agents I put in the Table for the tournament spotted

it. Nothing solid enough to toss him in the can, but enough to make him quit. Probably cost him a hundred bucks a day for three days. He doesn't like me."

"Oh."

"We'll get it back. When you make up the bill, slap it on the expense account."

"With glee." She looked at her wrist watch. "Burl, I like being out, going around with you on this one. But shouldn't there be somebody in the office?"

"What for?" he asked in a dry voice. "To handle all the new clients? Forget it. We'll take a ride."

"Oh?"

"Grand tour of the getaway car route. How are you at bird watching?"

She stared. "All right. Don't be cute."

"I don't think they switched that body to the other car. I say they dumped it someplace along the road."

"Oh, joy." She grimaced.

"Know what a vulture looks like?"

CHAPTER 6

Stannard drove rapidly through the village and cut down the hill. The late summer sun was warm, and the small beach had drawn a few swimmers and a lot of sunbathers. He slowed and watched a lithe, tanned girl with sun-bronzed hair spread oil over her body. There was a golden shine to her, and she was young and healthy and right for this beach.

Lee Ellen followed his gaze. She shook her head and said, "Wrong body."

Stannard pushed the accelerator a little harder. "I didn't see anything wrong with it." When the beach was behind them, he worked a cigarette out of a mashed pack and lit it. A belt of sand dunes, sparsely covered with tough grass and scrubby bushes, rose in a series of low humps between the narrow road and the rocks along the rim of the ocean. There were no houses in sight, no other cars on the road. He pulled the hand throttle out a fraction of an inch and dropped the Ford into low gear. The car bucked and settled down to a crawl.

"It could be anywhere from here on," he said. "You watch that side of the road for any sign of a car pulling off or something being dragged over the ground. It wouldn't be much—grass bent over, maybe an indentation in the sand."

"Then you were kidding about the vultures." She sounded relieved.

"No joke. Those two were in a hurry. I doubt if they took time to bury their buddy. Their problem was to dump him where he wouldn't be found right away. It was dark, and they couldn't take a chance on using a light. I know this whole area, and darned if I can think of any place that would be just right." His black eyes speared at each irregularity along the road. "He'll be found sooner or later. Either by men or birds or animals."

The beach merged into forest land again, and the road curled up the steep hill. They crossed the Coast Highway and entered the canyon where the getaway car had been abandoned. A single police evidence technician slouched in the seat of his station wagon. The back end was piled with equipment, and a box beside him held a couple of dozen small white envelopes. The man was carefully marking each one.

Stannard parked the Ford, and they got out. He leaned on the wagon, nodded at the envelopes, and asked, "Anything?"

"*Nada*," the cop said morosely. "They didn't leave much behind them, Burl. Go get us some people and there *might* be enough here so I can say whether they were or weren't on the spot. You know."

"Yeah. Well, nothing for us here; we might as well try it the other way."

He turned the Ford around, and they started back the way they had come.

"Aren't you even going to look?"

"No point to it. If the lab men say there's nothing, there's nothing. If I tried to go over the ground the police are already covering, I'd just be wasting time. And it would take me a month to do what's been done already. I've got a couple of things to concentrate on. A match folder, which could be a dud. And a body that nobody's found yet. If they dumped that body the way I think they did, we could find it in a couple of hours. All we need is about two hundred men and a few dogs," he said.

"Can't Moss arrange that?"

Stannard got another cigarette going. "Impossible. There aren't that many men in the combined police and sheriff's departments. They could get volunteers, but then any evidence around the body could be tracked up. And from Moss's viewpoint, the body isn't top priority yet. Right now the cops are killing themselves on routine stuff that is ninety-nine per cent useless but has to be done anyway. They're checking the license numbers of every car that went through any of the five Forest gates for five or six hours after the robbery. If those guys doubled back like I think, it could turn up a lead.

"The Forest has darned near two thousand employees and executives, what with the Lodge, three golf courses, shops, stables, bars, and all. Everyone has to be checked out. There are detectives doing nothing but sitting around every place people get together, listening for somebody who sounds as though he might have seen something or heard something that isn't in the file already. Most of it turns out to be junk."

The car had reached the edge of the wooded area south of the beach while he talked. Stannard pulled off the road and stared at the sand dunes, listening to the crash of waves against the huge rocks on the far side. "I'm going for a hike. You can cruise the road and keep an eye out for anything we missed."

"I wouldn't know it if I saw it." She pulled her high-heeled shoes off and wiggled her toes.

"That sand gets hot," he told her.

"I've been to the beach before."

By the time they had climbed the first dune, Stannard wished he had left his own shoes at the car. The sand filled them, biting at his skin, shifting treacherously under his weight. He began to sweat.

They walked the ridge of the dunes slowly, not talking. Stannard became impressed with the futility of it. The killers had forty acres of dunes to work with if they had disposed of the body here. With their bare hands, they could have scooped out a shallow grave in a minute or two. The sun and wind would have erased any traces of the grave hours ago.

The wind came in unhurried gusts, tangling Stannard's hair, molding Lee Ellen's dress tight against her body. The ocean was salted with whitecaps, and rollers exploded high in the air when they hit the rocks. The wind brought the sharp yelping of a herd of sea lions which had established a rookery on one of the wide, flat rocks a hundred yards offshore.

The sand was a broad, warm carpet as they started down the seaward side of the dunes toward the rocks. There was no beach here—just the dark, shark's-tooth crags beyond the shelf of rock that was the shore line.

Lee Ellen was saying something, speaking quietly, her voice lost in the whine of the wind.

"Huh?" Stannard muttered, taking his eyes from the ground.

She laughed. "Just talking to myself. Wondering why a lot of sand and sky and sun and beautiful bleakness brings out a sort of pagan urge."

"Hah!" It was Stannard, ex-cop speaking. "If you mean why do so many people make love on the beach, I can tell you. Because they can't afford a motel, think some cop will put the light on the car when they're in the throes, are afraid the neighbors will talk. All kinds of reasons."

There was a rise of color in her tanned cheeks, a critical narrowness to the sea-blue eyes. "I guess a man learns a lot of truths by the time he's a lieutenant." She stood close to him, fists doubled on her hips. "You've seen everything, so you have an answer for everything. But have you ever *done* anything?"

Her hair was almost white, flowing and alive, in the sun. She was breathing rapidly now, her breasts tightening against her thin cotton dress. Stannard thought this girl was fine and incredibly beautiful when she was angry. His hands began to move slowly toward her. Then he remembered that he was thirty-three and she was twenty-three, remembered that he was Burl Stannard, employer, and she was Lee Ellen Underwood, employee and his hands dropped to his sides again, and his mouth tightened. Slowly, deliberately, he said, "I'll tell you something about this beautiful sand, kid. You thump around on it a couple of minutes, and it packs down so hard you think you've got one of those rocks out there under you."

She stepped back then. He watched her fists unclench, become hands, drop futilely to her thighs, clutching until the dress was tight to her legs. There was a moistness in the corners of her eyes, and he couldn't tell whether it came from whatever she was feeling or the buffeting wind.

"I'm sorry for you, Burl," she said softly. "If you were with a girl and something like that stuck in your mind, I'm sorry for you."

She turned and walked away. He stood motionless for a few seconds, wanting to call her back, say it was a lie he had told because there had to be a certain distance between them. He held back, knowing that if he did the distance would not be there anymore; knowing that he would kiss her and draw her down to the sand; knowing that she would let him because of what he had said.

He swore at himself and at the sand in his shoes and followed at a distance. They moved along the low sandstone bluff at the water's edge, and he kept his eyes on the surge of white water over rocks.

Here the ocean had chewed away at the land, seeking the softer veins of stone, creating little inlets anywhere from ten to a hundred feet long. The sandstone shelf sloped down to water level in spots and in others rose a few feet above high-tide line. There were occasional potholes in the shelf. Known locally as blowholes, these resulted when the sea had tunneled a cave into the shelf and the ground surface that was the roof of the cave had been eroded from below and fallen in. At high tide the ocean would surge through the tunnel and erupt through the blowholes. There were occasional signs warning against going close to them. The rims were slick and grown over with a sea vegetation. Stannard knew that every few years somebody managed to fall into one. In each case the victim had been battered to death against the rocks before rescuers could reach him.

Stannard watched a heavy roller boil down an inlet. It came on with a sound like a subway train, and a moment later foam and spray boiled in the air high above the hole.

A flock of sea birds rode out with it, wings flapping, complaining in their shrill voices. They rode the air currents briefly, then floated down into the blowhole again. Stannard watched, then his eyes moved thoughtfully up and down the shore line.

A sea gull, wings beating furiously, rose from the hole, gulping a small silver fish as it flew. It made a circle and plunged downward again. None of the birds seemed to be working any other hole.

Lee Ellen was about fifty feet away, stalking along the sand, head down.

"Hey—wait," he shouted.

She stopped, stared, went on.

He ran after her, blocked her path. She moved to go around him, and he grabbed her shoulder. "You can take a walk and cool off. Back to the car. You'll find a coil of rope and some old coveralls in the trunk. Bring them. I think that body is feeding the fish over there."

She looked at him then and at the wet mouth of the hole. "If it is, I'd better go to town for help. You'd kill yourself if you tried going into one of those things alone."

"I don't dare call Moss away from what he's doing without being sure. Now do it."

She began to climb the dune. Stannard sat on the shelf, removed his shoes and socks, and stripped to the waist. He searched until he found a twisted scrub of a tree solidly rooted in a crevice. When Lee Ellen came back with the rope, he knotted an end securely to the tree and threw his weight hard against it. It showed no inclination to become uprooted. He unfolded the coveralls, then unsnapped his belt.

"Look at the pretty ocean a minute," he ordered.

She turned her back, and he shed his slacks and got into the coveralls. He rigged the rope as a mountain climber does, across the chest, over the shoulder, and around a leg and walked out until he was near the rim of the hole. He lay on his stomach and inched forward, giving out a few inches of line at a time, probing for indentations in the rock with his toes. Slick wetness soaked through the coveralls, and globs of slime attached themselves to his face. The express train roared through the tunnel again, and Stannard lay without moving until the spray had run off and the eruption of birds had subsided.

Stannard grabbed for the rim of the hole, eased off on the rope, and dragged himself forward. He looked over the edge. The hole was about ten feet deep. He saw a lump of something pounding against the jagged stone with each movement of the ebbing water. It was a body. Stannard swallowed the sickness that boiled in his throat; then, using both hands on the rope, he inched back. A cormorant flapped down over the body and stabbed with its beak at one of the small silver fish.

When the shelf was no longer wet under him, Stannard stood and drew a deep breath. The air didn't seem so clean as it had a few minutes earlier.

Lee Ellen started toward him.

"I'll wait here," he said thickly. "You take the car and find a phone."

CHAPTER 7

They came within a half-hour. Captain Jim Moss and the lab crew and the inspector from Homicide and the sheriff's men (because this was in the county area) and the Highway Patrol (to keep the siren chasers moving) and the newspaper and television men and the coroner. Burl Stannard shivered in the wet coveralls and sucked on a cigarette while they decided nobody could go down into the hole without being ground to hamburger on the rocks. Finally the phone company came through with a cherry-picker truck.

It churned over the dunes and backed around on the shelf, lifting the thin scorpion's tail of its boom up and over the hole, the homicide inspector and his assistant riding the bucket. They drew the body out with a grappling iron and dumped it on a tarpaulin spread on the ground.

The men ringed it, eyes dead, faces blanching. Lee Ellen lit a smoke from Stannard's pack and walked away along the bottom of the dune.

"Make him, Burl?" Moss asked.

"Nobody gets a make on something like that just by looking," Stannard said roughly. The surging water and sharp rocks and hungry fish had done their job, ribboning the face and body flesh. Stannard crouched down and tore the shredded jacket. "Those look like chopper holes to me. And the clothes are about right."

Moss turned a dead hand over and shook his head. "Play hell getting a print here."

Stannard tugged the jacket collar back, looked, then did the same with the ragged waistband of the trousers. "Label's torn out. Might get some laundry marks off the shirt and skivvies, but I doubt it." He scowled. "Doc," he said to the pathologist, "when will you be able to tell us something about this stiff?"

"Six or eight hours. And then it might not amount to much."

Moss stood, brushing his clothes. "This is your territory," he said to the sheriff's deputy.

The deputy looked with distaste at the body. "You can have him."

The coroner supervised loading the body into a wicker basket. It was stowed on a Jeep and hauled away. Stannard went behind the phone truck and changed clothes. Then he whistled and waved, and the small figure of Lee Ellen turned and started back along the shore. He waited, and they hiked across the dunes to the car together, Stannard carrying his shoes and socks.

"You cold?" he asked.

"I'm all right."

"Drive us by my place. I've got to get a shower and a drink, or I'm due for pneumonia."

She was in the tiny kitchen when he wrapped a robe around himself and hunted for fresh clothes. He found a frayed pair of slacks, a sports shirt, a baggy tweed jacket.

"If this keeps up another day, I'll have to buy a wad of clothes," he grumbled.

"Here." She handed him a steaming mug. "Hot rum toddy."

He took a swallow, puckering his mouth at the heat. They went into the small combination living room-bedroom. The studio couch was still covered with the rumpled electric blanket. He sat on one end, stretching his legs.

"No place else to sit, girl. You can stand or jump in bed with me." He intended the words to be light, bantering, but when he spoke he was remembering the tight time on the beach, and they didn't sound right.

"I'm afraid you wouldn't know how to enjoy it," she said crisply. She sat, keeping some distance between them, tucking the long, tanned legs under her.

Stannard gulped what was left in the cup. He felt the trembling begin in his belly and spread. His hand flashed out and his fingers were in her hair and he was pulling her down on the couch. She twisted on the loose blanket and tried to say something in the instant before his mouth crushed against hers. He felt her fingernails dig at his face for a moment. Then the nails were gone, and there was the light touch of fingers in their place. He could feel her full breasts through his shirt. His fingers were still in her hair, clenched, and he ran his free hand slowly over the back of her neck, touching the sensuous smoothness of her warm, soft skin.

There was no measuring of time. It could have been two minutes or an hour later when the phone beside the day bed buzzed. Stannard rolled up on an elbow and reached across Lee Ellen to snag the receiver from the low table beside the couch. He growled into the mouthpiece as Lee Ellen stirred and blinked her eyes. Her mouth soundlessly asked, "who?" and he held the phone so that she could hear.

"Burl, it's Tam." She sounded sober. If she remembered and resented being bounced out of bed, she showed no indication of it in her words. "How soon can you come by the house?"

Lee Ellen was shaking her head in a violent "no." Stannard grinned and stroked her back with his free hand.

"I don't know. Frankly, it's been a hell of a day, Mrs. Bacher."

"Ouch!" There was a soft, throaty laugh. "You made your point once. You can call me Tam safely from now on. But, Burl, it looks like the Major's hound dogs may have treed themselves a coon. They think they found the house the killers used."

"Hey!" Stannard slapped Lee Ellen's hip lightly and cupping his hand over the mouthpiece, whispered, "We've gotta go." She eased herself from the couch, and he spoke into the phone again. "All I'd heard from out there was that Deck and Taggart were irritating people. Let me talk to one of them."

"You can't," Tam replied. "We've got five bathtubs in this ark of a house. Will and Jack and two other old war buddies walked their legs numb for you today, and they're in four of them with big drinks. My darling husband, who directed the campaign from a command post in the gameroom bar, is just numb. He's in the other one."

"And what about his fatheaded, jug-eared little friend who damn near blew my head off yesterday? Scrubbing his back?"

"Oh, God!" She was laughing now. "Husted is staking the place out, whatever that may mean. Anyway, he's watching it."

"Yeah. How do I find it? I'll meet Deck and Taggart there."

"Just come to our place. I'd like to watch the Major huff and puff when he tries to explain how something like this could happen; but, Burl—it's the house next door!"

Stannard cradled the phone on her laughter, then waited while Lee Ellen raked a comb through the disorder of her hair and built a new red mouth. In the car she turned his face toward her with cool fingers.

He brushed a wisp of hair from her forehead and pressed his lips against the smooth warmth of her throat.

She held him tight, then pulled away and rested her head on the back of the seat. "We'd better go, lover," she said.

Major Harry Bacher spilled whiskey from a decanter into a tall glass and sipped it neat. "You probably think I'm a stupid ass, Stannard, for not thinking sooner about people being in that house. But for the last month I've done nothing but work on that damned tournament. Haven't been to the office, haven't sold a piece of property, haven't even *shown* one."

"Don't beat yourself over the head, Major," Stannard said. "You had no reason to think anything was up." They were grouped around the big poker table in Bacher's gameroom.

Will Deck and Jack Taggart didn't look like men who had spent a full day tramping from house to house, pumping questions at people, mulling the answers, pumping more questions. Deck's blond hair was faultlessly brushed; his charcoal suit, tab-collar shirt, and narrow, regimental-striped tie held by a platinum clip were casually perfect. Taggart leaned back in a captain's chair, his slender face a mask. He wore a turtleneck sweater and navy blazer with silver buttons.

There were two whom Stannard had not met before, less elegant men who drank beer from bottles and spoke without taking their cigarettes from their mouths. Both had served with Bacher as enlisted men. Claude Davis was short and heavy-set, with eyes that were mild behind thick lenses. Marvin Marsh was a thin man with the sad eyes and long face of a hound.

Stannard leaned on the table, shoulders hunched. "Tell me about it."

"The whole routine or just high lights?" Deck asked.

"High spots for now. How you got onto it, what you found."

Deck took a small leather-bound notebook from his pocket. "At 9:10 A.M. Davis and I called at the house which we later learned was and is owned by Charles Hartley. Hartley is a semiretired mining engineer and so far as we know is presently in Canada or Alaska checking up on some projects. We got no answer, and the house showed no signs of occupancy, and we went on. Later we made contact with a Vincent Eagles. Eagles is a landscape gardener for a number of homes in the Forest. Eagles informed us that three or four days ago, when he went to work at the Hartley place, he found it occupied by three men. One was evidently a chauffeur and houseman, the second a secretary of some sort, and the third their employer. The chauffeur told him his boss was some business associate of Hartley's and had the use of the place because of it."

"Eagles accepted this?" Stannard asked.

"According to him, Hartley often did this. The men involved acted as though they belonged there, and there was a Rolls Royce sedan in the drive. Friend, a gardener just does not question a Rolls."

"OK. This Eagles actually saw three men. Would he know them again?"

Deck dropped the notebook on the green-felt tabletop. "He couldn't swear to it in court. He puts them somewhere between five-eight and six feet, light to medium builds. One or two had mustaches—he thinks. All three wore sun goggles and some kind of hat or cap. Not much help."

"I saw that much in the holdup," Stannard retorted. "You go back?"

"We did," Deck continued. "No answer. I worked on a side-door lock for a couple of minutes, and we took a quick look around. They'd cleaned out and cleaned up after themselves. Hard to tell that anybody had been in the place for months. Want to take a look?"

"Sure," Stannard said. "You notify the police?" Jack Taggart's mouth curled into a mocking smile for an instant. "We aren't popular with your police. Some of the fine folks hereabouts apparently took umbrage at our questions this morning, and we got a cease-and-desist warning from some city dick. If they should find out we were in that house, we'll probably see the inside of your jail."

"It can be squared," Stannard told them. "Let's go."

Nobody moved, nobody spoke.

"Well?" Stannard shoved his chair back. "You found it. Going with me or not?"

Deck twisted the lodge ring on the third finger of his right hand. "We discussed it and came to the conclusion it would be best for us to fade away. We've antagonized your local police. Better all around if you tell them you found the house. They could make trouble for us in Indiana."

Stannard shrugged. "Suit yourself. Thanks for the assist."

"If there's anything else we can do, call," Deck told him.

"Sure."

Stannard found Lee Ellen at the bar leafing through a realtor's looseleaf binder of property listings and photos.

When they drove off in the Ford, it was already dusk. Stannard put the spotlight on a Cadillac hard-top that was pulled off the road several hundred yards ahead. Dick Husted squinted his little eyes at them.

"You can knock off now," Stannard said.

Husted didn't answer. He started the Cadillac, tramped on the gas, and cut the heavy car around the Ford.

"I suppose his stomach bothers him," Lee Ellen said as Stannard turned into the graveled drive that twisted through the oak grove.

Stannard braked the Ford near the front door of the Hartley house, checked his revolver, and pulled a flashlight from the glove compartment. "I want to give the joint a quick toss before anyone else gets into it. Wait for me to get the door open, then drive on into the Lodge and call Moss. Get him in person."

He went up the broad flagstone steps, worked on the door a half-minute with a lock pick, and stepped inside. When he heard the Ford move away, he used the flashlight, found light switches, and went to work.

There were dust covers on the furniture in the big living room and a small amount of ashes from what could have been papers in a fireplace big enough to hold a grand piano. The air was musty, but not with the dead, flat odor that comes when a house has been completely closed for months. Stannard spent little time in the living room, a library that held scores of volumes on mining and engineering, a formal dining room, and a den that smelled of rich, well-cared-for leather.

Footprints showed faintly in a thin layer of dust that covered the kitchen floor. He checked the refrigerator. It had been turned off, but there was water in the ice trays. The glass tray under the freezing compartment was dry. He ran a finger through it and examined a faint gray smudge of dust. He found several cabinets stocked with canned goods. A trash can was lined with a five-day-old newspaper. A set of copper skillets and pans hung from a rack by the big electric stove, their bottoms gleaming like a matched set of setting suns.

Stannard frowned, ran his fingers through his hair, felt the scab where the bullet had furrowed him. So far, the house was as clean as if a platoon of scrub-women had gone through it. The killers were evidently patient, methodical men; they must have cleaned it up before they pulled the job which could mean they hadn't returned afterward and Stannard was just wasting more time.

He hunted up a door leading to a fenced-off area behind the kitchen. It held two galvanized-iron garbage cans and a large wooden box, apparently intended for trash. All three were empty.

The bedrooms were equally unproductive. Of six in the main house, four were made up, ready for occupancy. Only one of the servants' bedrooms had sheets and blankets in place. Three of those in the main house had obviously been dusted recently, and the spreads were not quite even on the beds.

Somebody pounded on the front door. Stannard sighed and went downstairs. Captain Moss was doing the pounding. Lee Ellen and a detective team were with him.

Moss hurried into the house and looked the big living room over quickly. "You toss it already?"

"Yeah." Stannard fired a cigarette. "It might as well have been three ghosts for all they left behind."

"There's always something," Moss retorted.

"Try the fireplace. They burned something there. Take a good look at the rest of it, and you'll see what I mean. No food scraps, no tin cans, no soap in the johns. Even made the beds," Stannard growled.

Moss nodded to the detectives. "Shake it."

"Better have a landscape gardener named Eagles picked up. He's the one who claims to have seen three men here," Stannard said.

Moss tilted his hat back on his ears, frowning. "I've been meaning to ask you how you got onto this place. I had a dozen men out here today. They didn't find Eagles."

Stannard decided Moss would find out eventually. He grinned and said, "Der elves did it."

"You mean those bastards Bacher turned loose?" Moss demanded.

"Those same bastards. They tipped me and said they'd prefer to stay out of it."

"And I'll tip you to something, Burl. You we know and like downtown. Outside private eyes we don't know and we sure as hell don't like. I got a wire off to Terre Haute this afternoon to check them out."

"Gift horse," Stannard said, shrugging. "Come on, I'll show you around this barn."

He counted twenty rooms before they finished. Reinforcements arrived from headquarters, and Moss left to take charge. Stannard found a cubbyhole fitted out with a small desk and metal filing cabinet in the servants' wing. There was a legal-size folder in a drawer. He leaned against the wall and flipped through the pages stapled inside. He looked up to find Lee Ellen watching.

"You should be such a housekeeper. This thing's an inventory, probably made up when they closed the house. From the looks of it, the old gal counted the toothpicks," he said.

"God spare me, lover. I'm lucky if I know when the beer gets low."

Stannard nibbled his lower lip. "Let's go take another look at those bedrooms. I just had a wild thought, but it's out of my line."

"I'm glad you said that without a smirk." She followed him upstairs, into what was evidently the master bedroom.

Carefully, Stannard drew the spread and blankets back from one side, exposing starched sheets. "Take a good look," he instructed. "Tell me, has that bed been slept in since it was made up?"

She looked, ran her hand over the sheets, inspected the fold at the top. "I'd say no. There aren't any of those little wrinkles people make. It's just a guess, but—"

"Yeah," he broke in. "I'm guessing, too." He knelt, squinted along the creases left in the sheet by the laundry iron. They were distinct but the ridges were not sharp. He thumbed through the inventory. "According to this thing there are two linen closets in this part of the house. One should have thirty-two sheets, ten of which will be in their original wrapping, and nineteen pillowcases. According to this there are two dozen sheets in the second and the same number of pillowcases."

"So?" she said doubtfully.

"Count 'em. Count every last bundling one."

"Burl, are you—"

"Don't argue. I know what bundling is. Hop to it before Moss gets the troops up here."

Stannard smoked a cigarette while he checked the other bedrooms. He could see no variation in the condition of the beds. They all looked fresh but not necessarily newly made up. He had returned to the master bedroom and was listening to the searching noises being made by the police crew downstairs when Lee Ellen returned.

She dusted her fingers. "Well, nobody snitched any sheets."

"They're all accounted for?"

"Every sheet, every pillowcase. There's even a notation that in addition three beds in the main house and one in the wing are made up."

He scuffed his feet on a hooked rug. "This is the damnedest. We've got a supposedly good report that three men lived here in this house. What traces do they leave? Just about nothing! I find a newspaper five days old in the garbage can. Dust in the defroster tray of the refrigerator. They must have run that thing if they were here that long, and it should be wet from the stuff melting off the coils. Not a scrap of food or a tin can in the trash. A few ashes in the fireplace. All linen present and accounted for and beds that look fresh. Dammit, I can see them hauling off their garbage and cleaning up a little. But not like this. Not bringing their own bed sheets!"

He stopped, realizing his voice had risen to a shout. He went to the dresser and banged the flat of his hand on the polished, dust-free surface. "I offer you a bet. Beer against a hole in a doughnut and half the hole back if you lose, girl."

She sank back on the bed, blond hair spraying across the pillow, red mouth laughing. "What's the bet?"

He stuck a cigarette between his lips and scraped a match into flame. "This is a phony. Somebody set it up. Don't ask me why; I don't know why. Maybe to make us think the killers got away clean. I'll find out."

"If you talk to Eagles—"

"I'll talk to Eagles. Sure. But you know what happens when a murder case breaks, who the cops look at first?"

She waited silently.

"The guy who found the body."

"But we found—"

"Sure," he interrupted. "I'm thinking about who found the house."

CHAPTER 8

Vincent Eagles was a widower, age fifty-seven, with two married daughters, three grandchildren, and another on the way. He lived alone in a board-and-bat house in the village beyond the Forest wall. His savings account was in the neighborhood of six thousand dollars. A three-year-old pickup truck and station wagon were paid for. He had worked at landscaping jobs in the area nearly thirty years. He had never been in trouble of any kind with the law.

Eagles sat in the wooden armchair across the office from Moss. He was an aging but powerful man with sun-leathered features. His stubby fingers were laced together across his waist, and his right thumb flipped the zipper of his windbreaker jacket as he talked.

"I told you boys four times what I saw," he said. "We going to keep this up all night?"

"Maybe you'll remember something else," Stannard said.

"There wasn't anything else," Eagles insisted. "If I think of something, I'll call you right away."

Moss sighed, checked his notes. "OK. It boils down to Friday. Three men; you wouldn't know them again. You saw them just once, but they could have been there other days; you just didn't happen to go back. You don't remember anything about the car except it was a Rolls. But you're sure it didn't belong around here. How's that?"

"A Rolls is pretty rare, even in the Forest," Eagles told them. "In all the years I've gardened here, I don't imagine more than a couple of dozen families had 'em. Probably think who they were if you gave me a few minutes. A few come down from the city pretty regular, but it wasn't one of them. Almost new."

"How new?" Stannard demanded.

Eagles shuffled his feet, eyes on the floor. "About a '37 model."

"What would you think was an old one?" Moss said caustically.

"Rolls built in '37 is just a pup."

"Oh, God," Moss muttered. "Skip it. Now you said one of those guys moved around funny and talked 'different.' What's that mean?"

"Know how a big cat kind of flows along, smooth and sleek? Well, like that. Talked about like Jack Paar does on TV. Soft, easy way."

"Could you pick the voice out again?" Stannard asked hopefully.

"Maybe. Wouldn't count on it though. Had a real bugger of a head cold then, and you know how it is: nothin' sounds the way it really is."

Moss stood and thrust his hands in his pockets. "OK, Vince. Thanks for coming down."

"Sure. Wish I could have helped more." He zipped the windbreaker and went out.

Moss stared at the closed door. He swore fervently and fluently. "Burl, in all my years I've *never* run into such a bunch of wiseacre bastards! Caddy carts! Rolls Royces! Live in a house like they owned it without leaving a trace! Haul a dead partner off and then dump him in a blowhole! Craziest goddamn—"

"Smartest goddamn," Stannard interrupted. "Take a good look at it, Jim. If they just pulled the stickup and tried to get out of the Forest in a car, they'd have never made it past the gatehouses. So they use the cart to shortcut across three or four hundred yards of golf course and go over the wall.

"They took their buddy with them because they figured if we made him, we'd make them. Finding him as quick as we did was pure luck, and even then, what did we get?"

"Not much," Moss agreed grudgingly. "Can't get one lousy fingerprint, no identifiable scars or other marks, face all chewed up, no bridgework, no nothing. Doc says he was a white male seventy inches tall with light brown hair and maybe weighed one fifty-five without the eight chopper slugs you put in him."

"The house and the Rolls were window dressing. They wanted to be seen so we'd find the place and no car and figure they're long gone. Run that car down and you'll probably find it was rented by a little old lady from Pasadena."

"So why in hell go to the trouble?" Moss demanded. "This thing happened over thirty hours ago, Burl. You can't find them. I can't find them. The Master of Fox Hounds and all his damned beagles couldn't find them. They made their point without screwing around with the house and Rolls. They went somewhere, and I'll admit it! So *why?*"

Stannard chuckled. He had not seen Moss so worked up since the night he quit the department. He sat on the edge of the battered desk and lit a cigarette.

"Want a wild one? I say they had to make it look like they took off because they can't take off. I think they're local and can't afford to disappear."

"You'll have to make a hard sell on that one," Moss argued. "One, none of our locals has ever used a shotgun. Norm Keyes was killed with one. Two, no local gunsel who comes close to the size and coloring of the one you plugged is unaccounted for. We've already run every character who ever took a fall for robbery around here through the chopper. Drew a blank. So?"

"So it was at least set up by a local boy, and he had to be one of the two who got away," Stannard said. "Dumping the stiff in the blowhole had to be a spur-of-the-moment move. Would imported talent have known about the thing being there in the first place and just how to find it in the second?"

"All *right!*" Moss slumped in his chair. His face was gray and creased by exhaustion. "I'll buy the local brain. So how do we root him out of his hole?"

Stannard yawned, reached for his hat. "I've got some ideas, but they haven't jelled. Get anything from Terre Haute on Bacher's house guests?"

"Not yet." Moss eyed him sharply. "You looking at them?"

"Why not? You are."

"Yeah," Moss admitted. "Anyway, I was. But hell, the more I look, the more it falls apart. Those dark glasses and caps they wore would fool a stranger, but that isn't much of a disguise to use when someone who's known you for years will be getting a look."

"Uh-huh," Stannard said noncommittally.

"Oh, hell," Moss went on. "Bacher's an arrogant blowhard, but you can't fit him into it. He's loaded with dough; he was with you in the car all through it; and he was riding behind Norm. The scatter-gun could have taken him just as easy. If Bacher was in it, he sure wouldn't have taken a chance on losing his own head. Would he?"

Stannard opened the door. "You tell me, Jim. But if I had a lot of men sitting around on their duffs, I might stake a couple out where they could keep an eye on the whole lashup."

After leaving Captain Moss, Stannard drove by his office: he found it dark. He went in and phoned Lee Ellen's apartment. "You eat yet?"

"I'm reheating a pot of spaghetti for the fourth straight day. There's garlic bread."

"I'll pick up some Dago red."

Stannard finished two platters of spaghetti, a half-loaf of the hot Italian bread, and a fifth of wine in a quarter of an hour. He was looking around for more when he realized he hadn't spoken a word since he sat down.

"You can sure cook," he said sheepishly.

"You can sure eat." Lee Ellen poured more wine. "When was the last time?"

He thought back. "English muffin for breakfast yesterday, I guess." He stood, pushed his chair back, and thumped his belly in satisfaction. Pain exploded under his ribs, and he doubled over, gasping for breath.

"Burl!" Lee Ellen was in front of him, supporting him by the shoulders, looking anxiously at the sudden gray of his face.

He drew a slow, careful breath and forced himself to stand erect. "It's OK just whacked the wrong spot." He looked for the door. "Good chow. Wish I could stay."

She twisted him around, walked him to the sofa, made him sit. She opened his shirt and peered and probed at the bruise left by the golf club.

"I'm going to call a doctor."

"You are not," Stannard protested. "Doctor would want to put me in bed for a week, and he'd be right. Not yet. No time." He could feel the Dago red going to work. "You think that looks bad, you should see ol' Norm Keyes's head. Lemme up!"

"No!" Her eyes were fierce. "You didn't have anything important to do, or you'd never have stopped to eat in the first place. You're hurt, Burl. Now you can rest long enough for me to put something on that. Please!"

The wine warmth was spreading through him. Combining with the heavy meal, it was pushing him toward sleep.

"Call Moss. Tell him I'm here if he needs me. OK?"

"All right. Take your shirt off."

He unbuttoned his shirt and jacket and slumped back. He kept his eyes open by concentrating on the pale shine of Lee Ellen's hair as she talked on the phone. Then the smell of liniment was sharp in his nostrils, and her fingers kneaded the bruised muscles. He was asleep by the time the towel-wrapped hot water bottle was in place.

The shrilling phone woke him. He pushed back the light blanket that covered him and heard her voice.

"...Yes, he's still here. Is it important enough to wake him?"

"I'm awake," he muttered, swinging his legs to the floor. "Moss wouldn't call unless it was."

She brought the phone. He propped it against an ear, motioned for a cigarette, and said, "For the record, I'm classed as walking wounded. Racked out on the couch and stinking of horse liniment." He winked. Gotta protect the gal's reputation. What's up, Jim?"

His shirt and jacket were folded across the back of the sofa. He reached for them as he listened. "She called you, huh? OK. Buzz her back. I'm on the way."

Lee Ellen took the phone away. Stannard stuffed his shirttail into his slacks, shrugged into the jacket, and combed his hair with his fingers. Lee Ellen watched, tall and slender, unsmiling, arms crossed over her breasts.

Stannard took her head in his hands and kissed her lightly on the lips. "I'm stepping out on you. The black-haired she-panther wants to see me. In a dim café with soft music."

She stepped away from his touch. "You're not funny. You're not built to be funny, Burl. If Tam Bacher wants to see you and you think it's business, that's good enough for me. Just don't needle me."

He drew her against him and kissed the soft hair by her ear. "She seems to think it's important. The cop watching the place said she drove off an hour ago and didn't put the headlights on until she was out of sight of the house. She went to see a lawyer and while she was with him called the station, asking to get in touch with me. Wouldn't tell Moss why."

She reached for his head and pulled his mouth down to hers. "Come home when you're finished," she whispered.

The Red Boar was a soldier's bar on the highway to the Army camp east of Peninsula City, a flat-roofed, clapboard-sided building that looked as though another room had been tacked on whenever the interior got too small to handle the weekend and payday crush of soldiers and tarts and the people who lived off them. There was a sleazy feeling to the place. A fat sergeant and a bartender in a dirty apron shook dice at the long bar. A woman with bleached hair and broad hips bulging under a too-tight skirt leaned on the juke, running her fingers over the buttons. Her broad rump bumped up and down to the music, and she drummed a run-over heel on the bare, warped boards of the floor. Stannard walked past a phalanx of neon Burgie and Coors and Regal and Lucky signs and one with fat glasses of Hamm's jumping out of a ridiculously blue lake and turned left, into an ell with a single row of high-sided booths. He found Tam Bacher in the farthest one. She looked up with the dark eyes and told him to sit.

Stannard slipped onto the opposite bench. He remembered the scene with the Round Table bartender and said, "You throw this party. I'm flat."

There was a glass of beer on the narrow table. The woman slid her purse beside it, fingered a cigarette from a platinum case, and waited for a light. Stannard held a match, and she blew smoke from her nostrils, appraised him, and said, "First, let's clear the air. About last night, I was drunk and upset and I acted like a tramp and I'm sorry."

Stannard shrugged. "Forget it. I have. What's on your mind now?"

"I want to hire you. As soon—"

She stopped talking as a cocktail waitress with deep-dish blouse, ample breasts, and a narrow waist cinched tight by a studded leather belt came up. She passed her eyes over Stannard but watched Tam Bacher from under heavy lids; Tam Bacher did not belong in the Red Boar.

"Cutty Sark. Bring the bottle," Stannard ordered. "Ice and a bottle of soda."

"Can't do it, mister. Gotta sell by the drink." The waitress drummed crimson fingernails on the table.

Stannard dug for his wallet. His badge flashed in the dim light as he fingered a business card out and flipped it across the table. "Tell Louie to make it a new bottle. Scram."

The waitress glanced at the card, tossed her dark hair, and stalked away, hips swinging. Stannard lit a cigarette, studied Tam Bacher for a moment, and asked: "Hire me for what? And why come to this dump to talk about it?"

"Harry wouldn't think of looking for me in a rat-hole like this." She tapped the ash from her smoke impatiently.

"Huh. Trouble with Harry," Stannard said without enthusiasm. "What's he do, beat you about the head and shoulders, drink his tea from a saucer, or what?" He wondered through what mental process Tam Bacher had concluded he'd drop murder and robbery for a crummy domestic beef. "Never mind. It doesn't matter, because I'm not available. I can refer you to a couple of good agencies."

The waitress returned, banged a tray containing a bottle of Cutty Sark, soda, ice, and glasses on the table, and went away. Stannard built two drinks.

"It can wait until you are available." Tam tested her drink, touched it with soda. "My lawyer recommended you."

"That's a surprise," Stannard said drily. The lawyer Tam had visited earlier had defended several people arrested by Stannard over the years. They'd been convicted anyway.

"He doesn't like you; in fact, he called you a complete bastard and told me when you build a case it holds up in any man's court."

"Against his defense maybe."

"No matter." She laughed without humor, and there was bitterness in her eyes. "It will take someone with a thick skin to dig into the double life of Major Harry Bacher."

"Oh," Stannard said mildly, "double life?"

"An exaggeration," she admitted. "The officer-and-gentleman routine is put on. If outsiders aren't looking, my husband is a different person. Stannard, he's a fortune hunter. A successful one."

"He's got a lot of company in the Forest."

"I couldn't care less," she retorted. "I do want to get my hands on what was mine to start with."

"Uh-huh."

"It should be about a third of a million dollars, Stannard. Mine. I want it back."

Stannard whistled softly. "Yeah. I can see where you would at that." He finished his drink and made another. "How come? I'd heard you were some kind of a refugee and you met your husband in Europe at the end of the war."

"True. My family was Polish. We had substantial properties, really, quite a bit of money even by today's standards. Before the Germans came whatever could be turned into cash was banked in Switzerland. I was seventeen years old at the time, and I was not the brave type. I slept with the Germans, and when the Russians kicked the Germans out, I slept with them. I stayed alive, but most of my family was dead before the war was over. They were the lucky ones. The others died in Soviet camps.

"My last Russian was a colonel, and he wasn't a member of the Party. He expected to be eliminated as soon as there was no more need for his ability to fight. He deserted, and I went with him. Poor fool, he thought he was safe when he reached American-held territory. An American officer who thought he was a Communist trying to infiltrate promptly handed him back to the Reds. He grabbed a guard's pistol and killed himself."

"Tough," Stannard said. "There was a lot of that."

"He was a good man. Much better man than the officer who sent him back."

Stannard stifled a yawn. "Maybe he had orders."

She said a four-letter word. "Harry Bacher was the officer. He could have interned the colonel, but that wouldn't have been convenient. The colonel had something Harry wanted. Me."

"Violin solo, full tremolo," Stannard replied. "You married him."

"I didn't have to," she said fiercely. "I could have gone back to Poland in a cattle car."

"I suppose so. Then what?"

"Harry kept me. I told him about the money in Switzerland, and there was no problem then. As a war bride, I could come to this country. Even without me, Harry would have done all right. His unit was assigned to breaking up black markets and recovering stolen property. If he'd stayed overseas another year, he'd have been a millionaire."

"Just like a lot of guys." Stannard dropped ice into the glasses and mixed fresh drinks. "So?"

"So I am through with him, which I believe is fine with the Major, but I want what is mine, and maybe some of his for putting up with him. He's concealed most of it. I want you to investigate, get something for my lawyer to work on. I'll pay you five per cent of whatever you recover, plus all your expenses."

"About a third of a million, huh?" Stannard did some fast mental calculation. "Tell you what. If a lawyer did the job, he'd get away with at least a quarter of whatever he recovered. Better make it ten per cent."

"It won't be a difficult job. But I want it done right."

"Maybe someone else will do it right for five. Try around."

"You—All right."

Stannard grinned. "I'll get started as soon as I can." He stood and stretched. "Don't forget to pay for the hooch on the way out."

Stannard called Captain Moss from a pay phone at a gas station. "Still got a stakeout at Bacher's?"

"Yeah. The man I got on his wife says she's been in the Red Boar with you. Do any good?"

"Don't know yet, Jim. We can kick it around later. But just for the hell of it, dig out whatever you can on the Major. And Mrs. B."

"God! We're pretty shorthanded, Burl."

"I know. Turn up anything at the Hartley place?"

"Nothing. The ashes in the fireplace were from a local paper. An old one. Why?"

"Nothing. Got it staked?"

"Yeah."

"Call him off. I'm going back for another look. Might stir up something."

CHAPTER 9

The big house showed no sign of the police search. Stannard wandered aimlessly through the rooms, flipping light switches on and off as he went. He had no idea what he was looking for—if, in fact, he was looking for anything. Shaking the Hartley house down again at least gave him the satisfaction of doing something.

And for the moment there was nothing else to do.

It would have been easier to sweat a hundred suspects one at a time, to pound on them with deadly monotonous questions, make them tell their stories over and over again, wait for a slip—anything to sink his teeth into.

What he had so far led nowhere. A dead man who still could not be identified but who was important because his partners had taken a risk to dispose of his body. A match cover that was one of thousands of match covers; it led nowhere but to an expensive bar patronized by hundreds of people. This house, where the killers may or may not have hidden out. A caddy cart, which made sense when its role was considered, and a Rolls Royce which was both unfound and unexplained. A couple of smooth private eyes from the Midwest who had injected themselves into the case and thus were worth looking into. Particularly because they had found the Hartley house. Tam Bacher's dangling a fat fee under his nose, wanting him to dig into her husband's alleged manipulations of God knew how much money. And a little matter of somebody's clouting him with a golf club and laying Ray Keene out and then taking off with a cash-register tape.

A real sackful of snipes.

Stannard's shoulders slumped as he came down the broad staircase and walked through the library and living room. He dug for a cigarette, found the pack empty, crushed it, and tossed it into the fireplace. There was a leather-covered box on the coffee table by the sofa. He raised the lid hopefully and found cigarettes and matches inside. He helped himself to one and got it going. Drawing smoke into his lungs, he saw the matches were from the Round Table, identical to the folder he'd seen in the caddy cart. There were two more in the box. He sucked on the cigarette and decided it tasted fresh.

He shoved the matches into his pocket, went out, and drove quickly to the Round Table.

The lounge was nearly empty. Charlie was on duty. Stannard found a dollar in his pocket, put it onto the bar, and ordered a beer.

"Looks like it's giving you a rough time," the barman said. "Those matches you were asking about fit into it?"

"They could." Stannard drank from the bottle. "Got some more?"

Charlie flipped a couple of books across the bar. Stannard looked them over and compared them with the folder from his pocket. The difference didn't strike him immediately, and when it did, there was no way of knowing whether it had any significance.

The folders were on heavy black stock with a rippled finish. A reproduction of an old-time golfing print was on the back. The front bore the Round Table name in raised letters and a coat of arms: silver lions rampant on a red field slashed by a naked sword. The field on the one Stannard had found at the house was scarlet. The other was a lighter shade, almost a vermillion.

"I want to check on something. Who buys this sort of stuff around here—the manager?"

"More likely the purchasing agent. I can get you his name."

"Never mind. I know who it is. Thanks." Stannard finished his beer and left. He drove rapidly out of the Forest and to police headquarters in Peninsula City.

Jim Moss was off duty. Stannard spent ten minutes arguing the deputy watch commander into opening the evidence locker long enough to let him have a look at what had been picked up so far. The match folder that had been in the caddy cart was there with its identifying tag. The red on the cover matched the shade of the one he'd picked up at the house exactly.

Stannard felt a little better. He thought about routing the purchasing agent out of bed, checked the clock, saw it was almost two A.M., and decided it could wait until morning.

He went home, plugged the electric blanket in, and crawled under it.

The purchasing agent grumbled, finished his third cup of coffee for the morning, and dug through the file cabinets. "The trouble with this place," he muttered, "everybody's got to be fancy. Couldn't just order matches. Had to get six different kinds for the six different bars. Here." He came up with a folder, then thumbed through order forms and invoices. "Round Table wanted one case. One lousy case, and then they screamed that the color was wrong and bounced it back at me. Nobody would have noticed, but what the hell, I'm the one that has to fight the salesmen, so why not. That what you wanted?"

"Partly. How much of that case went back?" Stannard asked.

The purchasing agent chewed the stem of an empty pipe. "One carton was gone. I checked the case before we sent it back. We got credit for the whole thing, though."

"I want to find that one carton. How many folders would have been in it?"

"Guess all this makes some sense to you. Darned if it does to me." The purchasing agent stuffed his pipe. "Would have been fifty folders. I wouldn't have any idea who took it or when. You might ask down at the Table."

"OK." Stannard eased his hat down on his still-tender head. "Thanks."

The day-shift bartender was also manager of the Round Table. He took Stannard into the small room that doubled as office and liquor storeroom. He dropped into a creaking swivel chair, rubbed his hand across his forehead, and said, "My God. After the busiest week in a year you expect me to remember some lousy matches."

"You sent them back. That should help."

"When I tell Purchasing I want something, I want it right. Hell, they'd have sent kitchen matches if they thought they could get away with it."

"OK, let's do it this way. Just one carton was missing, so the mistake was found quickly. Did you spot it?"

The manager thought a minute. "Not me, I'm just about color blind. Let's see, seems the cocktail girl did. She broke the case to fix up her station and set the tables up. Yeah. I'm sure it was Janie."

"Where do I find her?"

The manager checked a card index, wrote on a pad of paper, and tore the sheet off, handing it to Stannard. "Janie Morrill. Probably find her home now. She worked the late shift yesterday."

Stannard memorized the address, thanked the man, and left.

As he slowed for the gatehouse at the Village exit from the Forest, Stannard spotted a gray Dodge about two hundred feet behind him. He made a couple of random turns on the winding Village streets. The Dodge stayed with him.

He found the street he wanted, cruised slowly until he saw the house, drove past it, and swung into a U-turn at the next intersection. The Dodge passed him, still headed in the opposite direction, and he waved at the driver. The man at the wheel was chunky, with a swarthy face, heavy-rimmed glasses, and a bald spot showing through his black hair.

Stannard wondered who was interested enough in his movements to put Mario Pitarys on his trail. Mario was a private cop with an office in the same building Stannard used. They scratched each other's backs.

He was about to pull into the driveway that curved out of sight behind a clump of lilac bushes when the chromed nose of a Cadillac came out. Its tires howled as the driver trod on the gas and turned down the street. He wore dark glasses, but with the top down and the side of his face still discolored, there was no mistaking Major Harry Bacher.

Stannard clucked his tongue, eased the Ford to a stop in front of the cottage, and got out. It was a small house, rustic, with softly weathered exterior and climbing vines. There were a couple of hundred like it in the Village. Cheap and comfortable except when the chilling fog came up from the bay, and then miserable until oak logs burned in the fireplaces. He rapped on the door.

It was a dutch door, and the top half swung open almost immediately. The woman wore jeans and a sweat shirt. Her hair was prematurely gray, but her skin was unlined. Her features were regular, not unattractive. She waited.

"Miss Morrill?" Stannard touched the brim of his hat and introduced himself.

"I saw your picture in the paper, Mr. Stannard." She swung the lower half of the door open. "Would you like to come inside?"

Stannard went in, took a quick inventory of the house. The living room was small. The sofa and chairs had seen better days, but the slip covers on them were clean. There were prints and some charcoal sketches on the pine-paneled walls, and a small fire burned in the fireplace. Through an open door he saw a small kitchen with a coffeepot steaming on a two-burner stove.

"Coffee?" She was watching him with steady eyes that had a touch of sadness. "So we can act civilized."

"No thanks." Stannard mulled over possible reasons for Major Harry Bacher's scooting off in his convertible as he came up. "What's the crack about being civilized mean?"

Janie Morrill shrugged, disappeared into the kitchen. There was a comfortable roundness to her figure. She came back with a cup of black coffee and gestured toward an overstuffed chair. "Aren't you working for his wife? I can't think of any other reason for you to pop in right after Harry left except to confront me."

"Uh-uh," Stannard said tersely. "I'm working on murder and robbery. What Bacher does has no interest for me."

She smiled as if she didn't believe it. "Then why are you here?"

"Working on what could be a lead. Before I start I better warn you this might get dangerous. For your own good don't mention any of it to anyone. Including Bacher." He showed her the match cover without telling her its significance. "I understand you spotted the mistake. One carton of matches is missing. I want to find it."

She studied his face, nibbled her lip in thought, then shrugged. "Perhaps it makes sense to you. To me it doesn't. Anyway, there's no mystery about who made off with the matches. I took them because I was all out at home."

"I'd like to know how many you have left. Mind seeing?"

The woman went to the kitchen. He heard drawers being opened and shut, the soft slam of cupboard doors. She came back empty-handed.

"I can't find them. They're not in the drawer where they should be."

"Yeah. I thought it might be like that." Stannard got to his feet. "Where's your phone?"

"Now what—"

"If they're here, the cops should find them pretty quick. Maybe a few other things. Shouldn't take long to get a search warrant," he said curtly. "The phone."

"Just wait a minute, mister," she said angrily. "I don't know what you're thinking, but it doesn't sound good. I haven't a darned thing to hide from you or anybody else. So go ahead and turn the house upside down if you want. You don't need any warrant."

Stannard hesitated. Janie Morrill wouldn't have admitted taking the matches in the first place if she had anything to hide. He went into the kitchen and checked a drawer near the gas stove. There were several match folders in it, most of them partly empty. A couple were from the Round Table, but the cover design was different. None of the others appeared significant.

"All right. Maybe someone swiped them, which makes no sense at all. Suppose you didn't bring them home after all."

"But I did. I remember clearly. I had the carton in my right hand when we went out to the car—" Her voice trailed off in uncertainty.

"But you don't remember bringing them in. OK. Whose car was it?"

She shut her eyes, and her lips compressed. She did not reply.

"Bacher's, huh? Got to billing and cooing and it was dark and you just forgot them when you got out."

"No! You're saying Harry—"

"I'm not saying Harry did a damned thing. Except maybe drive off with the bloody matches. God only knows who wound up with them. I mean to find out."

He saw her eyes swing toward the phone that was on an end table by the sofa.

"Be smart," he growled. "Don't call Harry and tell him about this."

"Why shouldn't I!"

"Why?" Stannard paced the floor, glowering. "Because he wouldn't keep his mouth shut. You don't know who wound up with them, so you're safe. He might, and if he does, he's as good as dead if the killer gets to him before he tells me. Get it?"

She sank into a chair, eyes shut tight. Her hands locked together, and he could see the skin around the knuckles turn white.

Stannard went to the door and swung the bottom half shut behind him. Janie Morrill hadn't moved, and he figured she would keep her mouth shut.

He backed the Ford around and drove slowly from the driveway. Mario Pitarys and his gray Dodge waited under an acacia tree at the corner. Stannard parked behind the other car, walked up to it, and slid into the front seat.

"How come?" he asked.

Pitarys grinned. "Twenty-five a day and expenses. Know a better reason?"

"Who's paying?"

"I'll never tell."

Stannard dug his fingers into the heavy shoulder of the swarthy man. "I'm after a couple of killers, chumly. Plus better than four hundred grand. So I damn well want to know who sent you after me. Mario, you know I'll find out. If it means pounding on you, then you get pounded."

Pitarys tried to pull away from the steel fingers. "That straight? You sure you're not working for her?"

"I'm not working for anybody," Stannard retorted. "If you mean Tam Bacher, she made a pitch last night. I told her no go until I get my first job done."

"OK. I guess it figures. Her old man hired me."

"Bacher? How come?"

"She's stepping. He figures she's about to take him. He wants to know who the guy is. And you met her last night."

"Oh, God." Stannard got a cigarette going. "And I guess you figured it was me. Mario—"

"Course I know it ain't you," Pitarys protested. "But she shook me when I tried to tail her from that gin mill last night. Did the same for a city cop. Drives that Mercedes convert like it didn't run right under a hundred. Anyway, I didn't know what else to do this A.M., and when you headed over toward where I knew the Major was visiting his broad, I thought maybe you were working for her after all and about to catch him with the meat in his mouth."

"Oh, brother." Stannard puffed irritably on his cigarette. "I don't suppose you ever did pick her up again."

"Naw. I know when she got home. Four-thirty in the A.M. She was up to something."

"Brilliant."

"Oh, hell. I mean she had somebody with her. Not when she finally drove in. I heard the car drive up that road on the hill behind the house and stop a couple of minutes, then start up again. She looped around and came home."

"So find out who lives up there, and you've got the field narrowed down. At twenty-five a day it should take a couple of weeks," Stannard said.

"You don't care, huh?"

"I don't care one little bit." Stannard opened the door, got out, and went back to the Ford. He thought he might as well hunt up Major Harry Bacher. Bacher had had enough time to fret about why he had apparently been tailed to his girl friend's house.

Bacher slumped deep in the leather chair behind the sleek desk. He drummed his thick fingers nervously on the padding of the arms and worried the stub of a cigar with his teeth. His jaw clenched, and his eyes burned at Stannard. The steady sound of typewriters filtered through the wall between the inner and outer offices.

Stannard tossed his hat on the desk, settled into a chair, and waited.

"I've got nothing to say to you or any other goddamn snooper," Bacher rumbled.

"I wasn't tailing you," Stannard said mildly. "If you want to play house, that's your business."

"So why were you there?" Bacher leaned forward, spreading his hands on the glass over the desk. "Let me tell you something, Stannard. Leave Janie alone. Bother her one more time, and I'll beat the hide off you, old as I am. I mean it!"

"I guess you do at that," Stannard began. "But I—"

He was interrupted by the opening of the door. Dick Husted popped in, dismissed Stannard with a glance, and said, "Sir, we've got that Surfside escrow agreement ready to go, and I'd like—"

"I'd like you to get the hell out and do your own work, you fat idiot!" Bacher barked. "Every goddamn time—"

"Sorry—sorry. See you later." The door clicked shut, but not before Stannard saw the flush of anger on the chubby cheeks, the narrowing of the eyes in hate.

"Wouldn't stand up to a cocker spaniel pup!" Bacher snorted. He swung his glare back to Stannard. "Now that you and I understand each other, why don't you get the hell out, too?"

"Because I didn't come here for what you seem to think," Stannard retorted. "Suppose you shut up and listen. I'm not Husted, and I might just bust you one in the mouth if you don't."

Bacher grinned then. "Well, pick the side that isn't fat already. Go on— I'll listen."

Stannard asked about the carton of matches and warned Bacher to keep his mouth shut about them.

"Stannard, I was a provost marshal before you were old enough to play with toy soldiers. I know when to button up." He rocked back in the chair, eying the ceiling. "If you want the truth, I don't even remember seeing any matches. If Janie said she left 'em in the car, I believe it. But I had a busy week, and anybody could have picked them up."

"Name some names."

Bacher swung from side to side in the chair. "No point to it. I lent the car out a lot to people working on the tournament. Probably twenty times anyway. My wife has keys to it, of course, and I know it was used by our house guests from time to time."

"Oh." Stannard reached for his hat, wondering if there would be any lead in the case that didn't head to a blank wall. "Well, see you."

"Good enough." Bacher reached for a Manila folder, paused. "One more thing, Stannard. We seem to lock horns a lot. But don't think you want those hoods and the money a bit more than I do. OK?"

"Sure, Major." Stannard turned the doorknob.

"Oh—my boys turn up anything since the house?"

"If they have, I haven't heard."

"If it's there, they will. Will Deck's got a mind like an IBM machine. And Jack Taggart's not exactly stupid."

"You think a lot of them."

"I respect their ability," Bacher said softly. "But I never did like them worth a damn!"

CHAPTER 10

Stannard clucked his tongue. "People I don't like don't get invited to sleep in my house and drink my liquor."

Bacher rocked back in the chair and closed his eyes for a moment. "I didn't exactly invite them. But if they're going to be around the Peninsula, I'd just as soon have them where I can keep an eye open."

His eyes went to a framed picture on the desk, then he looked past Stannard out a large window that gave a view of the small bay and the mountains on the far side. Stannard dug his hands into his pockets and moved around until he could see the picture. It was a shot of Tam, in snug western riding clothes, astride a palomino horse.

"OK, Major. There's just the two of us. Let's wring it out." There was a quiet hardness to his words.

"I—I don't know—" Bacher crushed his cigar in a bronze ash tray, opened a drawer, and removed a bottle of Scotch and two glasses. Stannard shook his head, and Bacher poured a stiff shot. "Stannard, just what are you thinking?"

"That you've got a monkey on your back. Partly your wife. Partly your old buddies Deck and Taggart. You're afraid of them, Major. Not the way a coward is afraid maybe. But you expect something to happen. Something you can't stop. Or maybe it's already happened. How about that?"

"It's a personal thing," Bacher said wearily. "I don't discuss my personal affairs."

"This time you do," Stannard retorted. "You say you didn't invite Deck and Taggart, but they were here. OK, so your wife did. They're slick and smooth. Too damned slick and smooth. They push themselves into this case because they're such good friends of yours, and they turn up this hideout that still smells phony to me. You hire Mario Pitarys to keep an eye on your wife. And I can tell you something else, because if I take the job on you'd get the word as soon as I started digging: your wife thinks you've been ratholing her money and wants me to find it for her."

"The bitch." It was a sick whisper. Bacher gulped another shot.

"You better tell me about Deck and Taggart. Captain Moss is having the Indiana authorities take a good close look at them anyway." Stannard banged his fist on the desk and glowered at Bacher. "Yes or no—do you think that pair could have pulled that stickup and killed that cop?"

Bacher looked at Stannard with dead eyes. "No. I can't believe that."

"Why?"

"Because I know where at least one of them was at the time."

"Not of your own knowledge, you don't. You were in that car with me. Remember?"

"Nevertheless, I do know. I can prove it if necessary."

"Yeah? Which one?"

"Will Deck."

"We'll see. That still leaves Taggart. And those other two, as long as we're on the subject. What were their names, Davis and March or something?"

"Claude Davis and Marvin Marsh." A short, bitter laugh slipped through Bacher's lips. "Also present and accounted for. Actually, I don't know where Jack Taggart was, but it shouldn't be hard to find out. He played in the tournament. Good amateur. Finalist in the fifth flight. I'd guess he was having some drinks with other players when the holdup took place. Why don't you ask him?"

"I will maybe." Stannard sat down in a leather chair. "Tell me more about Deck and Taggart."

Bacher's shoulders rose and fell in a futile shrug. "They were in my outfit in Europe, as you know. Both excellent investigators. Black markets and theft of government property were our principal concern immediately after the fighting stopped. The materiel those two recovered amounted to millions. They also found some important people before the Russians did. Very cool operators. Intelligence happened to be looking for some German scientists. They were in the rocket business, although we didn't know it at the time. Deck and Taggart stumbled across them. There was no time for formality; the Russians were only a couple of hours behind. So they did a little job of kidnaping, stole a Flying Fort, and lit out for England."

"But you didn't like them. Or you don't like them now, anyway."

Bacher manufactured a weak smile. "You know what they say, Stannard. To catch a thief—"

"Uh-huh. Nobody caught them." Stannard was remembering what Tam had said about the Major's taking home his own share. "I take it they knew Mrs. Bacher in Europe."

"Yes."

The tone told Stannard Deck or Taggart or both had known her well.

"They couldn't have come out with too much, or they wouldn't be working as private cops now," Stannard said.

"Working?" Bacher snorted a little. "Their agency is one of the biggest in the Midwest. Offhand, I'd say it makes a fine cover. Branches from Chicago to Tulsa. I imagine they don't do much except supervise. They spend winters in California or Florida. Get the picture?"

"Yeah. How about Marsh and Davis. Same deal?"

Bacher shook his head. "They're the have-nots. I doubt if they made a dime out of the war. Marsh is a doorshaker in Los Angeles, and Davis is a house dick in a big hotel there."

"So why are they here? The old-home-week gag looks kind of thin about now."

Bacher pursed his lips. "They're here because Deck and Taggart are here." He stood abruptly. "Anything else?"

"Not at the moment." Stannard went to the door. "See you later, Major."

Bacher did not answer. He spun around suddenly in his chair and stared out the window.

As Stannard walked through the outer office, he heard Dick Husted giving a typist hell.

Captain Moss was wearing a glum expression, and he tapped a long finger nervously against the space bar of a typewriter. "Looks like the match thing might not do us much good, Burl."

"Yeah. I think we could find the rest of them without any strain. Probably in Bacher's house or maybe in his car, for that matter. Likely the killers just took a handful and left the rest. From what he says, a lot of people had access to them."

"So. Got anything else to work on?"

"Nothing." He stubbed out his cigarette. "You?"

"A little. Maybe."

"Give."

"I think we found the Rolls. Got a tentative make on the guy who rented it. Probably the one you shot, judging by his size."

Stannard pulled up a chair and waited. Moss slid the contents of a heavy envelope onto the desk.

"The car went out a week ago from an agency in San Fran. Customer gave the name of Fred Harrow, said he was a commercial photographer and wanted to use the car in an advertising series. Of course, there's no Fred Harrow at the address that was on the driver's license he showed, and Motor Vehicles records don't list any license ever issued under that name to anyone who fits his age and description. Anyway, the car was returned Saturday afternoon."

"Another dead end," Stannard groused.

Moss shrugged. "We never figured that car was used in the stickup anyway. But there's more. We've got a picture of the guy."

"*What!*" Stannard sat up straight in the chair.

"Here." He unclipped a small photo from some papers.

It showed a neatly dressed man, possibly close to forty years old, with a round face and eyes that were set close together. His hair was long and combed straight back. He was standing at a counter writing. Stannard had no recollection of having seen the man before.

"The one piece of luck we've had so far," Moss said. "Happens that a few times in the last couple of years smart characters rented cars from that agency with fake credentials and used them in committing crimes. So the manager hid a camera behind a partition, and he takes pictures of everybody that rents a car now. We shot copies off to Sacramento, and CID may turn up something in the next few hours."

"Let's hope. Give it to the papers yet?"

"No. I'm wondering if we should. *If* this is the dead guy, it might flush the others before we're ready for them."

"Uh-huh. We were guessing the killers were local and couldn't afford to leave this one behind when he was taken dead because we'd make them through him. Now I don't know. This is a pretty good picture, and he's a new one on me."

"Me too. We could sit on it a day or two longer. Photo lab's making up copies, and we'll show them around in the usual places just in case."

"Sounds good. Still staking Bacher's house out?"

Moss grimaced. "Hell, no. Do it right and you've got twenty men tied up around the clock."

"Nothing going on?"

"Too much going on. None of which looks like it's any of our business."

"Like?"

"Like this. His wife goes out, heads for the Hill gate. One of those guys that's staying there, the one that looks like a hound dog, tippytoes after her."

"That'd be Marsh."

"Yeah. Well, then Mario Pitarys drops out of a tree somewhere and takes off after both of them. Next we get Deck roaring off in the opposite direction with Bacher's *other* pal shadowing *him*. Twenty minutes later Deck and the broad are ordering lunch in Slat's place on the wharf, and the three shadows are drinking beer together across the street. And the guy I got on it is mad because he can't have a beer too. God!"

"See what you mean. They're having a little trouble at home. I squeezed Bacher, and he just about came out and said his wife and Deck had something going a long time back and managed to keep it alive. She's getting ready to clean him and dump him, and he brought up the others, Marsh and Davis, to root for his side."

"Uh. Taggart's the only one that makes sense. They tell me he doesn't do much but play golf."

"Supposed to be good. Hear from Indiana?"

Moss dug into another folder. "They look OK, damn it. Got several branches and apparently do a lot of go-between stuff recovering loot for insurance companies but don't cut too many corners. Both with bank accounts in the middle five figures. Too much money for the size of their agency, but they report it all to Internal Revenue. Taggart's married, got a couple of kids. Deck was but it didn't go."

Stannard frowned. "Damn it to hell. Until a couple of hours ago, I liked the idea of sitting that pair in some hard chairs and showing them some bright lights."

"But not anymore, huh?" Moss got a pipe out and scraped at the bowl with a knife. "How come?"

"Just the way they are. Too smug, too smooth, some damn thing. I put it on the line with Bacher, asked him if he thought they could have pulled it."

"He said no?"

"Grudgingly," Stannard replied. "I got the impression Deck and Tam were getting in a few chukkers of pillow polo about that time and Marsh and Davis were peeping."

"That just about cleans us out of people."

"Check. But if the dope I've got is straight, it has to be connected with Bacher somehow."

"You sure?"

"I'm sure of this much. There was just one carton of those wrong matches floating around. We found a pack in the golf cart. We can trace the carton as far as Bacher's car. Several more books were in the Hartley house. So?"

"How about Bacher's barmaid? Maybe you blew it with her when you asked about the matches in the first place."

"How so?" Stannard demanded.

"Look at it this way. The heist artists use her to get close to Bacher, find out just what his routine is. They're using the Hartley house, at least part-time. So she has these matches with her one night, and they get left there. Then you show up with your questions, and she does a little quick thinking, says she left them in the old boy's car. With all Bacher had to do, you think he'd be able to say she didn't?"

"You're probably right. He was too busy to notice if someone dumped a sea cow on him," Stannard admitted. "But she said at first she was sure they were in her house somewhere."

"Smoke screen. So she could think."

"You could bring her in and put her through the hoops."

Moss closed his eyes in thought. "I've known Janie Morrill a long time. Frankly, Burl, I just don't think she'd be in it at that." He reached for the phone. "But we'll just keep an eye on her for a while."

"Wouldn't hurt," Stannard agreed. He stood, reached for his hat, and said casually, "Don't suppose you've got any idea how all these fine people are doing financially."

"Of course not," Moss said. He flipped through some report forms. "Dumb cops would never think about an angle like that. Bacher looks in fair shape. I say looks because in the past fourteen months he liquidated a lot of securities. He lives on a pretty high plateau; probably spends a lot more than he makes from pushing real estate; and his wife isn't frugal either. How much he's got hidden I don't know, but what shows is a hell of a lot more than you'll make in one lifetime. Believe it?"

"Sure. I haven't drawn dishwasher's wages so far. Any idea what happened to make him dump his investments?"

"Probably just trying to come out whole when he and his wife get to the split point."

"She wants me to find that dough for her. Go on."

"Deck and Taggart you know about. Claude Davis has worked as a hotel dick for years. Lives in, eats in, owns a car, and has close to eight grand in checking and savings accounts. Marsh rattles doors and makes about the same as you."

"No wonder he looks sad."

"Well, that leaves Husted. He was a salesman, but I guess he couldn't sell women in a logging camp, so Bacher made him office manager. He's got a cottage in the Village and raises poodle dogs. He's got a few bucks."

Stannard's mouth curled in distaste. "I'd like it to be him, Jim, I really would. And damn it, he's clean."

"Well—"

"Sure he is," Stannard growled. "Think he'd have gone anywhere near that car if he thought a stickup was coming off? He would not."

"He had a gun."

Stannard felt his mending scalp. "He sure did. Probably thought it made him a big boy."

"Bacher doesn't seem the kind to keep a guy like Husted around," Moss said thoughtfully. "He's a blowhard, but he's a *tough* blowhard."

"He's an old soldier. He needs someone he can raise hell with without having the guy quit. Husted qualifies."

"Screwball—" Moss broke off as the phone rang. He spoke sharply, cradled it, and headed for the office door. "Well, they found the strongbox. Bushes back of the old caddy house."

"Just now?" Stannard pounded along the corridor, trailing Moss to the police garage.

"Call just came in." Moss cursed as he yanked the door of his car open and dug through his pockets for the keys. The siren howled, and the car rocketed up the concrete ramp. As they swung around the side of the building, Stannard saw two Homicide Division men trot toward a car that waited at the curb. The car bored into traffic behind them, red spotlight flashing. He swung around and watched it through the rear window.

"Yeah. We got the box. We also got another stiff," Moss growled. He swore at a woman driver who ignored the siren, and cut into the lanes of oncoming traffic to get around her.

CHAPTER 11

The caddy house was a weathered frame building, seldom used in the past few years since the new clubhouse had been built. It backed up to a small, brush-choked ravine, and undergrowth had been allowed to encroach on what had once been a broad lawn on the front and sides. Quail skittered through the brush as Stannard and Moss walked past the uniformed cop at the head of the pathway.

"Straight on back, Cap. Path goes around the end of the gulch," the cop said.

They threaded their way through gaunt, stunted trees. Bushes snagged their clothes. The air here was cool and damp and shadowed.

The body lay at the bottom of a sheer bank, the head jammed between two boulders. There was not much blood, but there was nothing neat about the face of Jack Taggart. He was dressed in tweed slacks, a poplin wind-breaker, polo shirt, and golf shoes. A stubby automatic pistol was on the ground a couple of feet from his outstretched right hand. A striped cap with buckle on the back was half concealed beneath the body.

The strongbox was a sullen gray shape nearby. Its lid was open, and it was empty.

Stannard knelt and felt the dead man's flesh. It was chilling but not yet cold. He straightened and stepped aside as the homicide men came down the path. One of them carried a camera. He adjusted the shutter and began taking pictures. Stannard went to the strongbox and looked it over, humming softly under his breath. He looked up at the top of the bank. It was about fifteen feet high at the point where the body lay—an almost vertical drop. Part of the rear wall of the building was visible through the bushes.

"Not too long dead," Stannard said. "Who found him?"

"Guy named Thomas did, about half an hour ago," a harness cop said. "I had him go wait in the cruiser up above."

Stannard approached the homicide team. "OK to look him over?"

One of the detectives glanced at Moss, then said, "Help yourself, Burl."

He rolled the body over carefully. The face and front of the skull were broken and disfigured, the flesh scraped down to raw bone. Only a small amount of blood had seeped onto the ground and the rocks it had hit. There was a slashed hole in the windbreaker, low and close to the center of the chest. Stannard slid the zipper down, stared at the spreading, darkening red wound.

"Knife," Moss grunted. "Straight in the ticker."

"Probably dead before he hit," Stannard agreed. He went to the box. Except for a few small dents, it appeared to be undamaged. There were no signs it had been broken open.

"Let's go see what the guy who found him has to say," Moss said.

W. P. Thomas was a tall man with a scrawny head of hair. He spoke slowly and concisely, as if keeping himself rigidly under control. He smoked a cigarette and looked frequently at his bony hands as he talked.

"I was just out hacking around alone. Just for the exercise. I sliced one good coming up on the eighteenth. Went up high, and the wind took it in through the trees. I was poking around, trying to find it, when I came on a bag full of clubs down in the brush. I thought that was kind of strange. They're good clubs, but even if they weren't, it would have been enough—Well, I looked around a little, didn't see anything until I looked down in that little ravine. I saw the man lying there. It took me a couple of minutes to walk around and get to him. I could see he was dead, and I saw the gun there. I got out of there fast and called the police."

Moss chewed his lower lip. "Mr. Thomas, did you move the body? Or touch anything?"

Thomas shook his head vigorously. "No, sir. I felt him and knew he was dead, and that gun didn't look good to me at all. I didn't waste any time." He crushed his cigarette out. "Somebody said he might have been one of the men in the holdup. That so?"

"Maybe," Moss said. "Come on. Show us just what you did."

They walked with Thomas as he retraced his movements. When they came to the golf bag, Stannard counted the clubs.

"All here," he said. "Looks like he spotted something and stashed his gear."

They went on around the building, walking slowly through the rough grass. Below them the homicide men were taking measurements of the distance between the body of Jack Taggart and the embankment. The dry grass and other vegetation showed no sign of a struggle.

"Will you need me anymore?" Thomas asked finally.

"We'll want a signed statement of what you told us," Moss said. "You can come by headquarters in a couple of hours if that's convenient."

Thomas said it would be and departed, visibly relieved. Stannard and Moss circled the caddy house. They peered through dusty windows at empty rooms. There was no sign that the building had been recently entered.

On the north side, where the brush was thickest, they found a wooden cover pulled off a crawlway opening. It gave access to the area below the house. Stannard knelt and used a pencil flashlight to peer inside. Cobwebs dangled from dusty floor beams, and there was the smell of earth that has been without sunlight for a long time. The light picked up two parallel gouges, each about an inch deep, running back from the opening.

"Well, now we know where they hid the loot," Moss said morosely.

"And not much more," Stannard replied. He pocketed the flashlight and dusted his hands. "If I was in charge of this case, which I'm not, I'd be inclined to haul everybody, and I do mean everybody, downtown."

"I might at that," Moss said wearily. "First I'd like to figure out just what happened here."

"So let's brainstorm it."

Brainstorming involved grabbing at whatever idea passed through their minds, however ridiculous it might appear on the surface, examining its possibilities, and setting aside for later consideration those which might have some value.

"Thieves fell out," Moss said.

"Taggart was in it. Either he tried to grab the loot from its hiding place and was caught by one of the others, or he caught someone doing that and got killed. Could be."

"Taggart wasn't in it but got onto someone who was and followed him. The other guy was faster," Moss said.

"Maybe he figured out where the box was stashed but didn't know who put it there, and he hid out in the brush waiting to see who'd come around." Stannard walked down a little slope to where the golf bag and clubs were concealed. The growth around it seemed to be flattened, as if a man had waited. He inspected the clubs. The four woods were capped with their little leather bags, and the irons showed no traces of recent contact with grass and dirt. "Your men said he spent his time on the course while the others were chasing each other around. Maybe this was the reason."

"A hole in the first part of that," Moss countered. "If he did get onto where the loot was, why leave it there and take a chance on missing whoever came to pick it up?"

"Ummmmm. A point," Stannard conceded. "Suppose Taggart had it figured but couldn't prove his case, decided the only way was to catch his man in the act."

"If he knew something, why didn't he bring it to me?"

"Grandstand play. He and Deck volunteered some help and got kissed off and told off," Stannard argued. "When they found the Hartley house, we treated the thing like it was a phony."

"It was a phony."

"But not *their* phony."

Moss stared at his feet, then cocked his hat over his eyes, walked slowly from the bushes, and swore heartily. "He wouldn't be dead if I hadn't pulled the tails off that bunch."

"If they were still being followed, they'd have stayed away from the money."

"That should make Taggart feel good," Moss retorted as he headed for the police car. "I don't want to take this bunch downtown yet, but I guess it's time for a little informal chat with all hands. I'll have them rounded up and brought to Bacher's place." He used the two-way radio and issued a blanket pick-up order. The headquarters radio operator acknowledged, then added a message from the Peninsula City hospital.

"Ray Keene is conscious, and the doctors say you can talk to him."

Stannard wondered again why hospitals had the reputation of being quiet. They walked through the long, sterile corridors, pursued by a public address system that clamored insistently for doctors and floor supervisors, past a room where equipment was being sterilized in a loud hissing of steam, past a ward where an old man who had lost most of a leg was loudly making plans with his neighbors for a barbecue when he got out.

A green-clad surgeon met them at the door to Keene's room. "Either of you guys bring a bottle?"

"No," Moss said curtly.

"Good. This guy should be dead. We took his head apart and found nothing but booze and little you-know-what's inside. He came out of it an hour ago, and he seems to want nothing but a jug and his nurse."

"OK. How long can we see him?"

The doctor wiped a bead of sweat from his forehead. "Long as you want. But finish the job up now, because we're going to have to put him under for a couple more days. Otherwise he'll get out of here."

"Good enough." Moss led the way into the room. Ray Keene was cranked up in the bed, a wide bandage around his head. He was smoking a cigar and reading his way through a stack of newspapers.

Keene put his paper down and talked without taking the cigar out of his mouth. "Book me or turn me loose, Cap."

Moss glared at him. "You're lucky to be alive."

"In *here*?" Keene lowered his voice and looked at Stannard. "You happen to bring a little jug maybe?"

"Uh-uh."

"What kind of a private dick are you?" Keene grinned and sank back against the pillows. "OK, what do you want to know?"

"Who clobbered you?" Stannard said.

"I'd like to find out too."

"You didn't get a look at him?"

"Nary a peek." Keene touched the bandage on his head and grimaced. "Didn't have any lights on except the one in the office. Got the safe open, dug out that tape, and then I guess I must have heard something or other, because I remember starting to turn. And then *puta*—I'd had it. Next thing I remember is waking up here a couple of hours ago."

"Not much help," Moss told him. "Any idea whether the guy was inside before you got there?"

Keene thought a moment. "He might have been. I would have heard the door open or him walking across the floor. He went south with the tape, huh?"

"Yeah," Stannard said. "You happen to think of anything that might have been on it?"

"Not a thing. Just figures. I think some guy was worried about nothing." Keene picked up his paper again. "Sure rates a lot of space. Getting anywhere?"

Stannard leaned on the edge of the bed. "Losing ground. Another killing this morning."

He told Keene briefly about Jack Taggart.

"Lousy bastards," Keene muttered. "Jack played a lot of golf."

"You knew him?"

"Hell, yes. Teamed with him in a couple of big tournaments a few years back. He could have made it as a pro. Played like a goddamn machine. Pressure didn't hurt his game at all." Keene's cigar had gone out. He scratched a match, relit it, and added: "This hood you killed—find out yet who he really was?"

Stannard shook his head.

"I knew him," Keene said.

"You what?" Stannard eyed him in disbelief. "You never saw him."

"I see his picture right here in the paper." He tossed the top paper on the pile to the foot of the bed.

It was a morning edition from San Francisco. There was a two-column cut of the picture taken by the car rental agency. The cut line tentatively identified the man in the picture as the hoodlum killed in the $403,000 robbery.

Stannard took a deep breath. "Every police department in the state is trying to make this guy, and you calmly say he's a pal of yours. *Who is he?*"

"No buddy of mine," Keene replied. "I don't remember his name, but it wasn't Fred Harrow. But I can tell you this much—he was a bartender out at the Lodge a few years back. Five, six, something like that."

"Then why hasn't somebody recognized him from the picture before this?" Stannard demanded.

"Probably nobody who'd remember him saw it yet. It's not in the local rag." Keene was silent a minute. "Maybe he didn't work around here long anyway. I sort of think I saw him later down south. Maybe San Diego. Hard to say. I meet a lot of bartenders."

"Yeah." Stannard ripped the photo from the paper. "But you don't remember his name, except that it wasn't Fred Harrow."

"That wasn't it, but it's not too far off. Most bartenders you just know by a first name anyhow." He closed his eyes and pressed his fingers against his forehead. "Frank. I think that was it. Frankie something—"

"That could be enough," Stannard said. "We can take it from there." He turned to Moss. "Want to roll it?"

"Might as well."

They said good-by to Keene and went out, gave the high-sign to the doctor they'd talked with earlier, and left the hospital.

"I'll call in and have somebody start looking for this dead bartender's trail," Moss said. "We can go see what stories our people have to tell about who killed Taggart."

"Why don't I try on Frankie while you start asking the questions?" Stannard said. "The business agent for the bartenders' union has been on the job since Repeal, and he owes me a favor."

"Might as well. It'll save briefing the headquarters men," Moss agreed. "But, Burl—no cutting corners. No chasing off by yourself if you turn something up."

Stannard sighed. "You don't trust me worth a damn."

Jim Moss grinned and walked down the hospital steps to his car. Stannard headed for the cabstand in front of the hospital. He had the cabbie take him to the union headquarters.

The business agent teetered in his creaking swivel chair, scratched his bald head, and inspected the flakes of dandruff under his fingernails. He tossed the photo across the desk and shook his head.

"No make on him?" Stannard said.

"Nope. We get a lot of floaters. Maybe I seen him once or twice, a long time back. Hard to say. Or he could have scabbed."

"We think he worked at the Lodge."

"Wasn't a scab then. Lodge's been under contract since we started the union." He lit a battered pipe. "Tell you what. We got files on everybody that ever paid dues here. You want to dig through a couple of thousand cards on guys named Frank for one who worked at the Lodge, help yourself. Find any that look likely, ask Annie out in the front office. She takes the dues, and her memory's a lot better than mine anyway."

Stannard considered the filing cabinets, they covered an entire wall of the front office. He checked them and saw that inactive memberships were filed on a month-to-month basis. It was a job which could take hours, possibly days. He telephoned his office and asked Lee Ellen to come over.

Her blond hair was drawn back in a pony tail, and she wore a blue angora sweater and simple black skirt. He thought he saw little ridges of tension around the corners of her eyes and mouth. She said hello in a voice that lacked emotion.

Stannard showed her the picture and explained what was needed. She nodded and went to the bank of file cabinets without speaking.

He sensed her anger as if it were a living thing. He walked up behind her, kept his voice low, and said, "Just what's eating on you, girl?"

"Nothing." She studied a card, then went on to the next one. "Nothing at all."

"Spill it. What's got you frosted?"

"You have, if you insist."

"That much I know. How come?"

She turned, slowly, and her body brushed lightly against his. She stepped back, as if the contact was distasteful, until her back was pressed against the cabinet. "You went out last night when Tam wanted to see you. That was the last I saw of you until now."

"Oh, for God's sake!" Stannard scowled in anger. "I listened to what she had to say. She went her way, and I checked out what looked like a lead and went home to bed!"

"Home?" There was an emptiness in the word.

"It was after two o'clock. I went to my apartment."

"I wasn't suggesting you did anything else." Her voice was lower, huskier. "You were hurt and sick when you left me. You'd been getting the first decent sleep you've had in a week when Captain Moss called. I didn't expect you to run right back to me. But you could have phoned to let me know you were all right."

"Yeah. It was late. I—"

"If you were concerned about waking me up, you shouldn't have been. I didn't sleep all night."

"All right. I'm sorry," he said urgently. "I'm so accustomed to being alone—"

She shut her eyes. "I realize it. If next time you'll remember—"

"I'll remember."

It was all right then. They went to work on the files.

CHAPTER 12

They worked more than two hours in busy silence before Lee Ellen showed him the card. Stannard had spotted several possibles by that time, only to have each rejected by the graying woman who presided over the front-office desk. The file card was accompanied by a form with the usual information about residence and family, age and physical description. Annie didn't recall the man named, but the record indicated he had worked in the area almost six years ago.

Stannard phoned headquarters, learned Moss was still at Bacher's, and reached him there with another call. "Any break?"

"No break, but nobody's cleared themselves on the Taggart kill yet."

"Got something here," Stannard said. He explained what they had found. "Either it's a fat coincidence, or it gives us our inside man," Moss said. "Think I should bring him in and put him in the sweatbox?"

"Not yet. If we run this one down, we might get a line on the killers without sweating him at all. How about a three-state bulletin asking for a check on all union records? Find out where he worked last, and that could give us the others."

"Good enough. Sign my name to the teletype."

"Check, Jim." Stannard thought a moment. "One more point, just to keep us legal. Suppose I pick up a fistful of search warrants?"

"OK. Have the watch commander swear them out."

Stannard and Lee Ellen went to headquarters, where he dictated the teletype which would go out to all law enforcement agencies in California, Arizona, and Nevada. He included the names of all others involved in the case with a request that whoever turned up anything on the dead man ascertain if he had any known connection with any of the others. It was marked *Urgent and Not for Release to News Media.*

He walked across the avenue to the Courthouse with the watch commander and waited while the municipal judge issued search warrants. He put the warrants into the pocket of his jacket and looked at the sun. About three hours of daylight remained.

"I've got nothing to do until we get some word back," he told the watch commander. "How about letting me take a radio car so you can get me when the word comes in?"

The officer shook his head. He was a lieutenant who had sometimes worked with Stannard, sometimes on other watches. "No can do, Burl. Like to, but you're still on the suspended list."

"OK. So I go get off it."

Lee Ellen waited in the reception room while Stannard went into the chief's office. The chief let him stand in front of the desk a full minute before taking his eyes from a stack of reports.

"What's on your mind, Stannard?" The chief's face was a little flushed, and Stannard guessed he was remembering the last time they had been in this office together.

"I need a radio car. I want to be reinstated for a few hours."

"Just like that." The chief chuckled. Then he laughed.

Stannard controlled his temper. "Captain Moss and I have been working together on this caper. I've spent most of the afternoon digging on something that could break in an hour or two. When the word comes, it'll come here, and I want to be available. I've got a pocketful of search warrants ready to serve."

"Even with you gone, Stannard, the department has better than eighty officers, all of whom can serve warrants. Just leave them on my desk as you go out."

"The hell with you," Stannard retorted. "I'll just trot down the street for a talk with the city editor of the *Herald.* He's got a couple of cars with police radios in them, and for a little of the inside on this case I guess he'll let me borrow one." He strode toward the door.

"Stannard!"

He stopped with his hand on the doorknob, knowing he had won. The chief had made it too difficult for too many *Herald* reporters on occasion. The newspaper would welcome any chance to raise merry hell with the department's administration.

"Yes," Stannard said mildly.

The chief yanked the center drawer of the desk open, grabbed a badge, and tossed it at Stannard. "It still reads 'Lieutenant' across the top, but you're a probationary patrolman on special assignment to me, personally. Get it?"

Stannard laughed, dropped the star in a pocket, tossed the chief a mock salute, and went out. He picked up the keys to an unmarked cruiser car at the dispatcher's desk, escorted Lee Ellen to the basement garage, and drove out.

"I saw his face when you came out," she said. "He could have a heart condition."

"It gets tired pumping blood through all that fat between his ears," Stannard said with a laugh. He turned the radio on and checked with the dispatcher to make sure it was working properly. "Could be a long time between meals. Like pizza?"

"Missing breakfast and lunch, I'd like anything."

He drove to an Italian place on the wharf and radioed his location to headquarters. They went in and dawdled over pizza and bottled beer. Stannard watched the swells surge along the tilted pilings of the wharf, with the sea birds wheeling overhead or floating on the blue-green surface of the water. A fat sea lion paddled around on his back, slapped his flippers, and barked at the tourists who were tossing small fish to him.

Stannard grew restless. After an hour and a half he paid the check, and he and Lee Ellen returned to police headquarters. He stared at the rolls of yellow paper feeding from the teletype printers.

"Nothing yet?" he demanded irritably of the clerk in charge of the machines.

"Negative reports from a dozen or so smaller places," the man said. "Nothing from any major cities."

He looked out the window at the late afternoon traffic, then turned to Lee Ellen. "Think you better go on back to the office. Or knock off for the day if you want."

"Why?" she retorted. "I'd like to see the end of this as much as you would."

"Sure. We don't know yet that the end's in sight. Our man may dummy up, and sweating it out of him could take days. Or there's just a thin chance it's all coincidence and he's clean."

"I don't mind waiting."

"I don't want you there anyway. It could get dangerous."

"I'm sure Captain Moss has enough men on the job to handle it."

Stannard shook his head firmly. "He hopes so. But these birds have killed two men already. They don't want to smell gas. If we can't spring it just right, they'll probably make a break, and there'll be hell to pay. And face it—we still don't know who they are."

"I'd stay out of the way."

"Staying out of the way of bullets can be tricky," Stannard said. "I'm not about to argue. Come on downstairs. I want to take a look at the limousine."

They went downstairs to the garage, where the wreck of the Cadillac was stored in a corner. Stannard borrowed a flashlight from the attendant, switched on the powerful overhead lights, and stared at what was left of the once-sleek black car.

There were dark brown stains on the front seat and upholstery and Stannard remembered the quick, violent death of Norm Keyes. Anger welled in him, and he thought impersonally that some of the blood was his own. He counted seven bullet holes through the body and window glass and thought of the way a couple of slugs had tugged at his clothes when the shooting began. He yanked the twisted right-hand front door open, and little pieces of broken glass dropped to the concrete floor. There was a bullet hole high in the dashboard, and he thought of Dick Husted and his damned .45 and the way Husted had yelled that he was going to get the robber who was coming in on them from the right.

Stannard thought ruefully that it was just as good that Husted had creased him with that first wild shot. Otherwise he'd have kept triggering his stubby .38 at the hood with the shotgun, and the second one would have filled him with lead from the other side. Stannard looked at a second bullet hole, lower, below the instrument panel. He smiled grimly.

"Lieutenant Stannard, teletype room, please."

Stannard slammed the door as the squawkbox blared his name. He took the stairs two at a time, Lee Ellen's heels rapping on the hard steps behind him. The message-center man handed him the carbon of a teletype from the Los Angeles Police Department's Hollywood Division.

"Call Captain Moss yet?" Stannard snapped as he read it.

"No, sir. Just about to do it."

"Don't," Stannard ordered. "That house is lousy with extension phones. I'll scram out there right now!" He ran for the exit leading to the parking lot.

"Burl—wait!" Lee Ellen was close behind him.

"Hey—forgot about you," he said, spinning around. "Come on." He grabbed her arm and ran her down a long corridor. He came to an interrogation room, pulled the door open, shoved her inside. "Sorry, kid."

The room had only the single door, and there was no knob on the inside. Stannard heard her beat on the door and call his name in fury. As he ran past Communications he yelled, "You can let her out in ten or fifteen minutes."

He drove the cruiser car hard on the four-mile run to the Hill Gate of the Forest, using one hand on the wheel as he radioed for additional cars to block the various exits. He let the siren die as the car slued between the stone wall and the gatehouse.

There were other cars parked in the circular driveway in front of the Bacher house. Jim Moss's, one from the dick bureau, a cruiser with white shield on the door, Bacher's Caddy convert, a station wagon, and Tam's Mercedes. Stannard took the keys from the ignition, re-read the teletype, left the car, and walked slowly up the broad steps to the impressive front entrance of the house. He checked his .38 to make sure it slid freely from its holster.

He opened the door, stepped inside, and saw the people grouped in the vast living room off the foyer. Major Harry Bacher pouring brandy from a decanter. Tam, tall and sleek, with the setting sun that shone through the window striking highlights in her black hair. Marvin Marsh sitting at one end of the leather sofa, looking as morose as ever, and Claude Davis beside him, blinking behind his glasses. Dick Husted, pouting, watching first one and then another distrustfully with his close-set eyes. Will Deck, tall and blond and looking like an ad from *Esquire*, but with a tight fury in his face. The dick bureau team with their heads together at a small writing table as they read over the pages of a shorthand notebook. A couple of uniformed cops, standing around and looking tense and bored at the same time.

Jim Moss came up to Stannard and took the teletype message from his outstretched hand. He read it, then gestured toward an adjoining room. They went in and shut the door behind them.

"I guess this gives us one," Moss said. "Our inside man. We can pound on him a little, and he'll tell us who the others are."

"If he knows," Stannard said doubtfully.

"Of course he knows. Why wouldn't he?"

"Because there's no need for him to know. He had just one purpose in this thing—timing it. I've been thinking about that business at the Hartley house some more. The more I look, the more I figure it wasn't intended to fool the police but to make our boy think the two bandits who got away were a couple of other guys. Look at it this way, Jim. If you were setting up a caper like this, would you expose yourself to the one guy who's going to stay behind? When that guy would probably break down under pressure? How about it?"

"Could be right," Moss said uncertainly. "Well, do we take him now or let that whole bunch stew some more?"

"How's it gone so far?"

"Lousy for us. Nobody's got a solid alibi for the Taggart kill. About the time it happened, the whole bunch was milling around the Lodge. Either in the bars or the shops or Bacher's office. All within a few hundred feet of the old caddy house. None can cover the entire half-hour or so when it happened. We can't pin it on any one of them or clear any one either."

"One of those things," Stannard said. "Well, I guess we've got to work it from the stickup itself. You can take one look at what the LAPD sent up and figure who the others are."

"Set yourself up for a jolt, Burl. We just spent a sickening hour and a quarter hearing why it couldn't be."

"You serious?"

"Yeah." Moss ran his fingers across his forehead. "We just played a tape recording that started half an hour before the stickup and finished about forty-five minutes after it. I don't know how the Major stood there and took it, but he did. Never flinched, never looked at them. Just poured a couple of drinks in a military manner."

"What is this?" Stannard demanded.

"His wife and Deck. While the Major and you and Husted were getting the money straightened out, they were up in her room. God, the sounds people make, the things they do with each other—Oh, hell. She was trying to finagle Deck into taking her with him. I guess they've done the sex bit before. She wasn't about to make the grade though. He kissed her off, but in a way that let her think there might be a chance later."

"Uh," Stannard said. "I suppose this recording was made by Marsh and Davis?"

"With pictures yet. Moving pictures. From the attic gable that looks in on her room. Christ!"

"So it looks like that takes care of everybody," Stannard grunted. "What's that leave? Grab our inside man, try to make a case on him? He could know more than we figure."

"I guess so." Moss handed Stannard a set of handcuffs. "You put the irons on him. I'll watch the rest of the faces."

"OK." Stannard hefted the cuffs. "Just for fun, you shake all hands down for artillery?"

"They're clean."

"Let's take him."

CHAPTER 13

Stannard went back to the living room and walked directly to the deep chair where Dick Husted sat. "Get up," he ordered. "Hold out your hands."

"Why—?" Husted's mouth twisted, and he seemed to sink deeper into the chair. His fingers splayed out on the arms, clutching for something solid.

Stannard grabbed him by the front of his coat and jerked him to his feet. Husted's arms flailed, and his fists beat uselessly on the big man. Stannard released him and drove a fist into Husted's midsection. Husted cried out and bent double, clutching at his stomach. Stannard clamped the cuffs on his wrists, then shoved him back into the chair.

He was aware of others crowding around, all talking at once in surprised voices. He saw tears well in Husted's eyes just before the fat man brought his hands up in front of his face.

Major Harry Bacher, still holding his glass of brandy looked hard at him and muttered, "My God—he couldn't have."

"The charge is murder and conspiracy to commit armed robbery," Stannard said, looking in turn at each of the shocked faces. "Want to tell us about it, Husted? Tell us who the others are?"

Husted lowered his hands. His eyes were red, bloated. "You can go to hell. I'm not saying anything without a lawyer."

Bacher stepped up to him. The hand which held the brandy shook for an instant, then hurled the liquid into Husted's face. He half-lifted Husted, shaking him, and barked, "You sniveling worm, if you've got anything to do with this, you better start talking quick because I'm going to pound you to jelly in about half a min—"

"You'll go sit down, Major," Captain Moss interrupted. He shoved between the two men, elbowing Bacher aside.

Bacher glowered, his fists clenched. "I don't see how he did it."

"We're not too sure," Moss admitted. He studied the intent faces. "We can make a few guesses right here."

Will Deck cleared his throat. His eyes were fixed on Husted. "One question, Captain," Deck said in a cold, controlled voice. "Do you mean *that* knifed my partner?"

Moss shrugged. "He could have. But as far as we've found out, so could a lot of other people, including yourself. The murder we're booking him on is that of Officer Norman Keyes."

"That's crazy!" Husted shouted. "I was with Stannard and the Major and the officer in the car! I tried to stop the killers. I shot it out with them, and

I could have been killed myself!"

Stannard snorted unpleasantly. "You damned near shot my head out from between my ears is what you mean!"

"No." Husted clenched his manacled hands, tried to rise, then fell back in the chair. "I was trying to save the money. I—"

"I just took a good look at that car," Stannard said flatly. "One of your slugs went low in the dashboard and the other punched through the floorboards. Tough to explain if you were aiming at someone outside the car. Yes?"

Husted began to sob. His heavy, flaccid body shook, and he sat forward, head held in his hands.

"Cop out," Stannard snapped. "They crossed you, didn't they? Told you it could be done without any shooting, that all you had to do was slow the money count so we'd be at the right place at the right time. Looked like no strain at all for you, no risk." Stannard shook his head, smiling grimly. "Didn't work, though. There was killing instead."

Husted shook his head, ran his fingers through his hair, then looked up and stared mutely at Stannard.

"A cop died. So did a bartender from LA. The hoods took him with them because they were afraid to let us find his body and identify him. Well, we found it, and we identified him. Know who it was?" Stannard grabbed a fistful of Husted's hair, twisted his head up until he was looking straight into the little wet eyes. "*Know who he was, Husted?*"

Husted swallowed noisily. He tried to shake his head.

"He used the name Fred Harrow. We figure he was Frank Husted. We figure he was your brother. Right?"

A tortured sound came from Husted's throat. He nodded his head violently. "My God—that's about it, damn you! *But I didn't kill anybody!*"

"Your guilt's the same as that of the man who used the shotgun, under the law," Stannard told him. "Play it right, tell us who the others are and turn state's evidence, and you might get off with twenty years. How about it?"

Husted removed his glasses and scrubbed awkwardly at his eyes with his knuckles. He replaced the glasses and looked intently at each of the people in the room. Stannard watched their faces as his eyes sought them, but he could read nothing positive in the expressions.

"I don't know," Husted blurted. "I'd tell you if I knew, but *I don't know!*"

"Maybe he'll remember before he gets to Death Row," Captain Moss interrupted. "Take him downtown."

"No—good God, I'm telling you the truth," Husted pleaded. "I never met any of them."

"Just your brother, huh?" Stannard said.

"Yes. Frank contacted me, said they had a way figured out to take the receipts and all I had to do was make sure we didn't leave too soon with the money. I never met the others." He gulped. "I never even saw the money—any of it!"

"You're a lousy liar," Stannard said mildly.

"I didn't!' Husted protested. "I'm telling you all—!"

"You're telling us a couple of killers whom you never saw and couldn't possibly identify were worried enough about your neck to stick theirs out and cart your brother's body away so there'd be no way to tie you into the job," Stannard barked.

"Yes!" Husted screamed the word.

"OK. Play it that way, and you're as good as sniffing gas. How about Taggart, you kill him?"

"No. I didn't even see him today."

"Let's go back to the night of the robbery. Who smacked Keene and me in the pro shop?"

"All right, I did that. Now will you believe me when I—"

"*Why?*" Stannard shot back.

Husted scrubbed his hands together and muttered, "I heard you call him from the Round Table. Frank was the one who went down and rented the cart. From what I overheard it sounded like you really had something. I got in there first and hit Keene after he got the safe open. If you'd been a couple of minutes later, I'd have been gone."

"You didn't know then that it was your brother I got with the chopper?" Stannard asked.

"No—I thought it might have been."

Captain Moss cleared his throat abruptly. "Sounds like he's ready for a ride downtown, Burl. Open charge," he added to the uniformed cops. "Take him in."

Husted tried to argue. A cop dragged him from the house by the collar. Stannard and Moss frowned as the car with the shield on the door backed around and moved down the drive.

"Couple of days and he'll break," Moss said softly.

"I think he broke already," Stannard replied. "He can't get himself in any deeper, and he's not the type to take a fall for anyone else."

Moss scowled. "Well, then all we've got for our trouble is a lousy accomplice. Still missing two gunmen, one of whom presumably used a knife on Taggart. And better than four hundred grand."

Stannard looked around the room. "Let's get away from these people and wring it out a little longer. Maybe we'll come up with something."

"Yeah. Bring the warrants?" Moss asked.

Stannard took them from his pocket. "Here. Want to shake the place down now?"

"Yeah," Moss said glumly. "But the best way to find that loot is find the guys who took it and beat on them until they decide to say where it is." He called Bacher and his wife over and handed them a search warrant. "We're going to search your house. Any objections?"

"I can't see where there's any reason for—" Tam began. Her eyes shifted to the tall figure of Will Deck and back.

Bacher's big right hand hit the side of her face with a sound like a rifle shot. Tam screamed and careened across the room, sprawled on the sofa. She lay there, her skirt riding up over her knees, hair streaming wild over her shoulders, eyes narrowed in fury.

"You can shut up," Bacher said curtly. "If the police don't want to talk to you, you can get out. I'll have your clothes shipped to you!"

Will Deck grinned and chuckled softly. Bacher started for him, but Moss blocked his way.

"Hold it, Major. You can settle your family matters later," the detective said.

"Of course," Bacher said, flushing. "I'm sorry."

Tam sprang from the sofa. She ran at Deck, and her fingers slashed at his face, and she screamed: "You weaseling bastard!"

Deck slapped her away and stepped back. His fingers touched his face and came away smeared with blood.

A cop grabbed Tam and pinned her arms behind her. She struggled momentarily, cursing steadily in a low voice. Then she quieted, stared at Moss and Stannard, and said, "You see how the civilized upper classes live in this lovely Forest. I think the Major is right, that I had better leave."

"Sit down and behave," Moss ordered. "I don't think we're letting anybody leave for a while." He called over the detectives, who had been taking shorthand notes, and instructed them to start searching the house and grounds. He took Bacher aside and said quietly, "Major, can we use a room for an hour or so?"

"Certainly. My study, at the end of the second-floor hall," Bacher replied. He chewed his cigar and looked at Moss thoughtfully. "I want to do anything I can to cooperate. But I want to protect myself, too."

"Meaning you want a lawyer?" Stannard asked dryly.

Bacher reddened. The muscles of his jaw bunched up, and he snapped, "I don't believe I'll need one."

"You can call any time you change your mind," Moss told him. "Let's go upstairs."

Bacher mixed a highball at the small bar in the study and climbed up on a stool. He lifted the glass and said bitterly, "Here's to me. My wife's a slut and my office manager's a thief and I'm an ass."

Stannard grinned in sympathy and said, "You didn't mention your old war buddies."

Bacher released an empty laugh. "Well, Taggart's a corpse and Deck's a lover and Davis and Marsh are—just Davis and Marsh, I guess."

"That all?" Stannard said softly.

Bacher swallowed most of his drink. "I can say one thing for Will and Tam, they deserve each other."

"Uh-huh," Stannard said. "Likely so. Tell you something else that's likely: one or more of them is involved in the robbery."

Bacher slammed his glass on the bar, dropped fresh ice into it, and poured more liquor. "I'm almost ready to wish it could be that way. But the only one who isn't positively accounted for at the time is dead."

"So Captain Moss said," Stannard replied. "Let's go over it now and see."

Bacher slid off his stool, walked to a window, motioned Stannard over, and pointed. "See that big casement window, third down in the left wing? My wife's room, Stannard." He pivoted and pointed upward at the sloping, gabled roof of the house. "See that attic window?"

"I see them."

"Well, you can look through the attic window and see anyone in the bedroom. Without going into unnecessary and embarrassing detail, I'll say my wife and her friend were in the bedroom. For a prolonged period. Davis and Marsh had rigged a tape recorder and equipped themselves with a motion picture camera. Result: everyone accounted for."

Stannard turned it over quickly in his mind. "All of which doesn't establish any time element at all as far as I'm concerned."

"If you're suggesting I faked—"

"I'm not suggesting anything yet," Stannard cut in. "But you've had some police experience, Major. Granted your wife and Deck engaged in a mutual display of affection. We can presume it wasn't the first time. Which makes it possible the pictures and recording were made earlier. Yes?"

Bacher turned away from the window and went back to the bar. "Oh, it wasn't the first time," he said quietly. "I imagine the first time was a good many years ago. I think Tam would have left me any time Will asked her to. But he's the type who won't buy a cow as long as he's getting free milk. Which is beside the point. The point is, there's no question of when the picture was made. Or the recording either."

"Tell me," Stannard said.

"Very well. There is a television set in my wife's bedroom. When they had nothing more interesting to do, they watched television. The tournament finals were being shown, and naturally the television sound is on the tape. And the screen is visible in the pictures. So the time element is pretty well established."

"I thought along the same lines, Burl," Moss said. "Until I listened and looked."

"OK, OK," Stannard snapped. He paced the floor, went to the bar, iced a glass, and poured a shot over it. "So Deck and the woman are in the clear. I'm not about to pass Davis and Marsh over on account of it."

"Good God, man," Bacher blurted. "Do you think they hired someone else to operate the recorder and camera while they went out to commit a robbery and kill an officer?"

Stannard tossed his drink down and grinned. "That would stretch it a little. I'm trying to think of a way they could have done it by remote control, but it's got me whipped so far." He poured another drink, lit a cigarette, and climbed onto a bar stool. "Just for kicks, let's go back a little. Tell us why each of these four men came to your house, Major."

Bacher's cigar had gone out, and he took his time relighting it. "You're pretty damned persistent," he finally muttered. "I thought Deck and Taggart were a couple of bulldogs, but you beat them any day, Stannard. All right—I hope this is the last time I have to tell it."

CHAPTER 14

"It started over a year ago," Bacher said. "I had a phone call from Davis in Los Angeles. He's security officer in one of the top hotels. He told me my wife was there. With Deck. He asked me if I wanted anything done about it. I was wild for a few minutes; then I calmed down and asked him to just keep an eye on them and see if they were up to anything beyond the obvious. It was just coincidence they had chosen that hotel, I'm sure. Anyway, Davis kept out of sight. He had their rooms bugged and picked up pieces of information from the bellhops and others on the hotel staff.

"It was quite a report. Will Deck has always had a lot of success with women. Tam was determined to leave me and go with him. Apparently Deck tried to discourage her. He's too smart to get himself too tangled up. Tam claimed she could give him much more than he'd ever make out of his agency. She told him she'd clean me out and then leave me to live with him. He treated it as a joke and told her to look him up when that happened. With that much to go on, I started to work."

"In what way, Major?" Stannard asked.

"Protecting myself. Tam came to you with some cock-and-bull story about me squirreling her money away. Let me tell you this, Stannard: what little money she had in her own name she spent years ago. This is a community property state, and unless I could make a pretty bad case against her in court, she'd be able to take me for at least half of what I'm worth. In the circumstances, I didn't intend to hold still for it. I've played dumb with her for over a year. In that year I've put well over a million dollars where my wife—or a court for that matter—will never get to it. It took time and it took patience and it's done right. If you don't believe it, try looking."

"Yeah," Stannard agreed. "But what's all this got to do with the case?"

"Just this. I decided the time had come to break it off in her. Jack Taggart was not only Deck's partner and close friend; he's a top golfer, and he was invited to the tournament. Naturally, I invited him to stay with us. Of course Deck would come too. I pretended I'd just heard from Claude Davis, who was in touch with Marsh. From there it wasn't too big a step to setting up a little reunion of men from the old CID outfit. Davis, Marsh, and I had it all planned. Give Tam and Will all the chances they'd need. Jack was playing golf all the time; I was manufacturing things to do on that idiotic committee; and they'd have this big beautiful ark of a house to themselves for hours at a time. I was sure that with any luck at all we'd get enough evidence to make Tam pack up and get out without making any trouble. It's worked just that way, too."

"Except there was a robbery in which a cop was killed, and Taggart's dead because he figured out who pulled it," Stannard said.

"I still don't see how there could be any connection," Bacher argued.

"Taggart's dead, isn't he?" Stannard growled. "And Dick Husted was up to his fat neck in the thing."

"But Husted was connected through his brother," Bacher said.

"Yeah. I'm thinking about that." Stannard lit a cigarette from the stub of the one in his mouth. "One point, you had the goods on your wife and Deck. No question about it. So why did you hire Mario Pitarys to keep an eye on her?"

"Misdirection. I just wanted him to be seen so that her mind wouldn't be on Davis and Marsh."

"Uh-huh. Well—" Stannard broke off as knuckles rapped on the door. The plain-clothesmen who had been searching the house came in.

Moss and Stannard stepped into the hall with them. The taller one shook his head and wiped at his forehead with a soiled handkerchief. "We don't see anything hot so far," he said. "Might take a full day to go through this place right though. And it would help if we knew just what to look for."

"We don't even know if there's *anything* to look for," Moss told him. "Just flounder around and hope."

"That we been doing," the detective said. "The old boy wasn't kidding when he said they set a trap for his old lady. You should see her room and the one Deck is using. Bugs, bugs, and more bugs."

"High stakes," Stannard said.

"We haven't looked in the attic yet. Door's locked," the detective replied.

Moss called Bacher from the study. "We'd like to take a look in the attic."

"All right. I'll have to get the key." He went off down the hall.

"Where are the others?" Moss asked.

"Downstairs. We restricted them to the living room. Davis and Marsh didn't squawk, but the wife yapped at us until we told her the houseboy could make drinks. Seems to be happy enough now."

Moss shook his head in bewilderment and muttered, "How that man controlled himself—"

"The cool cuckold," Stannard agreed in a whisper as Bacher returned. He showed them a key and led Stannard and Moss up a winding stairway that ended at a narrow door on the top level of the house. He turned the key in the lock, pushed the door open, and explained, "We kept it locked so nobody'd stumble onto the setup."

The attic was a cavernous dark space under the sloping roof. Fading daylight came through from the gable windows. Bacher touched a light switch, and two unshaded bulbs suspended from heavy beams lit up. There was the usual clutter of stored boxes and trunks and furniture. Near one gable an area had been cleared.

There were two old overstuffed chairs flanking a long table. On the table were a large tape recorder, its spools gone now; an electric percolator; the remains of several sandwiches; a large tin can converted into an ash tray; several books of matches; a pad of legal foolscap; and a big motion picture camera equipped with a telephoto lens. A tripod for the camera was under the table. A number of thin wires ran from the recorder to a wall and disappeared in the bare wood.

"You put a lot of dough into this setup," Stannard said.

"Hoping to save a lot," Bacher replied. "Anyway, it's all rented. Marsh and Davis put it together."

Stannard bent and peered through the window. He had a good view of the other wing of the house. He pointed to a window directly opposite but somewhat lower. "That it?"

"That's my wife's room," Bacher said wearily.

As he spoke, a light came on across the way, and Stannard saw one of the detectives who had reported to Moss earlier enter the room and stand, hands in pockets, as he looked around him curiously. Stannard picked the camera up, aimed it at the scene, and found it was sharp in the view finder. Suddenly he said, "How long has this setup been here?"

Bacher thought a moment. "Six days, I believe. Davis and Marsh arrived before the others and installed it. I don't think they got the mikes wired up the first day, however. That had to wait until we could be sure my wife wouldn't return to her room at the wrong time."

"OK," Stannard said. "Captain Moss and I will prowl around here a little longer. You can wait for us downstairs if you want."

Bacher started to reply, then nodded and went out through the narrow door.

Stannard shut it behind him, then walked back to the long table. He put his hands on his hips, clenched his fists, and scowled at Moss.

"These bastards did it," he said flatly.

"Just that easy," Moss said quietly. There was a weak smile on his mouth, and Stannard realized the older man's face seemed to be eroding with the passing hours. "How?"

"Damn it, if I knew how and could prove it, we'd be putting cuffs on them instead of jawing," Stannard retorted. "Take a look here."

He dug into a cardboard carton at the end of the table. It held a half-dozen boxes of recording tape, several reels of sixteen-millimeter film, pencils, scratch pads, and a partly empty box of paper matchbooks. He grabbed a fistful of the folders and held them under the nose of Jim Moss.

"Here they are—those damned matches we've looked all over for. The ones with the wrong color field on the coat of arms. See the scarlet? Should be vermillion."

Moss looked doubtfully at the match folders. "So what's it prove? You tried to run the things down and traced them from Janie Morrill to the Major's car and lost them there. Maybe this is your answer: Davis and Marsh just grabbed the box when they set this place up."

"Just the point," Stannard argued. "They rigged this thing days before the stickup. It figures they didn't make any more trips packing stuff upstairs than they absolutely had to. With what's here they could have staked out as long as they felt like it. There were fifty folders in that carton to begin with." He made a fast count. "OK. A dozen are gone. One turned up in the caddy cart after the stickup. There's maybe half a dozen in that cigarette box over in Hartley's house."

"So?"

"So if we go through that butt can they were using here, I'll bet we find in there all the others, or enough of them so it doesn't make any difference."

Moss closed his eyes in concentration. "It could be. But it's pretty thin, Burl." He took a cigarette from a half-empty pack on the table and lit it. "And you have the tape and movies. Pretty tough to fake, and—"

"Sure. That I know." Stannard felt the heat of excitement spread through him. "They went to a hell of a lot of trouble to cover themselves because they couldn't just take off after it was over. They had to stay around until they wrapped up the job for Bacher. I still haven't figured whether the setup at the Hartley house was supposed to fool us or Husted or both. But something just got through my thick skull a few minutes ago while we were talking to Bacher."

"Well?" Moss demanded as Stannard paused to organize his thoughts.

"First, you think those killers thought enough of Husted to pack his dead brother off and dump him in a blowhole just to cover Dickie? I don't—"

"Well, we agreed on that at the time—" Moss interrupted.

"Sure. So they were covering for themselves one way or another," Stannard said quickly. "Take a good look and it's not tough to figure what that is."

"Brain boy, I've had a tough couple of days."

"Well, the hotel where Davis is house dick. That's where the teletype from LA said Frank Husted was tending bar."

Moss sucked his breath in noisily, expelled it. "Well—that gives it a new look. Ties them up to Frank Husted nice and tight."

"Not by itself. But some routine questions in the right places should do it."

"OK. Let's collar that pair," Moss said, moving toward the door.

"Jim—we haven't got enough yet."

"For me it's enough," Moss insisted. "They'll be ready to tell us where the money is in a day or two."

"I want to know first which one killed Norm Keyes. Be nice to clean up the Taggart kill too."

"Yeah, I know what you want, Burl. Well, I want a nice quick and quiet pinch instead of a couple of dead hoods." He smiled. "And that's the way it's going to be. Coming?"

Stannard didn't answer. He followed the angular figure of Captain Moss along the carpeted hallways, down the broad staircase to the first floor. They stopped side by side in the curtained archway of the living room. Tam Bacher was sitting moodily on a window seat, the full, ripe curves of her body in profile as she stared out at the darkening night. Major Harry Bacher stood straight and solid at the opposite side of the room, within easy reach of the cellarette, his eyes dwelling on the flames that licked and curled around a stack of oak logs in the fireplace. Marvin Marsh, his long, sad face impassive, was sitting on the left end of the sofa; Davis, eyes lidded but alert, was down at the right end. Four or five feet of space separated the two. A single uniformed officer, heavy arms crossed over his chest, stood by the doorway.

"Captain Moss," Tam said, swinging around as they came in, "I feel you have no right to hold me prisoner in my own house."

"Probably don't at that," Moss said amiably. He turned to the uniformed officer and held out his hand. The man slipped his handcuffs from his gun-belt and gave them to the captain. Moss caught Stannard's eye and nod-ded at Davis.

Stannard's fingers brushed the bulk of his holstered .38 as he strode across the long room. Davis had his hands crossed in front of his belly, and he drew his feet in as Stannard approached.

"On your feet," Stannard ordered. "Move quick, killer." He was aware of eyes fastening on him as he spoke.

"Just what—" Davis began.

Stannard's big hands reached, caught the front of the man's sports jacket. From the corner or his eye he saw Moss leaning over to slam a cuff on Marvin Marsh. Davis lunged upward then, and the knife which had been sheathed in the left sleeve of his jacket was in his right hand, point pressing lightly against Stannard's abdomen.

"Hold it now," Davis said. His words were quick and quiet. "Anybody moves, you get it, Stannard."

Stannard swiveled his eyes, saw the uniformed cop, his face flushing with surprise and anger, reach for the service revolver on his right hip, then check his draw as Moss barked a single curt command. Moss was stepping back from Marsh, holding his hands away from his sides. Stannard released Davis, then stood rigid as the man reached under his coat and snapped the stubby .38 from its holster.

"You won't make it," Stannard said quietly.

"It's worth a try," Davis retorted. He flipped Stannard's gun along the sofa and spoke to Marsh without turning his head. "Clean 'em, Marv."

"One at a time," Marsh said to Moss and the uniformed cop. "Take your guns out, drop 'em on the floor, kick 'em over to me. Be smart about it." He looked around. "Then sit on the sofa and behave."

It became intensely still in the room. Stannard's nerves jumped as one of the burning logs popped. He heard the guns hit the floor with soft thumps. The knife was less than an inch from him. He looked at it, saw it was a balanced double-edged throwing blade. Stannard hated knives, particularly at close range. He was trained, he was fast, and if Davis had been hold-ing a gun against his belly, there were ways to go for it that would give him at least an even chance for survival. But there was virtually no chance at all with the knife. The best he could do was grab for the man's wrist, and before his fingers would close, the thin steel shaft would be slicing up un-der his rib cage, slashing his heart.

He controlled his breathing with intense effort and looked straight into Davis' eyes. He saw no sign of fear or hate or anything, except possibly the intent to get out of this room and this house regardless of cost.

"You got Taggart, I guess."

"I got Taggart," Davis agreed pleasantly. "He figured where the dough was. Trying to take us alone was his mistake."

"From up close, like this?"

Davis shook his head. "This is a throwing knife, fella. He never knew it was coming."

"You never did have any guts, Claude." Will Deck spoke from a corner of the room where there was little light. He stepped from the shadows and stood by the fireplace, still tall and controlled and almost elegant in a lean, well-tailored way. "Someday I'll kill you for that."

Davis laughed, and Stannard saw a quick narrowing of his eyes.

Marsh had collected the guns. He snapped the cylinders of the pistols out, let the bullets drop to the rug, and tossed the guns at the fireplace. He held Stannard's .38, still loaded, easily in his right hand. Stannard remembered the dumdum slugs and prayed Marsh wouldn't blow up and use the gun.

Davis eyed Will Deck intently, and Stannard knew Davis believed the thin blond man would hunt him down and kill him some day. If he was left alive. Watching Davis' eyes, Stannard read the decision: Will Deck was going to die. He was going to die by the knife.

Davis moved then, with surprising speed and agility. He leaped backward before Stannard could move and pivoted lightly. Marsh shifted a few feet to his left, swung the .38 in a tight quarter-circle to cover Stannard as well as the others in the room.

Davis wet his lips, forced a grin as he said, "Willie, you always were a tricky one. Wouldn't have a gun on you even now?"

Deck smiled, shook his head. Slowly he unbuttoned his jacket, held it open. He turned in a full circle, letting them see that the spring-clip holster under his left shoulder was empty. He let the coat drop back into place, then stood spraddlelegged, his thumbs hooked over his wide black belt.

"Here's your target, Claude," he said mockingly. "Going to toss it like you did with Jack? Or maybe with Marvin holding a rod on us, you'll get some guts. Enough to walk up and stick it in."

Davis wet his lips, said nothing.

Deck laughed then. "You better throw it, Claude. Because if you get close to me, I'm going to take it away from you. And then I'll cut your throat." He moved to his left, until Davis was between himself and Marsh. "Try me."

Davis swore. Stannard saw his hand flash, and then the knife was reversed as Davis' arm came up and he set himself for an overhand throw.

In that instant Stannard saw the fingers of Deck's right hand blur with speed. The hand never moved from his belt, but there was a gun in the fingers—a gun so small as to appear ridiculous in his big hand.

The tiny barrel flamed twice, the shots so close they seemed to make only one sound.

Claude Davis froze. The knife dropped from his fingers, and without a sound he fell. He dropped straight down, buckling at the knees and hips and landing hard on his rump and then flopping over onto his back. Blood welled from two small holes. One was under the left eye and the other high on his forehead, slightly to the right of center.

Stannard was moving as the first shot was fired.

Marvin Marsh was raising the stubby .38, pivoting to get a clear shot at Will Deck as Davis' body crumpled between them. The heavy gun went off with a deafening violence, but Deck was dropping to the floor behind the sofa then, rolling.

Stannard's two hundred pounds slammed into Marsh, and he grabbed for the hand that held the gun.

Captain Moss and the uniformed cop were piling off the sofa. They dove for the squirming men as the gun went off again. Stannard felt the slug chew through the left armpit of his jacket. There was a sharp, stinging sensation, and he knew it had grazed his flesh.

His fingers clawed, then closed on Marsh's wrist with a terrible force. There was a crunch of bone, and Marsh screamed. Stannard rolled on top of him, bringing the stiff fingers of his left hand down across Marsh's throat.

The scream choked off. He felt the man's body shudder, and Marsh's heels drummed wildly on the carpet in a final spasm.

Stannard raised his hand, ready for another chop. He saw the distorted face, the eyes rolling upward so that only the whites were visible. He checked the blow and rolled off Marsh's body. Moss and the uniformed cop helped him to his feet.

Stannard caught his breath. He looked at the dying man, at the body of Claude Davis, finally at Jim Moss.

"Sorry," he said. "It didn't work out clean and quiet."

Moss shook his head, shrugged. "We're lucky it worked out at all."

There was fresh silence. Major Harry Bacher looked impersonally at the two bodies. Without a word he poured a drink and tossed it off. Then he began to swear, softly, competently.

Tam Bacher remained on the window seat. There was a strange rigidity to her features. Her eyes rested on the dead men, passed over Stannard, and sought Will Deck.

Deck returned her stare. When her eyes dropped, he came up to Moss and handed him his gun. It was a thin .22 automatic just a fraction over three inches long.

"I'd like to have this baby back later," he said.

Moss hefted the gun. He released the clip and ejected the live shell from the chamber. "Guess we can arrange it. I'd like to know one thing though."

"Sure," Deck said.

"My men supposedly picked up all the artillery. One lousy .32 from Bacher was all they got."

Deck loosened his belt, grinning. He slipped it from the first two loops of his trousers and ran a finger into the slit of the watch pocket. He lifted a padded leather holster out. "Right here. There's a spring deal in it. One finger on the release and it pops the peashooter right out. Makes it nice for tight spots."

"Yeah. Nice that you know how to use it too. You may be cool, but you'll bleed as easy as the next guy with a knife or a slug in you."

Deck nodded. He turned away, found the brandy bottle, eyed a glass momentarily, then drank straight from the bottle. He swallowed four times before lowering it. He gasped, then blinked his eyes. "Want the truth? I've never been so damned scared in my life."

"I wondered," Moss said wearily. He looked at the bodies of Marsh and Davis. "Lousy cop killers," he said softly. "I just wish one of them stayed alive long enough to tell us where the loot is."

"Uh-huh," Stannard agreed. He picked up his gun from where it lay on the floor, ejected the cartridges, and reloaded it.

Two doors burst open simultaneously, and the plain-clothes officers who had been searching the house jumped into the room. One held a .38 and the other a riot gun. They looked around and lowered the guns.

"Hell of a time to show up," Moss barked. "Well?"

The one with the pistol holstered it. "We were up on the third floor when we heard shots, Captain. Ben went around to cover the outside, and I took this end. We didn't waste any time."

"Yeah. I guess not," Moss conceded. "All right. Call the coroner to come get these hoods, and tell headquarters to send us some men. We've got to turn this joint upside down and find the loot."

Tam Bacher left the window seat then. She crossed the room with long, graceful strides, without looking at the dead men. "I am leaving this house tonight," she said to Captain Moss. "May I go to my room and pack?"

Moss considered it. "I guess so. We'll want to know where you go."

"Of course, Captain. I believe I'll take a suite at the Lodge." She turned away and went up the stairs. The men watched. At the first landing she stopped and turned, the long, sleek line of her leg taut under her skirt. She smiled mockingly and went on.

Stannard felt a grudging admiration for her ability to carry herself with pride. He lit a cigarette and watched through the tall windows as cars turned into the drive. He saw the black wagon from the coroner's office, two cruiser cars, and his Ford.

Two men got out of the black truck and carried a pair of wicker baskets up the steps. The cruiser cars disgorged plain-clothesmen. Lee Ellen Underwood got out of the Ford and hurried after the men.

Stannard intercepted her at the door and steered her into a room which opened off the foyer. He found a light switch and saw they were in a library.

The girl caught him in her arms, hugged him to her. She kissed him quickly and half laughed, half cried as she said, "Thank God you're safe. But don't think I'm not furious with you for locking me in that room. Your friends stood around and laughed for a half-hour before they let me out."

"Two men died here," he said sternly. "I'd have been in a hell of a spot if I had to worry about you too."

"I know. I know, Burl."

"OK. We'll forget it." He worked her arms loose and stepped back. "Hear anything downtown?"

"They're still questioning Husted."

"How much is Husted going for?"

"Not very much," she told him. "He admits part of it. Just that he held up the counting so that the car would be at the right place at the right time. He claims he doesn't know who was in it except for his brother. Says he didn't even know just how it was going to be done or who planned it."

"He doesn't know Davis and Marsh are dead?"

"He hadn't been told when I left. I came away the minute I heard about it."

"Same story he told here," Stannard said glumly.

"Does it matter now whether he knew or not?" Lee Ellen asked. "The other three are dead."

"Maybe it doesn't," Stannard said. He was suddenly weary, and the pain in his side had started again, probably from flailing around on the floor with Marsh, he thought. "I guess nothing matters now except finding four hundred and three grand."

CHAPTER 15

The newspaper reporters and photographers and television men came and griped because they were not admitted to the house. Captain Moss stood on the front porch and told them what had happened. Flashbulbs flared as the wicker baskets were carried from the house.

Moss went from room to room checking on the progress of the search. Stannard went along, and finally they climbed to the attic and began digging through the stored boxes. Stannard burrowed into the carton on the table which held miscellaneous items Davis and Marsh had brought up there. He paused and frowned, looking out the gabled window. The light was on in Tam Bacher's room, and he could see the dark-haired woman picking clothes off a rack in the closet and carrying them to the big bed. There were two open suitcases on the bed.

Stannard tore the top off an envelope and took out a folded yellow paper. He opened it, read what was written there, and said, "Well, this explains some of it." He showed it to Moss. "Invoice from the place they rented the camera stuff."

"What's that mean?" Moss asked.

"You told me there wasn't any question of when the tape and movies were made, and if Davis and Marsh had made them, they'd have had an airtight alibi."

"One of the things I intend to find out when there's time is just who did that little chore for them," Moss said.

"They did it themselves. With the help of a gadget that's on this invoice as 'remote shutter control and automatic wind,' which sounds like something to make a movie camera run and keep itself wound up by long distance."

"Yeah?" Moss scratched his chin. "There's still the tape."

"So they rigged both of them to some timing gadget. One of those alarm clocks that turns the coffee pot on would do it." Stannard inspected the recorder and looked carefully at the wires leading from it to the wall.

As he spoke, the machine made a clicking sound. An amber light glowed, and one of the tape spindles began to turn.

"What the—!" There were earphones connected to the recorder. He put them on, listened, moved around until he could see through the window into Tam's room.

"Still hooked up?" Moss asked.

"Yeah," Stannard said softly. He listened to the tap of the woman's heels on the floor, heard her hum softly. He watched her switch off a small bedside lamp.

The sound stopped and the recorder's light went out.

Stannard yanked the earphones off. He hurried to the wall and traced the thin wires from the hole to the table. Four were connected to terminals on the machine. The ends of two were loose.

He squatted down, peered at the dusty floor until he could make out the three small circles where the legs of the camera tripod had been placed. He grabbed the tripod, carefully set it in the same position, and picked up the dangling wires. They reached the head of the tripod with several inches to spare.

"Fits much better now," he said. He ran for the door, with Moss close behind him.

"What bug's bit you now?" Moss demanded.

Stannard ignored him. He reached Tam's room, twisted the knob, and kicked the door open.

Tam was between the bed and closet. She screamed and dropped an armful of clothes. She saw Stannard's face and leaped for the huge bed, hand plunging under the nearest pillow.

The gun was a silver-plated .32 automatic with pearl grips. It was inches from Stannard's head when she pulled the trigger.

Nothing happened.

She said a short, explosive word and clutched the gun in both hands. Her face was contorted, and he could see the knuckle of her trigger finger was dead white.

Stannard was diving for her, grabbing for the gun with a big hand. He hit the bed, and his momentum carried them off the far side.

She was strong and limber, and Stannard had an impression of trying to capture a tiger bare-handed. She writhed against him and brought a knee up hard in his groin. Stannard gasped in pain and hung on, not wanting to hit her, trying only to hold her down and pin her arms. The gun raked his face, and he caught the hand that held it, twisted. The woman screamed, and the gun dropped from her fingers and bounced across the rug.

Stannard rolled, got his weight on her, fought her arms behind her back, and locked them there.

"Burl—for Chrissakes." Moss was circling them, amazement on his face.

"Shut up and get some irons on her!" Stannard shouted. She twisted her head up and sank her teeth into his right cheek. He yelled and jerked back.

Moss dropped to his knees and quickly manacled her wrists behind her back.

Stannard rolled away from her and got to his feet. Tam kicked at him and cursed in a foreign language. He stood there, chest heaving as he caught his breath. He heard booted feet pounding along the hallway as he said, "Kick and cuss all you want, woman. You're not going anywhere."

The room filled with people. Police and the houseboy and Major Harry Bacher and Will Deck. Tam picked herself up. The skirt which had been twisted around her thighs dropped into place, and she let herself fall across the bed. She began to cry.

Bacher stared at his wife, then at Stannard and Moss.

"Everybody outside," Moss ordered before Bacher could speak. "You can stay, Major. Deck, too, if you want."

The others went out, and the door closed. Moss eyed Stannard as if he wasn't sure just what to do next. Finally he said, "Let's hear it, Burl."

"Got to find a couple of things first," Stannard said. He went over the room quickly, found the place under the wall-to-wall carpeting where the thin wires led in. He followed each down, located a small microphone in the bookcase headboard of the bed. The headboard had two built-in reading lamps and an electric clock-radio. Two wires led to the base of a lamp and two others to one of the switches on the radio. He looked at the curious faces and at the bitter mask of Tam Bacher.

"The timing was too good," he said. "Once the Captain and I figured out Davis and Marsh didn't actually make the recording and those pictures, the timing was just too good. Conceivable they could have started the recorder before they went off on the stickup, but that camera was the final touch. It had an automatic wind and shutter release rigged, but the magazine holds only enough film for about four minutes' shooting. From what I understand, it picked four important minutes to work. Yes?"

Bacher shot a glance at Will Deck. He nodded curtly.

"Plus this. It began to look like somebody else was in the thing. Husted claims his only contact was through his brother. I'm inclined to believe it; he's not the kind to take anybody else's falls. Davis and Marsh couldn't have known enough about the way the tournament was being run to set the thing up. Remember, Dick Husted said his brother Frank came to *him* with the plan of how to work the stickup. So who had made the deal with Davis and Marsh?"

He looked directly at Tam. She compressed her lips into a bitter red line.

"Who needed money? Tam. Who was close enough to the Major to know just how everything was being handled? Tam. Who could set up a nice tight alibi for everybody by just turning a couple of switches in this room as she entertained Deck? You fill the rest in; I'm sick of it."

Moss studied the woman silently, then said, "I'll phone downtown for a matron."

"Just a second," Major Harry Bacher said quietly. He walked over to his wife. Red fury boiled in his heavy face as he picked her from the bed and stood her on her feet.

She tossed her black hair, stood with legs apart, and glared defiance.

The back of his hand slammed into her mouth. She screamed and fell back across the bed. Her dress flared over her knees, and blood gushed from her smashed lips.

Moss and Stannard grabbed for Bacher. He shook them off, yanked his wife from the bed, and hit her again.

"Speak, you bitch. Say what you did with the money, or I'll beat you to death, and no man in this room will stop me!" He grabbed her hair in his fist and twisted her head around until she was looking directly into his eyes. "Tell us!"

Blood leaked from her mouth. Her jaw worked once, twice, before she said, "The express office. In the city. Addressed to me."

Bacher dropped her and stalked to the door. He yanked it open, started out, then spun around. He met each of their eyes in turn. He drew himself up, a big, aging man stamped by the military life. "When you want me, I'll be waiting."

He went out, closing the door softly behind him.

"I guess I can go now, too," Stannard said. He did not look at the crying, bleeding woman on the bed.

Moss caught up with him at the door. "Burl. Sometime in the next week or so, how about stopping in at headquarters? I'd like to talk about you coming back to the department."

"I'll give it some thought, Jim. Thanks." He reached into his pocket and handed Moss the badge the chief had returned to him. "Better hold this for now."

They shook hands, and Stannard left the room. He walked slowly down the long hallway and followed the stairway to the front of the big house.

Bacher was in the living room sloshing brandy around in a snifter. Lee Ellen was there, too. She came up to Stannard with quick, graceful steps.

"It's finished?" she asked in a low voice. Her eyes moved to Bacher and back to Stannard's face.

He took her arm, and they headed for a side door. "Yeah. It's finished. Our part anyway. It wasn't pleasant. I'll tell you about it."

"Where, Burl?"

He held the door, then grabbed her by the wrist and looked deep into her eyes. "Home," he said.

"Home?"

"Yeah. Your place. Home."

THE END

Jay Flynn Bibliography
(1927-1985)

As J. M. Flynn:

The Deadly Boodle (Ace Double D-313, 1958)
Drink with the Dead (Ace Double D-379, 1959)
Terror Tournament (Mystery House [hardcover], 1959;
  Ace Double D-409 [paperback reprint, abridged], 1959)
The Hot Chariot (Ace Double D-447, 1960)
Ring Around a Rogue (Ace Double D-459, 1960)
One for the Death House (Ace Double D-511, 1961)
The Girl from Las Vegas (Ace Double F-111, 1961)
Deep Six (Ace Double F-125, 1961)
The Screaming Cargo (Ace Double F-130, 1962)
SurfSide 6 (Dell 8388; TV tie-in, 1962)
Assault No. 1: The Raid on Reichswald Fortress (Award, 1974)
Warlock (Pocket Books 80478, 1976)
Danger Zone (Belmont-Tower 51171, 1977;
  reprinted in Australia as *Jet Set Orgy*, Stag, 1979)

As Jay Flynn [McH = McHugh. JR = Joe Rigg. B = Bannerman]

McHugh (Avon T-377, 1959) McH
It's Murder, McHugh (Avon T-406, 1960) McH
A Body for McHugh (Avon T-444, 1960) McH
Viva McHugh (Avon T-466, 1960) McH
The Action Man (Avon T-500, 1961)
The Five Faces of Murder (Avon F-156; 1962) McH
Blood on Frisco Bay (Leisure 360, 1976) JR
Trouble Is My Business (Leisure 384, 1976) JR
Bannerman (Leisure 389, 1976) B
Border Incident (Leisure, 1976) B

Western novels [unverified]

Flynn has been credited with the following novels in the Lassiter series:

As Jack Slade:

Lust for Gold (Belmont-Tower 51127, 1977)
Hangman (Belmont-Tower 51146, 1977)
Wolverine (Belmont-Tower 51225, 1978)
Big Foot's Range (Belmont-Tower 51428, 1979)

Short story:
"The Badger Game," as by Jay Flynn (*Guilty Detective Story Magazine*, Nov. 1956)